The Stirling / South Carolina ... Hogg

General Editors: Douglas S. Mack and Gillian Hughes

Reviews

Chastity, carnality, carnage and carnivorousness are among his favourite subjects, and dance together in his writings to the music of a divided life. [...] The later eighteenth century was a time when [Scotland] had taken to producing writers and thinkers of world consequence. One of these—though long disregarded as such, long unimaginable as such—was Hogg.

(Karl Miller, *TLS*)

The new interest in Hogg that Mack's editions in particular have stimulated has been supported by an excellent annual periodical, *Studies in Hogg and his World*; and now Mack has persuaded Edinburgh University Press to start publishing a collected edition, which, if the earlier volumes are as success-ful as they deserve to be, will eventually run to some thirty volumes. The first three came out last year, and are magnifi-cent: spaciously designed, scrupulously edited and thought-fully introduced. **(John Barrell, *London Review of Books*)**

Simple congratulations are in order at the outset, to the edi-tors and publisher of these first three handsome volumes of the projected *Collected Works* of James Hogg. It has taken a long time for Hogg to be recognised as one of the most notable Scottish writers, and it can fairly be said that the process of getting him into full and clear focus is still far from complete. That process is immeasurably helped by the provision of proper and unbowdlerised texts (in many cases for the first time), and in this the ongoing *Collected Works* will be a mile-stone. [...] There can be little doubt that in the prose and verse of these three volumes we have an author of unique interest, force, and originality.

(Edwin Morgan, *Scottish Literary Journal*)

Edinburgh University Press are also to be praised for the el-egant presentation of the books. It is wonderful that at last we are going to have a collected edition of this important author without bowdlerisation or linguistic interference.

(Iain Crichton Smith, *Studies in Scottish Literature*)

Reviews of the Stirling / South Carolina Edition
(continued)

The Shepherd's Calendar, though still celebrating diversity, remains centred on Hogg's local landscape, and carries an inherent sense of order and cyclical repetition. From the very first paragraph, the limitations of official, public history are underlined by the assertion that storms 'constitute the various aeras of the pastoral life'. Although the reference to 'the pastoral' indicates Hogg's awareness of an alien and slightly patronizing audience, the notion of a society ancient enough to be constituted by 'aeras', and interpreting itself through natural phenomena rather than through periods of government or reigns, is also a statement of independence. The reader is not being treated to a quaint display of an outmoded lifestyle, but privileged with glimpses of a community possessed of special knowledge and internal laws. Hogg's shepherds are far removed from those of Virgil or Spenser, while even Wordsworth's Michael seems remote from the narrator who can describe the destruction of '12 scores of excellent ewes' with such calmness and compassion: 'when the snow went away they were discovered all lying dead with their heads one way as if a flock of sheep had dropped dead going from the washing'. [...]

As he introduces the tale of George Dobson, the narrator explicitly upholds the power of narrative over rational analysis. While the philosopher 'does not know what mind is; even his own mind, to which one would think he has the most direct access', the storyteller not only apprehends truths, but can communicate them to others. And thus we are told that 'it is on this ground that I like to contemplate, not the theory of dreams, but dreams themselves'. If Hogg was patronized in his lifetime, it was perhaps not after all because he knew too little, but for fear that he knew too much.

(**Fiona Stafford**, *Review of English Studies*)

An important and addictively readable addition to the Scottish canon. (**Christopher Harvie**, *Notes & Queries*)

JAMES HOGG

The Shepherd's Calendar

Edited by
Douglas S. Mack

With a Chronology
by Gillian Hughes

EDINBURGH UNIVERSITY PRESS
2002

© Edinburgh University Press, 2002

Edinburgh University Press
22 George Square
Edinburgh
EH8 9LF

Typeset at the University of Stirling
Printed by The Cromwell Press, Trowbridge, Wilts.

ISBN 0 7486 6316 9

A CIP record for this book is available from the British Library

Hogg Rediscovered

A New Edition of a Major Writer

This book forms part of a series of paperback reprints of selected volumes from the Stirling / South Carolina Research Edition of the Collected Works of James Hogg (S/SC Edition). Published by Edinburgh University Press, the S/SC Edition (when completed) will run to some thirty-four volumes. The existence of this large-scale international scholarly project is a confirmation of the current consensus that James Hogg (1770–1835) is one of Scotland's major writers.

The high regard in which Hogg is now held is a comparatively recent development. In his own lifetime, he was regarded as one of the leading writers of the day, but the nature of his fame was influenced by the fact that, as a young man, he had been a self-educated shepherd. The second edition (1813) of his long poem *The Queen's Wake* contains an 'Advertisement' which begins as follows.

> The Publisher having been favoured with letters from gentlemen in various parts of the United Kingdom respecting the Author of the *Queen's Wake*, and most of them expressing doubts of his being a Scotch Shepherd; he takes this opportunity of assuring the Public, that *The Queen's Wake* is really and truly the production of *James Hogg*, a common shepherd, bred among the mountains of Ettrick Forest, who went to service when only seven years of age; and since that period has never received any education whatever.

This 'Advertisement' is redolent of a class prejudice also reflected in the various early reviews of *The Private Memoirs and Confessions of a Justified Sinner*, the book by which Hogg is now best known. This novel appeared anonymously in 1824, but many of the early reviews identify Hogg as the author, and see the *Justified Sinner* as presenting 'an incongruous mixture of the strongest powers with the strongest absurdities'. The Scotch Shepherd was regarded as a man of powerful and original talent, but it was felt that his lack of education caused his work to be marred by frequent failures in discretion, in expression, and in knowledge of the world. Worst of all was Hogg's lack of what was called 'delicacy', a failing which caused him to deal in his writings with subjects (such as prostitution) that were felt to be unsuitable for mention in polite literature. Hogg was regarded by these reviewers, and by his contemporaries in general, as a man of undoubted genius, but his genius was felt to be seriously flawed.

A posthumous collected edition of Hogg was published in the late 1830s. As was perhaps natural in all the circumstances, the publishers (Blackie & Son of Glasgow) took pains to smooth away what they took to be the rough edges of Hogg's writing, and to remove his numerous 'indelicacies'. This process was taken even further in the 1860s, when the Rev. Thomas Thomson prepared a revised edition of Hogg's *Works* for publication by Blackie. These Blackie editions present a bland and lifeless version of Hogg's writings. It was in this version that Hogg was read by the Victorians, and, unsurprisingly, he came to be regarded as a minor figure, of no great importance or interest. Indeed, by the first half of the twentieth century Hogg's reputation had dwindled to such an extent that he was widely dismissed as a vain, talent-free, and oafish peasant.

Nevertheless, the latter part of the twentieth century saw a substantial revival of Hogg's reputation. This revival was sparked by the republication in 1947 of an unbowdlerised edition of the *Justified Sinner*, with an enthusiastic Introduction by André Gide. During the second half of the twentieth century Hogg's rehabilitation continued, thanks to the republication of some of his texts in new editions. This process entered a new phase when the first three volumes of the S/SC Edition appeared in 1995, and the S/SC Edition as it proceeds is revealing a hitherto unsuspected range and depth in Hogg's achievement. It is no longer possible to regard him as a one-book wonder.

Some of the books that are being published in the S/SC Edition had been out of print for more than a century and a half, while others, still less fortunate, had never been published at all in their original, unbowdlerised condition. Hogg is now being revealed as a major writer whose true stature was not recognised in his own lifetime because his social origins led to his being smothered in genteel condescension; and whose true stature has not been recognised since, because of a lack of adequate editions. The poet Douglas Dunn wrote of Hogg in the *Glasgow Herald* in September 1988: 'I can't help but think that in almost any other country of Europe a complete, modern edition of a comparable author would have been available long ago'. The Stirling / South Carolina Research Edition of James Hogg, from which the present paperback is reprinted, seeks to fill the gap identified by Douglas Dunn.

vii

Acknowledgements

The research for the early volumes of the Stirling / South Carolina Edition of James Hogg has been sustained by funding and other support generously made available by the University of Stirling and by the University of South Carolina. In addition, funding of crucial importance was received through the Glenfiddich Living Scotland Awards; this was particularly pleasant and appropriate, given Hogg's well-known delight in good malt whisky. Valuable grants or donations have also been received from the Carnegie Trust for the Universities of Scotland, from the Association for Scottish Literary Studies, and from the James Hogg Society. The work of the Edition could not have been carried on without the support of these bodies.

The Edition is also deeply indebted to many libraries for assistance of various kinds, not least for permission to use and quote from manuscripts in their possession. Particular thanks are expressed to libraries holding major collections of Hogg manuscripts: the Alexander Turnbull Library, Wellington; the Beinecke Library, Yale University; the Huntington Library, San Marino; and the National Library of Scotland, Edinburgh.

During the preparation of the present volume many people helped the work forward in various ways, and it is a pleassure to record my particular thanks to John Davidson, Peter Garside, Gill Hughes, Neil Keeble, Ian Landles, Fianach Lawry, Alison Lumsden, Emily Lyle, Wilma Mack, Margaret Mackay, Jean Moffat, Wilson Ogilvie, Elaine Petrie, Judy Steel, David Sweet, and Archie Turnbull. The volume was typeset by Gordon Mack, assisted by Douglas Ferguson and Gill Hughes. I am grateful to the Lilly Library, University of Indiana, and to the Trustees of the National Library of Scotland, for permission to quote from the Hogg manuscripts in their care.

Douglas S. Mack

Contents

Introduction

OVER a period of ten years beginning in 1819, a series of articles by James Hogg appeared in *Blackwood's Edinburgh Magazine* under the title 'The Shepherd's Calendar'. Hogg, by the 1820s, was a professional man of letters in his fifties; but for many years in his youth he had earned his living working as a shepherd in his native Ettrick in the Scottish Borders. He took a proper pride in his early life and family background, frequently using 'The Ettrick Shepherd' as his nom de plume. As one might expect in these circumstances, his 'Shepherd's Calendar' is, in one of its aspects, a vigorous and lively account of the experiences, beliefs, and customs of the people of Ettrick. This account is presented partly through reminiscences of Hogg's own early days, and partly through his attempts to re-create on paper the manner and the content of traditional Ettrick oral story-telling.

Hogg's celebration of the life and values of Ettrick was offered to a sophisticated and international readership through *Blackwood's Edinburgh Magazine*. During the 1820s, Edinburgh was one of the major literary and cultural centres of Europe. The Author of Waverley was producing works like *Redgauntlet*, *Kenilworth*, and *Quentin Durward* which aroused eager interest in Paris, New York, and beyond. At the same time, *The Edinburgh Review* was delivering its influential and magisterial commentaries on politics and on literature; while *Blackwood's Edinburgh Magazine* (Maga to its friends) offered a pungent, stimulating, and frequently scandalous alternative to its longer-established rival. In addition to such present glories, the city continued to bask in the afterglow of the achievements of the Scottish Enlightenment of the eighteenth century: figures from the comparatively recent past included such giants as David Hume, Adam Smith, James Hutton, and Joseph Black.

Robert Burns had visited Edinburgh as a poet and as a ploughman in the 1780s, at a period when the greatest days of the Enlightenment were already over. Robert Crawford has expressed the view that Enlightenment Edinburgh tended 'to categorize Burns rather patronizingly as a belated primitive curiosity', for example by applying to him the term 'a Scotch bard'. Burns, however, was a difficult man to patronise. Crawford describes the ploughman-poet's strategy, which was to appropriate the phrase with which the literati sought to keep him safely in his place:

> In adopting the description 'a Scotch bard' and calling it his
> 'highest pride', Burns attempts to valorize this patronizing
> term. It allows him again to side firmly with those supposedly
> rather primitive Ayrshire peasants from whose society he comes
> and whose language he often uses. As he negotiates with the
> term 'bard', Burns's invention of the mockingly inflated 'bard-
> ship', his deployment of the self-deprecating diminutive 'bar-
> die', and his adoption and celebration of the term 'a Scotch
> bard' show him well able to cope with the values of the metro-
> politan world of literature, and able to avoid being trapped in
> the potentially patronizing or embalming bardolatry of being
> simply a 'bard'. It is just such tactical canniness which he was
> to exhibit in his face-to-face dealings with the literati of
> Edinburgh, subverting and redeploying the power of their cul-
> ture while remaining on good terms with men whose linguistic
> and other ideals were very different from his own.[1]

Hogg, a generation later, performed much the same trick as he set
out to storm the capital in his capacity as successor to Burns, and
shepherd-poet to the Scottish nation. 'The Shepherd's Calendar'
played an important part in this campaign. These articles in *Blackwood's* are in fact much more than a pleasant exercise in nostalgia for
a fast-fading rural way of life. Rather, they become a celebration of
the worth to be found in the values of Ettrick, and a sophisticated
subversion of some of the assumptions of Enlightenment Edinburgh.

This process can be seen particularly clearly in the 'Shepherd's
Calendar' story now known as 'Mr Adamson of Laverhope', which
first appeared in the June 1823 number of *Blackwood's*. Published
around the time when Hogg was writing *The Private Memoirs and
Confessions of a Justified Sinner*, 'Mr Adamson of Laverhope' has a
narrator who offers the enlightened readers of *Blackwood's* an account
of an incident which, we are told, rekindled 'the still and drowsy
embers of superstition' among the simple country people. The story is
of a farmer, Mr Adamson, who is struck by lightning after acting
with great cruelty and injustice towards a poor neighbour; and the
narrator, 'though far from giving them as authentic', records the
beliefs of the country people about the events surrounding the death
of Adamson. In their view of the matter, the farmer was struck down
by an act of divine vengeance; and his soul was carried off to hell by
the Devil, present at the scene disguised as an old 'profane gaberlunzie'. As well as re-telling this traditional story, the narrator also

offers his readers a bland, sober and scientific account of the death by
lightning of the admirable 'Adam Copland, Esquire, of Minnigess'.
For the reader, however, this cool and rational anecdote about 'the
electric matter that slew Mr Copland' cannot begin to match the
power and conviction of the country people's version of the death of
Adamson. The two deaths are, as it were, mirror images of each
other. The story of the death of Copland is the modern, rational,
scientific, enlightened version, while the story of the death of Adamson is the primitive and superstitious version: and the primitive and
superstitious version wins hands down. As a result, the values of the
enlightened narrator are undermined in much the same way as the
values of the enlightened 'Editor' are undermined in the final pages
of the *Confessions*. In 'Mr Adamson of Laverhope' Hogg the trickster
is at his usual work of 'subverting and redeploying' the power of the
culture of the literati of Edinburgh; and the trick is performed in the
pages of one of the house journals of the literati, *Blackwood's Edinburgh
Magazine*.

In spite of the frequently subversive undercurrents of Hogg's
'Shepherd's Calendar' articles, *Blackwood's* provided what was in
some ways an appropriate and suitable home for them. William
Blackwood had founded his magazine in 1817 as a Tory rival to the
Whig *Edinburgh Review*; and as a result the new periodical's concerns
tended to lie with agriculture, the landed gentry, and rural affairs as
opposed to industry, trade, and urban affairs. Contributions by Hogg
on the quaint ways of the stalwart Ettrick peasantry (salt of the earth,
our loyal peasantry, just what we need to keep the Radicals at bay)
must have seemed a good idea in theory: but, as we shall see,
Blackwood sometimes tended to be somewhat unsettled and alarmed
by what he got in practice.

Another motive for welcoming articles by Hogg into the pages of
Blackwood's was provided by the appearance, from March 1822
onwards, of the hugely popular series of articles entitled 'Noctes
Ambrosianae'. The 'Noctes' are conversations at Ambrose's
Tavern, a haunt of the younger Tory wits; and they feature a regular
cast of characters based on key contributors to the magazine. Thus
'Christopher North' is a version of John Wilson, 'Odoherty' is based
upon William Maginn, and 'the Shepherd' is a beguiling fiction-
alised representation and distortion of certain aspects of Hogg's per-
sonality. Much of the success of *Blackwood's* depended on the
'Noctes'; and much of the popularity of the 'Noctes' derived from the
character of the Shepherd, a rural philosopher-clown who has been
aptly described by J.H. Alexander as 'a complex embodiment of

profoundly intuitive responses to experience'.[2] Clearly, the Shepherd's 'Calendar' would have a strong appeal for both the publishers and the readers of *Blackwood's Edinburgh Magazine*.

Towards the end of his life, Burns had devoted much time and energy to his efforts to collect and re-create the corpus of traditional Scottish song. 'The Shepherd's Calendar' can be seen as Hogg's attempt to perform a similar service to the tradition of Scottish oral storytelling, a tradition familiar to him from his youth upwards. It seems clear that this project was close to Hogg's heart; and in September 1825, when a number of 'Shepherd's Calendar' articles had already appeared, he set out to make arrangements for publication of the series in book form. In a letter to Blackwood of 1 September Hogg writes:

> Although in the throng of my harvest as well as the moor sports I will be in town next week if possibly I can, or next again at all events. But should I miss Mr Rees [of Hogg's London publishers, Longman] tell him that I am going to publish two small works about Martinmass about 7/6 each "The Shepherd's Callander" and "Some passages in the lives of eminent men" and he must send the paper for both on the instant. You and he agree about what share you are to have. (National Library of Scotland [NLS], MS 4014, fol. 289)

Hogg's *The Three Perils of Woman* (1823) and *The Private Memoirs and Confessions of a Justified Sinner* (1824) had both been unsuccessful as far as sales were concerned. Both had been published by Longman, and in 1825 that publisher proved to be unwilling to accept *The Shepherd's Calendar*. William Blackwood was the obvious choice as an alternative to Longman, but he gave the project only a cautious welcome. In a letter to Hogg of 24 June 1826, Blackwood stresses the need for 'corrections and alterations' before the tales can appear in book form. He then goes on to suggest that the task of revision should be entrusted to Hogg's nephew Robert Hogg, whom he describes as a young man of 'much tact and good taste' (NLS, MS 30309, fols 229–30).

This was a period of financial difficulty for Hogg, mainly because he was attempting to run the large farm of Mount Benger without sufficient capital. In a letter to Blackwood of 12 September 1826 (NLS, MS 4017, fol. 139), he speaks of being 'exceedingly ill set by reason of a few hundred pounds of debt'; and with this in mind he asks for the publication of *The Shepherd's Calendar* in book form. Hogg goes on to accept Blackwood's suggestion about Robert, albeit with some caution: 'I should like above all things that my nephew Robt took the charge of the edition but there are many large curtailments that I only can manage'.

A rather dampening reply from Blackwood is dated 23 September 1826: 'Every thing however is so dull and I have such heavy demands upon me that I cannot well venture upon much just now' (NLS, MS 30309, fol. 387). Nevertheless, Hogg continued to press for publication. For example, on 5 July 1827 he writes 'You must I think publish the Shepherd's callander in two vols at Martinmass I could get common conditions elsewhere but the truth is no body should or can publish it but yourself' (NLS, MS 4019, fol. 193). Blackwood replied promptly on 14 July 1827: 'I think the Calendar will do as a separate publication, and when you come to town we will have some talk about it. You know I must publish it' (NLS MS, 30310, p.182). Naturally enough, Blackwood did not wish another publisher to bring out a book containing the contributions to *Blackwood's Edinburgh Magazine* of the star turn of the 'Noctes Ambrosianae'.

This did not necessarily mean that he was eager to publish the book himself, however; and there was to be more urging by Hogg, and more procrastination by Blackwood, before *The Shepherd's Calendar* was finally published.[3] Hogg's deep commitment to the project comes over strongly in a letter to Blackwood of 5 January 1828:

> You must not on any account hesitate on publishing the Shepherd's Calender. There is an absolute necessity exclusive of all other concerns for the collecting of these varied pictures and details of pastoral life I must have them brought into some tangible form by one means or another else my conscience will not be at rest (NLS, MS 4021, fol. 271)

Hogg, no doubt, was anxious to secure the publication of *The Shepherd's Calendar* in book form on whatever terms he could obtain it; and he told Blackwood in a letter of 12 February 1828 that 'Robert [...] is at full liberty to prune as he likes and arrange as he likes' (NLS, MS 4021, fol. 275).

A year later, on 8 February 1829,[4] we find Hogg writing to Blackwood in a mixture of exasperation and desperation:

> Is the Shepherd's Calander ever to see the light? or is it fairly to be strangled in the birth once more. I never hear a word of it nor know I in the least what progress you are making but sure am I it might have been published long ago. (NLS, MS 4719, fol. 153)

The end was in sight, however. Blackwood replied to Hogg's letter of
8 February in a letter dated 28 February 1829. In this reply he
assures Hogg that publication of *The Shepherd's Calendar* in book form
is imminent. Blackwood's comments in this letter make it abundantly
clear that the preparation of the new two-volume set had been
decisively placed beyond Hogg's control:

> I at last send you The Shepherd's Calendar and I hope you will
> be pleased with the way in which your Nephew has arranged
> and corrected the whole. I left it entirely to himself. I shall
> publish on Monday. I have shipped copies for London, and
> I have written and sent presents to a number of friends there
> who I hope will make some exertion for it (NLS, MS 30311,
> fol. 220)

Why did Blackwood entrust the task of revision to Robert Hogg,
while excluding the author himself from the process? A clue is given
by an admonition to Hogg contained in a letter of 28 May 1828 from
Thomas Pringle, editor of the annual *Friendship's Offering*. Pringle
writes:

> But now, in regard to the Poem you have sent me I will tell you
> frankly my sentiments after a careful perusal. It is full of wild
> originality & bold striking imagery—but altogether it seems to
> me too strange & droll, & "high kiltit" for the very "gentie"
> publication now under my charge. Were it for a Magazine or
> some such work I should not feel so particular but for these
> "douce" & delicate publications the annuals I think it rather
> inappropriate [...] in elegant publications of this description I
> think it ought to be a rule (& I endeavour to make it one so far
> as I am concerned) to admit not a single expression which
> would call up a blush in the Cheek of the most delicate female if
> reading aloud to a mixt Company. (NLS, MS 2245, fols 122–
> 23)

Pringle comments, interestingly, that 'Were it for a Magazine or
some such work I should not feel so particular'; and it seems clear
that although Blackwood was willing to print Hogg's articles in his
Magazine, he was more particular when it came to publication in the
more prestigious form of a separate book. Blackwood and Robert
Hogg shared Pringle's nervousness about what they called Hogg's
'indelicacy', and some of the revisions made to *The Shepherd's Calendar*
seem designed to ensure that Hogg's book could not possibly give
offence to even the most prudish of readers.

Fortunately, Robert Hogg's own account of his practice in revising *The Shepherd's Calendar* is to be found in a letter he wrote to Blackwood on 9 February 1828.[5] Robert writes:

Sir,

I have drawn out a sketch of what appears to me the best arrangement for the articles of the Shepherd's Calendar, including the whole that can be introduced under that title. The omission of any of the pieces will not of course interfere with that arrangement.

I have also gone over a part of the articles, making such verbal alterations as appeared to improve the style, and striking out what was objectionable or superfluous. As the work proceeds, and when it is settled how much is to be taken, I can go over the remainder in the same way, before it is put into the hands of the compositor.

I am,
Sir,
Your obedient humble servant
Robert Hogg
Saturday.   9th. Feb.
William Blackwood, Esq.   (NLS, MS 4021, fol. 284)

In many of the stories of *The Shepherd's Calendar* Robert Hogg's cuts and revisions were very extensive. For example, in 'Mary Burnet' the cuts made for the 1829 republication amount in total to almost two thousand words. Another story, 'Tibby Hyslop's Dream and the Sequel', may be taken as a representative example of the revisions by Robert Hogg; and it is illuminating to examine the differences between the original *Blackwood's* text of this story, and the revised version of 1829.[6]

Like the rest of the 'Shepherd's Calendar' series, 'Tibby Hyslop's Dream and the Sequel' is informal and conversational in tone in Hogg's original version, and has the rhythms of the spoken rather than the written language. This is of course entirely appropriate in a story that seeks to capture on paper the manner and the content of traditional Ettrick oral storytelling; but many of Robert Hogg's revisions seem designed to convert his uncle's language into formal literary English. For example, in *Blackwood's* (p.664) the narrator tells us that Tibbie lived 'In a wee cottage'; while in Robert Hogg's 1829 version (p.212) this becomes 'In a cottage'. Likewise, the narrator tells us in *Blackwood's* that 'Her mother was married to a sergeant' (p.664); but in 1829 this becomes 'Her mother married a sergeant' (p.213). Similarly, in *Blackwood's* (p.665) we read:

> with that grandmother was she brought up to read her Bible, card and spin, and work at all kinds of country labour

In Robert Hogg's version (p.213) this becomes:

> with that grandmother was she brought up, and taught to read her Bible, to card, spin, and work at all kinds of country labour

Singly, such changes are of no great consequence. Cumulatively—and they are very numerous—they destroy the conversational tone of the *Blackwood's* version.

Much of 'Tibby Hyslop's Dream' turns on the sexual pursuit of Tibby by her employer, the farmer Gilbert Forret. Naturally, Robert Hogg was anxious to tone down his uncle's indelicacy in writing about such matters; and several cuts and revisions were made as a result. For example, in *Blackwood's* (p.665), Forret tells Tibby 'it is likely to be a long while before you and I part, if I get my will'; but Robert Hogg delicately removes 'if I get my will' (p.215). Likewise, in *Blackwood's* (p.668) the narrator writes as follows of the aftermath of an attempted seduction (or perhaps rape) of Tibby by Forret:

> Jane found her grand-daughter terribly flushed in the countenance, and flurried in her speech that day, but Jane's stupid head could draw no inferences from these, or anything else. She asked if she was well enough, and the other saying she was, Jane took it for granted that she was so, and only added,

After Robert Hogg has dealt with this passage, it becomes (p.221):

> Jane found her grand-daughter apparently much disturbed; but having asked if she was well enough, and receiving an answer in the affirmative, she was satisfied, and only added,

Examples could be multiplied—but in short Robert Hogg's extensive cuts and revisions remove much of the vigour and vitality of 'Tibby Hyslop's Dream and the Sequel'. In the nature of things, a story of a sexual pursuit loses someting if all the references to sex are carefully removed or defused.[7] A similar process of extensive bowdlerisation was imposed throughout *The Shepherd's Calendar*, and the mutilated texts which resulted were reprinted in all the various nineteenth-century editions of Hogg's works. As a result, *The Shepherd's Calendar* has been undervalued for more than a century and a half.

The present edition offers the first complete reprinting of the

Blackwood's 'Shepherd's Calendar' articles as Hogg wrote them, without his nephew's cuts and revisions. Some other stories by Hogg were published during his lifetime under the series title 'The Shepherd's Calendar'; and these stories, which will be included in due course in future volumes of the Stirling/South Carolina Edition, are discussed in the concluding section of the Notes at the end of the present volume.

The 'Shepherd's Calendar' stories from *Blackwood's* form a coherent group; and the present volume is offered in the belief that, if seen as a group and read in the original versions, they combine, like the stories of Joyce's *Dubliners*, into a resonant and convincing portrait of the life and spirit of a particular society.

Notes

1. Robert Crawford, *Devolving English Literature* (Oxford: Clarendon Press, 1992), p.95.

2. In 'The Noctes Ambrosianae: a New Selection', *Scotlit*, 7 (Spring 1992), 1.

3. *The Shepherd's Calendar*, 2 vols (1829), was published by William Blackwood in Edinburgh and T. Cadell in London. A more detailed account of Hogg's negotiations with Blackwood over its publication is given in Douglas S. Mack, 'Hogg, Blackwood and *The Shepherd's Calendar*', in *Papers Given at the Second James Hogg Society Conference (Edinburgh 1985)*, ed. by Gillian Hughes (Aberdeen: ASLS, 1988), pp.24–31.

4. The letter (NLS, MS 4719, fol. 153) is simply dated 8 February; but although no year is given it is clear that it must have been written in 1829. Blackwood's detailed reply, dated 28 February 1829, is to be found in NLS, MS 30311, fols 219–20.

5. The letter is simply dated 'Saturday. 9th. Feb.', but 1828 would appear to be the year involved. As we have seen, *The Shepherd's Calendar* was published in book form at the beginning of March 1829. Robert Hogg's comments in his letter of 'Saturday. 9th Feb.' suggest strongly that publication was still some way off; and so the letter must be earlier than 1829. Hogg's letter to Blackwood of 12 February 1828 (quoted above) indicates that Robert's involvement in revising *The Shepherd's Calendar* was under active discussion during February 1828; and a calculation, based on Appendix III of Sir Paul Harvey's *Oxford Companion to English Literature* (Oxford: Oxford University Press, 1967), confirms that 9 February fell on a Saturday in 1828.

6. 'The Shepherd's Calendar. Dreams and Apparitions.—Part II. Containing Tibby Hyslop's Dream, and the Sequel', *Blackwood's Edinburgh Magazine*, 21 (June 1827), 664–76; and 'Tibby Hyslop's Dream', *The Shepherd's Calendar*, (1829), 1, 212–46.

7. For a complete list of the verbal variants to be found in the two versions of 'Tibby Hyslop's Dream and the Sequel' published in Hogg's lifetime, see Douglas S. Mack, 'Editing James Hogg' (unpublished doctoral thesis, University of Stirling, 1984), pp.126–40.

The Development of
The Shepherd's Calendar

This paperback is a reprint of the hardback edition of *The Shepherd's Calendar* published in 1995 as part of the Stirling / South Carolina Research Edition of the Collected Works of James Hogg (S/SC Edition). However, this note is a new addition, written to give a concise overview of the development of Hogg's 'Shepherd's Calendar' project. Part of the evidence on which this overview is based is provided by a document that has been brought to light since 1995 as a result of the research being undertaken by Gillian Hughes for her forthcoming edition of Hogg's *Collected Letters*. Now in the Lilly Library (University of Indiana), the document in question is a letter to William Blackwood of 10 March 1829, in which Hogg gives his reaction to seeing the edition of *The Shepherd's Calendar* that had been published by Blackwood at the beginning of March 1829.

We shall return to this letter in due course, but our overview begins with Hogg's first use of the title 'The Shepherd's Calendar', which was in 'The Shepherd's Calendar. Storms', a two-part article published in the numbers of *Blackwood's Edinburgh Magazine* for April and May 1819. This title points to Edmund Spenser's well-known pastoral poem *The Shepheardes Calendar* (1579),[1] but it had a particular resonance and relevance when used by Hogg, whose pen-name 'The Ettrick Shepherd' was already well established in 1819. 'The Shepherd's Calendar. Storms' presents the reminiscences of the mature Ettrick Shepherd (now a famous literary figure) about his experiences as a young shepherd in Ettrick Forrest during the great snow storm of January 1794. The narrative voice in 'Storms' is therefore able to draw on direct personal experience in describing the pastoral life, while also able to achieve a detached, objective tone in its account of that life. Hogg continued to make use of this double perspective in his future 'Shepherd's Calendar' articles in *Blackwood's*.

However, Hogg next used the 'Shepherd's Calendar' title, not in *Blackwood's*, but for a five-chapter section in his *Winter Evening Tales*, a two-volume collection of novellas, stories, and poems published in 1820. It is apparent from Hogg's letters that *Winter Evening Tales* developed from a long-held wish to publish a collection of stories based on the traditional oral tales with which he had grown up in his Ettrick youth. Hogg had written to Archibald Constable about this project as early as 20 May 1813:

> I have for many years been collecting the rural and traditionary tales of Scotland and I have of late been writing them over again and new-modelling them, and have the vanity to suppose they will form a most interesting work.   (NLS, MS 7200, fol. 203)

This approach of 1813 failed to interest Constable, but Hogg later tried to find another publisher for the projected collection, to which, in his letters, he gives such names as 'Cottage Winter Nights', 'Cottage Tales', and 'The Rural and Traditionary Tales of Scotland'.[2] In response to Hogg's promptings about this project, William Blackwood eventually published *The Brownie of Bodsbeck; And Other Tales* (1818, two volumes), and in 1820 further 'rural and traditionary tales' were published by Oliver & Boyd as *Winter Evening Tales*.[3]

Hogg drew on various sources as he shaped his *Winter Evening Tales* into a coherent collection: for example, he reprinted or revised various stories he had previously published (sometimes anonymously) in magazines. This applies to the five 'Shepherd's Calendar' chapters in *Winter Evening Tales*, the first two of which reprint 'Storms' (1819) from *Blackwood's*, while the remaining three reprint a series of contributions Hogg had made to the first volume (1817) of *Blackwood's* (pp. 22–25, 143–47, and 247–50). These three contributions had appeared anonymously in 1817 under the series title 'Tales and Anecdotes of the Pastoral Life', and their subject-matter therefore has something in common with 'Storms'. In 'Tales and Anecdotes of the Pastoral Life', however, the unnamed narrator is presented as someone who observes the pastoral life as a gentlemanly outsider, rather than as someone who has himself been a shepherd. Nevertheless, combining these three stories with 'Storms' under the 'Shepherd's Calendar' title allowed Hogg to create a coherent grouping within *Winter Evening Tales*.

Hogg's next use of the 'Shepherd's Calendar' title came in the March 1823 number of *Blackwood's*, in a contribution entitled 'The Shepherd's Calendar. Class Second. Deaths, Judgments, and Providences'. The long gap after the publication of 'Storms' in the numbers for April and May 1819 can be explained in part by the fact that Hogg and Blackwood quarrelled seriously in the summer of 1821. Hogg's contributions to *Blackwood's* dried up for a time as a result, and the story published in the March 1823 number of *Blackwood's* not only marked Hogg's re-entry into *Blackwood's*, but

also in effect re-launched the magazine's 'Shepherd's Calendar' series. The re-launch was followed in the June 1823 number by another contribution by Hogg entitled 'The Shepherd's Calendar. Class
Second. Deaths, Judgments, and Providences': the March story was
later given the title 'Rob Dodds', and the June story was later given
the title 'Mr Adamson of Laverhope'. The momentum of the series
was maintained with 'The Shepherd's Calendar. Class IV. Dogs',
published in the number for February 1824, while the number of
Blackwood's for March 1824 contained the first instalment of 'The
Shepherd's Calendar. Class V. The Lasses'. The concluding portion of 'The Lasses' did not appear until the number for February
1825, however, and thereafter there was a gap until a rush of new
'Shepherd's Calendar' stories by Hogg appeared in *Blackwood's* in
1827 and 1828.

Hogg's letters show that in September 1825 he felt that he already had in hand the nucleus of a new book, *The Shepherd's Calendar*, which he hoped would be taken on by his usual London publishers Longman, in partnership with Blackwood in Edinburgh.
However, the Longman firm turned down *The Shepherd's Calendar*,
apparently because of the lack of commercial success of *The Private
Memoirs and Confessions of a Justified Sinner* and *Queen Hynde*, both of
which had been published by Longman in 1824 (see Introduction,
p. xiv above). In late 1825, therefore, Hogg found himself in a situation in which he could either entrust his projected new book to
Blackwood alone, or seek a new publisher. The middle years of the
1820s saw a period of general financial crisis in Britain: for example, the ruin of Sir Walter Scott took place in January 1826. At this
time Hogg and Blackwood were both facing financial stresses, and
this resulted in protracted manoeuvrings between the two, with regard to the proposed publication of *The Shepherd's Calendar* in book
form. In these manoeuvrings, Hogg and Blackwood each had his
own agenda. Hogg's priorities can be sensed from a letter he wrote
on 29 January 1828 from his Border farmhouse of Mount Benger to
Blackwood in Edinburgh:

> You should not forget the collection of your old friend's
> Calenders because he is not present to importune you The
> season I fear will be let slip as it was last year. Had they been
> published last year my other tales in six vols might have been
> required this year which might have been of great advantage to
> me Were these properly revised there is no doubt that they
> have more interest and nature than tales in general   (NLS,
> MS 4021 fols. 273–74)

Hogg desperately needed to get books published to help him cope with pressing debts, and he clearly hoped that a successful book publication of *The Shepherd's Calendar* would pave the way for a collected edition of his prose works. Such an edition would be a companion-piece to the four-volume edition of his *Poetical Works* that had been published by Archibald Constable in 1822.

For his part, however, Blackwood does not seem to have been particularly enthused by the idea of publishing *The Shepherd's Calendar* in book form, and he seems to have been even less enthusiastic about publishing a collected edition of Hogg's prose (see Introduction, pp. xiv–xv). Nevertheless, Blackwood could not afford to reject *The Shepherd's Calendar* out of hand. His main asset as a publisher was *Blackwood's Edinburgh Magazine*, and in the 1820s much of the popularity of the magazine derived from the 'Noctes Ambrosianae'. This long-running series of articles purported to record the table-talk of the magazine's major contributors, and much of the popularity of the 'Noctes' derived from 'The Shepherd', Hogg's persona within the series. Inevitably, Hogg's 'Shepherd's Calendar' contributions to *Blackwood's* were connected in readers' minds with the Shepherd of the 'Noctes', and it would therefore be damaging to Blackwood if *The Shepherd's Calendar* were to be published in book form by another publisher. However, Blackwood saw himself as a publisher of high-class books, and he emphatically did not regard Hogg as a high-class writer. As Blackwood saw it, the Ettrick Shepherd (that entertainingly coarse rustic) was an amusing character in the 'Noctes', but this boor's *Calendar* would have to be very carefully revised and corrected if it were to become a book fit to be published by the eminently respectable Blackwood firm. Astutely, Blackwood decided to allocate the task of revision and correction to Hogg's nephew Robert Hogg (1802–34). Hogg was fond of his nephew, a scholarly young man who was attempting to earn a living in the book trade by proofreading and similar work. If Robert were to be employed to revise his uncle's *Calendar*, family ties would mean that Hogg himself would not be in a position to protest too vigorously about the outcome.

Hogg wrote again to Blackwood about *The Shepherd's Calendar* on 12 February 1828. It appears from this letter that he was still thinking of the proposed book publication of *The Shepherd's Calendar* as a precursor of a collected edition of his 'other tales':

My dear sir
    I have got a long letter from Robert with a specimen of the printing of the Calender. I think the page rather crouded but

leave that to your better taste But I would never think of making *only one vol* I would far rather you made three which might
reduce the number of the other tales somewhat. Of all things in
the world I hate a dumpy vol of that size and would rather were
there only 400 pages instead of 580 make two vols, the expense of publishing is the same, the price better, and the circulating librarians purchase double the number because they get
double the price for perusal, and they will be almost the sole
purchasers of the work. Besides you have the whole Winter
Evening tales to pick and chuse upon; there are at least seven
which I will mention to Robert which naturally belong to that
publication therefore there is no occassion for an inferior tale
being admitted I would rather engage to write a half dozen more
in the time of publication. He is at full liberty to prune as he
likes and arrange as he likes and by all means let him leave out
the classes and give every tale a kind of appropriate name for
every tale must be distinct either as a chapter or *Tale* with a
beginning and an end. [...]   (NLS, MS 4021, fols 275–76)

Hogg then goes on to conclude this letter of 12 February 1828 with
a discussion of other matters. Robert Hogg had written to Blackwood
on 9 February 1828, reporting that 'I have drawn out a sketch of
what appears to me the best arrangement for the articles of the Shepherd's Calendar, including the whole that can be introduced under
that title' (see Introduction, p. xvii). Bearing this in mind, it is possible to sense that Hogg's letter of 12 February 1828 reflects his alarm
about the way plans for *The Shepherd's Calendar* were shaping up. It is
also possible to sense that this letter is an attempt to retrieve the
situation. Hogg says he will mention to Robert 'at least seven' items
that might be included from *Winter Evening Tales*, and he expresses a
willingness to write 'half a dozen' new stories in time for inclusion.
Clearly, in February 1828 Hogg did not have a fixed and final list of
contents in mind for *The Shepherd's Calendar*. Rather, his objective
seems to have been to get into print a coherent and high-quality
collection to be called *The Shepherd's Calendar*, the hoped-for success
of which would pave the way for a collected edition of his other
tales. For the new book, the 'Shepherd's Calendar' stories that he
had been publishing in *Blackwood's* could combine naturally with items
chosen from *Winter Evening Tales*, because these two sets of material
had both been produced in the spirit of his old 'rural and traditionary
tales' project.

    Hogg's letter of 12 February 1828 did bear fruit in one respect,
because, when *The Shepherd's Calendar* eventually appeared early in

March 1829, it occupied two volumes (of 341 and 326 pages) rather than the single 'crouded' and 'dumpy' volume originally envisaged. However, as we saw in the Introduction (pp. xv–xvi), Blackwood ensured that he kept firm control of what the 1829 volumes contained, in spite of Hogg's eagerness to make helpful suggestions to Robert. Blackwood's main concern in publishing *The Shepherd's Calendar* was to be seen to be the publisher, when the famous Ettrick Shepherd's well-known 'Shepherd's Calendar' articles in *Blackwood's Edinburgh Magazine* were reprinted in book form. Naturally, all the articles that had been published in *Blackwood's* under the 'Shepherd's Calendar' series title are included in the 1829 volumes. However, six additional items are also included, doubtless with a view to increasing the attractiveness and saleability of the new book.

The 'Advertisement' which follows the titlepage of the first volume of the 1829 edition claims that 'several Tales hitherto unpublished' are included in the collection. The sales pitch of the Blackwood firm is a little over-enthusiastic here, however. One of the additional six items, 'Nancy Chisholm', was indeed previously unpublished. Furthermore, while the opening section of 'A Strange Secret' had been published in the number of *Blackwood's* for June 1828 (albeit not as part of the 'Shepherd's Calendar' series), the concluding section was not published in the magazine, and made its first appearance in the 1829 *Shepherd's Calendar*. However, in spite of the Advertisement's claim, the remaining four additional items had all been previously published. 'The Prodigal Son' and 'The School of Misfortune' had appeared (anonymously) in 1821 in volume 9 of Constable's *Edinburgh Magazine* (a new series of *The Scots Magazine*): perhaps Blackwood hoped that these old anonymously-published stories would be taken for new work. Be that as it may, the remaining two items had been published comparatively recently in *Blackwood's* as Hogg's work, but not as part of the 'Shepherd's Calendar' series: 'The Marvellous Doctor' had appeared in the number for September 1827, and 'The Brownie of the Black Haggs' had appeared in the number for October 1828.

It would appear that Hogg was surprised and angry when he finally saw the contents of the 1829 *Shepherd's Calendar*, which happened when a printed copy was sent to him with William Blackwood's letter of 28 February 1829. In his reply to Blackwood of 10 March 1829 (mentioned above), Hogg focuses his anger on the rejection of his article 'Wat the Prophet', which he had offered for *Blackwood's*. In this vein, he tells Blackwood 'you are the crabbedest cappernoityest worst tempered deevil I ever saw', and adds that, on reading Blackwood's letter of 28 February 'I was within a hairs-breadth of writing in a great rage and breaking with all connections of Maga for ever'. Hogg continues:

> You know that I sent you both Nancy Chisholm and M,Corkingdale avowedly for the Magazine without once adverting to the need there might be for inserting them else-where and as I recieved no hint that they would be taken for the Calendar It was to them I adverted when I complained of your dilatoriness in publishing.   (English Literature MSS, Lilly Library, Indiana University [photocopy in British Library, R.P.1117])

There is something of a mystery about 'M,Corkingdale', because no tale of that name appears in the 1829 *Shepherd's Calendar*. Never-theless, it is clear from what Hogg says here that he had sent 'Nancy Chisholm' and 'M,Corkingdale' as ordinary contributions to *Blackwood's*, and that when he sent them he did not see them as part of the *Shepherd's Calendar* project. After some time, the two stories had not appeared in the magazine, and Hogg complained about Blackwood's 'dilatoriness in publishing'. He did so because he had no reason to suppose that 'Nancy Chisholm' was in fact going to be included in the 1829 *Shepherd's Calendar*.

Blackwood's edition of *The Shepherd's Calendar* was followed by an American edition (New York: A. T. Goodrich, 1829). After 1829 Hogg's 'Shepherd's Calendar' stories were not reprinted during his lifetime, but these stories were reprinted in their bowdlerised 1829 versions in all the various posthumous nineteenth-century collected editions of his writings. However, half a dozen of them were in-cluded in their pre-1829 unbowdlerised versions in Hogg, *Selected Stories and Sketches*, ed. by Douglas S. Mack (Edinburgh: Scottish Academic Press, 1982). This was the first printing since the 1820s of any of the pre-1829 versions of Hogg's 'Shepherd's Calendar' stories, and it was followed in 1995 by the S/SC Edition of *The Shepherd's Calendar*, on which the present paperback is based.

There is good reason to suppose that Hogg set a high value on his 'Shepherd's Calendar' stories (see Introduction, p. xv), and when the S/SC Edition was being planned it was felt that it would be ap-propriate if *The Shepherd's Calendar* were to be one of the first vol-umes to appear. But what would the contents of this volume be? It seems abundantly clear from the evidence quoted above that Robert Hogg and William Blackwood were responsible for the choice of material for the 1829 *Shepherd's Calendar*, as well as for bowdlerising

Hogg's text. Equally clearly, Hogg himself was not involved in the process of selection. In these circumstances, it did not seem appropriate to follow Robert Hogg's selection of material for the 1829 edition. It seemed more useful to produce a volume consisting of the stories Hogg himself wrote for publication under the 'Shepherd's Calendar' series title. This book therefore consists of the stories that Hogg wrote for his 'Shepherd's Calendar' series in *Blackwood's Edinburgh Magazine*. It includes 'The Brownie of the Black Haggs', because there is clear evidence from Hogg's letters that he wrote this story as part of the 'Shepherd's Calendar' series, even although it was not published under the 'Shephed's Calendar' title when it appeared in the number of *Blackwood's* for October 1828. This evidence is discussed in the Notes (see pp. 276–77, below).

As we have seen, *Winter Evening Tales* (1820) includes, under the 'Shepherd's Calendar' title, stories that had previously appeared anonymously in Blackwood's in 1817 under the series title 'Tales and Anecdotes of the Pastoral Life'. The inclusion of these stories in the 'Shepherd's Calendar' subsection of *Winter Evening Tales* makes sense in the context of that collection, but these stories were not written as part of the 'Shepherd's Calendar' series. They find their natural place in the S/SC Edition as part of the *Winter Evening Tales* volume. However, Hogg originally wrote 'Storms' as a 'Shepherd's Calendar' contribution to *Blackwood's*, but later included this text in *Winter Evening Tales*. As a result, in the S/SC Edition 'Storms' finds a place in both *Winter Evening Tales* and *The Shepherd's Calendar*.

In short, the present volume brings together all the stories Hogg wrote for publication under the 'Shepherd's Calendar' series title. It turns out to be a notably coherent and vibrant collection.

Notes

1   The title was also used by John Clare, whose cycle of poems *The Shepherd's Calendar* was completed in 1823, and was first published in 1827.
2   For a discussion of this, see Hogg, *The Brownie of Bodsbeck*, ed. by Douglas S. Mack (Edinburgh: Scottish Academic Press, 1976), pp. xvi–xvii.
3   For further details, see Hogg, *Winter Evening Tales*, ed. by Ian Duncan (Edinburgh: Edinburgh University Press, 2002).

Select Bibliography

Editions of *The Shepherd's Calendar*

Between 1819 and 1828 Hogg made a number of contributions to *Blackwood's Edinburgh Magazine* under the series title 'The Shepherd's Calendar'. The magazine series formed the basis of *The Shepherd's Calendar*, 2 vols (Edinburgh: William Blackwood, 1829), but the 1829 text offered a bowdlerised and distorted version of Hogg's collection (see Introduction, above, pp. xv–xix). However, the mutilated 1829 text was followed in the various posthumous Victorian collected editions of Hogg's writings. Hogg's original versions of his 'Shepherd's Calendar' stories began to re-emerge when half a dozen of them were included in James Hogg, *Selected Stories and Sketches*, ed. by Douglas S. Mack (Edinburgh: Scottish Academic Press, 1982), a volume that saw the first printings since the 1820s of items from 'The Shepherd's Calendar' in their unbowdlerised form. In 1995, one of the first volumes of the Stirling / South Carolina Edition of Hogg's collected works (see below) brought together all his 'Shepherd's Calendar' contributions to *Blackwood's*, and published these pieces in their original, unmutilated form. The present paperback is a reprint of this 1995 volume.

Collected Editions

The Stirling / South Carolina Research Edition of the Collected Works of James Hogg (Edinburgh: Edinburgh University Press, 1995–), now underway but not yet complete, is a modern scholarly edition. Previous editions which are useful but bowdlerised are *Tales and Sketches by the Ettrick Shepherd*, 6 vols (Glasgow: Blackie and Son, 1836–37), *The Poetical Works of the Ettrick Shepherd*, 5 vols (Glasgow: Blackie and Son, 1838–40), and *The Works of the Ettrick Shepherd*, ed. by Thomas Thomson, 2 vols (Glasgow: Blackie and Son, 1865).

Bibliography

Edith C. Batho's Bibliography in *The Ettrick Shepherd* (Cambridge: Cambridge University Press, 1927), is still useful, together with her supplementary 'Notes on the Bibliography of James Hogg, the Ettrick Shepherd', in *The Library*, 16 (1935–36), 309–26. Two more modern and reader-friendly bibliographies are Douglas S. Mack, *Hogg's Prose: An Annotated Listing* (Stirling: The James Hogg Society, 1985), and Gillian Hughes, *Hogg's Verse and Drama: A Chronological Listing*

(Stirling: The James Hogg Society, 1990). Subsequent information about recently-discovered Hogg items may be gleaned from various articles in *The Bibliotheck* and *Studies in Hogg and his World.*

Biography

There is as yet no modern Hogg biography, though Gillian Hughes is currently writing one: her *James Hogg: A Life* will be published by Edinburgh University Press. Hogg's life up to 1825 is covered by Alan Lang Strout's *The Life and Letters of James Hogg, The Ettrick Shepherd Volume 1 (1770–1825)*, Texas Technological College Research Publications, 15 (Lubbock, Texas: Texas Technological College, 1946). Much valuable information may be obtained from Mrs M. G. Garden's memoir of her father, *Memorials of James Hogg, the Ettrick Shepherd* (London: Alexander Gardner, 1885), and from Mrs Norah Parr's account of Hogg's domestic life in *James Hogg at Home* (Dollar: Douglas S. Mack, 1980). Also useful are Sir George Douglas, *James Hogg*, Famous Scots Series (Edinburgh: Oliphant Anderson & Ferrier, 1899), and Henry Thew Stephenson's *The Ettrick Shepherd: A Biography*, Indiana University Studies, 54 (Bloomington, Indiana: Indiana University, 1922).

General Criticism

Edith C. Batho, *The Ettrick Shepherd* (Cambridge: Cambridge University Press, 1927)

Louis Simpson, *James Hogg: A Critical Study* (Edinburgh and London: Oliver & Boyd, 1962)

Douglas Gifford, *James Hogg* (Edinburgh: The Ramsay Head Press, 1976)

Nelson C. Smith, *James Hogg*, Twayne's English Authors Series (Boston: Twayne Publishers, 1980)

David Groves, *James Hogg: The Growth of a Writer* (Edinburgh: Scottish Academic Press, 1988)

Thomas Crawford, 'James Hogg: The Play of Region and Nation', in *The History of Scottish Literature: Volume 3 Nineteenth Century*, ed. by Douglas Gifford (Aberdeen: Aberdeen University Press, 1988), pp. 89–105

Silvia Mergenthal, *James Hogg: Selbstbild und Bild*, Publications of the Scottish Studies Centre of the Johannes Gutenberg Universität Mainz in Germersheim, 9 (Frankfurt-am-Main: Peter Lang, 1990)

Penny Fielding, *Writing and Orality: Nationality, Culture, and Nineteenth-Century Scottish Fiction* (Oxford: Clarendon Press, 1996)

The Shepherd's Calendar
(Criticism and Source Material)

John Hyslop and Robert Hyslop, *Langholm as it Was: A History of Langholm and Eskdale from the Earliest Times* (Sunderland: Hills, 1912). [Includes (pp. 847–50) other accounts of the storms described by Hogg in 'Storms'.]

Douglas S. Mack, '*Blackwood's Edinburgh Magazine* and *The Shepherd's Calendar*', in Mack, 'Editing James Hogg' (unpublished doctoral thesis, University of Stirling, 1984), pp. 87–140. [Includes a complete list (pp. 126–40) of the verbal variants between 'The Shepherd's Calendar. Dreams and Apparitions.–Part II. Containing Tibby Hyslop's Dream, and the Sequel', *Blackwood's Edinburgh Magazine*, 21 (June 1827), 664–76; and 'Tibby Hyslop's Dream', *The Shepherd's Calendar* (Edinburgh: Blackwood, 1829), I, 212–46.]

Douglas S. Mack, 'The Laverhope Water-Spout', *Newsletter of the James Hogg Society*, 3 (1984), 15–16

Douglas S. Mack, 'Notes on Editing James Hogg's "Storms"', *The Bibliotheck*, 12 (1985), 140–49

Emma Letley, ' "The Management of the Tongue": Hogg's Literary Uses of Scots', in *Papers Given at the Second James Hogg Society Conference (Edinburgh, 1985)*, ed. by Gillian Hughes (Aberdeen: Association for Scottish Literary Studies, 1988), pp. 11–23

Douglas S. Mack, 'Hogg, Blackwood and *The Shepherd's Calendar*', in *Papers Given at the Second James Hogg Society Conference*, pp. 24–31

Magdalene Redekop, 'Trials, Dreams, and Endings in the Tales of James Hogg', in *Papers Given at the Second James Hogg Society Conference*, pp. 32–41

James Hogg, 'Pictures of Country Life. Nos. I and II. Old Isaac', ed. by Douglas S. Mack, *Altrive Chapbooks*, 6 (1989), 1–23

John MacQueen, 'James Hogg', in MacQueen, *The Rise of the Historical Novel* (Edinburgh: Scottish Academic Press, 1989), pp. 193–269

Barbara Bloedé, 'The Witchcraft Tradition in Hogg's Tales and Verse', *Studies in Hogg and his World*, 1 (1990), 91–102

Jill Rubenstein, 'Varieties of Explanation in *The Shepherd's Calendar*', *Studies in Hogg and his World*, 4 (1993), 1–11

Fiona Stafford, review article in *Review of English Studies*, new series, 50 (February 1999), 66–68

Chronology of James Hogg

1770 On 9 December James Hogg is baptised in Ettrick Church, Selkirkshire, the date of his birth going unrecorded. His father, Robert Hogg (*c.*1729–1820), a former shepherd, was then tenant of Ettrickhall, a modest farm almost within sight of the church. His mother, Margaret Laidlaw (1730–1813), belonged to a local family noted for their athleticism and also for their stock of ballads and other traditional lore. Hogg's parents married in Ettrick on 27 May 1765, and had four sons, William (b.1767), James (b.1770), David (b.1773), and Robert (b.1776).

1775–76 Hogg attends the parish school kept by John Beattie for a few months before his formal education is abruptly terminated by his father's bankruptcy as a stock-farmer and sheep-dealer and the family's consequent destitution. Their possessions are sold by auction, but a compassionate neighbour, Walter Bryden of Crosslee, takes a lease of the farm of Ettrickhouse and places Robert Hogg there as his shepherd.

1776–85 Due to his family's poverty Hogg is employed as a farm servant throughout his childhood, beginning with the job of herding a few cows in the summer and progressing as his strength increases to general farmwork and acting as a shepherd's assistant. He learns the Metrical Psalms and other parts of the Bible, listens eagerly to the legends of his mother and her brother William (*c.*1735–1829), of itinerants who visit the parish, and of the old men he is engaged with on the lightest and least demanding farm-work.

1778 Death on 17 September of Hogg's maternal grandfather, William Laidlaw, 'the far-famed Will o' Phaup', a noted athlete and reputedly the last man in the district to have spoken with the fairies.

***c.* 1784** Having saved five shillings from his wages, at the age of fourteen Hogg purchases an old fiddle and teaches himself to play it at the end of his day's work.

1785 Hogg serves a year from Martinmas (11 November) with Mr Scott, the tenant-farmer of Singlee, at 'working with horses, threshing, &c.'

1786 Hogg serves eighteen months from Martinmas with Mr Laidlaw at Elibank, 'the most quiet and sequestered place in Scotland'.

1788 The father of Mr Laidlaw of Elibank, who farms at Willenslee, gives Hogg his first engagement as a shepherd from Whitsunday (15 May); here he stays for two years and begins to read while tending the ewes. His master's wife lends him newspapers and theological works, and he also reads Allan Ramsay's *The Gentle Shepherd* and William Hamilton of Gilbertfield's paraphrase of Blind Harry's *The Life and Adventures of William Wallace*.

1790 Hogg begins a ten-years' service from Whitsunday as shepherd to James Laidlaw of Blackhouse farm, whose kindness he later described as 'much more like that of a father than a master'. Hogg reads his master's books, as well as those of Mr Elder's Peebles circulating library, and begins to compose songs for the local lasses to sing. He makes a congenial and life-long friend in his master's eldest son, William Laidlaw (1779–1845), and with his elder brother William and a number of cousins forms a literary society of shepherds. Alexander Laidlaw, shepherd at Bowerhope in Yarrow, is also an intimate friend who shares Hogg's efforts at self-improvement. 'The Mistakes of a Night', a Scots poem, is published in the *Scots Magazine* for October 1794, and in 1797 Hogg first hears of Robert Burns (1759–96) when a half-daft man named Jock Scott recites 'Tam o' Shanter' to him on the hillside. Towards the end of this period Hogg composes plays and pastorals as well as songs. His journeying as a drover of sheep stimulates an interest in the Highlands of Scotland, and initiates a series of exploratory tours taken in the summer over a succession of years.

1800 At Whitsunday Hogg leaves Blackhouse to look after his ageing parents at Ettrickhouse. Going into Edinburgh in the autumn to sell sheep he decides to print his poems: his *Scottish Pastorals* is published early in the following year and receives favourable attention in the *Scots Magazine* for 1801. More popular still is his patriotic song of 'Donald Macdonald' also composed at about this time, in fear of a French invasion.

1802 Hogg is recruited by William Laidlaw in the spring as a ballad-collector for Scott's *Minstrelsy of the Scottish Border*, and meets Walter Scott himself (1771–1832) later in the year. He begins to contribute to the *Edinburgh Magazine*, and keeps a journal of his Highland Tour in July and August that is eventually published in the *Scots Magazine*.

1803 The lease of Ettrickhouse expires at Whitsunday and Hogg uses his savings to lease a Highland sheep farm, signing a five-year lease for Shelibost in Harris on 13 July, to begin from Whitsunday 1804. On his journey home he stops at Greenock where he meets the future novelist John Galt (1779–1839) and his friend James Park. He is now a regular contributor to the *Scots Magazine*, and also earns prizes from the Highland Society of Scotland for his essays on sheep.

1804 Hogg loses his money and fails to gain possession of Shelibost through a legal complication, retiring into England for the summer. On his return home he fails to find employment, but occupies himself in writing ballad-imitations for the collection published in 1807 as *The Mountain Bard*.

1805–1806 Hogg is engaged from Whitsunday 1805 as a shepherd at Mitchelslacks farm in Closeburn parish, Dumfriesshire: his master Mr Harkness belongs to a local family famous for their support of the Covenanters. He is visited on the hillside by the young Allan Cunningham (1784–1842), and becomes friendly with the whole talented Cunningham family. Around Halloween 1806 (31 October) he becomes the lover of Catherine Henderson. Towards the end of the year Hogg signs leases on two farms in Dumfriesshire, Corfardin and Locherben, to begin from Whitsunday 1807.

1807 *The Mountain Bard* is published by Archibald Constable (1774–1827) in Edinburgh in February. At Whitsunday Hogg moves to Corfardin farm in Tynron parish. *The Shepherd's Guide*, a sheep-farming and veterinary manual, is published in June. Hogg acknowledges paternity of Catherine Henderson's baby, born towards the end of the summer and baptised Catherine Hogg on 13 December.

1808–09 As a result of trips to Edinburgh Hogg becomes acquainted with James Gray (1770–1830), classics master of the Edinburgh High School and his future brother-in-law. He also meets a number of literary women, including Mary Peacock, Jessie Stuart, Mary Brunton, and Eliza Izet. After the death of his sheep in a storm Hogg moves to Locherben farm and tries to earn a living by grazing sheep for other farmers. His debts escalate, he becomes increasingly reckless, and around Whitsunday 1809 becomes the lover of Margaret Beattie. In the autumn Hogg absconds from Locherben and his creditors, returning to Ettrick where he is considered to be disgraced and unemployable.

1810 In February Hogg moves to Edinburgh in an attempt to pursue a career as a professional literary man. In Dumfries-shire Margaret Beattie's daughter is born on 13 March, and her birth is recorded retrospectively as Elizabeth Hogg in June, Hogg presumably having acknowledged paternity. Later that year Hogg meets his future wife, Margaret Phillips (1789–1870), while she is paying a visit to her brother-in-law James Gray in Edinburgh. He explores the cultural life of Edinburgh, and is supported by the generosity of an Ettrick friend, John Grieve (1781–1836), now a prosperous Edinburgh hatter. A song-collection entitled *The Forest Minstrel* is published in August. On 1 September the first number of Hogg's own weekly periodical *The Spy* appears, which in spite of its perceived improprieties, continues for a whole year.

1811–12 During the winter of 1810–11 Hogg becomes an active member of the Forum, a public debating society, eventually being appointed Secretary. This brings him into contact with John M'Diarmid (1792–1852), later to become a noted Scottish journalist, and the reforming mental health specialist Dr Andrew Duncan (1744–1828). With Grieve's encouragement Hogg takes rural lodgings at Deanhaugh on the outskirts of Edinburgh and plans a long narrative poem centred on a poetical contest at the court of Mary, Queen of Scots.

1813 Hogg becomes a literary celebrity in Edinburgh when *The Queen's Wake* is published at the end of January, and makes new friends in R. P. Gillies (1788–1858) and John Wilson (1785–1854), his correspondence widening to include Lord Byron (1788–1824) early the following year. Hogg's mother dies in the course of the summer. Hogg tries to interest Constable in a series of Scottish Rural Tales, and also takes advice from various literary friends on the suitability of his play, *The Hunting of Badlewe*, for the stage. In the autumn during his customary Highland Tour he is detained at Kinnaird House near Dunkeld by a cold and begins a poem in the Spenserian stanza, eventually to become *Mador of the Moor*.

1814 Hogg intervenes successfully to secure publication of the work of other writers such as R. P. Gillies, James Gray, and William Nicholson (1782–1849). George Goldie publishes *The Hunting of Badlewe* in April, as the Allies enter Paris and the end of the long war with France seems imminent. During the summer Hogg meets William Wordsworth (1770–1850) in Edinburgh, and visits him and other poets in an excursion to the Lake District. He proposes a poetical repository, and obtains several promises of contributions from important contemporary poets, though the project leads to a serious quarrel with Scott in the autumn. The bankruptcy of George Goldie halts sales of *The Queen's Wake*, but introduces Hogg to the publisher William Blackwood (1776–1834). Having offered Constable *Mador of the Moor* in February, Hogg is persuaded by James Park to publish *The Pilgrims of the Sun* first: the poem is brought out by John Murray (1778–1843) and William Blackwood in Edinburgh in December. Towards the end of the year Hogg and his young Edinburgh friends form the Right and Wrong Club which meets nightly and where heavy drinking takes place.

1815 Hogg begins the year with a serious illness, but at the end of January is better and learns that the Duke of Buccleuch has granted him the small farm of Eltrive Moss effectively rent-free for his lifetime. He takes possession at Whitsunday, but as the house there is barely habitable continues to spend much of his time in Edinburgh. He writes songs for the Scottish collector George Thomson (1757–1851). Scott's publication of a poem celebrating the ending of the Napoleonic Wars with the battle of Waterloo on 18 June prompts Hogg to write 'The Field of Waterloo'. Hogg also writes 'To the Ancient Banner of Buccleuch' for the local contest at football at Carterhaugh on 4 December.

1816 Hogg contributes songs to John Clarke-Whitfeld's *Twelve Vocal Melodies*, and plans a collected edition of his own poetry. *Mador of the Moor* is published in April. Despairing of the success of his poetical repository Hogg turns it into a collection of his own parodies, published in October as *The Poetic Mirror*. The volume is unusually successful, a second edition being published in December. The Edinburgh musician Alexander Campbell visits Hogg in Yarrow, enlisting his help with the song-collection *Albyn's Anthology* (1816–18). William Blackwood moves into Princes Street, signalling his intention to become one of Edinburgh's foremost publishers.

1817 Blackwood begins an *Edinburgh Monthly Magazine* in April, with Hogg's support, but with Thomas Pringle and James Cleghorn as editors it is a lacklustre publication and a breach between publisher and editors ensues. Hogg, holding by Blackwood, sends him a draft of the notorious 'Chaldee Manuscript', the scandal surrounding which ensures the success of the re-launched *Blackwood's Edinburgh Magazine*. Hogg's two-volume

Dramatic Tales are published in May. Hogg spends much of the summer at his farm of Altrive, writing songs for *Hebrew Melodies*, a Byron-inspired collection proposed by the composer W. E. Heather. In October George Thomson receives a proposal from the Highland Society of London for a collection of Jacobite Songs, a commission which he passes on to Hogg.

1818 *The Brownie of Bodsbeck; and Other Tales* is published by Blackwood in March, by which time Hogg is busily working on *Jacobite Relics*, his major preoccupation this year. A modern stone-built cottage is built at Altrive, the cost of which Hogg hopes to defray in part by a new one guinea subscription edition of *The Queen's Wake*, which is at press in October though publication did not occur until early the following year.

1819 On a visit to Edinburgh towards the end of February Hogg meets again with Margaret Phillips; his courtship of her becomes more intense, and he proposes marriage. Hogg's song-collection *A Border Garland* is published in May, and in August Hogg signs a contract with Oliver and Boyd for the publication of *Winter Evening Tales*, also working on a long Border Romance. The first volume of *Jacobite Relics* is published in December.

1820 During the spring Hogg is working on the second volume of his *Jacobite Relics* and also on a revised edition of *The Mountain Bard*, as well as planning his marriage to Margaret Phillips, which takes place on 28 April. His second work of fiction, *Winter Evening Tales,* is published at the end of April. Very little literary work is accomplished during the autumn: the Hoggs make their wedding visits in Dumfriesshire during September, and then on 24 October Hogg's old father dies at Altrive.

1821 The second volume of *Jacobite Relics* is published in February and a third (enlarged) edition of *The Mountain Bard* in March. The inclusion in the latter of an updated 'Memoir of the Author's Life' raises an immediate outcry. Hogg's son, James Robert Hogg, is born in Edinburgh on 18 March and baptised on the couple's first wedding anniversary. Serious long-term financial troubles begin for Hogg with the signing of a nine-year lease from Whitsunday of the large farm of Mount Benger in Yarrow, part of the estates of the Duke of Buccleuch—Hogg having insufficient capital for such an ambitious venture. In June Oliver and Boyd's refusal to publish Hogg's

Border Romance, *The Three Perils of Man*, leads to a breach with the firm. Hogg also breaks temporarily with Blackwood in August when a savage review of his 'Memoir of the Author's Life' appears in *Blackwood's Edinburgh Magazine*, and begins again to write for Constable's less lively *Edinburgh Magazine*. In September there is a measles epidemic in Yarrow, and Hogg becomes extremely ill with the disease. By the end of the year Hogg is negotiating with the Constable firm for an edition of his collected poems in four volumes.

1822 The first of the 'Noctes Ambrosianae' appears in the March issue of *Blackwood's Edinburgh Magazine*: Hogg is portrayed in this long-running series as the Shepherd, a 'boozing buffoon'. June sees the publication of Hogg's four-volume *Poetical Works* by Constable, and Longmans publish his novel *The Three Perils of Man*. There is great excitement in Edinburgh surrounding the visit of George IV to the city in August, and Hogg marks the occasion with the publication of his Scottish masque, *The Royal Jubilee*. A neighbouring landowner in Ettrick Forest, Captain Napier of Thirlestane, publishes *A Treatise on Practical Store-Farming* in October, with help from Hogg and his friend Alexander Laidlaw of Bowerhope. James Gray leaves Edinburgh to become Rector of Belfast Academy.

1823 In debt to William Blackwood Hogg sets about retrieving his finances with a series of tales for *Blackwood's Edinburgh Magazine* under the title of 'The Shepherd's Calendar'. His daughter Janet Phillips Hogg ('Jessie') is born on 23 April. That summer a suicide is exhumed in Yarrow, and Hogg writes an account for *Blackwood's*. *The Three Perils of Woman*, another novel, is published in August, and Hogg subsequently plans to publish an eight-volume collection of his Scottish tales.

1824 Hogg is working on his epic poem *Queen Hynde* during the spring when his attention is distracted by family troubles. His once prosperous father-in-law is in need of a home, so Hogg moves his own family to the old thatched farmhouse of Mount Benger leaving his new cottage at Altrive for the old couple. *The Private Memoirs and Confessions of a Justified Sinner*, written at Altrive during the preceding months, is published in June. Hogg contributes to the *Literary Souvenir* for 1825, this signalling the opening of a new and lucrative market for his work in Literary Annuals. In November a major conflagration destroys part of Edinburgh's Old Town. *Queen Hynde* is published early in December.

1825 Another daughter is born to the Hoggs on 18 January and named Margaret Laidlaw Hogg ('Maggie'). Hogg turns his attention to a new work of prose fiction, 'Lives of Eminent Men', the precursor of his *Tales of the Wars of Montrose*. In December John Gibson Lockhart (1794–1854), Scott's son-in-law and a leading light of *Blackwood's*, moves to London to take up the post of editor of the *Quarterly Review*, accompanied by Hogg's nephew and literary assistant Robert Hogg.

1826 Hogg is in arrears with his rent for Mount Benger at a time which sees the failure of the Constable publishing firm, involving Sir Walter Scott and also Hogg's friend John Aitken. By July Hogg himself is threatened with arrestment for debt, while the Edinburgh book trade is in a state of near-stagnation. James Gray is also in debt and leaves Belfast for India, leaving his two daughters, Janet and Mary, in the care of Hogg and his wife.

1827 Hogg's financial affairs are in crisis at the beginning of the year when the Buccleuch estate managers order him to pay his arrears of rent at Whitsunday or relinquish the Mount Benger farm. However, 'The Shepherd's Calendar' stories are appearing regularly in *Blackwood's Edinburgh Magazine* and Hogg is confident of earning a decent income by his pen as applications for contributions to Annuals and other periodicals increase. The death of his father-in-law Peter Phillips in May relieves him from the expense of supporting two households. Hogg founds the St Ronan's Border Club, the first sporting meeting of which takes place at Innerleithen in September. The year ends quietly for the Hoggs, who are both convalescent—Margaret from the birth of the couple's third daughter, Harriet Sidney Hogg, on 18 December, and Hogg from the lameness resulting from having been struck by a horse.

1828 Although a more productive year for Hogg than the last, with the publication of his *Select and Rare Scotish Melodies* in London in the autumn and the signing of a contract with Robert Purdie for a new edition of his *Border Garland*, the book-trade is still at a comparative standstill. Hogg's daughter Harriet is discovered to have a deformed foot that may render her lame. A new weekly periodical entitled the *Edinburgh Literary Journal* is started in Edinburgh by Hogg's young friend, Henry Glassford Bell (1803–74).

1829 Hogg continues to write songs and to make contributions to Annuals and other periodicals, while the spring sees the pub-

lication of *The Shepherd's Calendar* in book form. Hogg continues to relish shooting during the autumn months and the country sports of the St Ronan's Border Club.

1830 Hogg's lease of the Mount Benger farm is not renewed, and
the family return to Altrive at Whitsunday. Inspired by the
success of Scott's *magnum opus* edition of the Waverley Novels,
Hogg pushes for the publication of his own tales in monthly
numbers. Blackwood agrees to publish a small volume of
Hogg's best songs, and Hogg finds a new outlet for his work
with the foundation in February of *Fraser's Magazine*. Towards
the end of September Hogg meets with Scott for the last time.

1831 *Songs by the Ettrick Shepherd* is published at the start of the year,
and a companion volume of ballads, *A Queer Book*, is printed,
though publication is held up by Blackwood, who argues that
the political agitation surrounding the Reform Bill is hurtful
to his trade. He is also increasingly reluctant to print Hogg's
work in his magazine. Hogg's youngest child, Mary Gray
Hogg, is born on 21 August. Early in December Hogg quarrels openly with Blackwood and resolves to start the publication of his collected prose tales in London. After a short stay
in Edinburgh he departs by sea and arrives in London on the
last day of the year.

1832 From January to March Hogg enjoys being a literary lion in
London while he forwards the publication of his collected prose
tales. Within a few weeks of his arrival he publishes a devo-
tional manual for children entitled *A Father's New Year's Gift*,
and also works on the first volume of his *Altrive Tales*, published in April after his return to Altrive. Blackwood, no doubt
aware of Hogg's metropolitan celebrity, finally publishes *A
Queer Book* in April too. The Glasgow publisher Archibald
Fullarton offers Hogg a substantial fee for producing a new
edition of the works of Robert Burns with a memoir of the
poet. The financial failure of Hogg's London publisher, James
Cochrane, stops the sale and production of *Altrive Tales* soon
after the publication of the first (and only) volume. Sir Walter
Scott dies on 21 September, and Hogg reflects on the subject
of a Scott biography. In October Hogg is invited to contribute
to a new cheap paper, *Chambers's Edinburgh Journal*.

1833 During a January visit to Edinburgh Hogg falls through the
ice while out curling and a serious illness results. In February
he tries to interest the numbers publisher Blackie and Son of
Glasgow in a continuation of his collected prose tales. He tries

to mend the breach with Blackwood, who for his part is seriously offended by Hogg's allusions to their financial dealings in the 'Memoir' prefacing *Altrive Tales*. Hogg sends a collection of anecdotes about Scott for publication in London but withdraws them in deference to Lockhart as Scott's son-in-law, forwarding a rewritten version to America in June for publication there. He offers Cochrane, now back in business as a publisher, some tales about the wars of Montrose, and by November has reached an agreement with Blackie and Son. The young Duke of Buccleuch grants Hogg a 99-year lease for the house at Altrive and a fragment of the land, a measure designed to secure a vote for him in elections but which also ensures a small financial provision for Hogg's young family after his death.

1834 Hogg's nephew and literary assistant Robert Hogg dies of consumption on 9 January, aged thirty-one. Hogg revises his work on the edition of Burns, now with William Motherwell as a co-editor. His *Lay Sermons* is published in April, and the same month sees the publication of his *Familiar Anecdotes of Sir Walter Scott* in America. When a pirated version comes out in Glasgow in June Lockhart breaks off all friendly relations with Hogg. The breach with William Blackwood is mended in May, but Blackwood's death on 16 November loosens Hogg's connection both with the publishing firm and *Blackwood's Edinburgh Magazine*.

1835 *Tales of the Wars of Montrose* is published in March. Hogg seems healthy enough in June, when his wife and daughter, Harriet, leave him at Altrive while paying a visit to Edinburgh. Even in August he is well enough to go out shooting on the moors as usual and to take what proves to be a last look at Blackhouse and other scenes of his youth. Soon afterwards, however, his normally excellent constitution begins to fail and by October he is confined first to the house and then to his bed. He dies on 21 November, and is buried among his relations in Ettrick kirkyard a short distance from the place of his birth.

Gillian Hughes

Storms

These constitute the various aeras of the pastoral life. They are the red lines in the shepherd's manual—the remembrancers of years and ages that are past—the tablets of memory by which the ages of his children the times of his ancestors and the rise and downfall of families are invariably ascertained. Even the progress of improvement in Scots farming can be traced traditionally from these, and the rent of a farm or estate given with precision, before and after such and such a storm, though the narrator be uncertain in what century the said notable storm happened. "Mar's year" and "that year the heelanders raide" are but secondary mementos to *the year Nine* and *the year Forty*—these stand in bloody capitals in the annals of the pastoral life as well as many more that shall hereafter be mentioned.

The most dismal of all those on record is *The Thirteen drifty days*. This extraordinary storm as near as I have been able to trace must have occurred in the year 1620. The traditionary stories and pictures of desolation that remain of it are the most dire imaginable and the mentioning of the thirteen drifty days to an old shepherd in a stormy winter night never fails to impress his mind with a sort of religious awe and often sets him on his knees before that Being who alone can avert such another calamity.

It is said that for thirteen days and nights the snow drift never once abated—the ground was covered with frozen snow when it commenced and during all that time the sheep never broke their fast. The cold was intense to a degree never before remembred and about the fifth and sixth days of the storm the young sheep began to fall into a sleepy and torpid state and all that were so affected in the evening died over night. The intensity of the frost wind often cut them off when in that state quite instantaneously. About the ninth and tenth days the shepherds began to build up huge semi-circular walls of their dead in order to afford some shelter for the remainder of the living but they availed but little for about the same time they were frequently seen tearing at one another's wool with their teeth.

When the storm abated, on the fourteenth day from its commencement, there was on many a high-lying farm not a living sheep to be seen. Large mishapen walls of dead, surrounding a small prostrate flock likewise all dead, and frozen stiff in their lairs, were all that remained to cheer the forlorn shepherd and his master and though on low-lying farms where the snow was not so hard before numbers of sheep weathered the storm yet their constitutions received such a shock that the greater part of them perished afterwards and the final consequence was that about nine tenths of all the sheep in the South of Scotland were destroyed.

In the extensive pastoral district of Eskdalemoor which maintains upwards of 20:000 sheep it is said none were left alive but forty young wedders on one farm and five old ewes on another. The farm of Phaup remained without a stock and without a tenant for twenty years subsequent to the storm, at length one very honest and liberal minded man ventured to take a lease of it at the annual rent of *a grey coat and a pair of hose.* It is now rented at £500. An extensive glen in Tweedsmuir belonging to Sir James Montgomery Bart. became a common at that time, to which any man drove his flocks that pleased, and it continued so for nearly a century. On one of Sir Patrick Scott of Thirlestane's farms, that keeps upwards of 900 sheep, they all died save one black ewe from which the farmer had high hopes of preserving a breed; but some unlucky dogs, that were all laid idle for want of sheep to run at, fell upon this poor solitary remnant of a good stock, and chased her into the lake where she was drowned. When word of this was brought to John Scott the farmer, commonly called gouffin' Jock, he is reported to have expressed himself as follows "Ochon ochon an' is that the gate o't?—a black beginning maks aye a black end" then taking down an old rusty sword he added, "come thou away my auld frien'—thou an' I maun e'en stock Bowrhope Law aince mair. Bessy my dow, how gaes the auld sang now? Gin ye'll gie me the words I'll sing't to you.

> There's walth o' kye i' bonny Braidlees
> There's walth o' yowes i' Tine
> There's walth o' gear i' Gowanburn
> An' thae shall a' be thine"

It is a pity that tradition has not preserved any thing further of the history of Gouffin' Jock than this one saying.

The next memorable event of this nature is *the Blast o' March,* which happened on the 24th day of that month in the year 16.. on a Monday's morning; and though it lasted only for one forenoon, it was calculated to have destroyed upwards of a thousand scores of sheep, as well as a number of shepherds. There is one anecdote of this storm that is worthy of being preserved as it is shows with how much attention shepherds as well as sailors should observe the appearances of the sky. The Sunday evening before was so warm that the lasses went home from church barefoot, and the young men threw off their plaids and coats and carried them over their shoulders. A large group of these younkers going home from the chuch of Yarrow equipped in this manner chanced to pass by an old shepherd on the farm of Newhouse named Walter Blake who had all his sheep gathered into the side of a wood. They asked at Watie, who was a very religious man, what could have induced him to gather his sheep on the Sabbath day? He answered that he had seen an ill-hued weather-gaw that morning and was afraid it was going to be a drift. They were so much amused at Watie's apprehensions that they clapped their hands and laughed at him and one pert girl cried

"Aye fie tak' care Watie; I wadna say but it may be thrapple deep or the morn." Another asked if he wasna rather feared for the sun burning the een out o' their heads? and· a third if he didna keep a correspondence wi' the thieves an' kend they were to ride that night. Watie was obliged to bear all this for the evening was fine beyond any thing generally seen at that season and only said to them at parting "Weel weel callans; time will try a; let him laugh that wins; but slacks will be sleek, a hogg for the howking; we'll a' get horns to tout on the morn." The saying grew proverbial but Watie was the only man who saved the whole of his stock in that country.

The years 1709–40 and 72 were all likewise notable years for severity and for the losses sustained among the flocks of sheep. In the latter the snow lay from the middle of December until the middle of April, and all the time hard frozen. Partial thaws always kept the farmer's hopes of relief alive and thus prevented him from removing his sheep to a lower situation, till at length they grew so weak that they could not be removed. There has not been such a general loss in the days of any man living as in that year. It is by these years that all subsequent hard winters have been measured, and of late by that of 1795, and when the balance turns out in favour of the calculator there is always a degree of thankfulness expressed, as well as a composed submission to the awards of Divine providence. The daily sense so naturally impressed on the shepherd's mind that all his comforts are so entirely in the hand of him that rules the elements, contributes not a little to that firm spirit of devotion for which the Scotish shepherd is so distinguished. I know of no scene so impressive as that of a family sequestered in a lone glen during the time of a Winter storm; and where is the glen in the kingdom that wants such a habitation? There they are left to the protection of heaven, and they know and feel it. Throughout all the wild vicissitudes of nature they have no hope of assistance from man, but are conversant with the Almighty alone.

Before retiring to rest, the shepherd uniformly goes out to examine the state of the weather, and make his report to the little dependant group within—nothing is to be seen but the conflict of the elements, nor heard but the raving of the storm—then they all kneel around him, while he reccommends them to the protection of heaven, and though their little hymn of praise can scarcely be heard even by themselves as it mixes with the roar of the tempest, they never fail to rise from their devotions with their spirits cheered, and their confidence renewed, and go to sleep with an exaltation of mind of which kings and conquerors have no share. Often have I been a sharer in such scenes; and never, even in my youngest years, without having my heart deeply impressed by the circumstances. There is a sublimity in the very idea. There we lived as it were inmates of the cloud and the storm, but we stood in a relationship to the ruler of these that neither Time nor Eternity could ever cancel. Wo to him that would weaken the bonds with which true Christianity connects us with Heaven and with each other.

But of all the storms that ever Scotland witnessed, or I hope ever will again behold, there is none of them that can once be compared with the memorable 24th of Janr 1794, which fell with such peculiar violence on that division of the South of Scotland that lies between Crawford-Moor and the Border. In that bounds there were 17 shepherds perished, and upwards of 30 carried home insensible who afterwards recovered; but the numbers of sheep that were lost far outwent any possibility of calculation. One farmer alone Mr. Thomas Beattie, lost 72 scores for his own share, and many others in the same quarter from 30 to 40 scores each. Whole flocks were overwhelmed with snow and no one ever knew where they were till the snow was disolved, that they were all found dead. I myself witnessed one particular instance of this on the farm of Thickside. There were 12 scores of excellent ewes all one age that were missing there all the time that the snow lay, which was only a week, and no traces of them could be found; when the snow went away they were discovered all lying dead with their heads one way as if a flock of sheep had dropped dead going from the washing. Many hundreds were driven into waters, burns, and ravines by the violence of the storm, where they were buried or frozen up, and these the flood carried away so that they were never seen or found by the owners at all. The following anecdote somewhat illustrates the confusion and devastation that it bred in the country. The greater part of the rivers on which the storm was most deadly run into the Solway Firth, on which there is a place called *the beds of Esk* where the tide throws out, and leaves, whatsoever is carried into it by the rivers. When the flood after the storm subsided, there were found on that place and the shores adjacent 1840 sheep, 9 black cattle, 3 horses, 2 men, 1 woman, 45 dogs, and 180 hares, besides a number of meaner animals.

To relate all the particular scenes of distress that occurred during this tremendeous hurricane is impossible—a volume would not contain them. I shall therefore, in order to give a true picture of the storm, merely relate what I saw, and shall in nothing exaggerate. But before doing this I must mention a circumstance, curious in its nature, and connected with others that afterwards occurred.

Some time previous to that, a few young shepherds, (of whom I was one, and the youngest, though not the least ambitious of the number), had formed themselves into a sort of literary society that met periodically at one or other of the houses of its members, where each read an essay on a subject previously given out; and after that every essay was minutely investigated, and criticised. We met in the evening and continued our important discussions all night. Friday the 23 of Janr was the day appointed for one of these meetings, and it was to be held at Entertrony a wild and remote sheiling at the very sources of the Ettrick, and now occupied by my own brother. I had the honour of having been named as preses, so leaving the charge of my flock with my master, off I set from Blackhouse on Thursday, a very ill day, with a flaming bombastical essay in my pocket, and my tongue trained to many wise and profound remarks to attend this extraordinary meeting, though the place lay at the distance of 20 miles over the wildest hills in the kingdom, and the time the depth of Winter.

I remained that night with my parents at Ettrick-House, and next day again set out on my journey. I had not however proceeded far before I percieved or thought I percieved symptoms of an approaching storm and that of no ordinary nature. I remember the day well: the wind which was rough on the preceding day had subsided into a dead calm; there was a slight fall of snow, which descended in small thin flakes that seemed to hover and reel in the air as if uncertain whether to go upward or downward; the hills were covered down to the middle in deep folds of rime, or frost-fog; in the cloughs that was dark, dense, and seemed as if it were heaped and crushed together; but on the brows of the hills it had a pale and fleecy appearance and altogether I never beheld a day of such gloomy aspect. A thought now began to intrude itself on me though I strove all that I could to get quit of it that it would be a wise course in me to return home to my sheep. Inclination urged me on, and I tried to bring reason to her aid by saying to myself "I have no reason in the world to be afraid of my sheep my master took the charge of them cheerfully there is not a better shepherd in the kingdom and I cannot doubt his concern in having them right." All would not do. I stood still and contemplated the day, and the more closely I examined it, the more was I impressed by the belief that some mischief was a brewing; so with a heavy heart, I turned on my heel, and made the best of my way back the road I came; my elaborate essay, and all my wise observations had come to nothing.

On my way home I called at a place called The Hope House to see a maternal uncle whom I loved. He was angry when he saw me, and said it was not like a prudent lad to be running up and down the country in such weather and at such a season and urged me to make haste home for it would be a drift before the morn. He accompanied me to the top of a height called The Black Gate-head and on parting he shook his head and said "Ah! it *is* a dangerous looking day! In troth I'm amaist fear'd to look at it." I said I would not mind it if any one knew from what quarter the storm would arise but we might in all likelihood gather our sheep to the place where they would be most exposed to danger. He bade me keep a good look out all the way home, and wherever I observed the first opening through the rime to be assured the wind would rise directly from that point. I did as he desired me but the clouds continued close set all around till the fall of evening and as the snow had been accummulating all day so as to render walking very unfurthersome it was that time before I reached home. The first thing I did was to go to my master and enquire where he had left my sheep—he told me, but though I had always the most perfect confidence in his experience I was not pleased with what he had done—he had left a part of them far too high out on the hills and the rest were not where I wanted them and I told him so. He said he had done all for the best but if there appeared to be any danger if I would call him up in the morning he would assist. We had two beautiful servant girls and with them I sat chatting till past 11 o'clock and then I went down to the old tower. What could have taken me to that ruinious habitation of The Black Douglasses at that untimeous hour I cannot reccollect but it certainly must have been from a supposition that one of the girls would follow me or else that I would see a hare both very unlikely events to have taken place on such a night. However certain it is that there I was at midnight and it was while standing on the top of the stair-case turret that I first beheld a bright bore through the clouds toward the north which reminded me of my uncle's apothegm. But at the same time a smart thaw had commenced and the breeze seemed to be rising from the south so that

I laughed in my heart at his sage rule and accounted it quite absurd —short was the time till aweful experience told me how true it was.

I then went to my bed in the bire loft where I slept with a neighbour shepherd named Borthwick but though fatigued with walking through the snow I could not close an eye so that I heard the first burst of the storm which commenced between one and two with a fury that no one can concieve who does not remember of it besides the place where I lived being exposed to two gathered winds as they are called by shepherds the storm raged there with redoubled ferocity. It began all at once with such a tremendeous roar that I imagined it was a peal of thunder until I felt the house trembling to its foundations. In a few minutes I went and thrust my naked arm through a hole in the roof in order if possible to ascertain what was going on without for not a ray of light could I see. I could not then nor can I yet express my astonishment. So completely was the air overloaded with falling and driving snow that but for the force of the wind I felt as if I had thrust my arm into a wreathe of snow. I deemed it a judgement sent from heaven upon us and lay down again in my bed trembling with agitation. I lay still for about an hour in hopes that it might prove only a temporary hurricane but hearing no abatement of its fury I awakened Borthwick and bade him get up for it was come on such a night or morning as never blew from the heavens. He was not long in obeying for as soon as he heard the turmoil he started from his bed and in one minute throwing on his clothes he hasted down the ladder and opened the door where he stood for a good while uttering exclamations of astonishment. The door where he stood was not above fourteen yards from the door of the dwelling-house but a wreath was already ammassed between them as high as the walls of the house and in trying to get round or through this Borthwick lost himself and could neither find the house nor his way back to the bire and about six minutes after I heard him calling my name in a shrill desperate tone of voice at which I could not refrain from laughing immoderately notwithstanding the dismal prospect that lay before us for I heard from his cries where he was. He had tried to make his way over the top of a large dunghill but going to the wrong side had fallen over and wrestled long among snow quite over the head. I did not think proper to move to his assistance but lay still and shortly after heard him shouting at the kitchen door for instant admittance. Still I kept my bed for about three quarters of an hour longer and then on reaching the house with much difficulty, found our master, the plowman, Borthwick and the two servant maids sitting round the kitchen fire with looks of dismay I may almost say despair. We all agreed at once that the sooner we were able to reach the sheep the better chance we had to save a remnant and as there were 800 excellent ewes all in one lot but a long way distant and the lot of most value of any on the farm we resolved to make a bold effort to reach them. Our master made family worship a duty he never neglected but that morning the manner in which he manifested our trust and confidence in heaven was particularly affecting. We took our breakfast—stuffed our pockets with bread and cheese—sewed our plaids around us—tied down our hats with napkins coming below our chins and each taking a strong staff in his hand we set out on the attempt.

No sooner was the door closed behind us than we lost sight of each other—seeing there was none—it was impossible for a man to see his hand held up before him; and it was still two hours till day. We had no means of keeping together but by following to one another's voices, nor of working our way save by groping with our staves before us. It soon appeared to me a hopeless concern, for ere ever we got clear of the houses, and hay-stacks, we had to roll ourselves over two or three wreaths which it was impossible to wade through; and all the while the wind and drift were so violent, that every three or four minutes we were obliged to hold our faces down between our knees to recover our breath.

We soon got into an eddying wind that was altogether insufferable, and at the same time we were struggling among snow so deep, that our progress in the way we purposed going, was indeed very equivocal, for we had by this time lost all idea of East West North or South. Still we were as busy as men determined on a business could be and persevered on we knew not whither sometimes rolling over the snow and sometimes weltering in it to the chin. The following instance of our successful exertions marks our progress to a tittle. There was an inclosure around the house to the Westward which we denominated *the Park* as is customary in Scotland. When we went away we calculated that it was two hours until day—the park did not extend above 300 yards and we were still engaged in that *Park* when day light appeared.

When we got free of the park we also got free of the eddy of the wind—it was now straight in our faces—we went in a line before each other and changed places every three or four minutes and at length after great fatigue we reached a long ridge of a hill where the snow was thinner having been blown off it by the force of the wind and by this we had hopes of reaching within a short space of the ewes which were still a mile and a half distant. Our master had taken the lead; I was next him and soon began to suspect from the depth of the snow that he was leading us quite wrong but as we always trusted implicitly to him that was foremost for the time I said nothing for a good while until satisfied that we were going in a direction very nearly right opposite to that we intended. I then tried to expostulate with him but he did not seem to understand what I said and on getting a glimpse of his countenance I percieved that it was quite altered. Not to alarm the others nor even himself I said I was becoming terribly fatigued and proposed that we should lean on the snow and take each a mouthful of whisky (for I had brought a small bottle in my pocket for fear of the worst) and a bite of bread and cheese. This was unanimously agreed to and I noted that he swallowed the spirits rather eagerly a thing not usual with him and when he tried to eat it was long before he could swallow any thing. I was convinced that he would fail altogether but as it would have been easier to have got him to the shepherd's house before us than home again I made no proposal for him to return. On the contrary I said if they would trust themselves entirely to me I would engage to lead them to the ewes without going a foot out of the way—the other two agreed to it and aknowledged that they knew not where they were, but he never opened his mouth, nor did he speak a word for two hours thereafter. It had only been a temporary exhaustion however for after that he recovered and wrought till night as well as any of us, though he never could reccollect a single circumstance that occurred during that part of our way nor a word that was said nor of having got any refreshment whatever.

At half an hour after ten we reached the flock and just in time to save them—but before that both Borthwick and the plowman had lost their hats notwithstanding all their precautions and to impede us still further I went inadvertantly over a precipice and going down head foremost between the scaur and the snow found it impossible to extricate myself for the more I struggled I went the deeper. For all our troubles I heard Borthwick above convulsed with laughter he thought he had got the affair of the dunghill paid back. By holding by one another and letting down a plaid to me they hauled me up but I was terribly incommoded by snow that had got inside my clothes.

The ewes were standing in a close body one half of them were covered over with snow to the depth of ten feet the rest were jammed against a brae. We knew not what to do for spades to dig them out; but to our agreeable astonishment when those before were removed they had been so close pent together as to be all touching one another and they walked out from below the snow after their neighbours in a body. If the snow-wreath had not broke and crumbled down upon a few that were hindmost we should have got them all out without putting a hand to them. This was effecting a good deal more than I or any of the party expected a few hours before—there were 100 ewes in another place near by but of these we could only get out a very few and lost all hopes of saving the rest.

It was now wearing towards mid day and there were occassionally short intervals in which we could see about us for perhaps a score of yards, but we got only one momentary glance of the hills around us all that day. I grew quite impatient to be at my own charge and leaving the rest I went away to them by myself that is I went to the division that was left far out on the hills while our master and the plowman volunteered to rescue those that were down on the lower ground. I found mine in miserable circumstances but making all possible exertion I got out about one half of them which I left in a place of safety and made towards home for it was beginning to grow dark and the storm was again raging without any mitigation in all its darkness and deformity. I was not the least afraid of losing my way for I knew all the declivities of the hills so well that I could have come home with my eyes bound up and indeed long ere I got home they were of no use to me. I was terrified for the water (Douglas Burn) for in the morning it was flooded and gorged up with snow in a dreadful manner and I judged that it would be quite impassible—at length I came to a place where I judged the water should be and fell a boring and groping for it with my long staff—No; I could find no water and began to dread that for all my accuracy I had gone wrong. I was terribly astonished and standing still to consider, I looked up towards heaven I shall not say for what cause and to my utter amazement thought I beheld trees over my head flourishing abroad over the whole sky. I never had seen such an optical delusion before it was so like enchantment that I knew not what to think but dreaded that some extraordinary thing was coming over me and that I was deprived of my right senses. I remember I thought the storm was a great judgement sent on us for our sins, and that this strange phantasy was connected with it; an illusion effected by evil spirits. I stood a good while in this painful trance—at length on making a bold exertion to escape from the fairy vision I came all at once in contact with the old tower. Never in my life did I experience such a relief I was not only all at once freed from the fairies but from the dangers of the gorged river—I had come over it on some mountain of snow I knew not how nor where nor do I know to this day. So that after all they were trees that I saw and trees of no great magnitude neither but their appearance to my eyes it is impossible to describe. They flourished abroad not for miles but for hundreds of miles to the utmost verges of the visible heavens. Such a day and such a night may the eye of shepherd never again behold. What befel to our literary meeting, and the consequences of the storm as I witnessed them must be deferred till a future number.

H.

Charles' Street
April 15th 1819

The Shepherds Calender
Continued from p.

"That night a child might understand
The Diel had business on his hand"

On reaching home I found our women fo'k sitting in woful plight. It is well known how wonderfully acute they generally are, either at raising up imaginary evils, or magnifying those that exist; and ours had made out a theory so fraught with misery and distress, that the poor things were quite overwhelmed with grief. "There were none of us ever to see the house again *in life*—There was no possibility of the thing happening, all circumstances considered—There was not a sheep in the country to be saved, nor a single shepherd left alive— Nothing but *women*! And there they were left, three poor helpless creatures, and the men lying dead out among the snow, and none to bring them home, Lord help them, what was to become of them!" They perfectly agreed in all this: there was no dissenting voice; and their prospects still continuing to darken with the fall of night, they had no other resource left them, long before my arrival, but to lift up their voices and weep. The group consisted of a young lady, our master's neice, and two servant girls, all of the same age, and beautiful as three spring days, every one of which are mild and sweet but differ only a little in brightness. No sooner had I entered than every tongue and every hand was put in motion, the former to pour forth queries faster than six tongues of men could answer them with any degree of precision, and the latter to rid me of the incumbrances of snow and ice with which I was loaded. One slit up the sewing of my frozen plaid, another brushed the icicles from my locks, and a third unloosed my clotted snow boots: we all arrived within a few minutes of each other, and all shared the same kind offices, and heard the same kind enquiries, and long string of perplexities narrated: even our dogs shared of their carresses and ready assistance in ridding them of the frozen snow, and the dear consistent creatures were six times happier than if no storm or danger had existed. Let no one suppose that even amid toils and perils the shepherd's life is destitute of enjoyment.

Borthwick had found his way home without losing his aim in the least. I had deviated but little, save that I lost the river, and remained a short time in the country of the fairies; but the other two had a hard struggle for life. They went off, as I said formerly, in search of 17 scores of my flock that had been left in a place not far from the house, but being unable to find one of them, in searching for these they lost themselves while it was yet early in the afternoon. They supposed that they had gone by the house very near to it, for they had toiled till dark among deep snow in the burn below; and if John Burnet, a neighbouring shepherd had not heard them calling, and found and conducted them home, it would have stood hard with them indeed, for none of us would have looked for them in that direction. They were both very much exhausted, and the goodman could not speak above his breath that night.

Next morning the sky was clear, but a cold intemperate wind still blew from the North. The face of the country was entirely altered— The form of every hill was changed, and new mountains leaned over every valley. All traces of burns, rivers and lakes were obliterated, for the frost had been commensurate with the storm, and such as had never been witnessed in Scotland. Some registers that I have seen place this storm on the 24 of Decr, a month too early, but that day was one of the finest winter days I ever saw.

There having been thus 340 of my flock that had never been found at all during the preceding day, as soon as the morning dawned we set all out to look after them. It was a heideous looking scene—no one could cast his eyes around him and entertain any conception of sheep being saved. It was one picture of desolation. There is a deep glen lies between Blackhouse and Dryhope called The Hawkshaw Cleuch, which is full of trees. There was not the top of one of them to be seen. This may convey some idea how the country looked; and no one can suspect that I would state circumstances otherwise than they were, when there is so many living that could confute me.

When we came to the ground where these sheep should have been, there was not one of them above the snow. Here and there, at a great distance from each other, we could percieve the head or horns of stragglers appearing, and these were easily got out, but when we had collected these few we could find no more. They had been lying all abroad in a scattered state when the storm came on, and were covered over just as they had been lying. It was on a kind of slaunting ground, that lay half beneath the wind, and the snow was uniformly from six to eight feet deep. Under this the hoggs were lying scattered over at least 100 acres of heathery ground. It was a very ill looking concern. We went about boring with our long poles, and often did not find one hogg in a quarter of an hour. But at length a white shaggy colley, named Sparkie, that belonged to the cow-herd boy seemed to have comprehended something of our perplexity, for we observed him plying and scraping in the snow with great violence and always looking over his shoulder to us. On going to the spot we found that he had marked straight above a sheep. From that he flew to another, and so on to another, as fast as we could dig them out, and ten times faster, for he sometimes had twenty or thirty holes all marked before hand.

We got out 300 of that division before night, and about half as many on other parts of the farm, in addition to those we had rescued the day before, and the greater part of these would have been lost had it not been for the voluntary exertions of Sparkie. Before the snow went away (which lay only eight days) we had got every sheep on the farm out, either dead or alive, except four; and that these were not found was not Sparkie's blame, for though they were buried below a mountain of snow at least 50 feet deep, he had again and again marked on the top of it above them. The sheep were all living when we found them, but those that were buried in the snow to a certain depth, being I suppose in a warm half suffocated state, though on being taken out they bounded away like roes yet the sudden change of atmosphere instantly paralized them, and they fell down deprived of all power in their limbs. We had great numbers of these to carry home and feed with the hand, but others that were very deep buried died outright in a few minutes. We did not however lose above 60 in all, but I am certain Sparkie saved us at least 200.

We were for several days utterly ignorant how affairs stood with the country around us, all communication between farms being cut off, at least all communication with such a wild place as that in which I lived; but John Burnet, a neighbouring shepherd on another farm, was remarkably good at picking up the rumours that were afloat in the country which he delighted to circulate without abatement. Many people tell their stories by halves, and in a manner so cold and indifferent that the purport can scarcely be discerned and if it is cannot be believed; but that was not the case with John; he gave them with *interest* and we were very much indebted to him for the intelligence that we daily recieved that week for no sooner was the first brunt of the tempest got over than John made a point of going off at a tangent every day to learn and bring us word what was going on. The accounts were most dismal; the country was a charnel-house. The first day he brought us tidings of the loss of thousands of sheep, and likewise of the death of Robert Armstrong a neighbour shepherd, one whom we all well knew, he having but lately left the Blackhouse to herd on another farm. He died not above 300 paces from a farm house while at the same time it was known to them all that he was there. His companion left him at a dike side, and went in to procure assistance; yet, nigh as it was, they could not reach him, though they attempted it again and again; and at length they were obliged to return, and suffer him to perish at the side of the dike. There were three of my own intimate acquaintances perished that night. There was another shepherd named Watt, the circumstances of whose death were peculiarly affecting. He had been to see his sweetheart on the night before with whom he had finally agreed and settled every thing about the marriage; but it so happened in the inscrutable awards of providence, that at the very time when the banns of his marriage were proclaimed in the church of Moffat, his companions were carrying him home a corpse from the hill.

It may not be amiss here to remark that it was a recieved opinion all over the country, that sundry lives were lost, and a great many more endangered by the administering of ardent spirits to the sufferers while in a state of exhaustion. It was a position against which I entered my vehement protest, nevertheless the voice of the multitude should never be disregarded. A little bread and sweet milk, or even a little bread and cold water, it was said, proved a much safer restorative in the fields. There is no denying that there were some who took a glass of spirits that night, that never spoke another word, even though they were continuing to walk when their friends found them. On the other hand, there was one woman who left her children, and followed her husband's dog, who brought her to his master lying in a state of insensibility. He had fallen down bareheaded among the snow, and was all covered over save one corner of his plaid. She had nothing better to take with her when she set out than a bottle of sweet milk and a little oatmeal cake, and yet with the help of these she so far recruited his spirits as to get him safe home, though not without long and active perseverence. She took two little vials with her, and in these she heated the milk in her bosom. That man would not be disposed to laugh at the silliness of the fair sex for some time.

It is perfectly unaccountable how easily people died that night. The frost must certainly have been prodigious; so intense as to have seized on the vitals of those that overheated themselves by wading and toiling too impatiently among the snow, a thing that is very aptly done. I have conversed with five or six that were carried home in a state of insensibility that night who never would again have moved from the spot where they lay, and were only brought to life by rubbing and warm applications, and they uniformly declared that they felt no kind of pain or debility, farther than an irressistable desire to sleep. Many fell down while walking, and speaking, in a sleep so sound as to resemble torpidity, and there is little doubt that those who perished slept away in the same manner. I knew a man well whose name was Andrew Murray, that perished in the snow on Minch-moor, and he had taken it so deliberately that he had buttoned his coat, and folded his plaid, which he had laid beneath his head for a bolster.

But it is now time to return to my notable literary society. In spite of the heideous appearances that presented themselves, the fellows actually met, all save myself, in that solitary sheiling before mentioned. It is easy to concieve how they were confounded, and taken by surprise, when the storm burst forth on them in the middle of the night, while they were in the heat of sublime disputation. There can be little doubt that there was part of loss sustained in their respective flocks, by reason of that meeting, but this was nothing compared with the obloquy to which they were subjected on another account, and one which will scarcely be believed, even though the most part of the members be yet alive to bear testimony to it.

The storm was altogether an unusual convulson of nature. Nothing like it had ever been seen, or heard of in Britain before; and it was enough of itself to arouse every spark of superstition that lingered among these mountains—It did so—It was universally viewed as a judgement sent by God for the punishment of some heineous offence, but what that offence was, could not for a while be ascertained: but when it came out, that so many men had been assembled, in a lone unfrequented place, and busily engaged in some mysterious work at the very instant that the blast came on, no doubts were entertained that all had not been right there, and that some horrible rite, or correspondence with the powers of darkness had been going on. It so happened too, that this sheiling of Entertrony was situated in the very vortex of the storm; the devastations made by it extended all around that, to a certain extent; and no farther on any one quarter than another. This was easily and soon remarked, and upon the whole the first view of the matter had rather an equivocal appearance to those around who had suffered so severely by it. But still as the rumour grew the certainty of the event gained ground—new corroborative circumstances were every day divulged, till the whole district was in an uproar, and several of the members began to meditate a speedy retreat from the country; some of them I know would have fled, if it had not been for the advice of the late worthy and judicious Mr. Bryden of Crosslee. The first intimation that I had of it was from my friend John Burnet, who gave it me with his accustomed energy, and full assurance. He came over one evening, and I saw by his face he had some great news; I think I remember, as I well may, every word that past between us on the subject.

"Weel chap" said he to me "we hae fund out what has been the cause of a' this mischief now."

"What do you mean John?"

"What do I mean? It seems that a great squad o' birkies that ye are conneckit wi', had met that night at the herds house o' Ever Phaup, an had raised the deil amang them."

Every countenance in the kitchen changed; the women gazed at John and then at me, and their lips grew white. These kind of feelings are infectious, people may say what they will; fear begets fear as naturally as light springs from reflection. I reasoned stoutly at first against the veracity of the report, observing that it was utter absurdity, and a shame and disgrace for the country to cherish such a rediculous lie.

"Lie!" said John. "It's nae lie; they had him up amang them like a great rough dog at the very time that the tempest began, and were glad to draw cuts, an' gie him ane o' their number to get quit o' him again."

Lord how every hair of my head, and inch of my frame crept at hearing this sentence; for I had a dearly loved brother who was one of the number, several full cousins, and intimate acquaintances; indeed I looked on the whole fraternity as my brethren, and considered myself involved in all their transactions. I could say no more in defence of the society's proceedings, for to tell the truth, though I am ashamed to acknowledge it, I suspected that the allegation might be too true.

"Has the deil actually ta'en awa ane o' them bodily?" said Jean. "He has that" returned John "an' it's thought the skaithe wadna hae been grit, had he ta'en twa or three mae o' them. Base villains! That the hale country should hae to suffer for their pranks! But however the law's to tak its course on them, an' they'll find or a' the play be played, that he has need of a lang spoon that sups wi' the deil."

The next day John brought us word that it was *only* the servant maid that the *ill thief* had taen away; and the next again that it was actually Bryden of Glenkerry; but finally he was obliged to inform us

"That a' was exactly true as it was first tauld, but only that Jamie Bryden, after being a wanting for some days, had casten up again."

There has been nothing since that time, that has caused such a ferment in the country—nought else could be talked of; and grievious was the blame attached to those who had the temerity to raise up the devil to waste the country. If the effects produced by the Chaldee Manuscript had not been fresh in the minds of the present generation, they could have no right conception of the rancour that prevailed against a number of individuals; but the two scenes greatly resembled each other, for in that case as well as the latter one, legal proceedings, it is said, were meditated, and attempted; but lucky it was for the shepherds that they agreed to no reference, for such were the feelings of the country and the opprobrium in which the act was held, that it is likely it would have fared very ill with them; at all events, it would have required an arbiter of some decision and uprightness to have dared to oppose them. Two men were sent to come to the house as by chance, and endeavour to learn from the shepherd, and particularly from the servant maid, what grounds there were for inflicting legal punishments: but before that happened I had the good luck to hear her examined myself, and that in a way by which all suspicions were put to rest, and simplicity and truth left to war with superstition alone. I deemed it very curious at the time, and shall give it verbatim as nearly as I can reccollect.

Being all impatience to learn particulars, as soon as the waters abated so as to become fordable, I hasted over to Ettrick, and the day being fine, I found numbers of people astir on the same errand with myself—the valley was moving with people, gathered in from the glens around, to hear, and relate the dangers and difficulties that were just overpast. Among others, the identical girl who served with the shepherd in whose house the scene of the meeting took place, had come down to Ettrick schoolhouse to see her parents. Her name was Mary Beattie, a beautiful, sprightly lass, about twenty years of age, and if the devil had taken her in preference to any one of the shepherds his good taste could scarcely have been disputed. The first person I met was my friend the late Mr. James Anderson, who was as anxious to hear what had passed at the meeting as I was, so we two contrived a scheme whereby we thought we would hear every thing from the girl's own mouth.

We sent word to the Schoolhouse for Mary to call at my father's house on her return up the water, as there was a parcel to go to Phawhope. She came accordingly, and when we saw her approaching we went into a little sleeping apartment, where we could hear every

thing that passed, leaving directions with my mother how to manage
the affair. My mother herself was in perfect horrors about the business, and believed it all; as for my father he did not say much either
the one way or the other, but bit his lip, and remarked that "fo'k wad
find it was an ill thing to hae to do wi' *the Enemy*."

My mother would have managed extremely well, had her own
early prejudices in favour of the doctrine of all kinds of apparitions not
got the better of her. She was very kind to the girl, and talked with her
about the storm, and the events that had occurred, till she brought
the subject of the meeting forward herself, on which the following
dialogue commenced.

"But dear Mary, my woman, what were the chiels a met about that
night?"

"Oo they were just gaun through their papers an' arguing."

"Arguing? What were they arguing about?"

"I have often thought about it sin' syne, but really I canna tell
preceesely what they were arguing about."

"Were you wi' them a' the time?"

"Yes a' the time but the wee while I was milkin' the cow."

"An' did they never bid ye gang out?"

"Oo no; they never heedit whether I gaed out or in."

"It's queer that ye canna mind ought ava. Can ye no tell me ae
word that ye heard them say?"

"I heard them sayin' something about the fitness o' things."

"Aye, that was a braw subject for them! But Mary; did ye no hear
them sayin nae ill words?"

"No."

"Did ye no hear them speaking naething about the deil?"

"Very little."

"What were they saying about *him*?"

"I thought I aince heard Jamie Fletcher sayin that there was nae
deil ava."

"Ah! the unwordy rascal! How durst he for the life o' him! I
wonder he didna think shame."

"I fear aye he's something regardless Jamie."

"I hope nane that belangs to me will ever join him in sic wickedness! But tell me Mary my woman did ye no see nor hear naething
uncanny about the house yoursel' that night?"

"There was something like a plover cried twice i' the peat neuk, in
at the side o' Will's bed."

"A plover! His presence be about us! There was never a plover at
this time o' the year. And in the house too! Ah Mary I'm feared an'

concerned about that nights wark! What thought ye it was that cried?"

"I didna ken what it was, it cried just like a plover."

"Did the callans look as they war fear'd when they heard it?"

"They lookit gay an' queer."

"What did they say?"

"Ane cried, 'What is that?' an' another said, 'What can it mean.' 'Hout,' quo Jamie Fletcher, 'it's just some bit stray bird that has lost itsel.' 'I dinna ken,' quo your Will, 'I dinna like it unco weel.'"

"Think ye did nane o' the rest see ony thing?"

"I believe there was something seen."

"What was't?" (in a half whisper with manifest alarm)

"When Will gaed out to try if he could gang to the sheep, he met wi' a great big rough dog, that had very near worn him into a lin in the water."

My mother was now deeply affected, and after two or three smothered exclamations, she fell a whispering; the other followed her example, and shortly after they rose and went out, leaving my friend and me very little wiser than we were for we had heard both these incidents before with little variation. I accompanied Mary to Phawhope and met with my brother, who soon convinced me of the falsehood and absurdity of the whole report; but I was grieved to find him so much cast down and distressed about it. None of them durst well show their faces at either kirk or market for a whole year, and more. The weather continuing fine, we two went together and perambulated Eskdale Moor, visiting the principal scenes of carnage among the flocks, where we saw multitudes of men skinning and burying whole droves of sheep, taking with them only the skins and tallow.

I shall now conclude this long account of the storm and its consequences, by an extract from a poet for whose works I always feel disposed to have a great partiality, and whoever reads the above will not doubt on what incident the discription is founded, nor yet deem it greatly overcharged.

* * * * * * * *

"Who was it reared those whelming waves?
    Who scalp'd the brows of old Cairngorm,
And scoop'd these ever yawning caves?
    'Twas I, the Spirit of the Storm!"

He waved his sceptre north away,
　The arctic ring was rift asunder;
And through the heaven the startling bray
　Burst louder than the loudest thunder.

The feathery clouds, condenced and furled,
　In columns swept the quaking glen;
Destruction down the dale was hurled,
　O'er bleating flocks and wondering men.

The Grampians groan'd beneath the storm;
　New mountains o'er the correi lean'd;
Ben-Nevis shook his shaggy form,
　And wonder'd what his sovereign mean'd.

Even far on Yarrow's fairy dale
　The shepherd paused in dumb dismay,
And cries of spirits in the gale
　Lured many a pitying hind away.

The Louthers felt the tyrant's wrath;
　Proud Hartfell quaked beneath his brand,
And Cheviot heard the cries of death,
　Guarding his loved Northumberland.

But O as fell that fateful night,
　What horrors Avin wilds deform,
And choak the ghastly lingering light!
　There whirled the vortex of the storm.

Ere morn the wind grew deadly still,
　And dawning in the air updrew
From many a shelve and shining hill,
　Her folding robe of fairy blue.

Then what a smoothe and wonderous scene
　Hung o'er Loch Avin's lonely breast!
Not top of tallest pine was seen,
　On which the dazzled eye could rest.

But mitred cliff, and crested fell,
　In lucid curls her brows adorn;
Aloft the radiant crescents swell,
　All pure as robes by angels worn.

Sound sleeps our seer, far from the day,
　Beneath yon sleek and writhed cone;
His spirit steals unmiss'd away,
　And dreams across the desart lone.

Sound sleeps our seer!—the tempests rave,
　And cold sheets o'er his bosom fling;
The moldwarp digs his mossy grave;
　His requiem Avin eagles sing.

* * * * * *

Altrive April 14th 1819　　　　　　　　　　　James Hogg

Class Second.
Deaths, Judgments, and Providences.

Rob Dodds

It was on the 13th of February 1823, on a cold stormy day, the snow lying from one to ten feet deep on the hills, and nearly as hard as ice, when an extensive store-farmer in the outer limits of the county of Peebles went up to one of his led farms to see how his old shepherd was coming on with his flocks. A partial thaw had blackened some scraps on the brows of the mountains here and there, and over these the half-starving flocks were scattered, picking up a scanty sustenance, while all the hollow parts, and whole sides of mountains that lay sheltered from the winds on the preceding week when the great drifts blew, were heaped and over-heaped with immense loads of snow, so that every hill appeared to the farmer to have changed its form. There was a thick white haze on the sky, corresponding exactly with the wan frigid colour of the high mountains, so that in casting one's eye up to the heights, it was not apparent where the limits of the earth ended, and the heavens began. There was no horizon—no blink of the sun looking through the pale and impervious mist of heaven; but there, in that elevated and sequestered *hope*, the old shepherd and his flock seemed to be left out of nature and all its sympathies, and embosomed in one interminable chamber of waste desolation.—So his master thought; and any stranger beholding the scene, would have been still more deeply impressed that the case was so in reality.

But the old shepherd thought and felt otherwise. He saw God in the clouds, and watched his arm in the direction of the storm. He perceived, or thought he perceived, one man's flocks suffering on account of their owner's transgression; and though he bewailed the hardships to which the poor harmless creatures were reduced, he yet acknowledged in his heart the justness of the punishment. "These temporal scourges are laid upon sinners in mercy," said he, "and it will be well for them if they get so away. It will learn them in future how to drink and carouse, and speak profane things of the name of Him in whose hand are the issues of life, and to regard his servants as the dogs of their flock."

Again, he beheld from his heights, when the days were clear, the flocks of others more favourably situated, which he attributed as a reward for their acts of charity and benevolence; for this old man believed that all temporal benefits were sent to men as a reward for good works; and all temporal deprivations as a scourge for evil ones, and that their effects in spiritual improvement or degradation were rare and particular.

"I hae been a herd in this *hope*, callant and man, for these fifty years now, Janet," said he to his old wife, "an' I think I never saw the face o' the country look waur."

"Hout, goodman, it is but a cludd o' the despondency o' auld age come ower your een, for I hae seen waur storms than this, or else my sight deceives me. This time seven and twenty years, when you and I were married, there was a deeper and a harder snaw baith than this. There was mony a burn dammed up wi' dead hogs that year. And what say ye to this time nine years, goodman?"

"Ay, ay, Janet, these were hard times when they were present. But I think there's something in our corrupt nature that gars us aye trow the present burden is the heaviest. However, it is either my strength failing, that I canna won sae weel through the snaw, or I never saw it lying sae deep before. I canna steer the poor creatures frae ae knowe-head to another, without rowing them ower the body. And some-times when they wad spraughle away, then I stick firm an' fast mysel', an' the mair I fight to get out, I gang aye the deeper. This same day, nae farther gane, at ae step up in the gait cleugh, I slumpit in to the neck. Peace be wi' us, quo' I to mysel', where am I now? If my auld wife wad but look up the hill, she wad see nae mair o' her poor man but the bannet. Ah! Janet, Janet, I'm rather feared that our Maker has a craw to pook wi' us even now!"

"I hope no, Andrew; we're in good hands; and if he should e'en see meet to pook a craw wi' us, he'll maybe fling us baith the bouk an' the feathers at the end. Ye shoudna repine, goodman. Ye're something ill for thrawing your mou' at Providence now and then."

"Na, na, Janet, far be't frae me to grumble at Providence. I ken ower weel that the warst we get is far aboon our demerits. But it's no for the season that I'm sae feared; that's ruled by ane that canna err; only, I dread that there's something rotten in the government or the religion of the country, that lays it under his curse. There's my fear, Janet. The scourge of a land often fa's on its meanest creatures first, and advances by degrees to gie the boonmost orders o' society war-ning and time to repent. There, for instance, in the saxteen and seventeen, the scourge fell on our flocks and our hirds. Then, in aughteen and nineteen, it fell on the weavers, they're the neist class, ye ken; then our merchants, they're the neist again; and last o' a' it has

fallen on the farmers and the shepherds, they're the first and maist
sterling class o' a country. Na, ye needna smudge and laugh at me
now, Janet; for it's true. They *are* the boonmost, and hae aye been the
boonmost sin' the days o' Abel, an that's nae date o' yesterday. An'
ye'll observe, Janet, that whenever they began to fa' low, they gat aye
another lift to keep up their respect. But I see our downfa' coming on
us wi' rapid strides.—There's a heartlessness and apathy croppen in
amang the sheep farmers, that shews their warldly hopes to be nearly
extinct. The maist o' them seem no to care a bodle whether their
sheep die or live. There's our master, for instance, when times were
gaun weel, I hae seen him up ilka third day at the farthest in the time
of a storm, to see how the sheep were doing; an' this winter I hae never
seen his face sin' it came on. He seems to hae forgotten that there are
sic creatures existing in this wilderness as the sheep and me. His
presence be about us, gin there be nae the very man come bye the
window!"

Janet sprung to her feet, swept the hearth, set a chair on the
cleanest side, and wiped it with her check apron, all ere one could well
look about him.

"Come away, master; come in by to the fire here; lang-lookit-for
comes at length."

"How are you, Janet? still living, I see. It is a pity that you had not
popped off before this great storm came on."

"Dear, what for, master?"

"Because Andrew would have been a great deal the better of a
young soncy quean to have slept with him in such terrible weather.
And then if you should take it into your head to coup the creels just
now, you know it would be out of the power of man to get you to a
Christian burial. We would be obliged to huddle you up in the nook of
the kail-yard."

"Ah, master, what's that you're saying to my auld wife? Aye the
auld man yet, I hear! A great deal o' the leaven o' corrupt nature aye
sproutin' out now and then. I wonder you're no fear'd to speak in that
regardless manner in these judgment-looking times!"

"And you are still the old man too, Andrew; a great deal of cant
and hypocrisy sprouting out at times. But tell me, you old sinner, how
has your Maker been serving you this storm? I have been right
terrified about your sheep; for I know you will have been very
impertinent with him of evenings."

"Hear to that now! There's no hope, I see! I thought to find you
humbled wi' a' thir trials and warldly losses, but I see the heart is
hardened like Pharaoh's, and you will not let the multitude o' your

sins go. As to the storm, I can tell you my sheep are just at ane mae wi't. I am waur than ony o' my neighbours, as I lie higher on the hills; but I may hae been as it chanced for you, for ye hae never lookit near me mair than you had had no concern in the creatures."

"Indeed, Andrew, it is because neither you nor the creatures are much worth looking after now-a-days. If it hadna been the fear I was in for some mishap coming over the stock, on account of these hypocritical prayers of yours, I would not have come to look after you so soon."

"Ah, there's nae mense to be had o' you! It's a good thing I ken the heart's better than the tongue, or ane wad hae little face to pray either for you, or aught that belangs t'ye. But I hope ye hae been nae the waur o' auld Andrew's prayers as yet. An some didna pray for ye, it wad maybe be the waur for ye. I prayed for ye when ye coudna pray for yoursel', an' had hopes when I turned auld and doited, that you might say a kind word for me. But I'm fear'd that warld's wealth and warld's pleasures hae been leading you ower lang in their train, and that ye hae been trusting to that which will soon take wings and flee away."

"If you mean riches, Andrew, or warld's walth, as you call it, you never said a truer word in your life; for the little that my forbears and I have made, under the influence of these long prayers of yours, is actually melting away from among my hands faster than ever the snaw did from the dike."

"It is perfectly true, what you're saying, master. I ken the extent o' your bits o' sales weel enough, an' I ken your rents; an' weel I ken you're telling me nae lee. An' it's e'en a hard case. But I'll tell you what I would do. I would throw their tacks in their teeth, an' let them mak' aught o' them they likit."

"Why, that would be ruin at once, Andrew, with a vengeance. Don't you see that stocks of sheep are fallen so low, that if they were put to sale, they would not pay more than the rents, and some few arrears that every one of us have got into; and thus by throwing up our farms, we would throw ourselves out beggars. We are all willing to put off the evil day as long as we can, and rather trust to long prayers for a while."

"Ah! you're there again, are you? Canna let alane profanity! It's hard to gar a wicked cout leave off funking. But I can tell you, master mine—An you farmers had made your hay when the sun shone, ye might a' hae suttin independent o' your screwin' lairds, wha are maistly sair out at elbows; an' ye ken, sir, a hungry louse bites wicked sair. But this is but a just joodgment come on you for your behaviour.

Ye had the gaun days o' prosperity for twenty years! But instead o'
laying by a little for a sair leg, or making provisions for an evil day, ye
gaed on like madmen. Ye biggit houses, and ye plantit vineyards, an'
threw away money as ye had been sawing sklate-stanes. Ye drank
wine, an' ye drank punch; and ye roared and ye sang, and spake
unseemly things. An' did ye never think there was an ear that heard,
an' an ee that saw a' thae things? An' did ye never think that they
wad be revisited on your heads some day when ye couldna play paw
to help yoursels? If ye didna think sae then, ye'll think sae soon. An'
ye'll maybe see the day when the like o' auld Andrew, wi' his darned
hose, an' his cloutit shoon; his braid bannet, instead of a baiver; his
drink out o' the clear spring, instead o' the punch bowl; an' his good
steeve aitmeal parritch and his horn spoon, instead o' the drap suds o'
tea, that costs sae muckle—I say, that sic a man wi' a' thae, an' his
worthless prayers to boot, will maybe keep the crown o' the causey
langer than some that carried their heads higher."

"Hout fie, Andrew!" quoth old Janet; "Gudeness be my help, an' I
dinna think shame o' you! Our master may weel think ye'll be
impudent wi' your Maker, for troth you're very impudent wi' himsel;
dinna ye see that ye hae made the douse sonsy lad that he disna ken
where to look?"

"Ay, Janet, your husband may weel crack. He kens he has
feathered his nest off my father and me. He is independent, let the
world wag as it will."

"It's a' fairly come by, master, an' the maist part o't came through
your ain hands. But my bairns are a' doing for themsels, in the same
way that I did; an' if twa or three hunder pounds can beet a mister for
you in a strait, ye sanna want it, come of a' what will."

"It is weel said o' you, Andrew, and I am obliged to you. There is
no class of men in this kingdom so independent as you shepherds. You
have your sheep, your cow, your meal and potatoes; a regular income
of from sixteen to thirty pounds yearly, without a farthing of expen-
diture, except for shoes; for your clothes are all made at home. If you
would even wish to spend it, you cannot get an opportunity, and
every one of you is rich, who has not lost money by lending it. It is
therefore my humble opinion, that all the farms over this country will
soon change occupants; and that the shepherds must ultimately
become the store-farmers."

"I hope in God I'll never live to see that, master, for the sake of
them that I and mine hae won our bread frae, as weel as some others
that I hae a great respect for. But that's no the thing that hasna
happened afore this day. It is little mair than 140 years, sin' a' the

land i' this country changed masters already; sin' every farmer in it was reduced, and the farms were a' ta'en by common people and strangers at half naething. The Welches came here then out of a place they ca' Wales, in England; the Andersons came frae a place they ca' Kamsagh, some gate i'the north; an' your ain set came first to this country then frae some bit lairdship near Glasgow. There were a set o' M'Gregors and M'Dougals, said to have been great thieves, came into Yarrow then, and changed their names to Scotts; but they didna thrive; for they warna likit, and the hinderend o' them were in the Catslackburn. They ca'd them aye the Pinolys, frae the place they came fra; but I dinna ken where it was. The Ballantynes came frae Galloway; and for as flourishin' fo'ks as they are now, the first o' them came out at the Birkhill-path, riding on a heltered poney, wi' a goat-skin aneath him for a saddle. The Cunninghams, likewise, began to spread their wings at the same time; they came a' frae a little fat curate that came out o' Glencairn to Etterick. But that's nae disparagement to ony o' thae families; for an there be merit at a' inherent in man as to warldly things, it is certainly in raising himsel frae naething to respect. There is nae very ancient name amang a' our farmers now, but the Tweedies an' the Murrays; I mean that anciently belonged to this district. The Tweedies are very auld, and took the name frae the water. They were lairds o' Drumelzier hunders o' years afore the Hays got it, and hae some o' the best blood o' the land in their veins; and sae also were the Murrays; but the maist part o' the rest are upstarts and come-o'-wills. Now ye see, for as far outbye as I live, I can tell ye some things that ye dinna hear amang your drunken cronies."

"It is when you begin to these old traditions that I like to listen to you, Andrew. Can you tell me what was the cause of such a complete overthrow of the farmers of that age?"

"O I canna tell, sir—I canna tell. Some overturn o' affairs, like the present, I fancy. The farmers had outhir lost a' their sheep, or a' their siller, as they are like to do now; but I canna tell how it was; for the general change had ta'en place, for the maist part, afore the Revolution. My ain grandfather, who was the son of a great farmer, hired himsel for a shepherd at that time to young Tam Linton, and mony ane was wae for the downcome. But, speaking o' that, of a' the downcomes that ever a country kenn'd in a farming name, there has never been ought like that o' the Lintons. When my grandfather was a young man, and ane o' their herds, they had a' the principal store-farms o' Etterick Forest, and a part in this shire. They had, when the great Mr Boston came to Etterick, the farms o' Blackhouse,

Dryhope, Henderland, Chapelhope, Scabcleugh, Shorthope, Midge-hope, Meggatknowes, Buccleuch, and Gilmainscleugh, that I ken of, and likely as mony mae; and now there's no a man o' the name in a' the bounds aboon the rank of a cow-herd. Thomas Linton rode to kirk an' market, wi' a liveryman at his back; but where is a' that pride now? A' buried in the mools wi' the bearers o't! an' the last repre-sentative o' that great overgrown family, that laid house to house, an' field to field, is now sair gane on a wee, wee farm o' the Duke o' Buccleuch's. The ancient curse had lighted on these men, if ever it lighted on men in this world. And yet they were reckoned good men, and kind men in their day; for the good Mr Boston wrote an epitaph on Thomas, in metre, when he died; an' though I have read it a hunder times in St Mary's kirkyard, where it is to be seen to this day, I canna say it ower. But it says that he was eyes to the blind, and feet to the lame, and that the Lord would requite him in a day to come, or something to that purpose. Now that said a great deal for him, master, although Providence has seen meet to strip his race o' a' their worldly possessions. But take an auld fool's advice, and never lay ye farm to farm, even though a fair opportunity should offer; for, as sure as He lives who pronounced that curse, it will take effect. I'm an auld man, an' I hae seen mony dash made that way, but I never saw ane o' them come to good! There was first Murray of Glenvath; why, it was untelling what land that man possessed. Now his family has not a furr in the twa counties. Then there was his neighbour Simpson of Posso: I hae seen the day that Simpson had two-and-twenty farms, the best o' the twa counties, an' a' stockit wi' good sheep. Now there's no a drap o' *his* blood has a furr in the twa counties. Then there was Grieve of Willenslee; ane wad hae thought that body was gaun to take the hale kingdom. He was said to hae had ten thousand sheep, a' on good farms, at ae time. Where are they a' now? Neither *him* nor *his* hae a furr in the twa counties. Let me tell ye, master—for ye're but a young man, an' I wad aye fain have ye to see things in a right light—that ye may blame the wars; ye may blame the government; an' ye may blame the parliamenters; but there's a hand that rules higher than a' these; an' gin ye dinna look to that, ye'll never look to the right source either o' your prosperity or adversity. An' I sairly doubt that the pride o' the farmers was raised to ower great a pitch, that Providence has been brewing a day of humiliation for them, and that there will be a change o' hands aince mair, as there was about this time hunder an' forty years."

"Then I suppose you shepherds expect to have century about with us, or so? Well, I don't see anything very unfair in it."

"Ay, but I fear we will be as far aneath the right medium for a while, as ye are startit aboon it. We'll make a fine hand doing the honours o' the grand mansion-houses that ye hae biggit for us; the cavalry exercises; the guns an' the pointers; the wine an' the punch drinking; an' the singing o' the deboshed sangs. But we'll just come to the right set again in a generation or twa, and then as soon as we get ower hee, we'll get a downcome in our turn.—But, master, I say, how will you grand gentlemen take wi' a shepherd's life? How will ye like to be turned into reeky holes like this, where ye can hardly see your fingers afore ye, an' be reduced to the parritch and the horn-spoon?"

"I cannot tell, Andrew. I suppose it will have some advantages. It will teach us to say long prayers to put off the time; and if we should have the misfortune afterwards to pass into *the bad place* that you shepherds are all so terrified about, why, we will scarcely know any difference. I account that a great advantage in dwelling in such a place as this. We'll scarcely know the one place from the other."

"Ay, but O what a surprise ye will get when ye step out o' ane o' your grand palaces into hell! An' gin ye dinna repent in time, ye'll maybe get a little experiment o' that sort. Ye think ye hae said a very witty thing there; but a' profane wit's sinfu', an' whatever is sinfu' is shamefu'; and therefore it never suits to be said either afore God or man. Ye are just a good standin' sample o' the young tenantry o' Scotland at this time. Ye're ower genteel to be devout, an' ye look ower high, and depend ower muckle on the arm o' flesh, to regard the rod and Him that hath appointed it. But it will fa' wi' the mair weight o' that! A blow that is seen coming may be wardit off; but if ane's sae proud as no to regard it, 'tis the less scaith that he be knockit down."

"I see not how any man can ward off this blow, Andrew. It has gathered its overwhelming force in springs over which we have no control, and is of that nature that no industry of man can aught avail. It is merely as a drop in the bucket; and I greatly fear that this grievous storm is come to lay the axe to the root of the tree."

"I'm glad to hear, however, that ye hae some scripture phrases at your tongue roots. I never heard you use ane in a serious mood before; an' I hope there will be a reformation yet. If adversity will hae that effect, I shall submit to my share o' the loss that the storm should lie still for a while, and cut off a wheen o' the creatures that ye aince made eedals o', and now dow hardly bide to see. But that's the gate wi' a' things that ane sets up for warldly worship in place o' the true object; they turn a' out curses and objects o' shame and disgrace. As for warding off the blow, master, I see no resource but throwing up the farms ilk ane, and trying to save a remnant out o' the fire. The lairds want naething better than for ye to rin in arrears; then they will get a' your stocks for neist to naething, and have the land stockit themsels as they had langsyne; and you will be their keepers, or vassals, the same as we are to you at present. As to hinging on at the present rents, it is madness—the very extremity of madness. I hae been a herd here for fifty years, an' I ken as weel what the ground will pay at every price of sheep as you do, and I daresay a great deal better. When I came here first, your father paid less than the third of the rent that you are bound to pay; sheep of every description were dearer, lambs, ewes, and wedders; and I ken weel he was making no money of it, honest man, but merely working his way, with some years a little over, and some naething. And how is it possible that you can pay three times the rent at the same prices o' sheep? I say the very presumption of the thing is sheer madness. And it is not only this farm, but you may take it as an average of all the farms in the country, that *before the French war began, the sheep were dearer than they are now—the farms were not above one-third of the rents at an average, and the farmers were not making any money.* They have lost their summer day during the French war, which will never return to them; and the only resource they have, that I can see, is to abandon their farms in time, and try to save a remnant. Things will come to their true level presently, but not afore the auld stock o' farmers are crushed past rising again. An' then I little wat what's to come o' ye; for an we herds get the land, we *winna* employ you as our shepherds, that you may depend on."

"Well, Andrew, these are curious facts that you tell me of the land having all changed occupiers about a certain period. I wish you could have stated the causes with certainty. Was not there a great loss on this farm once, when it was said the burn was so dammed up with dead carcases that it changed its course?"

"Ay, but that's quite a late story. It happened in my own day, and I believe mostly through mischance. That was the year Rob Dodds was lost in the Carny Cleuch. I remember of it, but cannot tell what year it was, for I was but a little bilsh o' a callant then."

"Who was Rob Dodds? I never heard of the incident before."

"Ay, but your father remembered weel o't; for he sent a' his men mony a day to look for the corpse, but a' to nae purpose. I'll never forget it; for it made an impression on me sae deep that I coudna get rest i' my bed for months and days. He was a young handsome bonny lad, an honest man's only son, and was herd wi' Tam Linton in the Birkhill. The Lintons were sair come down then; for this Tam was a herd, and had Rab hired as his assistant. Weel, it sae happen'd that Tam's wife had occasion to cross the wild heights atween the Birkhill

and Tweedsmuir, to see her mother, or sister, on some express; and
Tam sent the young man wi' her to see her ower the Donald's Cleuch
edge. It was in the middle o' winter, and, if I mind right, this time
sixty years. The morning was calm, frosty, and threatening snaw, but
the ground clear of it at the time they set out. Rob had orders to set his
mistress to the height, and return home; but by the time they had got
to the height, the snaw had come on, so the good lad went all the way
through Guemshope with her, and in sight of the water o' Frood. He
crossed all the wildest o' the heights on his return in safety; and on the
middle-end, west of Loch-Skene, he met with Robin Laidlaw, that
went to the Highlands and grew a great farmer after that. Robin was
gathering the Balmoody ewes; and as they were neighbours, and both
herding to ae master, Laidlaw testified some anxiety that the young
man might not find his way hame, for the blast had then come on very
severe. Dodds leugh at him, an' said, 'he was nae mair feared for
finding the gate hame, than he was for finding the gate to his mouth
when he was hungry.' 'Weel weel,' quo' Robin, 'keep the band o' the
hill a' the way, for I hae seen as clever a fellow warred on sic a day; an'
be sure to hund the ewes out o' the Brand Law scores as ye gang by.'
'Tammy charged me to bring a backfu' o' peats wi' me,' said he, 'but I
think I'll no gang near the peat stack the day.' 'Na,' quo' Robin, 'I
think ye'll no be sae mad.' 'But, O man,' quo' the lad, 'hae ye ony bit
bread about your pouches, for I'm unco hungry. The wife was in sic a
hurry that I had to come away without getting ony breakfast, an' I
had sae far to gang wi' her, that I'm grown unco toom i' the inside.'
'The fiend ae inch I hae, Robie, my man, or ye should hae had it,'
quo' Laidlaw. 'But an that be the case, gang straight hame, and never
heed the ewes, come o' them what will.' 'O there's nae fear!' said he,
'I'll turn the ewes, and be hame in good time too.' And with that he
left Laidlaw, and went down the Middle-Craig-end, jumping and
playing in a frolicsome way ower his stick. He had a large lang-nebbit
staff in his hand, which Laidlaw took particular notice of, thinking it
would be a good help for the young man in the rough way he had to
gang.

"There was never another word about the matter till that day
eight days. The storm having increased to a terrible drift, the snaw
had grown very deep, and the herds, wha lived about three miles
sindry, hadna met for a' that time. But that day Tam Linton an'
Robin Laidlaw met at the Tail Burn; an' after cracking a lang time
thegither, Tam says to the tither, just as it war by chance, 'Saw ye
naething o' our young dinnagood this day eight days, Robin? He
gaed awa that morning to set our goodwife ower the height, an' has

never mair lookit near me, the careless rascal!'

" 'Tam Linton, what's that you're saying? what's that I hear ye saying, Tam Linton?' quo' Robin, wha was dung clean stupid wi' horror. 'Hae ye never seen Rob Dodds sin' that morning he gaed away wi' your wife?'

" 'Na, never,' quo' the tither.

" 'Why then, sir, let me tell ye, that you'll never see him again in this world alive,' quo' Robin, 'for he left me on the Middle-end on his way hame that day at eleven o'clock, just as the day was coming to the warst.—But, Tam Linton, what was't ye war saying? Ye're telling me a great lee, man.—Do ye say that ye haena seen Rob Dodds sin' that day?'

" 'Haena I tauld ye that I hae never seen his face sinsyne!' quo' Tammie.

" 'Sae I hear ye saying,' quo' Robin again. 'But ye're tellin' me a downright made lee. The thing's no possible; for ye hae the very staff i' your hand that he had in his, when he left me in the drift that day.'

" 'I ken naething about sticks or staves, Robin Laidlaw,' says Tam, lookin' rather like ane catched in an ill turn. 'The staff wasna likely to come hame without the owner; and I can only say, I hae seen nae mair o' Rob Dodds sin' that morning; an' I had thoughts that, as the day grew sae ill, he had hadden forrit a' the length wi' our wife, and was biding wi' her fo'ks a' this time to bring her hame again when the storm had settled.'

" 'Na na, Tammie, ye needna get into ony o' thae lang-windit stories wi' me,' quo' Robin. 'For I tell ye that's the staff that Rob Dodds had in his hand when I last saw him; sae ye have either seen him dead or living—I'll gie my oath to that.'

" 'Ye had better take care what ye say, Robin Laidlaw,' says Tam, vera fiercely, 'or I'll maybe make ye blithe to eat in your words again.'

" 'What I hae said, I'll stand to, Tammy Linton,' says Robin. 'An' mair than that,' says he, 'if that good young man has come to an untimely end, I'll see his blood requited at your hand.'

"Then there was word sent away to the Hopehouse to his parents, and ye may weel ken, master, what heavy news it was to them, for Rob was their only son; they had gien him a good education, an' muckle muckle they thought o' him; but naething wad serve him but he wad be a shepherd. His father came wi' the maist part o' Etterick parish at his back; and mony sharp and threatening words there past atween him and Tam; but what could they make o't? The lad was lost, and nae law, nor nae revenge could restore him again; sae they had naething for't, but to spread athwart a' the hills looking for the corpse. The hale country raise for ten miles round, on ane or twa good days that happened; but the snaw was still lying, an' a' their looking was in vain. Tam Linton wad look nane. He took the dorts, and never heeded the fo'k mair than they hadna been there. A' that height atween Loch-Skene an' the Birkhill was just movin' wi' fo'k for the space o' three weeks, for the twa auld fo'k, the lad's parents, coudna get ony rest, an' fo'k sympathized unco sair wi' them. At length the snaw gaed maistly away, an' the weather turned fine, an' I gaed out ane o' the days wi' my father to look for the body. But, aih wow! I was a feared wight! whenever I saw a bit sod, or a knowe, or a grey stane, I stood still an' trembled for fear it was the dead man, and no ae step durst I steer farther, till my father gaed up to a' thae things. I gaed nae mair back to look for the corpse; for I'm sure if we had found the body I wad hae gane out o' my judgment.

"At length every body tired o' looking, but the auld man himsel. He travelled day after day, ill weather and good weather, without intermission. They said it was the waesomest thing ever was seen, to see that good auld grey-headed man gaun sae lang by himsel', looking for the remains o' his only son. The maist part o' his friends advised him at length to gie up the search, as the finding o' the body seemed a thing a'thegither hopeless. But he declared he wad look for his son till the day o' his death; and if he could but find his bones, he would carry them away from the wild moors and lay them in the grave where he was to lie himsel'. Tam Linton was apprehended, and examined on oath afore the sheriff; but there was nae proof could be led against him, an' he wan off. He swore that, as far as he remembered, he got the staff standing at the mouth o' the peat stack; and that he conceived that either the lad or himsel' had left it there some day when bringing away a burden of peats. The shepherds' peats had not been led home that year, and the stack stood on a hill head, half a mile frae the house, and the herds were obliged to carry them home as they needed them.

"But there was a mystery hung over that lad's death that was never cleared up, nor ever will a' thegither. Every man was convinced, in his own mind, that Linton knew of the body a' the time; and also, that the young man had not come by his death fairly. It was proven that the lad's dog had come hame several times, and that Tam Linton had been seen kicking it frae about his house; and as the dog could be no where all that time, but waiting on the body, if that had not been concealed in some more than ordinary way, the dog would at least have been seen. At length, it was suggested to the old man, that there were always dead lights hovered over a corpse by night, if the body was left exposed to the air; and it was a fact that two drowned men had been found in a field of whins, where the water had left the bodies, by means of the dead lights, a very little while before that. On the first calm night, therefore, the old desolate man went to the Merkside-edge, to the top of a high hill that overlooked all the ground where there was ony likelihood that the body would be lying. He watched there the lee-lang night, keeping his eye constantly roaming ower the broken waste over against him, but he never noticed the least glimmer of the dead lights. About midnight, however, he heard a dog barking; it likewise gae twa or three melancholy yowls, and then ceased. Robin Dodds was convinced it was his son's dog; but it was at such a distance, being about twa miles off, that he coudna be sure where it was, or which o' the hills on the opposite side it was on. The second night he kept watch on the Path Knows, a hill which he supposed the howling o' the dog came frae. But that hill being all surrounded to the west and north by tremendous ravines and cat-aracts, he heard nothing o' the dog. In the course of the night, however, he saw, or fancied he saw, a momentary glimmer o' light, in the depth of the great gulf immediately below where he sat; and that at three different times, always in the same place. He now became convinced that the remains o' his dear son were in the bottom of the linn, a place which he conceived inaccessible to man; it being so deep from the summit where he stood, that the roar o' the waterfall only reached his ears now and then wi' a loud *whush!* as if it had been a sound wandering across the hills by itsel'. But sae intent was Robin on this Willie-an-the-wisp light, that he took landmarks frae the ae summit to the other, to make sure o' the place; and as soon as daylight came, he set about finding a passage down to the bottom of the linn. He effected this by coming to the foot of the linn, and tracing its course backward, sometimes wading in water, and sometimes clambering over rocks, till at length, with a beating heart, he reached the very spot where he perceived the light; and in the grey o' the morning, he saw there was something lying there that differed in colour from the iron-hued stones, and rocks, of which the linn was composed. He was in great astonishment what this could be; for, as he came closer on it, he saw it had no likeness to the dead body o' a man, but rather appeared to be a heap o' bed-clothes. And what think you it turned out to be? For I see ye're glowring as your een were gaun to loup out. Just neither mair nor less than a strong mineral well; or what the doctors ca' a callybit spring, a' boustered about wi' heaps o' soapy, limy kind o' stuff, that it seems had thrown out a sort o' fiery vapours i' the night-time.

"However, Robin being unable to do ony mair in the way o' searching, had now nae hope left but in finding his dead son by some kind o' supernatural means. Sae he determined to watch a third night, and that at the very identical peat-stack where it had been said his son's staff was found. He did sae; an' about midnight, ere ever he wist, the dog set up a howl close beside him. He called on him by his name, and the dog came and fawned on his old acquaintance, and whimpered, and whinged, an' made sic a wark, as cou'd hardly hae been trowed. Robin keepit him in his bosom a' the night, and fed him wi' pieces o' bread, and said mony kind things to him; and then as soon as the sun rose, he let him gang; and the poor affectionate creature went straight to his dead master; who, after all, was lying in a little green sprithy hollow, not above a musket-shot from the peat-stack. This rendered the whole affair more mysterious than ever; for Robin Dodds himself, and above twenty men beside, could all have made oath that they had looked into that place again and again, and that so minutely, that a dead bird could not have been in it, that they would not have seen. However, there the body of the youth was gotten, after having been lost for the long space of ten weeks; and not in a state of great decay neither, for it rather appeared swollen, as if it had been lying among water.

"Conjecture was now driven to great extremities in accounting for all these circumstances. It was manifest to every one, that the body had not been all the time in that place. But then, where had it been? Or what could have been the reasons for concealing it? These were the puzzling considerations. There were a hunder different things suspectit; and mony o' them, I dare say, a hunder miles frae the truth; but on the whole, Tammy was sair lookit down on, and almaist perfectly abhorred by the country; for it was weel kenn'd that he had been particularly churlish and severe on the young man at a' times, and seemed to have a peculiar dislike to him. An it hadna been the wife, wha was a kind considerate sort o' a body, if gi'en Tam his will, it was reckoned he wad hae hungered the lad to dead. After that, Tammy left the place, an' gaed away, I watna where; and the country, I believe, came gayan near to the truth o' the story at last. There was a girl in the Birkhill house at the time, whether a daughter o' Tam's, or no, I hae forgot, though I think otherwise. However, she durstna for her life tell a' she kenn'd as lang as the investigation was gaun on; but it at last spunkit out that Rob Dodds had got hame safe eneugh; and that Tam got into a great rage at him, because he had not brought a burden o' peats, there being none in the house. The youth excused himself on the score of fatigue and hunger; but Tammy swore at him, and said, 'The de'il be in your teeth, gin they shall break bread, till ye gang back out to the hill-head and bring a burden o' peats.' Dodds refused; on which Tam struck him, and forced him away; and he went crying an' greetin' out at the door, but never came back. She also told, that after poor Rob was lost, Tam tried several times to get at his dog to fell it with a stick, but the creature was terrified for him, and made its escape. It was therefore thought, an' there was little doubt, that Rob, through fatigue and hunger, and reckless of death at the way he had been guidit, went out to the hill, and died at the peat-stack, the mouth of which was a shelter from the drift-wind; and that his cruel master, conscious o' the way he had used him, and dreading skaith, had trailed away the body, and sunk it in some pool in these unfathomable linns, or otherwise concealed it, wi' the intention, that the world might never ken whether the lad was actually dead or had absconded. If it had not been for the dog, from which it appears he had been unable to conceal it, and the old man's perseverance, to whose search there appeared to be no end, it is probable he would never have laid the body in a place where it could have been found, otherwise than by watching and following the dog. By that mode, the intentional concealment of the corpse would have been discovered, so that Tammy all that time could not be quite at his ease, and it was no wonder he attempted to fell the dog. But where the body could have been deposited, that the faithful animal was never discovered by the searchers, during the day, for the space of ten weeks, that baffled a' the conjectures that ever could be tried.

"The two old people, the lad's father and mother, never got over their great and cruel loss. They never held up their heads again, nor joined in society ony mair, except in attending divine worship. It might be truly said o' them, that they spent the few years that they survived their son in constant prayer and humiliation; but they soon died, short while after ane anither. As for Tam Linton, he left this part of the country; but it was said there was a curse hung over him an' his a' his life, an' that he never did mair weel. That was the year, master, on which our burn was dammed wi' the dead sheep; and in fixing the date, you see, I hae been led into a lang story, and am just nae farther wi' the main point than when I began."

"I wish from my heart, Andrew, that you would try to fix a great many old dates in the same manner; for I confess I am more interested in your lang stories, than in either your lang prayers, or your lang sermons, about repentance and amendment. But pray, you were talking of the judgments that overtook Tam Linton—Was that the same Tam Linton that was precipitated from the Brand Law by the break of a snaw wreathe, and he and all his sheep jammed into the hideous gulf, called The Grey Mare's Tail?"

"The very same, sir; and that might be accountit ane o' the first judgments that befel him, for there were many of his ain sheep in the flock. Tam asserted all his life, that he went into the linn along with his hirsel, but no man ever believed him; for there was not one of the sheep came out alive, and how it was possible for the carl to have come safe out, naebody could see. It was, indeed, quite impossible; for it had been such a break of snaw as had scarcely ever been seen. The gulf was crammed sae fu', as that ane could hae gane ower it like a pendit brigg; and no a single sheep could be gotten out, either dead or living. When the thaw came, the burn wrought a passage for itself below the snaw, but the arch stood till summer. I have heard my father oft describe the appearance of that vault as he saw it on his way from Moffat fair. Ane hadna gane far into it, he said, till it turned darkish, like an ill-hued twilight; an' sic a like arch o' carnage he never saw! There were limbs o' sheep hingin' in a' directions, the snaw was wedged sae firm. Some hale carcases hung by the neck, some by a spauld; then there was a hale forest o' legs sticking out in ae place, an' horns in another, terribly mangled an' broken; an' it was a' thegither sic a frightsome-looking place, that he was blithe to get out o't again."

After looking at the sheep, tasting old Janet's best kebbuck, and oatmeal cakes, and preeing the whisky bottle, the young farmer again set out through the deep snaw, on his way home. But Andrew made him promise, that if the weather did not amend, he was to come back in a few days and see how the poor sheep were coming on; and, as an inducement, promised to tell him a great many old anecdotes of the shepherd's life.

Mr Adamson of Laverhope

ONE of those judgments that have made the deepest impression on the shepherds' minds for a century bygone, seems to have been the fate of Mr Adamson, who was tenant in Laverhope for the space of twenty-seven years. That incident stands in the calendar as an æra from whence to date summer floods, water spouts, hail and thunderstorms, &c; and appears from tradition to have been attended with some awful circumstances, expressive of divine vengeance. This Adamson is represented, as having been a man of an ungovernable temper—of irritability so extreme, that no person could be for a moment certain to what excesses he might be hurried. He was otherwise accounted a good and upright man, and a sincere christian; but in these out-breakings of temper he often committed acts of cruelty and injustice, for which any good man ought to have been ashamed. Among other qualities, he had an obliging turn of disposition, there being few men to whom a poor man would sooner have applied in a strait. Accordingly, he had been in the habit of assisting a poorer neighbour of his with a little credit for many years. This man's name was Irvine, and though he had a number of rich relations, he was never out of difficulties. Adamson, out of some whim, or caprice, sued this poor farmer for a few hundred merks, taking legal steps against him, even to the very last measures short of poinding and imprisonment. Irvine paid little attention to this, taking it for granted that his neighbour took these steps only for the purpose of inducing his debtor's friends to come forward and support him.

It happened one day about this period, that a thoughtless boy belonging to Irvine's farm dogged Adamson's cattle in a way that gave great offence to their owner, on which the two farmers differed, and some hard recriminating words and terms passed between them. The next day Irvine was seized and thrown into jail, and shortly after his effects were poinded, and sold by auction for ready money. They were consequently thrown away, as the neighbours, not having been forewarned of such an event, were wholly unprovided with ready money, and unable to purchase at any price. Mrs Irvine came to the enraged creditor with a child in her arms, and begged and implored of him to put off the sale for a month, that she might try amongst her friends what could be done to prevent a wreck so irretrievable. He was on the very point of yielding, but some bitter reminiscences coming over his mind at the moment, stimulated his spleen against her husband, and the sale was ordered to go on. William Carrudders of Grindiston heard the following dialogue between them, and he said that his heart almost trembled within him, for Mrs Irvine was a violent woman, and her eloquence did more evil than good.

"Are ye really gaun to act the part of a devil the day, Mr Adamson, an' turn me and thae bairns out to the bare high-road, helpless as we are? Oh, man, if your bowels be nae seared in hell fire already, take some compassion; for an ye dinna, they *will* be seared afore baith men and angels yet, till that hard and cruel heart o' yours be nealed to an izle."

"I'm gaun to act nae part of a devil, Mrs Irvine; I'm only gaun to take my ain in the only way I can get it. I'm no baith gaun to tine my siller, an' hae my beasts abused into the bargain."

"Ye sal neither lose plack nor bawbee o' your siller, man, if ye will gie me but a month to make a shift for it—I swear to you, ye sal neither lose, nor rue the deed. But if ye winna grant me that wee wee while, when the bread of a hale family depends on it, ye're waur than ony deil that's yammerin' and cursin' i' the bottomless pit."

"Keep your ravings to yoursel, Mrs Irvine, for I hae made up my mind what I'm to do, and I'll do it; sae it's needless for ye to pit yoursel into a bleeze; for the surest promisers are aye the slackest payers; it isna likely that your bad language will gar me alter my purpose."

"If that *be* your purpose, Mr Adamson, and if you put that purpose in execution, I wadna change conditions wi' you the day for ten thousand times a' the gear ye are worth. Ye're gaun to do the thing that ye'll repent only aince—for a' the time that ye hae to exist baith in this warld and the neist, an' that's a lang lang look forrit an' ayond. Ye have assisted a poor honest family for the purpose of taking them at a disadvantage, and crushing them to beggars; and when ane thinks o' that, what a heart you must hae! Ye hae first put my poor man in prison, a place where he little thought, and less deserved, ever to be; an' now ye are reaving his sackless family out o' their last bit o' bread. Look at this bit bonny innocent thing in my arms, how it is smiling on ye. Look at a' the rest standin' leaning against the wa's, ilka ane wi' his een fixed on you by way o' imploring your pity. If ye reject thae looks, ye'll see them again in some trying moments, that will bring this ane back to your mind. Ye will see them i' your dreams; ye will see them on your death-bed, an' ye will *think* ye see them gleaming on ye through the reek o' hell, but it winna be them."

"Haud your tongue, woman, for ye make me feared to hear ye."

"Ay, but better be feared in time, than torfelled for ever! Better conquer your bad humour for aince, than be conquessed for it through sae many lang ages. Ye pretend to be a religious man, Mr Adamson, an' a great deal mair sae than your neighbours. Do you think that religion teaches you acts o' cruelty like this? Will ye hae the face to kneel afore your Maker the night, and pray for a blessing on you and yours, and that He will forgive you your debts as you forgive your debtors? I hae nae doubt but ye will. But aih! How sic an appeal will heap the coals o' divine vengeance on your head, an' tighten the belts o' burning yettlin round your hard heart! Come forret, ye hallanshaker-like tikes, an' speak for yoursels ilk ane o' ye."

"O, Mr Adamson, ye maunna turn my father an' mother out o' their house an' their farm, or what think ye is to come o' us?" said Thomas.

"Maissa Adamson, an ye da tun my faddy an' moddy out o' dem's house, when oul John tulns a geat, muckle, big, stong man, John fesh youd skin to you—let you take tat," said John, and in the meantime he nodded his head, and shook his tiny fist at the farmer, who called him an impertinent brat, and said he deserved his cuffs.

The sale went on; and still, on the calling off of every favourite animal, Mrs Irvine renewed her anathemas.

"Gentlemen, this is the mistress's favourite cow, and gives thirteen pints of milk every day. She is valued in my roup-roll at fifteen pounds, but we shall begin her at ten. Does anybody say ten pounds for this excellent cow? ten pounds, ten pounds? Nobody says ten pounds? Gentlemen, this is extraordinary! Money is surely a scarce article here to-day. Well, then, does any gentleman say five pounds to begin this excellent cow that gives twelve pints of milk daily? Five pounds? Only five pounds! Nobody bids five pounds? Well, the stock must positively be sold without reserve. Ten shillings for the cow—ten shillings—ten shillings—Will nobody bid ten shillings to set the sale a-going?"

"I'll gie five-an'-twenty shillings for her," cried Adamson.

"Thank you, sir. One pound five—one pound five, and just a-going. Once—twice—*thrice*. Mr Adamson, one pound five."

Mrs Irvine came forward, drowned in tears, with the babe in her arms, and patting the cow, she said, "Ah, poor lady Bell, this is my last sight o' you, and the last time I'll clap your honest side! An' hae we really been deprived o' your support for the miserable sum o' five and twenty shillings; my curse light on the head o' him that has done

it! In the name of my destitute bairns I curse him; an' does he think
that a mother's curse will sink fizzenless to the ground? Na, na! I see
an ee that's lookin' down here in pity and in anger; an' I see a hand
that's gathering the bolts o' Heaven thegither, for some purpose that I
could divine, but darena utter. But that hand is unerring, and where
it throws the bolt, there it will strike. Fareweel, poor beast! ye hae
supplied us wi' mony a meal, but ye will never supply us wi' anither."

This sale at Kirkheugh was on the 11th of July. On the day
following, Mr Adamson went up to the folds in the hope, to shear his
sheep, with no fewer than twenty-five attendants, consisting of all his
own servants and cottars, and about as many neighbouring shepherds
whom he had collected; it being customary for the farmers to assist
one another reciprocally on these occasions. Adamson continued
more than usually capricious and unreasonable all that forenoon. He
was discontented with himself, and when a man is ill pleased with
himself, he is seldom well pleased with others. He seemed altogether
left to the influences of the wicked one, running about in a fume of
rage, finding fault with everything, and every person, and at times
cursing bitterly, a crime to which he was not usually addicted; so that
the sheep-shearing that wont to be a scene of hilarity among so many
young and old shepherds, lads, lasses, wives, and callants, was that
day turned into one of gloom and dissatisfaction.

After a number of provoking outrages, he at length, with the
buisting-iron that he held in his hand, struck a dog that belonged to
one of his own shepherd boys, till the poor animal fell senseless on the
ground, and lay sprawling as in the last extremity. This brought
matters to a point that threatened nothing but anarchy and confusion, for every shepherd's blood boiled with indignation, and each
almost wished in his heart that the dog had been his own, that he
might have retaliated on the tyrant. The boy was wearing one of the
fold-doors, and perceiving the plight of his faithful animal, he ran to
its assistance, lifted it in his arms, and holding it up to recover its
breath, he wept and lamented over it most piteously. "My poor poor
little Nimble!" cried he; "I am feared that mad body has killed ye,
and then what am I to do wanting ye? I wad ten times rather he had
strucken mysel."

He had not the words said out ere his master had him by the hair of
the head with the one hand, with which he fell a swinging him round,
and with the other began a threshing him most unmercifully. When
the boy left the fold door, the sheep broke out and got away to the hill
among the lambs and the clippies, and the farmer being in one of his
"mad tantrums," as the servants called them, the mischance had

almost put him beside himself; and that boy, or man either, is in a
ticklish case who is in the hands of an enraged person far above him in
strength.

The sheep-shearers paused, and the girls screamed, when they saw
their master lay hold of the boy. But Robert Johnston, a shepherd
from an adjoining farm, flung the sheep from his knee, made the
shears ring against the fold-dike, and in an instant had the farmer by
both wrists, and these he held with such a grasp that he took the
power out of his arms, for Johnston was as far above the farmer in
might, as the latter was above the boy.

"Mr Adamson, what are ye about?" cried he; "hae ye tint your
reason awthegither, that ye are gaun on rampauging like a madman
that gate? Ye hae done the thing, sir, in your ill-timed rage, that ye
ought to be ashamed of baith afore God and man."

"Are ye for fighting, Rob Johnston?" said the farmer, struggling to
free himself. "Do ye want to hae a fight, lad? Because if ye do, I'll
maybe gie you enough o' that."

"Na, sir, I dinna want to fight, but I winna let you fight either,
unless wi' ane that's your equal; sae gie ower spraughling, and stand
still till I speak to ye, for an ye winna stand to hear reason, I'll gar ye
lie till ye hear it. Do ye consider what ye hae been doing even now? Do
ye consider that ye hae been striking a poor orphan callant, wha has
neither father nor mother to protect him, or to right his wrangs? An'
a' for naething, but a wee bit start o' natural affection. How wad ye
like, sir, an ony body were to guide a bairn o' yours that gate? and ye
as little ken what they are a' to come to afore their deaths, as that
boy's parents did when they were rearing and fondling ower him. Fie
for shame, Mr Adamson! Fie for shame! Ye first strak his poor dumb
brute, which was a greater sin than the tither, for it didna ken what ye
were striking it for; and then, because the callant ran to assist the only
creature he has on the earth, an' I'm feared the only true and faithfu'
friend beside, ye claught him by the hair o' the head, an' fa' to the
dadding him as he war your slave! Od, sir, my blood rises at ye for sic
an act o' cruelty and injustice; and gin I thought ye worth my while, I
wad tan ye like a pellet for it."

The farmer struggled and fought so viciously, that Johnston was
obliged to throw him down twice over, somewhat roughly, and hold
him by main force. But on laying him down the second time, Johnston
said, "Now, sir, I just tell ye, aince for a', that if I hae to lay ye down
the third time, ye shall never rise again till the day o' joodgment. Ye
deserve to hae your hide weel throoshen; but ye're nae match for me,
an' I'll scorn to lay a tip on ye. I'll leave ye to him who has declared

himself the stay and shield of the orphan, and gin some visible testimony o' his displeasure dinna come ower ye for the abusing of his ward, I am right sair mista'en."

Adamson, finding himself fairly mastered, and that no one seemed disposed to take his part, was obliged to give in, and went sullenly away to tend the hirsel that stood beside the fold. In the meantime the sheep-shearing went on as before, with a little more of hilarity and glee. It is the business of the lasses to take the ewes, and carry them from the fold to the clippers; and now might be seen every young shepherd's sweetheart, or favourite, tending on him, helping him to clip, or holding the ewes by the hind legs to make them lie easy, a great matter for the furtherance of the operator. Others again, who thought themselves slighted, or loved a joke, would continue to act in the reverse way, and plague the youths by bringing such sheep to them as it was next to impossible to clip.

"Aih, Jock lad, I hae brought you a grand ane for this time! Ye will clank the shears ower her, an' be the first done o' them a'."

"My truly, Jessy, but ye hae gi'en me my dinner! I declare the beast is woo to the cloots an' the een holes, an' afore I get the fleece broken up, the rest will be done. Ah, Jessy, Jessy! ye're working for a mischief the day, an' ye'll maybe get it."

"She's a braw sonsie sheep, Jock. I ken ye like to hae your arms weel filled. She'll amaist fill them as weel as Tibby Tod."

"There's for it now! There's for it! What care I for Tibby Tod, dame? Ye are the most jealous elf, Jessy, that ever drew coat ower head. But wha was't that sat half a night at the side of a grey stane wi' a crazy cooper? An' wha was't that gae the poor precentor the whiskings, and reduced a' his sharps to downright flats? An ye cast up Tibby Tod ony mair to me, I'll tell something that will gar thae wild een reel i' your head, Mistress Jessy."

"Wow, Jock, but I'm unco wae for ye now. Poor fellow! It's really very hard usage! If ye canna clip the ewe, man, gie me her, an' I'll tak her to anither; for I canna bide to see ye sae sair put about. I winna bring ye anither Tibby Tod the day, take my word on it. The neist shall be a real May Henderson, a Firthhope-cleuch ane, ye ken, wi' lang legs, a short tail, an' a good lamb at her fit."

"Gudesake, lassie, haud your tongue, an' dinna affront baith yoursel and me. Ye are fit to gar ane's cheek burn to the bane. I'm fairly quashed, an' darena say anither word. Let us therefore hae let-a-be for let-a-be, which is good bairns' greement, till after the close o' the day sky, and then I'll tell ye my mind."

"Ay, but whilk o' your minds will ye tell me, Jock? For ye will be in five or six different anes afore that time. Ane, to ken your mind, wad need to be tauld it every hour o' the day, and then cast up the account at the year's end. But how wad she settle it then, Jock? I fancy she wad hae to multiply ilk year's minds by dozens, and divide by four, and then we a' ken what wad be the quotient."

"Aih wow, sirs! heard ever ony o' ye the like o' that? For three things the sheep-fauld is disquieted, and there are four which it cannot bear."

"An' what are they, Jock?"

"A witty wench, a woughing dog, a waukit-woo'd wedder, an' a pair o' shambling shears."

After this manner did the gleesome chat go on, now that the surly goodman had withdrawn from the scene. But this was but one couple; every pair being engaged according to their biasses, and after their kind—some settling the knotty points of divinity; others telling auld warld stories about persecutions, forays, and fairy raids; and some whispering, in half sentences, the soft breathings of pastoral love.

But the farmer's bad humour, in the mean while, was only smothered, not extinguished; and, like a flame that is kept down by an overpowering weight of fuel, wanted but a breath to rekindle it; or like a barrel of gunpowder, that the smallest spark will set up in a blaze. That spark unfortunately fell upon the ignitible heap too soon. It came in the form of an old beggar, ycleped Patie Maxwell, a well known, and generally a welcome guest over all that district. He came up to the folds for his annual bequest of a fleece of wool, which had never before been denied him; and the farmer being the first person he came to, he made up to him, as in respect bound, accosting him in his wonted obsequious way.

"Weel, goodman, how's a wi' ye the day?"—(No answer.)—"This will be a thrang day w'ye. How are ye getting on wi' the clipping?"

"Nae the better o' you, or the like o' you. Gang away back the gate ye came. What are ye coming doiting up through the sheep that gate for, putting them a' tersyversy?"

"Tut, goodman, what does the sheep mind an auld creeping body like me? I hae done nae ill to your pickle sheep, man. An' as for ganging back the road I cam, I'll do that whan I like, and no till than."

"But I'll make you blithe to turn back, auld vagabond. Do ye imagine I'm gaun to hae a' my clippers, an' grippers, buisters, an' binders, laid half idle, gaffing and giggling wi' you?"

"Why, than, speak like a reasonable man, an' a courteous Christian, as ye used to do, an' I'se crack wi' yoursel, and no gang near them."

"I'll keep my Christian cracks for others than auld Papist dogs, I trow."

"Wha do ye ca' auld Papist dogs, Mr Adamson?—Wha is it that ye mean to denominate by that fine sounding title?"

"Just you, and the like o' ye, Pate. It is weel ken'd that ye are as rank a Papist as ever kissed a crosier, an' that ye were out in the very fore end o' the unnatural rebellion, in order to subvert our religion, and place a Popish tyrant on the throne. It is a shame for a Protestant parish like this to support ye, an' gie you as liberal awmosses as ye were a Christian saint. For me, I can tell you, ye'll get nae mae at my hand, nor nae rebel Papist loun amang ye."

"Dear sir, ye're surely no yoursèl the day? Ye hae ken'd I professed the Catholic religion these thretty years. It was the faith I was brought up in, and that in which I shall dee; and ye ken'd a' that time that I was out in the forty-five wi' Prince Charles, and yet ye never made mention o' the facts, nor refused me my awmos till the day. But as I hae been obliged t'ye, I'll haud my tongue; only, I wad advise ye as a friend, that whenever ye hae occasion to speak of ony community of brother Christians, that ye will in future hardly make use o' siccan harsh epithets. Or, if ye will do't, tak care wha ye use sic terms afore, an' let it no be to the nose o' an auld veteran."

"What, ye auld beggar worm that ye are!—ye profane wafer-eater, and worshipper of graven images, dare ye heave your pikit kent at me?"

"I hae heaved baith sword and spear against mony a better man, and, in the cause o' my religion, I'll do it again."

He was proceeding, but Adamson's choler rising to an ungovernable height, he drew a race, and coming against the gaberlunzie with his whole force, he made him fly heels-over-head down the hill. The old man's bonnet flew off, his meal-pocks were scattered abroad, and his old mantle, with two or three small fleeces of wool in it, rolled down into the burn.

The servants perceived the attack made on the old man, and one elderly shepherd said, "In troth, sirs, our master is not himself the day. He maun really be looked to. It appears to me, that sin' he roupit out yon poor but honest family yesterday, the Lord has ta'en his guiding arm frae about him. Rob Johnston, ye'll be obliged to rin to the assistance of the auld man."

"I'll trust the auld Jacobite for another shake wi' him yet," said Rob, "afore I steer my fit; for it strikes me, if he hadna been ta'en unawares, he wad hardly hae been sae easily coupit."

The beggar was considerably astounded and stupified when he first got up his head; but finding all his bones whole, and his old frame disencumbered of every superfluous load, he sprung to his feet, shook his grey burly locks, and cursed the aggressor in the name of the Holy Trinity, the Mother of our Lord, and all the blessed Saints above. Then approaching him with his cudgel heaved, he warned him to be on his guard, or make out of his reach, else he would send him to eternity in the twinkling o' an ee. The farmer held up his staff across, to defend his head against the descent of old Patie's piked kent, and, at the same time, made a break in, with intent to close with him; but, in so doing, he held down his head for a moment, on which the gaber-lunzie made a jerk to one side, and lent Adamson such a lounder over the neck, or back part of the head, that he fell violently on his face, after running two or three steps precipitately forward. The beggar, whose eyes gleamed with wild fury, while his grey locks floated over them like a winter cloud over two meteors of the night, was going to follow up his blow with another more efficient one on his prostrate foe; but the farmer, perceiving these unequivocal symptoms of danger, wisely judged that there was no time to lose in providing for his own safety, and, rolling himself rapidly two or three times over, he got to his feet, and made his escape, though not before Patie had hit him what he called "a stiff lounder across the rumple."

The farmer fled along the brae, and the gaberlunzie pursued, while the people at the fold were absolutely like to burst with laugh-ter. The scene was highly picturesque, for the beggar could run none, and still the faster that he essayed to run, he made the less speed. But ever and anon he stood still, and cursed Adamson in the name of one or other of the Saints or Apostles, brandishing his cudgel, and tramping with his foot. The other, keeping still at a small distance, pretended to laugh at him, and at the same time uttered such bitter and unhallowed epithets on the Papists, and on old Patie in partic-ular, that, after the latter had cursed himself into a proper pitch of indignation, he always broke at him again, making vain efforts to reach him one more blow. At length, after chasing him by these starts about half a mile, the beggar returned, gathered up the scattered implements and fruits of his occupation, and came to the fold to the busy group.

Patie's general character was that of a patient, jocular, sarcastic old man, whom people liked, but dared not much to contradict; but that day his manner and mien had become so much altered, in consequence of the altercation and conflict that had just taken place, that the people were almost frightened to look at him; and as for social converse, there was none to be had with him. His countenance was grim, haughty, and had something Satanic in its lines and deep wrinkles; and ever as he stood leaning against the fold, he uttered a kind of hollow growl, with a broken interrupted sound, like a war-horse neighing in his sleep, and then muttered curses on the farmer.

The old shepherd before-mentioned, ventured, at length, to caution him against such profanity, saying, "Dear Patie, man, dinna sin away your soul, venting siccan curses as these. They will a' turn back on your ain head; for what harm can the curses of a poor sinfu' worm do to our master?"

"My curse, sir, has blasted the hopes of better men than either you or him," said the gaberlunzie, in an earthquake voice, and shivering with vehemence as he spoke. "Ye may think the like o' me can hae nae power wi' heaven; but an I hae power wi' hell, it is sufficient to cow ony that's here. I sanna brag what effect my curse will have, but I shall say this, that either your master, or ony o' his men, had as good have auld Patie Maxwell's blessing as his curse ony time, Jacobite and Roman Catholic though he be."

It now became necessary to bring the sheep into the fold that the farmer was wearing, and they were the last hirsel that was to shear that day. The farmer's face was red with ill-nature, but yet he now appeared to be somewhat humbled by reflecting on the figure he had made. Patie sat on the top of the fold dike, and from the bold and hardy asseverations that he made, he seemed disposed to provoke a dispute with any one present who chose to take up the cudgels; but just while the shepherds were sharping the shears, a thick black cloud began to rear itself over the height to the southward, the front of which seemed to be boiling—both its outsides rolling rapidly forward, and again wheeling in toward the centre. I have heard old Robin Johnston, the stout young man mentioned above, but who was a very old man when I knew him, describe the appearance of the cloud as greatly resembling a whirlpool made by the eddy of a rapid tide, or flooded river; and he declared, to his dying day, that he never saw aught in nature have a more ominous appearance. The gaberlunzie was the first to notice it, and drew the attention of the rest towards that point of the heavens by the following singular and profane remark: "Aha, lads! see what's coming yonder. Yonder's Patie Maxwell's curse coming rowing an' reeling on ye already; and what will ye say an the curse of God be coming backing it?"

"Gudesake, haud your tongue, ye profane body, ye mak me feared to hear ye," said one. "O, it's a strange delusion to think that a Papist can hae ony influence wi' the Almighty, either to bring down his blessing or his curse."

"Ye speak ye ken nae what, man," answered Pate; "ye hae learned some rhames frae your poor cauld-rife Protestant whigs about Papists, and Antichrist, and children of perdition; yet it is plain to the meanest capacity, that ye hae nae ane spark o' the life or power o' religion in your whole frames, an' dinna ken either what's truth or what's falsehood. Ah! yonder it is coming, grim an' gurly! Now, I hae called for it, an' it is coming; let me see if a' the Protestants that are of ye can order it back, or pray it away again. Down on your knees, ye dogs, an' set your mou's up against it, like as many spiritual whig cannon, an' let me see if you have influence wi' Heaven to turn aside ane o' the hailstanes that the deils are playing at chucks wi' in yon dark chamber."

"I wadna wonder if our clipping were cuttit short," said one.

"Na, but I wadna wonder if something else were cuttit short," said Patie; "What will ye say an some o' your weazons be cuttit short. Hurraw! yonder it comes! Now, there will be sic a hurly-burly in Laverhope as never was sin' the creation o' man."

The folds of Laverhope were situated on a gently sloping plain, in what is called the forkings of a burn. Laver burn runs to the eastward, and Widehope burn runs north, meeting the other at a right angle, a little below the folds. It was around the head of this Widehope that the cloud first made its appearance, and there its vortex seemed to be impending. It descended lower and lower, and that too with uncommon celerity, for the elements were in a turmoil. The cloud laid first hold of one height, then of another, till at length it closed over and around the pastoral group, and the dark hope had the appearance of a huge chamber hung with sackcloth. Then the big clear drops of rain began to descend, on which the shepherds gave over clipping, and covered up the wool with blankets, then huddled together below their plaids at the side of the fold, to eschew the speat, which they saw was going to be a terrible one. Patie still kept undauntedly to the top of the dike, and Mr Adamson stood cowering at the side of it, with his plaid over his head, at a little distance from the rest. The hail and rain mingled, now began to descend in a way that had been seldom witnessed; but it was apparent to them all that it was ten times worse up in Widehope-head to the southward.—Anon a whole volume of lightning burst from the bosom of the darkness, and quivered through the gloom, dazzling the eyes of every beholder; even old Maxwell clapped both his hands on his eyes for a space—a crash of thunder followed the flash, that made all the mountains chatter, and shook the firmament so, that the density of the cloud was broken up; for, on the instant that the thunder ceased, a rushing sound began up in Wide-hope, that soon increased to a loudness equal with the thunder itself, but it resembled the noise made by the sea in a storm. "Mother of God!" exclaimed Patie Maxwell, "What is this? What is this? I declare we're a' ower lang here, for the dams of heaven are broken up;" and with that he flung himself from the dike, and fled toward the top of a rising hillock. He knew that the sound proceeded from the descent of a tremendous water-spout; but the rest, not conceiving what it was, remained where they were. The storm increased every minute, and in less than a quarter of an hour after this retreat of the Gaberlunzie, they heard him calling out with the most desperate bitterness, and when they eyed him, he was jumping like a madman on the top of the knowe, waving his bonnet, and screaming out, "Run, ye deil's buckies! Run for your bare lives." One of the shepherds, jumping up on the dike, to see what was astir, beheld the burn of Widehope coming down in a manner that could be compared to nothing but an ocean, whose boundaries had given way, descending into the abyss. It came with a cataract front more than twenty feet deep, as was afterwards ascertained by measurment, for it left sufficient marks wheresoever it reached, to enable men to do this with precision. The shepherd called for assistance, and flew into the fold to drive out the sheep; and just as he got the foremost of them to take the door, the flood came upon the head of the fold, on which he threw himself over the side-wall, and escaped in safety, as did all the rest of the people.

Not so Mr Adamson's ewes; the greater part of the hirsel being involved in this mighty current. The big fold next the burn was levelled with the earth in one second. Stones, ewes, and sheep-house, all were carried before it, and all seemed to bear the same weight. It must have been a dismal sight, to see so many fine animals tumbling and rolling in one irresistible mass. They were strong, however, and a number of them plunged out, and made their escape to the east-ward—a greater number were carried headlong down, and thrown out on the other side of Laver-burn, upon the side of a dry hill, to which they all escaped, some of them considerably maimed; but the greatest number of all were lost, being overwhelmed among the rubbish of the fold, and entangled so among the falling dikes, and the torrent wheeling and boiling amongst them, that escape was impossible. The wool was totally swept away, and all either lost, or so much wasted, that, when afterwards recovered, it was unsalable.

When the flood broke first in among the sheep, and the women began to run screaming to the hills, and the despairing shepherds a-flying about, unable to do any thing, Patie began a-laughing with a loud and a hellish gaffaw, and in that he continued to indulge till quite exhausted. "Ha, ha, ha, ha! what think ye o' the auld beggar's curse now? Ha, ha, ha, ha! I think it has been backit wi' God's an' the deil's baith. Ha, ha, ha, ha!" And then he mimicked the thunder with the most outrageous and ludicrous jabberings, turning occasionally up to the cloud streaming with lightning and hail, and calling out,— "Louder yet, deils! louder yet! Kindle up your crackers, and yerk away! Rap, rap, rap, rap—Ro-ro, ro, ro—Roo—Whugh."

"I daresay that body's the vera devil himsel in the shape o' the auld Papist beggar!" said one, not thinking that Patie could hear at such a distance.

"Na, na, lad, I'm no the deil," cried he in answer; "but an I war, I wad let ye see a stramash. It is a sublime thing to be a Roman Catholic amang sae mony weak apostates; but it is a sublimer thing still to be a deil—a master-spirit in a forge like yon. Ha, ha, ha, ha! Take care o' your heads, ye cock-chickens o' Calvin. Take care o' the auld coppersmith o' the black cludd."

From the moment that the first thunder-bolt shot from the cloud, the countenance of the farmer was changed. He was manifestly alarmed in no ordinary degree, and when the flood came rushing from the dry mountains, and took away his sheep and his wool before his eyes, he became as a dead man, making no effort to save his store, or to give directions how it might be done. He ran away in a cowering posture, as he had been standing, and took shelter in a little green hollow, out of his servants' view.

The thunder came nigher and nigher to the place where the astonished hinds were, till at length they perceived the bolts of flame striking the earth around them, in every direction; at one time tearing up its bosom, and at another splintering the rocks. Robin Johnston said, that "the thunner bolts" (so the country people always denominate the electrical flame) "came shimmering out o' the cludd sae thick, that they appeared to be linkit thegither, an' fleeing in a' directions. There war some o' them blue, some o' them red, an' some o' them like the colour o' the lowe of a candle. Some o' them diving into the earth, an' some o' them springing up out o' the earth and darting into the heaven." I cannot vouch for the truth of this, but I am sure my informer thought so, or he would not have said it; and he said farther, that when old Maxwell saw it, he cried—"Fie, tak care, cubs o' hell! fie, tak care! cower laigh, an' sit sicker, for your auld dam is aboon ye, an' aneath ye, an' a' round about ye. O for a good wat nurse to spean ye, like John Adamson's lambs! Ha, ha, ha!" The lambs, it must be observed, had been turned out of the fold at first, and none of them perished with their dams.

But just when the storm was at the height, and apparently passing the bounds ever witnessed in these northern climes; when the embroiled elements were in the state of hottest convulsion, and when our little pastoral group were every moment expecting the next to be their last, behold all at once a lovely "blue bore," fringed with downy gold, opened in the cloud behind, and in five minutes after that, the sun again appeared, and all was beauty and serenity. What a contrast to the scene so lately witnessed!—they were like scenes of two different worlds, or places of abode which it would be unmeet to contrast together.

The greatest curiosity of the whole to a stranger would have been the contrast between the two burns. The burn of Laverhope never changed its colour, but continued pure, limpid, and so shallow, that a boy might have stepped over it dry shod, all the while that the other burn was coming in upon it like an ocean broken loose, and carrying all before it. In mountainous districts, however, instances of the same kind are quite frequent in times of summer speats.

There were some other circumstances connected with this storm, at the description of which I could not help laughing immoderately, forty years after they had taken place; and, dismal as the catastrophe turned out to be, whenever they present themselves to my imagination, I cannot answer for myself doing the same to this day. The storm coming from the south, over a low-lying, wooded, and populous district, the whole of the crows inhabiting it, posted away up the glen of Laver-hope to avoid the fire and fury of the storm. "There were thoosands o' thoosands came up by us," said Robin, "a' laying theirsels out as they had been mad. An' then whanever the bright bolt played flash through the darkness, ilk ane o' them made a dive an' a wheel to avoid the shot. Aih wow! I never saw as mony as feared beasts, an' never will again. Od, sir, I was persuaded that they thought a' the artillery an' a' the musketry o' the hale coontry were loosed on them, an that it was time for them to tak the gait. There were likewise several colly dogs came by us in great extremity, hingin' out their tongues, an' lookin' aye ower their shoulders, rinning straight on they kendna where; an' among other things, there was a black Highland cow came roaring up the glen wi' her stake hanging at her neck."

The gush of waters soon subsiding, all the group, men and women, were soon employed in pulling out dead sheep from rubbish of stones, banks of gravel, and pools of the burn; and many a row of carcases was laid out, which at that season were of no use whatever, and of course utterly lost. But all the while that they were so engaged, Mr Adamson came not near them, at which they wondered, and some of them remarked, that "they thought their master was fey the day, mae ways than ane."

"Ay, never mind him," said the old shepherd, "he'll come when he thinks it his ain time; he's a right sair humbled man the day, an' I hope by this time he has been brought to see his errors in a right light. But the gaberlunzie is lost too. I think he be sandit in the yird, for I hae never seen him sin' the last great crash o' thunner."

"He'll be gane into the howe to wring his duds," said Robert Johnston, "or maybe to make up matters wi' your master. Gude sauf us, what a profane wretch the auld creature is! I didna think the muckle horned deil himsel could hae set up his mou to the heaven, an' braggit an' blasphemed in sic a way. He gart my heart a' grue within me, and dirle as it had been bored wi' red-het elsins."

"Oh, what can ye expect else of a papist?" said the auld herd, with a deep sigh. "They're a' the deil's bairns ilk ane, an' a' employed in carrying on their father's wark. It is needless to expect gude branches frae sic a stock, or gude fruit frae siccan branches."

"There's ae wee bit text that focks should never lose sight o'," said Robin, "an' it's this,—'Judge not, that ye be not judged.' I think," said Robin, when he told the story, "I think that steekit their gabs!"

The evening at length drew on; the women had gone away home, and the neighbouring shepherds had scattered here and there to look after their own flocks. Mr Adamson's men alone remained, lingering about the brook and the folds, waiting on their master. They had seen him go into the little green hollow, and they knew he was gone to his prayers, and were unwilling to disturb him. But they at length began to think it extraordinary that he should continue at his prayers the whole afternoon. As for the beggar, though acknowledged to be a man of strong sense and sound judgment, he had never been known to say prayers all his life, except in the way of cursing and swearing a little sometimes, and none of them could conjecture what was become of him. Some of the rest, as it grew late, applied to the old shepherd before oft mentioned, whose name I have forgot, but he had herded with Adamson twenty years—some of the rest, I say, applied to him to go and bring their master away home, for that perhaps he was taken ill.

"O, I'm unco laith to disturb him," said the old man; "he sees that the hand o' the Lord has fa'n heavy on him the day, an' he's humbling himsel afore him in great bitterness of spirit, I daresay. I count it a sin to brik in on sic devotions as thae."

"Na, I carena if he should lie and pray yonder till the morn," said a young lad, "only I wadna like to gang hame an' leave him lying on the hill, if he should hae chanced to turn no weel. Sae, if nane o' ye will gang an' bring him, or see what ails him, I'll e'en gang mysel;" and away he went, the rest standing still, to await the issue.

When the lad went first to the brink of the little slack where Adamson lay, he stood a few moments, as if gazing or listening, and then turned his back and fled. The rest, who were standing watching his motions, wondered at this; and they said, one to another, that the master was angry at him for disturbing him, and that he had been threatening the lad so rudely, that it had caused him to take to his heels for it. But what they thought most curious, was, that the lad did not fly toward them, but straight to the hill; nor did he ever so much as cast his eyes toward them; so deeply did he seem to be impressed with what had passed between him and his master. Indeed, it rather appeared that he did not know what he was doing, for, after running a space with great violence, he stood and looked back, and then broke to the hill again—always looking first over the one shoulder, and then over the other. Then he stopped a second time, and returned cautiously toward the spot where his master reclined, and all the while he never so much as once turned his eyes toward his neighbours, or seemed to remember that they were there. His motions were strikingly erratic; for all the way, as he returned to the spot where his master was, he continued to advance by a zigzag direction, like a vessel beating up by short tacks; and several times he stood still, as on the very point of retreating. At length he vanished from their sight in the little hollow; and they said one to another, that he was gone in to sit beside the master, or to pray with him, after all.

It was not long, however, till the lad again made his appearance, shouting and waving his cap for them to come likewise, on which they all went away to him as fast as they could, in great amazement what could be the matter. But when they came to the green hollow, a shocking spectacle presented itself. There lay the body of their master, who had been struck dead by the lightning; and, his right side having been torn open, his bowels had gushed out, and were lying beside the body. The earth was rutted and ploughed close to his side, and at his feet there was a hole scooped out, a full yard in depth, and very much resembling a grave. He had been cut off in the act of prayer, and the body was still lying in the position of a man praying in the field. He had been on his knees, with his elbows leaning on the brae, and his brow laid on his folded hands; his plaid was drawn over his head, and his hat below his arm; and this affecting circumstance proved a great source of comfort to Mrs Adamson afterward, when the extremity of her suffering had somewhat abated.

There was no such awful visitation of Providence had ever been witnessed or handed down to our hinds on the ample records of tradition, and the impression that it made, and the interest that it excited, were also without a parallel. Thousands visited the spot, to view the devastations made by the flood, and the furrows formed by the electrical matter; and the smallest circumstances were inquired into with the most minute curiosity: above all, the still and drowsy embers of superstition were rekindled by it into a flame, than which none had ever burnt brighter, not even in the darkest days of gospel ignorance; and by the help of it a theory was made out and believed, that for horror is absolutely unequalled. But as it was credited in its fullest latitude by my informant, and always added by him as the summary of the tale, I am bound to mention the circumstances, though far from giving them as authentic.

It was asserted, and pretended to have been proven, that old Peter Maxwell *was not in the glen of Laverhope that day*, but at a great distance in a different county, and that it was the devil who had attended the folds that day in his likeness. It was farther believed by all the people at the folds, that it was the last explosion of the whole that had slain Mr Adamson, for they had then observed the side of the brae, where the little green slack was situated, at that time covered with a sheet of flame for a moment. And it so happened, that from that moment the profane gaberlunzie had been no more seen; and therefore they said, and there was the horror of the thing, that there was no doubt of his being the devil waiting for his prey, and that he fled away in that sheet of flame, carrying the soul of John Adamson along with him.

I never saw old Pate Maxwell, for I believe he died before I was born, but Robin Johnston said, that he denied to his dying day, having been within forty miles of the folds of Laverhope on the day of the thunder storm, and was exceedingly angry when any one pretended to doubt the assertion. It was likewise reported, that at six o'clock afternoon a stranger had called on Mrs Irvine, and told her, that John Adamson, and a great part of his stock, had been destroyed by the lightning and the hail. Mrs Irvine's house was five miles distant from the folds,—and more than that, his death was not so much as known of by mortal man until two hours after Mrs Irvine received this information. It was a great convulsion of the elements, exceeding anything remembered, either for its violence or consequences, and these mysterious circumstances having been bruited abroad as connected with it, gave it a hold on the minds of the populace, never to be erased but by the erasure of existence. It fell out on the 12th of July, 1753.

The death of Mr Copland of Minnigess forms another era of the same sort in Annandale. It happened, if I mistake not, on the 18th of July, 1804. It was one of those days by which all succeeding thunder storms have been estimated and compared, and from which they are dated, both as having taken place so many years before as well as after.

Adam Copland, Esquire, of Minnigess, was a gentleman esteemed by all who knew him. Handsome and comely in his person, and elegant in his manners; he was the ornament of rural society, and the delight of his family and friends; therefore his loss was felt as no common misfortune. As he occupied a pastoral farm of considerable extent, his own property, he chanced likewise to be out at his folds on the day above-mentioned, with his own servants, and some neighbours, speaning a part of his lambs, and shearing a few sheep. About mid-day the thunder, lightning, and hail, came on, and deranged their operations entirely; and, among other things, there was a set of the lambs broke away from the folds, and being in great fright, they continued to run on. Mr Copland and a shepherd of his own, named Thomas Scott, pursued them, and, at the distance of about half a mile from the folds, they turned them, mastered them, after some running, and were bringing them back together toward the fold, when the dreadful catastrophe happened. Thomas Scott was the only person present, of course; and though he was within a few steps of him at the time, he could give no account of anything. I am well acquainted with Scott, and have questioned him about the particulars fifty times; but he could not so much as tell me how he got back to the fold; whether he brought the lambs with him or not; how long the storm continued; nor indeed anything after the time that his master and he turned the lambs. That he remembered perfectly, but thenceforward his mind seemed to have become a blank. I should likewise have mentioned, as an instance of the same kind, that, on the young lad who went first to the body of Adamson being questioned why he fled from the body at first, he denied that ever he fled. He was not conscious of having fled a foot, and never would have believed it had he not been seen by four eye-witnesses. The only things of which Thomas Scott had any impressions were these: that, when the lightning struck his master, he sprung a great height into the air, much higher, he thought, than it was possible for any man to leap by his own exertion. He also thinks, that the place where he fell dead was at a considerable distance from that on which he was struck and leaped from the ground; but when I inquired if he judged that it would be twenty yards or ten yards, he could give no answer—he could not tell. He only had an impression that he saw his master spring into the air, all on fire; and, on running up to him, he found him quite dead. If Scott was correct in this, and he being a man of plain good sense, truth, and integrity, there can scarce be a reason for doubting him, the circumstance would argue that the electric matter that slew Mr Copland had issued out of the earth. He was speaking to Scott with his very last breath; but all that the survivor could do, he could never remember what he was saying. There were some melted drops of silver standing on the case of his watch, as well as on some of his coat-buttons; and the body never stiffened like other corpses, but remained as supple as if every bone had been softened to jelly. He was a married man, scarcely at the prime of life, and left a young widow and only son to lament his loss. On the spot where he fell there is now an obelisk erected to his memory, with a warning text on it, relating to the shortness and uncertainty of human life.

H.

Class IV.

Dogs

THERE being no adage more generally established, or better founded, than that the principal conversation of shepherds meeting on the hills is either about DOGS or LASSES, I shall make each of these important topics a head, or rather a *knag*, in my Pastoral Calendar, whereon to hang a few amusing anecdotes; the one of these forming the chief support, and the other the chief temporal delight, of the shepherd's solitary and harmless life.

Though it may appear a singular perversion of the order of nature to put the dogs before the lasses, I shall nevertheless begin with the former. I think I see how North will chuckle at this, and think to himself how this is all of the Shepherd being fallen into the back ground of life, (by which epithet he is pleased to distinguish the married state,) for that he had seen the day he would hardly have given angels the preference to lasses, not to speak of a parcel of tatted towsy tykes!

I beg your pardon, sir, but utility should always take precedency of pleasure. A shepherd may be a very able, trusty, and good shepherd, without a sweetheart—better, perhaps, than with one. But what is he without his dog? A mere post, sir—a nonentity as a shepherd—no better than one of the grey stones upon the side of his hill. A literary pedlar, such as yourself, Sir Christy, and all the thousands beside who deal in your small wares, will not believe, that a single shepherd and his dog will accomplish more in gathering a stock of sheep from a Highland farm, than twenty shepherds could do without dogs. So that you see, and it is a fact, that, without this docile little animal, the pastoral life would be a mere blank. Without the shepherd's dog, the whole of the open mountainous land in Scotland would not be worth a sixpence. It would require more hands to manage a stock of sheep, gather them from the hills, force them into houses and folds, and drive them to markets, than the profits of the whole stock were capable of maintaining. Well may the shepherd feel an interest in his dog; he is indeed the fellow that earns the family's bread, of which he is himself content with the smallest morsel; always grateful, and always ready to exert his utmost abilities in his master's interest. Neither hunger, fatigue, nor the worst of treatment, will drive him from his side; he will follow him through fire and water, as the saying is, and through every hardship, without murmur or repining, till he literally fall down dead at his foot. If one of them is obliged to change masters, it is sometimes long before he will acknowledge the new one, or condescend to work for him with the same avidity as he did for his former lord; but if he once acknowledge him, he continues attached to him till death; and though naturally proud and high-spirited, in as far as relates to his master, these qualities (or rather failings) are kept so much in sub-ordination, that he has not a will of his own. Of such a grateful, useful, and disinterested animal, I could write volumes; and now that I have got on my hobby, I greatly suspect that all my friends at Ambrose's will hardly get me off again.

I once sent you an account of a notable dog of my own, named Sirrah, which amused a number of your readers a great deal, and put their faith in my veracity somewhat to the test; but in this district, where the singular qualities of the animal were known, so far from any of the anecdotes being disputed, every shepherd values himself to this day on the possession of facts far outstripping any of those recorded by you formerly. With a few of these I shall conclude this paper.

But, in the first place, I must give you some account of my own renowned Hector,* which I promised long ago. He was the son and immediate successor of the faithful old Sirrah; and though not nearly so valuable a dog as his father, he was a far more interesting one. He had three times more humour and whim about him; and though exceedingly docile, his bravest acts were mostly tinctured with a grain of stupidity, which shewed his reasoning faculty to be laughably obtuse.

I shall mention a striking instance of it. I was once at the farm of Shorthope, on Ettrick head, receiving some lambs that I had bought, and was going to take to market, with some more, the next day. Owing to some accidental delay, I did not get final delivery of the lambs till it was growing late; and being obliged to be at my own house that night, I was not a little dismayed lest I should scatter and lose my lambs, if darkness overtook me. Darkness did overtake me by the time I got half way, and no ordinary darkness for an August evening. The lambs having been weaned that day, and of the wild black-faced breed, became exceedingly unruly, and for a good while I lost hopes of mastering them. Hector managed the point, and we got them safe home; but both he and his master were alike sore fore-foughten. It had become so dark, that we were obliged to fold them

* See the Mountain Bard.

with candles; and after closing them safely up, I went home with my father and the rest to supper. When Hector's supper was set down, behold he was wanting! and as I knew we had him at the fold, which was within call of the house, I went out, and called and whistled on him for a good while, but he did not make his appearance. I was distressed about this; for, having to take away the lambs next morning, I knew I could not drive them a mile without my dog, if it had been to save me the whole drove.

The next morning, as soon as it was day, I arose and inquired if Hector had come home. No; he had not been seen. I knew not what to do; but my father proposed that he would take out the lambs and herd them, and let them get some meat to fit them for the road; and that I should ride with all speed to Shorthope, to see if my dog had gone back there. Accordingly, we went together to the fold to turn out the lambs, and there was poor Hector sitting trembling in the very middle of the fold door, on the inside of the flake that closed it, with his eyes still stedfastly fixed on the lambs. He had been so hardly set with them after it grew dark, that he durst not for his life leave them, although hungry, fatigued, and cold; for the night had turned out a deluge of rain. He had never so much as lain down, for only the small spot that he sat on was dry, and there had he kept watch the whole night. Almost any other colley would have discerned that the lambs were safe enough in the fold, but honest Hector had not been able to see through this. He even refused to take my word for it, for he durst not quit his watch though he heard me calling both at night and morning.

Another peculiarity of his was, that he had a mortal antipathy at the family mouser, which was ingrained in his nature from his very puppyhood; yet so perfectly absurd was he, that no impertinence on her side, and no baiting on, could ever induce him to lay his mouth on her, or injure her in the slightest degree. There was not a day, and scarcely an hour passed over, that the family did not get some amusement with these two animals. Whenever he was within doors, his whole occupation was watching and pointing the cat from morning to night. When she flitted from one place to another, so did he in a moment; and then squatting down, he kept his point sedulously, till he was either called off or fell asleep.

He was an exceedingly poor taker of meat, was always to press to it, and always lean; and often he would not taste it till we were obliged to bring in the cat. The malicious looks that he cast at her from under his eyebrows on such occasions, were exceedingly ludicrous, considering his utter incapability of wronging her. Whenever he saw her, he drew near his bicker, and looked angry, but still he would not taste till she was brought to it; and then he cocked his tail, set up his birses, and began a lapping furiously, in utter desperation. His good nature was so immoveable, that he would never refuse her a share of what he got; he even lapped close to the one side of the dish, and left her room—but mercy as he did ply!

It will appear strange to you to hear a dog's *reasoning faculty* mentioned, as I have done; but, I declare, I have hardly ever seen a shepherd's dog do anything without perceiving his reasons for it. I have often amused myself in calculating what his motives were for such and such things, and I generally found them very cogent ones. But Hector had a droll stupidity about him, and took up forms and rules of his own, for which I could never perceive any motive that was not even farther out of the way than the action itself. He had one uniform practice, and a very bad one it was, during the time of family worship, and just three or four seconds before the conclusion of the prayer, he started to his feet, and ran barking round the apartment like a crazed beast. My father was so much amused with this, that he would never suffer me to correct him for it, and I scarcely ever saw the old man rise from the prayer without his endeavouring to suppress a smile at the extravagance of Hector. None of us ever could find out how he knew that the prayer was near done, for my father was not formal in his prayers; but certes he did know,—of that we had nightly evidence. There never was anything for which I was so puzzled to discover a motive as this; but, from accident, I did discover it, and, however ludicrous it may appear, I am certain I was correct. It was much in character with many of Hector's feats, and rather, I think, the most *outré* of any principle he ever acted on. As I said, his great daily occupation was pointing the cat. Now, when he saw us kneel all down in a circle, with our faces couched on our paws, in the same posture with himself, it struck his absurd head, that we were all engaged in pointing the cat. He lay on tenters all the time, but the acuteness of his ear enabling him, through time, to ascertain the very moment when we would all spring to our feet, he thought to himself, "I shall be first after her for you all."

He inherited his dad's unfortunate ear for music, not perhaps in so extravagant a degree, but he ever took care to exhibit it on the most untimely and ill-judged occasions. Owing to some misunderstanding between the minister of the parish and the session clerk, the precenting in church devolved on my father, who was the senior elder. Now, my father could have sung several of the old church tunes middling well, in his own family circle; but it so happened, that, when mounted in the desk, he never could command the starting notes of any but one (St Paul's), which were always in undue readiness at the root of his tongue, to the exclusion of every other semibreve in the whole range of sacred melody. The minister giving out psalms four times in the course of every day's service, consequently, the congregation were treated with St Paul's, in the morning, at great length, thrice in the course of the service, and then once again at the close. Nothing but St Paul's. And, it being of itself a monotonous tune, nothing could exceed the monotony that prevailed in the primitive church of Ettrick. Out of pure sympathy for my father alone, I was compelled to take the precentorship in hand; and, having plenty of tunes, for a good while I came on *as well as could be expected*, as men say of their wives. But, unfortunately for me, Hector found out that I attended church every Sunday, and though I had him always closed up carefully at home, he rarely failed in making his appearance in church at some time of the day. Whenever I saw him a tremor came over my spirits, for I well knew what the issue would be. The moment that he heard my voice strike up the psalm, "with might and majesty," then did he fall in with such overpowering vehemence, that he and I seldom got any to join in the music but our two selves. The shepherds hid their heads, and laid them down on the backs of the seats rowed in their plaids, and the lasses looked down to the ground and laughed till their faces grew red. I despised to stick the tune, and therefore was obliged to carry on in spite of the obstreperous accompaniment; but I was, time after time, so completely put out of all countenance with the brute, that I was obliged to give up my office in disgust, and leave the parish once more to their old friend, St Paul.

Hector was quite incapable of performing the same feats among sheep that his father did; but, as far as his judgment served him, he was a docile and obliging creature. He had one singular quality, of keeping true to the charge to which he was set. If we had been shearing, or sorting sheep in any way, when a division was turned out, and Hector got the word to attend to them, he would have done it pleasantly, for a whole day, without the least symptom of weariness. No noise or hurry about the fold, which brings every other dog from his business, had the least effect on Hector, save that it made him a little troublesome on his own charge, and set him a running round and round them, turning them in at corners, out of a sort of impatience to be employed as well as his baying neighbours at the fold. Whenever old Sirrah found himself hard set, in commanding wild sheep on steep ground, where they are worst to manage, he never failed, without any hint to the purpose, to throw himself wide in below them, and lay their faces to the hill, by which means he got the command of them in a minute. I never could make Hector comprehend this advantage, with all my art, although his father found it out entirely of himself. The former would turn or wear sheep no other way, but on the hill above them; and though very good at it, he gave both them and himself double the trouble and fatigue.

It cannot be supposed that he could understand all that was passing in the little family circle, but he certainly comprehended a good part of it. In particular, it was very easy to discover that he rarely missed aught that was said about himself, the sheep, the cat, or of a hunt. When aught of that nature came to be discussed, Hector's attention and impatience soon became manifest. There was one winter evening, I said to my mother that I was going to Bowerhope for a fortnight, for that I had more conveniency for writing with Alexander Laidlaw, than at home; and I added, "But I will not take Hector with me, for he is constantly quarrelling with the rest of the dogs, singing music, or breeding some uproar."—"Na, na," quoth she, "leave Hector with me; I like aye best to have him at hame, poor fallow."

These were all the words that passed. The next morning the waters were in a great flood, and I did not go away till after breakfast; but when the time came for tying up Hector, he was wanting.—"The d——'s in that beast," said I, "I will wager that he heard what we were saying yesternight, and has gone off for Bowerhope as soon as the door was opened this morning."

"If that should really be the case, I'll think the beast no canny," said my mother.

The Yarrow was so large as to be quite impassable, so that I had to go up by St Mary's Loch, and go across by the boat; and, on drawing near to Bowerhope, I soon perceived that matters had gone precisely as I suspected. Large as the Yarrow was, and it appeared impassable by any living creature, Hector had made his escape early in the morning, had swum the river, and was sitting, "like a drookit hen," on a knoll at the east end of the house, awaiting my arrival with great impatience. I had a great attachment to this animal, who, with a good deal of absurdity, joined all the amiable qualities of his species. He was rather of a small size, very rough and shagged, and not far from the colour of a fox.

His son, Lion, was the very picture of his dad, had a good deal more sagacity, but also more selfishness. A history of the one, however, would only be an epitome of that of the other. Mr William Nicholson took a fine likeness of this latter one, which that gentleman still possesses. He could not get him to sit for his picture in such a position as he wanted, till he exhibited a singularly fine picture of his, of a small dog, on the opposite side of the room. Lion took it for a real animal, and, disliking its fierce and important look exceedingly, he immediately set up his ears and his shaggy birses, and fixing a stern eye on the picture, in manifest wrath, he would then sit for a whole day, and point his eye at it, without budging or altering his position.

It is a curious fact, in the history of these animals, that the most useless of the breed have often the greatest degree of sagacity in trifling and useless matters. An exceedingly good sheep dog attends to nothing else, but that particular branch of business to which he is bred. His whole capacity is exerted and exhausted on it, and he is of little avail in miscellaneous matters; whereas, a very indifferent cur, bred about the house, and accustomed to assist with everything, will often put the more noble breed to disgrace, in these paltry services. If one calls out, for instance, that the cows are in the corn, or the hens in the garden, the house-colley needs no other hint, but runs and turns them out. The shepherd's dog knows not what is astir; and, if he is called out in a hurry for such work, all that he will do is to break to the hill, and rear himself up on end, to see if no sheep are running away. A bred sheep-dog, if coming ravening from the hills, and getting into a milk-house, would most likely think of nothing else than filling his belly with the cream. Not so his uninitiated brother. He is bred at home, to far higher principles of honour. I have known such lie night and day, among from ten to twenty pails full of milk, and never once break the cream of one of them with the tip of his tongue, nor would he suffer cat, rat, or any other creature, to touch it. This latter sort, too, are far more acute at taking up what is said in a family. There was a farmer of this country, a Mr Alexander Cuninghame, who had a bitch that, for the space of three or four years, in the latter part of her life, met him always at the foot of his farm, about a mile and a half from his house, on his way home. If he was half a day away, a week, or a fortnight, it was all the same; she met him at that spot, and there never was an instance seen of her going to wait his arrival there on a wrong day. If this was a fact, which I have heard averred by people who lived in the house at that time, she could only know of his coming home by hearing it mentioned in the family. The same animal would have gone and brought the cows from the hill when it grew dark, without any bidding, yet she was a very indifferent sheep-dog.

The anecdotes of these animals are all so much alike, that were I but to relate the thousandth part of those I have heard, they would often look very much like repetitions. I shall therefore only in this paper mention one or two of the most singular, which I know to be well authenticated.

There was a shepherd lad near Langholm, whose name was Scott, who possessed a bitch, famed over all the West Border for her singular tractability. He could have sent her home with one sheep, two sheep, or any given number, from any of the neighbouring farms; and in the lambing season it was his uniform practice to send her home with the kebbed ewes just as he got them.—I must let the town reader understand this. A kebbed ewe is one whose lamb dies. As soon as such is found, she is immediately brought home by the shepherd, and another lamb put to her; and this lad, on going his rounds on the hill, whenever he found a kebbed ewe, he immediately gave her in charge to his bitch to take home, which saved him from coming back that way again, and going over the same ground he had looked before. She always took them carefully home, and put them into a fold which was close by the house, keeping watch over them till she was seen by some one of the family; and then that moment she decamped, and hasted back to her master, who sometimes sent her three times home in one morning, with different charges. It was the custom of the farmer to watch her, and take the sheep in charge from her; but this required a good deal of caution; for as soon as she perceived that she was seen, whether the sheep were put into the fold or not, she conceived her charge at an end, and no flattery could induce her to stay and assist in folding them. There was a display of accuracy and attention in this, that I cannot say I have ever seen equalled.

The late Mr Steel, flesher in Peebles, had a bitch that was fully equal to the one mentioned above, and that in the very same qualification too. Her feats in taking home sheep from the neighbouring farms into the flesh-market at Peebles by herself, form innumerable anecdotes in that vicinity, all similar to one another. But there is one instance related of her, that combines so much sagacity with natural affection, that I do not think the history of the animal creation furnishes such another.

Mr Steel had such an implicit dependence on the attention of this animal to his orders, that whenever he put a lot of sheep before her, he took a pride of leaving it to herself, and either remained to take a glass with the farmer of whom he had made the purchase, or took another road, to look after bargains or other business. But one time he chanced to commit a drove to her charge at a place called Willenslee, without attending to her condition, as he ought to have done. This farm is five miles from Peebles, over wild hills, and there is no regularly defined path to it. Whether Mr Steel remained behind, or took another road, I know not; but on coming home late in the

evening, he was astonished at hearing that his faithful animal had
never made her appearance with the drove. He and his son, or
servant, instantly prepared to set out by different paths in search of
her; but on their going out to the street, there was she coming with the
drove, no one missing; and, marvellous to relate, she was carrying a
young pup in her mouth! She had been taken in travail on these hills;
and how the poor beast had contrived to manage her drove in her
state of suffering, is beyond human calculation; for her road lay
through sheep the whole way. Her master's heart smote him when he
saw what she had suffered and effected; but she was nothing daunted;
and having deposited her young one in a place of safety, she again set
out full speed to the hills, and brought another, and another, till she
brought her whole litter, one by one; but the last one was dead. I give
this as I have heard it related by the country people; for though I
knew Mr Walter Steel well enough, I cannot say I ever heard it from
his own mouth. I never entertained any doubt, however, of the truth
of the relation, and certainly it is worthy of being preserved, for the
credit of that most docile and affectionate of all animals—the shepherd's dog.

The stories related of the dogs of sheep-stealers are fairly beyond all
credibility. I cannot attach credit to those without believing the
animals to have been devils incarnate, come to the earth for the
destruction of both the souls and bodies of men. I cannot mention
names, for the sake of families that still remain in the country; but
there have been sundry men executed, who belonged to this department of the realm, for that heinous crime, in my own time; and others
have absconded, just in time to save their necks. There was not one of
these to whom I allude who did not acknowledge his dog to be the
greatest aggressor. One young man, in particular, who was, I believe,
overtaken by justice for his first offence, stated, that after he had
folded the sheep by moonlight, and selected his number from the flock
of a former master, he took them out, and set away with them towards
Edinburgh. But before he had got them quite off the farm, his
conscience smote him, as he said, (but more likely a dread of that
which soon followed,) and he quitted the sheep, letting them go again
to the hill. He called his dog off them; and mounting his poney, he
rode away. At that time he said his dog was capering and playing
around him, as if glad of having got free of a troublesome business;
and he regarded him no more, till, after having rode about three
miles, he thought again and again that he heard something coming
up behind him. Halting, at length, to ascertain what it was, in a few
minutes there comes his dog with the stolen drove, driving them at a

furious rate to keep up with his master. The sheep were all smoking, and hanging out their tongues, and their driver was fully as warm as they. The young man was now exceedingly troubled; for the sheep having been brought so far from home, he dreaded there would be a pursuit, and he could not get them home again before day. Resolving, at all events, to keep his hands clear of them, he corrected his dog in great wrath, left the sheep once more, and taking his dog with him, rode off a second time. He had not ridden above a mile, till he perceived that his dog had again given him the slip; and suspecting for what purpose, he was terribly alarmed as well as chagrined; for the day-light approached, and he durst not make a noise calling on his dog, for fear of alarming the neighbourhood, in a place where both he and his dog were known. He resolved therefore to abandon the animal to himself, and take a road across the country which he was sure his dog did not know, and could not follow. He took that road; but being on horseback, he could not get across the enclosed fields. He at length came to a gate, which he closed behind him, and went about half a mile farther, by a zigzag course, to a farm-house where both his sister and sweetheart lived; and at that place he remained until after breakfast time. The people of this house were all examined on the trial, and no one had either seen sheep, or heard them mentioned, save one man, who came up to the aggressor as he was standing at the stable-door, and told him that his dog had the sheep safe enough down at the Crooked Yett, and he needed not hurry himself. He answered, that the sheep were not his—they were young Mr Thomson's, who had left them to his charge; and he was in search of a man to drive them, which made him come off his road.

After this discovery, it was impossible for the poor fellow to get quit of them; so he went down and took possession of the stolen drove once more, carried them on, and disposed of them; and, finally, the transaction cost him his life. The dog, for the last four or five miles that he had brought the sheep, could have no other guide to the road his master had gone, but the smell of his poney's feet. I appeal to every unprejudiced person if this was not as like one of the deil's tricks as an honest colley's.

It is also well known that there was a notorious sheep-stealer in the county of Mid-Lothian, who, had it not been for the skins and sheep's-heads, would never have been condemned, as he could, with the greatest ease, have proved an *alibi* every time on which there were suspicions cherished against him. He always went by one road, calling on his acquaintances, and taking care to appear to everybody by whom he was known; while his dog went by another with the stolen sheep; and then on the two felons meeting again, they had nothing more ado than turn the sheep into an associate's enclosure, in whose house the dog was well fed and entertained, and would have soon taken all the fat sheep on the Lothian edges to that house. This was likewise a female, a jet-black one, with a deep coat of soft hair, but smooth headed, and very strong and handsome in her make. On the disappearance of her master, she lay about the hills and the places where he had frequented; but she never attempted to steal a drove by herself, nor yet anything for her own hand. She was kept a while by a relation of her master's; but never acting heartily in his service, soon came to an untimely end privately. Of this there is little doubt, although some spread the report that one evening, after uttering two or three loud howls, she had vanished!—From such dogs as these, good Lord deliver us!

H.

ALTRIVE, *Feb.* 2*d*, 1824.

Class V.

The Lasses.

GREAT have been the conquests, and grievous the deray wrought in the human heart by some of these mountain nymphs. The confusion that particular ones have sometimes occasioned for a year or two almost exceeds credibility. Every young man in the bounds was sure either to be in love with her, or believed himself to be so; and as all these would be running on a Friday's evening to woo her, of course the pride and vanity of the fair was raised to such a height that she would rarely yield a preference to any, but was sure to put them all off with gibes and jeers. This shyness, instead of allaying, never fails to increase the fervour of the flame; an emulation, if not a rivalship, is excited among the younkers, until the getting a single word exchanged with the reigning beauty becomes a matter of thrilling interest to many a tender-hearted swain; but, generally speaking, none of these admired beauties are married till they settle into the more quiet vale of life, and the current of admiration has turned toward others. Then do they betake themselves to sober reflection, listen to the most rational, though not the most youthful of their lovers, and sit down, contented through life to share the toils, sorrows, and joys of the married life, and the humble cot.

I am not now writing of ladies, nor of "farmers' bonny daughters;" but merely of country maidens, such as ewe-milkers, hay-workers, har'st-shearers, the healthy and comely daughters of shepherds, hinds, country tradesmen, and small tenants; in short, all the rosy, romping, and light-hearted dames that handle the sickle, the hoe, the hay-raik, and the fleece. And of these I can say, to their credit, that there is rarely an instance happens of a celebrated beauty among them turning out a bad, or even an indifferent wife. Whether it is owing to the circumstance of their never marrying very young, (for a youthful marriage of a pair who have nought but their experience and a good name to depend on for the support of a family, is far from being a prudent, or highly commendable step,) or whether it be that these belles having had too much experience in the follies and flippancies of youthful love, and youthful lovers, make their choice at last on principles of reason, suffice it, that the axiom is a true one. But there is another reason which must not be lost sight of. That class of young men never flock about, or make love to a girl who is not noted for activity as well as beauty. Cleverness is always the first recommendation; and consequently, when such a one chooses to marry, it is natural to suppose that her good qualities will then be exerted to the utmost, which before were only occasionally called into exercise. Experience is indeed the great teacher among the labouring class, and her maxims are carried down from father to son in all their pristine strength. Seldom are they violated in anything, and never in this. No young man will court a beautiful daw, unless he be either a booby, or a rake, who does it for some selfish purpose, not to be mentioned nor thought of in the annals of virtuous love.

In detailing the ravages of country beauty, I will be obliged to take fictitious or bynames to illustrate true stories, on account of many circumstances that have occurred at periods subsequent to the incidents related. Not the least of these is the great change that time has effected in every one of those pinks of rustic admiration. How would it look if ODoherty or yourself, at your annual visit here, were to desire me to introduce you to one of these by her name and sirname, and I were to take you to see a reverend grannie; or at best, a russet dame far advanced in life, with wrinkles instead of roses, and looks of maternal concern instead of the dimpling smile, and glance of liquid beauty? Ah, no, dear sir! let us not watch the loveliest of all earthly flowers till it becomes degraded in our eyes by a decay which it was born to undergo. Let it be a dream in our philosophy that it still remains in all its prime, and that so it will remain in some purer clime through all the vicissitudes of future ages.

As I have not been an eye-witness to many of the scenes I mean to detail, I judge it best to give them as the relation of the first person, in the same manner as they have been rehearsed to me, whether that person chanced to be the principal or not. Without this mode I might make a more perfect arrangement in my little love stories, but could not give them any degree of the interest they appeared to me to possess, or define the characters by letting them speak for themselves.

"Wat, what was the matter wi' you, that ye never keepit your face to the minister the last Sabbath day? Yon's an unco unreverend gate in a kirk, man. I hae seen you keep a good ee on the preacher, an' take good tent o' what was gaun too; and troth I'm wae to see ye altered to the waur."

"I kenna how I might chance to be lookin', but I hope I was listening as weel as you, or ony that was there. Heighow! It's a weary warld this!"

"What has made it siccan a weary warld to poor Wat? I'm sure it wasna about the ills o' life that the minister was preachin' that day, that has gart ye change sae sair? Now, Wat, I tentit ye weel a' the day, an' I'll be in your debt for a toop lamb at Michaelsmass, gin ye'll just tell me ae distinct sentence o' the sermon on Sabbath last."

"Hout, Jock, man! ye ken I dinna want to make a jest about ony saucred or religious thing; an' as for your paulie toop lamb, what care I for it?"

"Ye needna think to win aff that gate, callant. Just confess the truth, that ye never yet heard a word the good man said, for that baith your heart an' your ee was fixed on some object in the contrair direction. An' I may be mistaen, but I think I could guess what it was."

"Whisht, lad, an' let us alane o' your sinfu' surmeeses. I might turn my back on the minister during the time o' the prayer, but that was for getting a lean on the seat, an' what ill was in that?"

"Ay, an' ye might likewise hirsel yoursel up to the corner o' the seat a' the time o' baith the sermons, an' lean your head on your hand, an' look through your fingers too. Can ye deny this? Or that your een were fixed the hale day on ae particular place?"

"Aweel, I winna gie a friend the lee to his face. But an ye had lookit as weel at a' the rest as at me, ye wad hae seen that a' the men in the kirk were lookin' the same gate."

"An' a' at the same object too? An' a' as deeply interested in it as you? Isna that what ye're thinkin? Ah, Wat, Wat! love winna hide! I saw a pair o' slae-black een that threw some gayan saucy disdainfu' looks up the kirk, an' I soon saw the havoc they were makin', an' had made, i' your simple honest heart. Wow, man! but I fear me you are in a bad predickiment."

"Ay, ay. Between twa friends, Jock, there never was a lad in sic a predickiment as I am. I needna keep ought frae you; but for the life that's i' your bouk dinna let a pater about it escape frae atween your lips. I wadna that it were kend how deeply I am in love, an' how little it is like to be requited, for the hale warld. But I am this day as miserable a man as breathes the breath o' life. For I like yon lass as man never likit another, an' a' that I get is scorn, an' gibes, an' mockery in return. O Jock, I wish I was dead in an honest natural way, an' that my burial day were the morn!"

"Weel, after a', I daresay that is the best way o' winding up a hopeless love scene. But only it ought surely to be the last resource. Now, will ye be candid, and tell me gin ye hae tried all lawful endeavours to preserve your ain life, as the commandment requires us to do, ye ken? Hae ye courtit the lass as a man ought to hae courtit her who is in every respect her equal?"

"Oh, yes, I have! I have told her a' my love, an' a' my sufferings; but it has been only to be mockit, an' sent about my business."

"An' ye wad whine, an' make wry faces, as you are doing just now? Na, na, Wat, that's no the gate o't;—a maid maun just be wooed in the same spirit that she shews, an' when she shews sauciness, there's naething for it but taking a step higher than her in the same humour, letting her always ken, an' always see, that you are naturally her superior, an' that you are even stooping from your dignity when you condescend to ask her to become your equal. If she refuse to be your joe at the fair, never either whine or look disappointed, but be sure to wale the bonniest lass in the market, an' lead her to the same party where your saucy dame is. Take her to the top o' the dance, the top o' the table at dinner, an' laugh, an' sing; an' aye between whisper your bonny partner; an' if your ain lass disna happen to be unco weel buckled, it is ten to ane she will find an opportunity of offering you her company afore night. If she look angry or affronted at your attentions to others, you are sure o' her. They are queer creatures the lasses, Wat, an' I rather dread ye haena muckle skill or experience in their bits o' wily gates. For, to tell you the truth, there's naething pleases me sae weel as to see them begin to pout, an' prim their bits o' gabs, an' look sulky out frae the wick o' the ee, an' gar ilka feather an' flower-knot quiver wi' their angry capers. O the dear, sweet jewels! When I see ane o' them in sic a key, I could just take her a' in my arms!"

"If you had ever loved as I do, Jock, ye wad hae found little comfort in their offence. For my part, every disdainfu' word that yon dear, lovely lassie says, goes to my heart like a red-hot spindle. My life is bound up in her favour. It is only in it that I can live, move, or breathe; an' whenever she says a severe or cutting word to me, I feel as if ane o' my members were torn away, and am glad to escape as lang as I am onything ava; for I find, if I war to remain, a few mae siccan sentences wad soon annihilate me."

"O sic balderdash! In three months' time I shall take in hand to bring her to your ain terms, if you will take my advice. When I speak o' *your ain terms*, mind I take it for granted that you will never propose ony that are not strictly honourable."

"That you may rely on. I would sooner think of wranging my own flesh an' blood than suffer a thought to waver about my heart to her prejudice. But, O man, speak; for ye are garring a' the blood in my veins rin up to my head, as gin it war a thousand ants running races."

"Weel, Wat, in the first place, I propose to gang down yonder a night by mysel', an' speak baith to her father an' her, to find how the land lies; an' after that we can gang down baith thegether, an' gie her a fair broadside. The deil's in't, if we sanna bring her to reason."

Wat scratched his head, and pulled the grass (that was quite blameless in the affair) furiously up by the roots, but made no answer. On being urged to declare his sentiments, he said, "I dinna ken about that way o' ganging down your lane; I wish you maunna stick by the auld fisher's rule, 'Every man for his ain hand.' That I ken weel, that nae man alive can see her, an' speak to her, and no be in love wi' her."

"It is a good thing in love affairs, Wat, that there are hardly two in the world wha think the same way."

"Ay, but this is a particular case, for a' the men in the country think the same gate here, an' rin the same gate to the wooing. It is impossible to win near the house on a Friday night without rinning your head against that of some rival, like twa toops fightin' about a ewe. Na, na, John, this plan o' gangin' down by yoursel' winna do. An' now when I think on't, ye had better no gang down ava, for if we gang down friends, we'll come up enemies, an' that wadna be a very agreeable catastroff."

"Now shame fa' me gin ever I heard sic nonsense! To think that a' the warld see wi' your een! Hear ye, Wat.—I wadna gie that snap o' my fingers for her. I never saw her till Sunday last, when I came to your kirk ance errand for that purpose, an' I wadna ken her again gin I war to meet her here come out to the glen wi' your whey—what ails you, fool, that you're dightin' your een?"

"Come out to the glen wi' *my* whey! Ah, man! the words gaed through me like the stang of a bumbee. Come out to the glen wi' my whey! Gude forgie my sin, what is the reason I canna thole that thought? That were a consummation devoutly to be wussed, as the soloquy in the Collection says. I fear I'll never see that blessed an' lovely sight! But, Jock, take my advice; stay at hame, an' gangna near her, gin ye wad enjoy ony peace o' conscience."

"Ye ken naething about the women, Wat, an' as little about me. If I gang near her, it will only be to humble her a wee, by mocking at her influence among the young men, an' bringing her to reason, for your sake. Jock the Jewel wadna say *'wae's me!'* for the best lass's frown in a' the kingdom o' Britain. Whatever some o' them might do for his, that's no his right to say."

Jock the Jewel went down in all his might and high experience to put everything to rights between his friend Wat and the bonny

Snaw-fleck, as this spink of a mountain damsel was called, for every girl in the whole parish was named after one of the birds of the air; and every man, too, young and old, had his by-name, by which we shall distinguish them all for the present. The Snaw-fleck's father was called Tod-Lowrie, (the fox;) his eldest daughter, the Eagle; the second, the Sea-maw; and his only son was denominated the Fou-mart, (polecat;) from a notable hunt he once had with one of these creatures in the middle of the night, in a strange house; and it was the worst name I ever heard for a young man. Our disconsolate lover was called Window Wat, on account of his bashful nature, and, as they alleged, for hanging always about the windows when he went a-courting, and never venturing in. It was a good while after this first rencounter before the two shepherds met again with that convenience so as to resume their love affairs. But at length an occasion offered, and then——But we must suffer every man to tell his own tale, else the sport will be spoilt.

"Weel, Wat, hae ye been ony mair down at Lowrie's Lodge, sin' I saw you?"

"An' if I hae, I hae been little the better o' you. I heard that you were there before me, an' sinsyne too."

"Now, Wat, that's mere jealousy an' suspicion, for ye didna see the lass to ken whether I was there or not. I ken ye wad be hingin' about the window-soles as usual, keekin' in, feastin' your een, seein' other woosters beikin' their shins at the ingle, but for a' that durstna venture ben. Come, I dinna like siccan sackless gates as thae. I *was* down, I'se no deny't, but I gaed to wark in a different manner. Unco cauldrife wark that o' standin' peengin' about windows, man. Come, tell me a' your expedition, an' I'll tell mine, like friends, ye ken."

"Mine's no ill to tell. I gaed down that night after I saw you, e'en though Wednesday be the widower's night; there were more there than I, but I was fear'd ye had got there afore me, and then, wi' your great skill o' the ways o' women, ye might hae left me nae chance at a'. I was there, but I might as weel hae staid at hame, for there were sae mony o' the out-wale wallietragle kind o' wooers there, like mysel, a' them that canna win forret on a Friday night, that I got the back o' the hallan to keep; but there's ae good thing about the auld Tod's house, they never ditt up their windows. Ane sees aye what's gaun on within doors. They leave a' their actions open to the ee o' God an' man, yon family, an' I often think it is nae ill sign o' them. Auld Tod-Lowrie himsel sometimes looks at the window in a kind o' considering mood, as if doubtful that at that moment he is both overheard and overseen; but, or it is lang, he cocks up his bonnet and cracks as crouse as ever, as if he thought again, 'There's aye ae ee that sees me at a' times, an' a ear that hears me, an' when that's the case, what need I care for a' the birkies o' the land!' I like that open independent way that the family has. But O, they are surely sair harassed wi' wooers."

"The wooers are the very joy o' their hearts, excepting the Foumart's; he hates them a' unless they can tell him hunders o' lies about battles, bogles, an' awfu' murders, an' persecutions. An' the leaving o' the windows open too is not without an aim. The Eagle's beginning to weary for a husband; an' if ye'll notice how dink she dresses hersel ilka night, an' jinks away at the muckle wheel as she war spinning for a wager. They hae found out that they are often seen at night yon lasses; and though they hae to work the foulest work o' the bit farm a' the day when naebody sees them, at night they are a' dressed up like pet-ewes for a market, an' ilka ane is acting a part. The Eagle is yerkin' on at the wheel, and now and then gi'en a smirk wi' her face to the window. The Snaw-fleck sits busy in the neuk, as sleek as a kinnen, and the auld clocker fornent her, admirin' an' misca'in' her a' the time. The white Seamaw flees up an' down the house, but an' ben, ae while i' the spense, ane i' the awmrie, an' then to the door wi' a soap-suds. Then the Foumart, he sits knitting his stocking, an' quarrelling wi' the hale tot o' them. The feint a haed he minds but sheer ill nature. If there be a good body i' the house, the auld Tod is the ane. He is a gayan honest, downright carle, the Tod."

"It is hardly the nature o' a tod to be sae; an' there's no ae bit o' your description that I gang in wi'! It is a fine, douse family.

> 'But O the Snaw-fleck!
> The bonny bonny Snaw-fleck!
> She is the bird for me, O!' "

"If love wad make you a poeter, Wat, I wad say it had wrought miracles. Ony mair about the bonny Snaw-fleck, eh? I wonder how you can make glowin' love-sangs stan'in' at a cauld window—No the way that, man. Tell me plainly, did ye ever get a word o' the bonny lass ava?"

"Hey how me!—I can hardly say that I did; an' yet I hae been three times there sin' I saw you."

"An' gat your travel for your pains a' the times?"

"No sae bad as that, neither. I had the pleasure o' seeing her, bonny, braw, innocent, an' happy, busy working her mother's wark. I saw her smile at her brother's crabbit words, and I saw the approving glances beam frae the twa auld focks' een. When her father made family-worship, she took her Bible, and followed devoutly wi' her ee the words o' holy writ, as the old man read them; and her voice in singing the psalm was as mellow an' as sweet as the flute playing afar off. Ye may believe me, Jock, when I saw her lift up her lovely face in sweet devotion, I stood on the outside o' the window, an' grat like a bairn. It was mair than my heart could thole; an' gin it warna for shame, I wad gang every night to enjoy the same heavenly vision."

"As I'm a Christian man, Wat, I believe love *has* made a poeter of you. Ye winna believe me, man, that very woman is acting her part. Do you think she didna ken that ye saw her, an' was makin' a' thae fine murgeons to throw glamour in your een, an' gar you trow she was an angel? I managed otherwise; but it is best to tell a' plain out, like friends, ye ken. Weel, down I goes to Lowrie's Lodge, an', like you, keeks in at the window, and the first thing I saw was the auld Tod toving out tobacco-reek like a moorburn. The hale biggin was sae choke fu' o' the vapour, it was like a dark mist, an' I could see naething through it but his ain braid bonnet moving up and down like the tap o' the smith's bellows, at every poogh he gave. At length he handit by the pipe to the auld wife, and the reek soon turned mair moderate. I could then see the lasses a' dressed out like dolls, and several young boobies o' hinds, threshers, an' thrum-cutters, sitting gashin' and glowrin' amang them. I shall soon set your backs to the wa', thinks I, if I could get ony possible means o' introduction. It wasna lang till ane offered; out comes a lass wi' a cog o' warm water, an' she gars it a' clash on me. 'Thanks t'ye for your kindness, my woman,' says I. 'Ye canna say I hae gi'en ye a cauld reception,' says she. 'But wha the widdy are ye standin' like a thief i' the mirk for?' 'Maybe kenn'd fo'k, gin it war daylight,' quo' I. 'Ye had better come in by, an' see gin candle-light winna beet the mister,' says she. 'Thanks t'ye,' says I; 'but I wad rather hae you to come *out by*, an' try gin stern-light winna do!' 'Catch me doing that,' cried she, and bounced into the house again.

"I then laid my lug close to the window, an' heard ane askin' wha that was she was speakin' to? 'I dinna ken him,' quo' she; 'but I trow I hae gi'en him a mark to ken him by; I hae gi'en him a balsam o' boiling water.'

" 'I wish ye may hae peeled a' the hide aff his shins,' quo' the Foumart, an' he mudged and leugh; 'haste ye, dame, rin awa out an' lay a plaister o' lime and linseed-oil to the lad's trams,' continued he.

" 'I can tell ye wha it is,' said ane o' the hamlet wooers; 'it will be Jock the Jewel comed down frae the moors, for I saw him waiting about the chop an' the smiddy till the darkness came on. If ye hae disabled him, lady sea-bird, the wind will blaw nae mair out o' the west.'

"I durstna trust them wi' my character and me in hearing; sae, without mair ado, I gangs bauldly ben.—'Gude e'en to ye, kimmers a' in a ring,' says I.

" 'Gude-e'en t'ye, honest lad,' quo' the Eagle. 'How does your cauld constitution an' our potatoe-broo sort?'

" 'Thanks t'ye, bonny lass,' says I. 'I hae gotten a right sair skelloch; but I wish I warna woundit nae deeper somewhere else than i' the shin-banes, I might shoot a flyin' erne for a' that's come an' gane yet.'

" 'That's weel answered, lad,' quo' the Tod. 'Keep her down, for she's unco glib o' the gab, especially to strangers.'

" 'You will never touch a feather o' her wing, lad,' quo' she. 'But if ye could——I'll say nae mair.'

" 'Na, na, Mistress Eagle, ye soar o'er high for me,' says I. 'I'll bring down nae sky-cleaving harpies to pick the e'en out o' my sheep, an' my ain into the bargain, maybe. I see a bit bonny norlan' bird in the nook here, that I would rather woo to my little hamely nest. The Eagle maun to her eiry; or, as the auld ballant says—

'Gasp and speel to her yermit riven,
Amid the mists an' the rains of heaven.'

It is the innocent, thrifty, little Snaw-fleck that will suit me, wi' the white wings an' the blue body. She's pleased wi' the hardest and hameliest fare; a pickin o' the seeds o' the pipe bent is a feast to her.' "

"Now, by the faith o' my body, Jewel, that wasna fair. Was that preparing the way for your friend's success?"

"Naething but sheer banter, man; like friends, ye ken. But ye sall hear. 'The Snaw-fleck's a braw beast,' said I, 'but the Eagle's a waster and a destroyer.'

" 'She's true to her mate, though,' said the dame; 'but the tither is a bird o' passage, and mate to the hale flock.'

"I was a wee startled at this observe, when I thought of the number of wooers that were rinning after the bonny Snaw-fleck. However, I didna like to yield to the jocular and haughty Eagle; and I added, that I wad take my chance o' the wee Snaw-bird, for though she war ane of a flock, that flock was an honest ane. This pleased them a'; and the auld slee Tod, he spak up an' said, he hadna the pleasure o' being acquaint wi' me, but he hoped he shouldna hae it in his power to say sae again. Only there was ae thing he beggit to

remind me o', before I went any farther, and that was, that the law of
Padanaram was established in his family, an' he could by no means
give a younger daughter in marriage before one that was elder.

" 'I think you will maybe keep them for a gay while, then,' said the
Foumart. 'But if the Sea-gull wad stay at hame, I carena if the rest
were at Bamph. She's the only usefu' body I see about the house.'

" 'Haud the tongue o' thee, thou illfa'red, cat's-witted serf,' said
the auld wife. 'I'm sure ony o' them's worth a faggald o' thee. An'
that lad, gin I dinna forecast aglee, wad do credit to ony kin.'

" 'He's rather ower weel giftit o' gab,' quo' the menseless thing.
That remark threw a damp on my spirits a' the night after, an' I
rather lost ground than gained ony mair. The ill-hued weazel-blawn
thing of a brother, never missed an opportunity of gieing me a yerk
wi' his ill-scrapit tongue, an' the Eagle was aye gieing hints about the
virtues o' potatoe-broo—how it improved the voice for singin', an'
gae ane a chance o' some advancement in the dominions o' the
Grand Turk. I didna ken what she meant, but some o' the rest did,
for they leugh as they had been kittled; and the mirth and humour
turned outrageous, aye seemingly at my expense. The auld Tod
chewed tobacco an' threw his mouth, lookit whiles at ane and whiles
at another, an' seemed to enjoy the joke as muckle as ony o' them. As
for the bonny Snaw-bird, she never leugh aboon her breath, but sat
as mim an' as sleek as a moudie. There were some very pretty smiles
an' dimples gawn, but nae gaffawing. She is really a fine lass."

"There it goes now! I tauld you how it wad be! I tell you, Jewel,
the deil a bit o' this is fair play."

"Ane may tell what he thinks—like a friend, ye ken. Weel—to
make a lang tale short—I couldna help seeing a' the forenight that
she had an ee to me. I couldna help *that*, ye ken. Gat mony a sweet
blink an' smile thrawn o'er the fire to me—couldna help that either,
ye ken—never lost that a friend gets. At length a' the douce wooers
drew off ane by ane—saw it was needless to dispute the point wi' me
that night. Ane had to gang hame to supper his horses, another to
fodder the kye, and another had to be hame afore his master took the
book, else he had to gang supperless to bed. I sat still—needless to
lose a good boon for lack o' asking. The potatoes were poured an'
champit—naebody bade me bide supper, but I sat still; an' the auld
wife she slippit away to the awmrie, an' brought a knoll o' butter like
ane's nieve, an' slippit that into the potatoe pot hidling ways, but the
fine flavour that filled the house soon outed the secret. I drew in my
seat wi' the rest, resolved to hae my share o' the cheap, healthfu', and
delightfu' meal, an' I maun say that I never enjoyed ane a' my life wi'

mair satisfaction. I saw that I had a hearty welcome frae them a' but the Foumart, an' I loot him girn an' snivel as muckle as he liket. Weel, I saw it was turning late, and there was a necessity for proceeding to business, else the books an' the prayers wad be on. Sae I draws to my plaid an' staff, an' I looks round to the lasses; but in the meantime I dropt half a wink to the Snaw-fleck, an' I says, 'Weel, wha o' you bonny lasses sets me the length o' the townhead yett the night?'

" 'The feint a ane o' them,' quo' the Foumart wi' a girn.

" 'The townhead yett the night, honest lad?' quo' the wife. 'Be my certy, thou's no gaun nae siccan a gate. Dis thou think thou can gang to the muirs the night? Nay, nay, thou shalt take share of a bed wi' our son till it be day, for the night's dark an' the road's eiry.'

" 'He needna stay unless he likes,' quo' the Foumart. 'Let the chap tak his wull, an' gang his gates.'

" 'Haud thy ill-faur'd tongue,' said the wife. I sat down again, an' we grew a' unco silent. At length the Eagle rose an' flew to the door. It wadna do—I wadna follow; sat aye still, and threw another straight wink to the bonny Snaw-fleck, but the shy shirling sat snug in her corner, an' wadna move. At length the Eagle comes gliding in, an' in a moment, or ever I kend what I was doing, claps down a wee table at my left hand, an' the big Bible an' psalm-book on't. I never gat sic a stound, an' really thought I wad drap down through the floor; an' when I saw the lasses shading their faces wi' their hands, I grew waur.

" 'What ails thee, honest lad, that thou looks sae baugh?' said the auld wife. 'Sure thou's no ashamed to praise thy Maker? for an thou be, I shall be ashamed o' thee. It is an auld family custom we hae, aye to gie a stranger the honour o' being our leader in this bit e'ening duty; an' gin he refuse that, we dinna countenance him ony mair.'

"That was a yerker! I now fand I was fairly in the mire. For the saul o' me I durstna take the book; for though I had a good deal o' good words, an' blads o' scripture, an' religious rhames, a' by heart, I didna ken how I might gar them compluther. An' as I took this to be a sort o' test to try a wooer's abilities, I could easily see that my hough was fairly i' the sheep crook, an' that what wi' sticking the psalm, bungling the prayer, potatoe-broo an' a' thegither, I was like to come badly off. Sae I says, 'Goodwife, I'm obliged t'ye for the honour ye hae offered me; an' sae far frae being ashamed o' my Maker's service, I rejoice in it; but I hae mony reasons for declining the honour. In the first place, war I to take the task out o' the goodman's hand, it wad be like the youngest scholar o' the school pretending to teach his master;

an' war I to stay here a' night, it wad be principally for the purpose of enjoying his family worship frae his ain lips. But the truth is, an' that's my great reason, I *can not* stay a' night. I want just ae single word o' this bonny lass, an' then I maun take the road, for I'm far o'er late already.'

" 'I bide by my text, young man,' says the Tod; 'the law of Padanaram is the law of this house.'

" 'An', by the troth o' me, thou'lt find it nae bad law for thee, honest lad,' said the wife; 'our eldest will mak the *best* wife for thee—tak thou my word for that.'

" 'I am thinkin' I wad,' said the Eagle; 'an' I dinna ken but I might hae taen him too, if it hadna been—an accident.' Here she brak aff, an' a' the house set up a giggle of a laugh, an' the goodman turned his quid an' joined in it. I forced on a good face, an' added, 'Ah! the Eagle! the Eagle's a deil's bird—she's no for me. I want just a single word wi' this dink chicken; but it isna on my ain account—it is a word frae a friend, an' I'm bound in honour to deliver it.'

" 'That is spoken sae like an honest man, an' a disinterested ane,' quo' the Tod, 'that I winna refuse the boon. Gae your ways ben to our little ben-end, an' say what ye hae to say, for I dinna suffer my bairns to gang out i' the dark wi' strangers.'

" 'Come away, then, hinny,' says I. She rose wi' slow an' ill will, for I saw she wad rather I had been to speak for mysel'; an' as I perceived this, as soon as I got her ben the house, an' the door fairly steekit, I says till her, says I, 'Now, bonny lassie, I never saw your face afore but ance, an' that day I gaed mony fit to see't. I came here the night ance errand to speak a word for a friend, but really'—Here she interrupted me as soon as she heard *but really.*

" 'Could your friend no speak his word himself?' said she.

" 'As you say,' says I; 'that is good sense—I ca' that good, sound common sense; for a man does always his own turn best; an' therefore I maun tell you, that I am fairly fa'en in love wi' you mysel', an' am determined to hae ye for my ain, cost what it will.' "

At this part of the story, Wat sprung to his feet—"Did you say sae, sirrah?" said he. "If ye did, ye are a fause loun, an' a villain, an' I am determined to hae pennyworths o' *you*, cost what it will."

"Hout, fych fie, Wat, man! dinna be a fool. Sit down, an' let us listen to reason, like friends, ye ken. Ye sall hear, man— ye sall hear."

"I winna hear another word, Jewel. Up to your feet; either single-stick or dry nieves, ony o' them ye like. Ye gat the lass ben the house on the credit o' my name, an' that was the use ye made o't! Ye dinna ken how near my heart, an' how near my life, ye war edging then, an' I'll break every bane in your bouk for it; only ye shall hae fair play, to smash mine, gin ye can. Up, I say; for yon was a deed I winna brook."

"Perhaps I was wrang, but I'll tell the truth. Sit down an' ye shall hear—an' then, gin we maun fight, there's time enough for it after. If I had thought I acted wrang, I wadna hae tauld it sae plain out; but when twa folks think the saam gate, it isna a good sign. 'I'm in love wi' you, an' am determined to hae you,' says I.

" 'I winna hear a single word frae ane that's betraying his friend,' said she;—'not one word, after your avowal to my father. If he hae ony private word, say it—an' if no, good night.' "

"Did she say that, the dear soul? Heaven bless her bonny face!"

" 'I did promise to a particular friend o' mine to speak a kind word for him,' said I. 'He is unco blate an' modest, but there's no a better lad; an' I never saw ane as deeply an' distractedly in love; for though I feel I *do* love, it is with reason and moderation.' "

"There again!" cried Wat, who had begun to hold out his hand— "There again! I'm distracted, but you are a reasonable being!"

" 'Not a word of yourself,' said she. 'Who is this friend of yours? And has he any more to say by you? Not one word more of yourself —at least not to-night.' "

"At least not to-night!" repeated Wat again and again—"Did she say that? I dinna like the addition ava."

"That was what she said; an' naething could be plainer than that she was inviting me back; but as I was tied down, I was obliged to say something about you. 'Ye ken Window Wat?' says I. 'He is o'er sight and judgment in love wi' you, an' he comes here ance or twice every week, just for the pleasure o' seeing you through the window. He's a gay queer compost—for though he is a' soul, yet he wants spirit.' "

"Did ye ca' me a compost? That was rather a queer term for a wooer, begging your pardon," says Wat.

" 'I hae seen the lad sometimes,' says she. 'If he came here to see me, he certainly need not be sae muckle ashamed of his errand as not to shew his face. I think him a main saft ane.'

" 'Ye're quite i' the wrang, lass,' says I. 'Wat's a great dab. He's an arithmeticker, a stronomer, a historian, and a grand poeter, an' has made braw sangs about yoursel'. What think ye o' being made a wife to sic a hero as him? Od help ye, it will raise ye as high as the moon.' "

"I'll tell ye what it is, Jock the Jewel. The neist time ye gang to court, court for yoursel', for a' that ye hae said about me is downright mockery, an' it strikes me that you are baith a selfish knave and a gommeril. Sae good e'en t'ye for the present. I owe you a good turn

for your kind offices down bye. I'll speak for mysel in future, and do
ye the same—*like friends, ye ken*—that's a' I say."

"If I speak for mysel', I ken wha will hae but a poor chance," cried
Jock after him.

The next time our two shepherds met, where was it but in the
identical smithy adjoining to Lowrie's Lodge, and that at six o'clock
on a December evening. The smith smelt a rat, looked exceedingly
wise, and when he heard the two swains begin to cut and sneer at one
another, it was delicate food for Vulcan. He puffed and blew at the
bellows, and thumped at the stithy, and always between put in a
disjointed word or two.—"Mae hunters! mae hunters for the Tod's
bairns—hem, phoogh, phoogh—will be worried now!—phoogh"—
thump, thump—"will be run down now—hem!"

"Are ye gaun far this way the night, Jewel, an ane may spier?"

"Far enough for you, Wat, I'm thinkin'. How has the praying
been coming on this while bygane?"

"What d'ye mean, Mr Jewel? If ye will speak, let it no be in
riddles. Rather speak nonsense, as ye used to do."

"I'm speakin' in nae riddles, lad. I wat weel a' the country side
kens that ye hae been gaun learnin' prayers aff Hervey's Meditations,
an' crooning them o'er to yoursel' in every cleuch o' the glen, a' to
tame a young she-fox wi'."

"An' that ye hae been lying under the hands o' the moor doctor
for a month, an' submitting to an operation, frae the effects o'
somebody's potatoe-broo—isna that as weel kent?"

"Till't, lads, till't!" cried the smith—"that's the right way o'
ganging to wark—phoogh!"—clink, clink—"pepper away!"—clink,
clink—"soon be baith as het as nailstrings—phoogh!"

The potatoe-broo rather settled Jock's sarcasm, for he had suffered
some inconvenience from the effects of it, and the circumstance had
turned the laugh against him among his companions in a very
particular manner. After all, his right ankle only was blistered a little
by the burning; but, according to the country gossips, matters were
bad enough, and it proved a sore thorn in Jock's side. It was not long
after this till he glided from the smithy like a thing that had vanished,
and after that Wat sat in the fidgets for fear his rival had effected a
previous engagement with the Snow-fleck. The smith perceiving it,
seized him in good humour, and turned him out at the door. "Nae
time to stay now, lad—nae time to wait here now. The hunt will be
up, and the young Tod holed, if ye dinna make a' the better speed."
Then, as Wat vanished down the way, the smith imitated the sound
of the fox-hounds and the cries of the huntsmen. "Will be run down

now, thae young Tods—heavy metal laid on now—we'll have a scalding heat some night, an the track keep warm," said the smith, as he fell to the big bellows with both hands.

When Wat arrived at Lowrie's Lodge, he first came in contact with one wooer, and then another, hanging about the corners of the house; but finding that none of them was his neighbour and avowed rival, he hasted to his old quiet station at the back window, not the window where the Jewel stood when he met with his mischance, but one right opposite to it. There he saw the three bonniest birds of the air surrounded with admirers, and the Jewel sitting cheek by cheek with the lovely Snow-bird. The unbidden tears sprung to Wat's eyes, but it was not for jealousy, but from the most tender affection, as well as intense admiration, that they had their source. The other wooers that were lingering without, joined him at the window; and Wat feeling this an incumbrance, and eager to mar his rival's success, actually plucked up courage, and strode in amongst them all. This was a great effort indeed, and it was the first time he had ever dared such a piece of desperate temerity. But the efforts of that eventful night, and the consequences that followed, must needs be reserved for another Number.

Class V

The Lasses
(Continued)

"How came the twa moorland chiels on at the courting the other night?"

"It's hard to say; there are various accounts about the matter."

"What does the smith say?—for, though his sentences are but short, he says them loud enough, and often enough ower, an' fo'ks reckon there's aye some truth in the foundation."

"I can tell ye what he says, for I heard him on the subject oftener than aince, and his information was precisely as follows:—'The Tod's bairns maun gang now, lads—I'm saying, the Tod's bairns maun gang now—eh, Menye?—fairly run down. Half-a-dozen tykes ower sair for ae young Tod—eh? Fairly holed the young ane, it seems—I'm saying, the young ane's holed. Nought but a pick and shool wantit to howk her. Jewel has gi'en mouth there—I'm saying, auld Jewel has gi'en mouth there. Poor Wat has been obliged to turn to the auld ane—he's on the full track o' her—I'm saying, he's after her, full trot. But some thinks she'll turn her tail to a craig, an' wear him up. It was Wat that got the honour o' the beuk, though—I'm saying, it was him that took the beuk—wan gloriously through, too. The saxteenth o' the Romans, without a hamp, hinny. Was that true, think ye?—I'm saying, think ye that was true? Cam to the holy kiss, a' the wooers' teeth watered—eh?—Think ye that was true, hinny? The Jewel was amaist comed to grips at that verse about the kiss— eh?—I'm saying, the Jewel closed wi' the beauty there, I'm saying— Ha! ha!—I think that wadna be true.'—This is the length the smith's information gangs."

"I'm sure, gin the Snawfleck take the Jewel in preference to Wat, it will show a strange perversion of taste."

"O, there's naebody can answer for the fancies of a woman. But they're a gayan auld-farrant set the Tods, an' winna be easily out-witted. Did ye no hear ought of a moonlight-match that was to be there?"

"Not a word; and if I had, I wadna hae believed it."

"The Jewel has been whispering something to that effect; he's sae uplifted, he canna haud his tongue, an' I dinna wonder at it. But, for a' the offers the bonny lass had, to fix on him, is a miracle. Time tries a'; an' Jock may be cheated yet."

Yes, time is the great trier of human events. Let any man review his correspondences for ten years back, and he will then see how widely different his own prospects of the future have been from the lessons taught him by that hoary monitor Time. But, for the present, matters turned out as the fortunate wooer had insinuated; for, in a short month after this confabulation had taken place, the auld Tod's helpmate arose early one morning, and began a-bustling about the house in her usual busy way, and always now and then kept giving hints to her bonny lasses to rise and begin to their daily tasks.— "Come, stir ye, stir ye, my bonny bairns. When the sterns o' heaven hae gane to their beds, it is time the flowers o' the yird war rising— Come, come!—No stirring yet?—Busk ye, busk ye, like thrifty bairns, an' dinna let the lads say that ye are sleepy dowdies, that lie in your beds till the sun burns holes in your coverlets. Fie, fie!—There has been a reek i' Jean Lowrie's lum this half-hour. The moor-cock has crawed, the mawkin cowered, and the whaup yammered abune the flower. Streek your young limbs—open your young een—a foot on the cauld floor, an' sleep will soon be aboon the cludds.—Up, up, my winsome bairns!"

The white Lady-seabird was soon afoot, for she slept by herself, but the old dame still kept speaking away to the other two, at one time gibing, at another coaxing them to rise, but still there was no answer. "Peace be here, Helen, but this is an unco sleep-sleeping!" added she.—"What has been asteer owernight? I wish your twa titties haena been out wi' the men?"

"Ay, I wish they binna out wi' them still; for I heard them steal out yestreen, but I never heard them steal in again."

The old wife ran to the bed, and in a moment was heard exclaiming,—"The sorrow be i' my een gin ever I saw the like o' that! I declare the bed's as cauld as a curling-stane.—Ay, the nest's cauld, and the birds are flown. Oh, wae be to the day! wae be to the day! Gudeman, gudeman, get up and raise the parishen, for our bairns are baith stown away!"

"Stown away!" cried the father—"What does the woman mean?"

"Ay, let them gang," cried the son; "they're weel away, gin they bide; deil speed the gate to the hallikit hempies!"

"Tewhoo! hoo-hoo!" cried the daughter, weeping,—"That comes o' your laws o' Padan-aram! What had ye ado with auld Laban's rules? Ye might hae letten us gang as we could win aff.—There, I am left to spin tow, wha might hae been married the first, had it no been for your daft laws o' Padan-aram."

The girl cried, the son laughed, the old woman raved and danced through very despair, but the goodman took the matter right calmly, as if determined to wait the issue with resignation, for better or worse.

"Haud your tongues, ilk ane o' ye," said he—"What's a' the fy-gae-to about? I hae that muckle to trust to my lasses, that I can lippen them as weel out o' my sight as in my sight, an' as weel wi' young men as wi' auld women.—Bairns that are brought up in the fear, nurture, and admonition o' their Maker, will aye swee to the right side, and sae will mine. Gin they thought they had a right to chuse for themselves, they war right in exercising that right; an' I'm little feared that their choices be bad anes, or yet that they be adverse to my opinion. Sae I rede you to haud a' your tongues, an' tak nae mair notice o' ought that has happened, than it hadna been. We're a' in gude hands to guide us; an' though we whiles pu' the reins out o' His hand to tak a gallop our ain gate, yet He winna leave us lang to our ain direction."

With these sagacious words, the auld sly Tod settled the clamour and outcry in his family that morning; and the country has never doubted to this day, that he plowed with his own heifers.

On the evening previous to this colloquy, the family of the Tods went to rest at an early hour. There had been no wooers admitted that night; and no sooner had the two old people begun to breathe deep, than the eldest and youngest girls, who slept in an apartment by themselves, and had everything in readiness, eloped from their father's cot, the Eagle with a lightsome heart and willing mind, but the younger with many fears and misgivings. For thus the matter stood:—Wat sighed and pined in love for the maiden, but he was young and modest, and could not tell his mind; but he was such a youth as a virgin would love,—handsome, respectable, and virtuous; and a match with him was so likely, that no one ever supposed the girl would make objections to it. Jock, on the other hand, was nearly twice her age, talkative, forward, and self-conceited; and, it was thought, rather wanted to win the girl for a brag, than for any great love he bore her. But Jock was rich; and when one has told that, he has told enough. In short, the admired, the young, the modest, and reserved Snawfleck, in order to get quit of her father's laws of Padan-aram, agreed to make a run-away marriage with Jock the Jewel. But what was far more extraordinary, her youthful lover agreed to accompany her as bridesman, and, on that account, it may possibly be supposed, her eldest sister never objected to accompany her as maid.

The shepherds had each of them provided himself with a good horse, saddle, and pillion; and, as the custom is, the intended bride was committed to the care of the best-man, and the Eagle was mounted behind her brother-in-law that was to be. It was agreed before mounting, that in case of their being parted in the dark by *a pursuit*, or any other accident, their place of rendezvous was to be at the Golden Harrow, in the Candlemaker-Row, towards which they were to make with all speed.

They had a wild moorland path to traverse for some space, on which there were a multiplicity of tracks, but no definite road. The night was dark and chill, and, on such ground, the bride was obliged to ride constantly with her right hand round Wat's waist, and Wat, from sheer instinct, was obliged to press that hand to his bosom, for fear of its being cold—on all such occasions, he generally magnified the intemperance of the night at least seven-fold. When pressing that fair hand to his bosom, Wat sometimes thought to himself, what a hard matter it was that it should so soon be given away to another; and then he wiped a tear from his eye, and did not speak again for a good while. Now the night, as was said, being very dark, and the bride having made a pleasant remark, Wat spontaneously lifted that dear hand from his bosom, in order to attempt passing it to his lips, but (as he told me himself) without the smallest hope of being permitted. But behold, the gentle ravishment was never resisted! On the contrary, as Wat replaced the insulted hand in his bosom, he felt the pressure of his hand gently returned.

Wat was confounded, electrified! and felt as the scalp of his head had been contracting to a point. He felt, in one moment, as if there had been a new existence sprung up within him, a new motive for life, and every great and good action; and, without any express aim, he felt a disposition to push onward. His horse soon began to partake of his rider's buoyancy of spirits, (which a horse always does,) so he cocked up his ears, mended his pace, and, in a short time, was far ahead of the heavy, stagnant-blooded beast on which the Jewel bridegroom and his buxom Eagle rode. She had *her* right arm round *his* waist too, of course; but her hand lacked the exhilarating qualities of her lovely sister's; and yet one would have thought that the Eagle's looks were superior to those of most young girls outgone thirty.

"I wish thae young fools wad take time an' ride at leisure; we'll lose them on this black moor a'thegither, an' then it is a question how we may foregather again," said the bridegroom; at the same time making his hazel sapling play yerk on the hind-quarters of his nag. "Gin the gouk let aught happen to that bit lassie o' mine under cloud o' night, it wad be a' ower wi' me—I could never get aboon that. There are some things, ye ken, Mrs Eagle, for a' your sneering, that a man can never get aboon."

"No very mony o' them, gin a chield hae ony spirit," returned the Eagle. "Take ye time, an' take a little care o' your ain neck an' mine. Let them gang their gates. Gin Wat binna tired o' her, an' glad to get quat o' her, or they win to the ports o' Edinburgh, I hae tint my computation."

"Na, if he takes care o' *her*, that's a' my dread," rejoined he, and at the same time kicked viciously with both heels, and applied the sapling with great vigour. But "the mair haste the waur speed" is a true proverb, for the horse, instead of mending his pace, slackened it, and absolutely grew so frightened for the gutters on the moor, that he would hardly be persuaded to take one of them, even though the sapling was sounding as loud and as thick on his far loin as ever did the whip of a Leith carter. He tried this ford, and the other ford, and smelled and smelled with long-drawn breathings. "Ay, ye may snuff!" cried Jock, losing all patience; "the deil that ye had ever been foaled! Hilloa! Wat Scott, where are ye?"

"Hush, hush, for gudesake," cried the Eagle; "ye'll raise the country, and put a' out thegither."

They listened for Wat's answer, and at length heard a far-away whistle. The Jewel grew like a man half distracted, and, in spite of the Eagle's remonstrances, thrashed on his horse, cursed him, and bellowed out still the more; for he suspected what was the case, that, owing to the turnings and windings of his horse among the haggs, he had lost his aim altogether, and knew not which way he went. Heavens! what a stentorian voice he sent through the moor before him! but he was only answered by the distant whistle, that still went farther and farther away.

When the bride heard these loud cries of desperation so far behind, and in a wrong direction, she was mightily tickled, and laughed so much that she could hardly keep her seat on the horse; at the same time, she continued urging Wat to ride, and he seeing her so much amused and delighted at the embarrassment of her betrothed and sister, humoured her with equal good will, rode off, and soon lost all hearing of the unfortunate bridegroom. They came to the high road at Middleton, cantered on, and reached Edinburgh by break of day, laughing all the way at their unfortunate companions. Instead, however, of putting up at the Golden Harrow, in order to render the bridegroom's embarrassment still more complete, at the bride's suggestion, they went to a different corner of the city, namely, to the White Horse, Canongate. There the two spent the morning, Wat as much embarrassed as any man could be, but his lovely companion in fidgets of delight at thinking of *what* Jock and her sister *would do*. Wat could not understand her for his life, and he conceived that she did not understand herself; but perhaps Wat Scott was mistaken. They breakfasted together; but for all their long and fatiguing journey, neither of them seemed disposed to eat. At length Wat ventured to say, "We'll be obliged to gang to the Harrow, an' see what's become o' our friends."

"O no, no! by no means!" cried she fervently; "I would not, for all the world, relieve them from such a delightful scrape. What the two *will do* is beyond my comprehension."

"If ye want just to bamboozle them a'thegither, the best way to do that is for you and me to marry," said Wat, "an' leave them twa to shift for themselves."

"O that wad be so grand!" said she.

Though this was the thing nearest to honest Wat's heart of all things in the world, he only made the proposal by way of joke, and as such he supposed himself answered. Nevertheless, the answer made the hairs of his head creep once more. "My truly, but that wad gar our friend Jock loup twa gates at aince!" rejoined Wat.

"It wad be the grandest trick that ever was played upon man," said she.

"It wad mak an awfu' sound in the country," said Wat.

"It wad gang through the twa shires like a hand-bell," said she.

"I really think it is worth our while to try't," said he.

"O by a' manner o' means!" cried she, clasping her hands together for joy; "for heaven's sake let us do it."

Wat's breath cut short, and his visage began to alter. He was like to pop into the blessing of a wife rather more suddenly than he anticipated, and he began to wish to himself that the girl might be in her perfect senses. "My dear M—," said he, "are you serious? would you really consent to marry me?"

"Would I consent to marry you!" reiterated she. "That is sickan a question to speer!"

"It is a question," says Wat, "an' I think a very natural ane."

"Ay, it is a question, to be sure," said she; "but it is ane that ye ken ye needna hae put to me to answer, at least till ye hae tauld me whether ye wad marry me or no."

"Yes, faith, I will—there's my hand on it," says Wat. "Now, what say ye?"

"O, Wat, Wat!" exclaimed she, leaning to his arm; "ask the bee if it will hae the flower, ask the lamb if it will hae the ewe that lambed it, or ask the chicken if it will cower aneath the hen—Ye may doubt ony o' thae, but no that I wad take you, far, far, far, in preference to ony other body."

"I wonder ye war sae lang o' thinking about that," said Wat. "Ye ought surely to hae tauld me sooner."

"Sae I wad if ever ye had speered the question," said she.

"What a stupid idiot I was!" exclaimed Wat, and rapped on the floor with his stick for the landlord. "An it be your will, sir, we want a minister," says Wat.

"There's one in the house, sir," said the landlord, chuckling with joy at the prospect of some fun. "Keep a daily chaplain here—Thirlstane's motto, 'Aye ready.' Could ye no contrive to do without him?"

"Na, na, sir, we're folks o' conscience," said Wat; "we hae comed far and foul gate for a preevat but honest hand-fasting."

"Quite right, quite right," said my landlord. "Never saw a more comely country couple. Your business is done for you at once;" at the same time he tapped on the hollow of his hand, as much as to say, some reward must be forthcoming. In a few minutes he returned, and setting the one cheek in at the side of the door, said, with great rapidity, "Could not contrive to do without the minister, then? Better? Kiss, an' come again—eh? what say ye to that? Now's the time—no getting off again. Better?—what?—Can't do without him?"

"O no, sir," said Wat, who was beginning a long explanatory speech, but my landlord cut him short, by introducing a right reverend divine, more than half-seas over. He was a neat, well-powdered, cheerful, little, old gentleman, but one who never asked any farther warrant for the marrying of a couple than the full consent of parties. About this he was very particular, and advised them, in strong set phrases, to beware of entering rashly into that state ordained for the happiness of mankind. Wat thought he was advising him against the match, but told him he was very particularly situated. Parties soon came to a right understanding, the match was made, the minister had his fee, and afterwards he and the landlord invited themselves to the honour, and very particular pleasure, of dining with the young couple at two.

What has become of Jock the Jewel and his copartner all this while? We left them stabled in a mossy moor, surrounded with haggs, and bogs, and mires, every one of which would have taken a horse over the back; at least so Jock's great strong plough-horse supposed, for he grew that he absolutely refused to take one of them. Now, Jock's horse happened to be wrong, for I know the moor very well, and there is not a bog on it all, that will hold a horse still. But it was the same thing in effect to Jock and the Eagle—the horse would have gone eastward or westward along and along the sides of these little dark stripes, which he mistook for tremendous quagmires; or if Jock would have suffered him to turn his head homeward, he would, as Jock said, have galloped for joy; but northwards towards Edinburgh the devil a step would he proceed. Jock thrashed him at one time, stroked his mane at another, at one time coaxed, at another cursed him, till, ultimately, on the horse trying to force his head homeward in spite of Jock's teeth, the latter, in high wrath, struck him a blow on the far ear with all his might. This had the effect of making the animal take the motion of a horizontal wheel, or millstone. The weight of the riders fell naturally to the outer side of the circle—Jock held by the saddle, and the Eagle held by Jock—till down came the whole concern with a thump on the moss. "I daresay, that beast's gane mad the night," said Jock; and, rising, he made a spring at the bridle, for the horse continued still to reel; but, in the dark, our hero missed his hold—off went the horse, like an arrow out of a bow, and left our hapless couple in the midst of a black moor.

"What shall we do now?—shall we turn back?" said Jock.

"Turn back!" said the maid; "certainly not, unless you hae ta'en the rue."

"I wasna thinkin' o' that ava," said he; "but, O, it is an

unfortunate-like business—I dinna like their leaving o' us, nor can I ken what's their meaning."

"They war fear'd for being catched, owing to the noise that you were making," said she.

"And wha wad hae been the loser gin we had been catched? I think the loss then wad hae faun on me," said Jock.

"We'll come better speed wanting the beast," said she; "I wadna wonder that we are in Edinburgh afore them yet."

Wearied and splashed with mud, the two arrived at the Harrow-inn a little after noon, and instantly made inquiries for the bride and best man. A description of one man answers well enough for another to people quite indifferent. Such a country gentleman as the two described, the landlady said, had called twice in the course of the day, and looked into both rooms, without leaving his name. They were both *sure* it was Wat, and rested content. The gentleman came *not* back, so Jock and the Eagle sat and looked at one another. "They will be looking at the grand things o' this grand town," said the maid.

"Ay, maybe," said Jock, in manifest discontent. "I couldna say what they may be looking at, or what they may be doing. When focks gang ower the march to be married, they should gang by themselves twa. But some wadna be tauld sae."

"I canna comprehend where he has ta'en my sister to, or what he's doing wi' her a' this time," said the Eagle.

"I canna say," said Jock, his chagrin still increasing, a disposition which his companion took care to cherish, by throwing out hints and insinuations that kept him constantly in the fidgets, and he seemed to be ruing heartily of all his measures. A late hour arrived, and the two having had a sleepless night and toilsome day, ordered some supper, and separate apartments for the night. They had not yet sat down to supper, when the landlord requested permission for two gentlemen, acquaintances of his, to take a glass together in the same room with our two friends, which being readily granted, who should enter but the identical landlord and parson who had so opportunely buckled the other couple! They had dined with Wat and his bride, and the whisky-toddy had elicited the whole secret from the happy bride-groom. The old gentlemen were highly tickled with the oddity of the adventure, and particularly with the whimsical situation of the pair at the Harrow, and away they went at length on a reconnoitring expedition, having previously settled on the measures to be pursued.

My landlord of the White Horse soon introduced himself to the good graces of the hapless couple by his affability, jokes, quips, and quibbles, and Jock and he were soon as intimate as brothers, and the

maid and he as sweethearts, or old intimate acquaintances. He
commended her as the most beautiful, handsome, courteous, and
accomplished country-lady he ever had seen in his life, and at length
asked Jock if the lady was his sister. No, she was not. Some near
relation, perhaps, that he had the charge of.—No.—"Oh! Beg
pardon—perceive very well—plain—evident—wonder at my blind-
ness," said my landlord of the White Horse—"sweetheart—sweetheart? Hope 'tis to be a match? Not take back such a flower to the
wilderness unplucked—unappropriated that is—to blush unseen—
waste sweetness on the desert air? What? Hope so? Eh? More sense
than that, I hope?"

"You mistak, sir; you mistak. My case is a very particular ane,"
said Jock.

"I wish it were mine, though," said he of the White Horse.

"Pray, sir, are you a married man?" said the Eagle.

"Married? Oh yes, mim, married—to a white horse," returned he.

"To a grey mare, you mean," said the Eagle.

"Excellent! superlative!" exclaimed my landlord. "Minister, what
think you of that? I'm snubbed—cut down—shorn to the quick!
Delightful girl. I declare she is something favoured like the young
country bride we dined with to-day. What say you, minister? Prettier, though—decidedly prettier. More animation, too. Girls from
the same country-side have always a resemblance."

"Sir, did you say you dined with a bride from our country-side?"
said Jock.

"Did so—did so."

"What was the bridegroom like?"

"A soft soles—milk-and-water."

"And his name? You will not tell, maybe,—a W and an S?"

"The same—the same—mum!—W.S., writer to the signet. The
same. An M and a T, too. You understand. Mum."

"Sir, I'll be muckle obliged to you, gin ye'll tak me to where they
are. I hae something to say to them," said Jock, with great emphasis.

"Oh! you are the father, are you? Minister, I'll take you a bet this
is the bride's father and sister. You are too late, sir; far too late. They
are bedded long ago!"

"Bedded? Where bedded?" cried Jock.

"In a hotel, sir," cried the other, in the same tone.

"In hot hell, sir, did you say? Dinna be in a rage, sir. That is a
dreadfu' answer. But an ye'll tak me to where they are bedded, I sall
gar *him* come ower the bed like a lampereel—that's a'."

"What! make a fool of both yourself and others? No, no, the case is past redemption now. A father is to be pitied: but—"

"Sir, you mistak'—I'm not her father."

"What! not her father? Hope you are not the injured husband, sir? What!"

"One that should have been so, however."

"What! should have been an injured husband? O Lord!"

About this stage of the conversation, a letter was handed in "to Miss Tod, at the Golden Harrow;" but the bearer went off, and waited no answer. The contents were as follows:—

> "Dear Sister,
>
> This cometh to let you know, that I have married Wat, thinking you and Jock had turned on the height, and that he had taken the rue; so I thought, after leaving the country to be married, I could never set up my face in it again, without a man; for you know a woman leaving home with a man, as we both have done, can never be received into a church or family again, unless she be married on him; and you must consider of this; for if you are comed to Edinburg with a man, you need never go home again. John hath used me bad, and made me do the thing I may rue, but I could not help it. I hope he will die an old batchelor, as he is, and never taste the joys of the married state. We will remain here another night, for some refreshment, and then I go home to his mother. This business will make a terrible noise in the country. I would not have gone home a maiden for all the whole world."

When the Eagle read this, she assumed symptoms of great distress, and after much beseeching and great attention by the two strangers, she handed the letter to Jock, shewing him that she could never go home again after what had happened. He scratched his head often, and acknowledged that "Maggy's was a ticklish case," and then observed that he would see what was to be done about it to-morrow. My landlord called for a huge bowl of punch, which he handed liberally around. The matter was discussed in all its bearings. The minister made it clearly out, that the thing had been fore-ordained, and it was out of their power to counteract it. My landlord gave the preference to the Eagle in every accomplishment. Jock's heart grew mellow, while the maid blushed and wept; and, in short, they went to their beds that night a married couple, to the great joy of the Eagle's heart; for never one doubted that the whole scheme was a con-trivance of her own. A bold stroke to get hold of the man with the money. She knew Wat would grip to her sister at a word or hint, and

then the Jewel had scarcely an alternative. He took the disappointment and affront so much to heart, that he removed with his Eagle
to America, at the Whitsunday following, where their success was
beyond anticipation, and where they were both living at an advanced age about twelve years ago, without any surviving family.
It is a pity I should have been so long with this story, which forms
such a particular era in the Shepherd's Love Calendar.

Altrive Lake, January 27, 1825.

General Anecdotes.

Sheep.

THE sheep has scarcely any marked character, save that of natural affection, of which it possesses a very great share. It is otherwise a stupid, indifferent animal, having few wants, and fewer expedients. The old black-faced, or forest breed, have far more powerful capabilities than any of the finer breeds that have been introduced into Scotland, and therefore the few anecdotes that I have to relate, shall be confined to them.

The most singular one that I know of, to be quite well authenticated, is that of a black ewe, that returned with her lamb from a farm in the head of Glen-Lyon, to the farm of Harehope, in Tweeddale, and accomplished the journey in nine days. She was soon missed by her owner, and a shepherd followed her all the way to Crieff, where he turned, and gave her up. He got intelligence of her all the way, and every one told him that she absolutely persisted in travelling on—She would not be turned, regarding neither sheep nor shepherd by the way. Her lamb was often far behind, and she had constantly to urge it on, by impatient bleating. She unluckily came to Stirling on the morning of a great annual fair, about the end of May, and judging it imprudent to adventure through the crowd with her lamb, she halted on the north side of the town the whole day, where she was seen by hundreds lying close by the road side. But next morning, when all grew quiet, a little after the break of day, she was observed stealing quietly through the town, in apparent terror of the dogs that were prowling about the street. The last time she was seen on the road, was at a toll-bar near St Ninian's; the man stopped her, thinking she was a strayed animal, and that some one would claim her. She tried several times to break through per force when he opened the gate, but he always prevented her, and at length she turned patiently again. She had found some means of eluding him, however, for home she came on a Sabbath morning, the 4th of June; and she left the farm of Lochs, in Glen-Lyon, either on the Thursday afternoon, or Friday morning, the week previous but one. The farmer of Harehope paid the Highland farmer the price of her, and she lived on her native farm till she died of old age, in her seventeenth year.

I have heard of sheep returning from Yorkshire to the Highlands; but then I always suspected that they might have been lost by the way. But this is certain, that when once one, or a few sheep, get away from the rest of their acquaintances, they return homeward with great eagerness and perseverance. I have lived beside a drove-road the better part of my life, and many stragglers have I seen bending their steps northward in the spring of the year. A shepherd rarely sees these journeyers twice; if he sees them, and stops them in the morning, they are gone long before night; and if he sees them at night, they will be gone many miles before morning. This strong attachment to the place of their nativity, is much more predominant in our own aboriginal breed, than in any of the other kinds with which I am acquainted.

There is another peculiarity in their nature, of which I have witnessed innumerable instances. I shall only relate one, for they are all alike, and show how much the sheep is a creature of habit.

A shepherd in Blackhouse bought a few sheep from another in Crawmel, about ten miles distant. In the spring following, one of the ewes went back to her native place, and yeaned on a wild hill called Crawmel Craig. On a certain day, about the beginning of July following, the shepherd went and brought home his ewe and lamb— took the fleece from the ewe, and kept the lamb for one of his stock. The lamb lived and throve, became a hog and a gimmer, and never offered to leave home; but when three years of age, and about to have her first lamb, she vanished; and the morning after, the Crawmel shepherd, in going his rounds, found her with a new-yeaned lamb on the very gair of the Crawmel Craig, where she was lambed herself. She remained there till the first week of July, the time when she was brought a lamb herself, and then she came home with hers of her own accord; and this custom she continued annually with the greatest punctuality as long as she lived. At length her lambs, when they came of age, began the same practice, and the shepherd was obliged to dispose of the whole breed.

But with regard to their natural affection, the instances that might be mentioned are without number, stupid and fushionless creatures as they are. When one loses its sight in a flock of short sheep, it is rarely abandoned to itself in that hapless and helpless state. Some one always attaches itself to it, and by bleating calls it back from the precipice, the lake, the pool, and all dangers whatever. There is a disease among sheep, called by shepherds the Breakshugh, a sort of deadly dysentery, which is as infectious as fire in a flock. Whenever a sheep feels itself seized by this, it instantly absents itself from all the rest, shunning their society with the greatest care; it even hides itself, and is often very hard to be found. Though this propensity can hardly be attributed to natural instinct, it is, at all events, a provision of nature of the greatest kindness and beneficence.

There is another manifest provision of nature with regard to these animals, which is, that the more inhospitable the land is on which they feed, the greater their kindness and attention to their young. I once herded two years on a wild and bare farm called Willenslee, on the border of Mid-Lothian, and of all the sheep I ever saw, these were the kindest and most affectionate to their young. I was often deeply affected at scenes which I witnessed there. We had one very hard winter, so that our sheep grew lean in the spring, and the thwarter-ill (a sort of paralytic affection) came among them, and carried off a number. Often have I seen these poor victims, when fallen down to rise no more, even when unable to lift their heads from the ground, holding up the leg, to invite the starving lamb to the miserable pittance that the udder still could supply. I had never seen aught more painfully affecting.

It is well known that it is a custom with shepherds, when a lamb dies, if the mother have sufficiency of milk, to bring her in and put another lamb to her. I have described the process somewhere else;—it is done by putting the skin of the dead lamb upon the living one; the ewe immediately acknowledges the relationship, and after the skin has warmed on it, so as to give it something of the smell of her own progeny, and it has sucked her two or three times, she accepts and nourishes it as her own ever after. Whether it is from joy at this apparent reanimation of her young one, or a little doubt remaining on her mind that she would fain dispel, I cannot decide; but, for a number of days, she shows far more fondness, more bleating, and caressing, over this one, than she did formerly over the one that was really her own.

But this is not what I wanted to explain; it was, that such sheep as thus lose their lambs, must be driven to a house with dogs, so that the lamb may be put to them; for they will only take it in a dark confined place. But here, in Willenslee, I never needed to drive home a sheep by force, with dogs, or in any other way than the following: I found every ewe, of course, standing hanging her head over her dead lamb, and having a piece of twine with me for the purpose, I tied that to the lamb's neck, or foot, and trailing it along, the ewe followed me into any house or fold that I chose to lead her. Any of them would have followed me in that way for miles, with her nose close on the lamb, which she never quitted for a moment, except to chase the dog, which she would not suffer to walk near me. I often, out of curiosity, led them in to the side of the kitchen fire by this means, into the midst of servants and dogs; but the more that dangers multiplied around the ewe, she clung the closer to her dead offspring, and thought of nothing but protecting it.

That same year there was a severe blast of snow came on by night about the latter end of April, which destroyed several scores of our lambs; and as we had not enow of twins and odd lambs for the mothers that had lost theirs, of course we selected the best ewes, and put lambs to them. As we were making the distribution, I requested of my master to spare me a lamb for a hawked ewe which he knew, and which was standing over a dead lamb in the head of the hope, about four miles from the house. He would not do it, but bid me let her stand over her lamb for a day or two, and perhaps a twin would be forthcoming. I did so, and truly she did stand to her charge; so truly, that I think the like never was equalled by any of the woolly race. I visited her every morning and evening, and for the first eight days never catched her above two or three yards from the lamb; and always, as I went my rounds, she eyed me long ere I came near her, and kept tramping with her foot, and whistling through her nose, to fright away the dog. He got a regular chase twice a-day as I passed by, but however excited and fierce a ewe may be, she never offers any resistance to mankind, being perfectly and meekly passive to them. The weather grew fine and warm, and the dead lamb soon decayed, which the body of a dead lamb does particularly soon; but still this affectionate and desolate creature kept hanging over the poor remains with an affection that seemed to be nourished by hopelessness. It often drew the tears from my eyes to see her hanging with such fondness over a few bones, mixed with a small portion of wool. For the first fortnight she never quitted the spot, and for another week she visited it every morning and evening, uttering a few kindly and heart-piercing bleats each time; till at length every remnant of her offspring vanished, mixing with the soil.

Prayers.

THERE is, I believe, no class of men professing the Protestant faith, so truly devout as the shepherds of Scotland. They get all the learning that the parish schools afford; are thoroughly acquainted with the Scriptures of truth; deeply read in theological works, and really, I am sorry to say it, generally much better informed than their masters. Every shepherd is a man of respectability—he must be so, else he must cease to be a shepherd. His master's flock is entirely committed to his care, and if he does not manage it with constant care, caution, and decision, he cannot be employed. A part of the stock is his own, however, so that his interest in it is the same with that of his master; and being thus the most independent of men, if he cherishes a good behaviour, and the most insignificant if he loses the esteem of his employers, he has every motive for maintaining an unimpeachable character.

It is almost impossible, also, that he can be other than a religious character, being so much conversant with the Almighty in his works, in all the goings-on of nature, and the control of the otherwise resistless elements. He feels himself a dependent being, morning and evening, on the great Ruler of the universe; he holds converse with him in the cloud and the storm—on the misty mountain and the darksome waste—in the whirling drift and the overwhelming thaw —and even in voices and sounds that are only heard by the howling cliff or solitary dell. How can such a man fail to be impressed with the presence of an eternal God, of an omniscient eye, and an almighty arm?

The position generally holds good; for, as I have said, the shepherds are a religious and devout set of men, and among them the antiquated but delightful exercise of family worship is never neglected. It is always gone about with decency and decorum, but formality being a thing despised, there is no composition that I ever heard so truly original as these prayers occasionally are; sometimes for rude eloquence and pathos, at other times for a nondescript sort of pomp, and not unfrequently for a plain and somewhat unbecoming familiarity.

One of the most notable men for this sort of family eloquence was Adam Scott, in Upper Dalgliesh. I had an uncle who herded with him, and from him I had many quotations from Adam Scott's prayers:—a few of them are as follow.

"We particularly thank thee for thy great goodness to Meg, and that ever it came into your head to take any thought of sic an useless baw-waw as her." (This was a little girl that had been somewhat miraculously saved from drowning.) "For thy mercy's sake—for the sake of thy poor sinfu' servants that are now addressing thee in their ain shilly-shally way, and for the sake o' mair than we dare weel name to thee, hae mercy on Rob. Ye ken yoursell he is a wild mischievous callant, and thinks nae mair o' committing sin than a dog does o' licking a dish; but put thy hook in his nose, and thy bridle in his gab, and gar him come back to thee wi' a jerk that he'll no forget the langest day he has to leeve."

"Dinna forget poor Jamie, wha's far away frae amang us the night.

Keep thy arm o' power about him, an' O, I wish ye wad endow him wi' a little spunk and smeddum to act for himsell. For if ye dinna, he'll be but a bauchle in this world, and a back-sitter in the neist."

"We desire to be submissive to thy will and pleasure at a' times, but our desires are like new-bridled colts, or dogs that are first laid to the brae; they run wild frae under our control. Thou hast added one to our family—so has been thy will, but it would never hae been mine—if it's of thee, do thou bless and prosper the connexion; but if the fool hath done it out of carnal desire, against all reason and credit, may the cauld rainy cloud of adversity settle on his habitation, till he shiver in the flame that his folly hath kindled." (I think this was said to be in allusion to the marriage of one of his sons.)

"We're a' like hawks, we're a' like snails, we're a' like slogie riddles;—like hawks to do evil, like snails to do good, and like slogie riddles, that let through a' the good, and keep the bad."

"Bring down the tyrant and his lang neb, for he has done muckle ill the year, and gie him a cup o' thy wrath, and gin he winna tak that, gie him kelty."

Kelty signifies double, or two cups. This was an occasional petition for one season only, and my uncle never could comprehend what it meant.—The general character of Scott was one of decision and activity; constant in the duties of religion, but not over strict with regard to some of its moral precepts.

I have heard the following petitions sundry times in the family prayers of an old relation of my own, long since gone to his rest.

"And moreover and aboon, do thou bless us a' wi' thy best warldly blessings—wi' bread for the belly an' theeking for the back, a lang stride an' a clear ee-sight. Keep us from a' proud prossing and upsetting—from foul flaips, and stray steps, and from all unnecessary trouble."

But, in generalities, these prayers are never half so original as when they come to particular incidents that affect only the petitioners; for there are some things happening to them daily, which they deem it their bounden duty to remember before their Maker, either by way of petition, confession, or thanksgiving. The following was told to me as a part of the same worthy old man's prayer occasionally, for some weeks before he left a master, in whose father's service and his own the decayed shepherd had spent the whole of his life.

"Bless my master and his family with thy best blessings in Christ Jesus. Prosper all his worldly concerns, especially that valuable part which is committed to my care. I have worn out my life in the service of him and his fathers, and thou knowest that I have never bowed a knee before thee without remembering them. Thou knowest, also, that I have never studied night's rest, nor day's comfort, when put in competition with their interest. The foulest days and the stormiest nights were to me as the brightest of summer; and if he has done weel in casting out his auld servant, do thou forgive him. I forgive him with all my heart, and will never cease to pray for him; but when the hard storms o' winter come, may he miss the braid bonnet and the gray head, and say to himself, 'I wish to God that my auld herd had been here yet.' I ken o' neither house nor habitation this night, but for the sake o' them amang us that canna do for themsells, I ken thou wilt provide ane; for though thou hast tried me with hard and sair adversities, I have had more than my share of thy mercies, and thou ken'st better than I can tell thee that thou hast never bestowed them on an unthankful heart."

This is the sentence, exactly as it was related to me, but I am sure it is not correct; for, though very like his manner, I never heard him come so near the English language in one sentence in my life. I once heard him say, in allusion to a chapter he had been reading about David and Goliath, and just at the close of his prayer: "And when our besetting sins come bragging and blowstering upon us, like Gully o' Gath, O enable us to fling off the airmer and hairnishin' o' the law, whilk we haena proved, an' whup up the simple sling o' the gospel, and nail the smooth stanes o' redeeming grace into their foreheads."

Of all the compositions, for simple pathos, that I ever saw or heard, his prayer, on the evening of that day on which he buried his only son, excelled; but at this distance of time, it is impossible for me to do it justice; and hoping that it is recorded in heaven, I dare not take it on me to garble it. He began the subject of his sorrows thus:—

"Thou hast seen meet, in thy wise providence, to remove the staff out of my right hand, at the very time when, to us poor sand-blind mortals, it appeared that I stood maist in need o't. But O it was a sicker ane, an' a sure ane, an' a dear ane to my heart! an' how I'll climb the steep hill o' auld age an' sorrow without it, thou may'st ken, but I dinna."

His singing of the psalms beat all exhibitions that ever were witnessed of a sacred nature. He had not the least air of sacred music; there was no attempt at it; it was a sort of recitative of the most grotesque kind; and yet he delighted in it, and sung far more verses every night than is customary. The first time I heard him I was very young; but I could not stand it, but leaned myself back into a bed, and laughed till the sweat ran off me in streams. He had likewise an out-of-the-way custom, in reading a portion of Scripture every night, of always making remarks as he went on. And such remarks! There was one evening I heard him reading a chapter—I have forgot where it was—but he came to words like these: "And other nations, whom the great and noble Asnapper brought over"——John stopped short, and, considering for a little, says: "Asnapper! whaten a king was he that? I dinna mind o' ever hearing tell o' him afore."

"I dinna ken," said one of the girls; "but he has a queer name."— "It is something like a goolly knife," said a younger one. "Whisht, dame," said John, and then went on with the chapter. I believe it was about the fourth or fifth chapter of Ezra. He seldom missed a few observations of this sort for a single night.

There was another night, not long after the time above noticed, that he was reading of the feats of one Sanballat, who set himself against the building of the second Temple. On closing the Bible John uttered a long hemh! and then I knew there was something forthcoming. "He has been another nor a gude ane that," added he; "I hae nae brow o' their Sandy-ballat."

There was another time that he stopped in the middle of a chapter and uttered his "hemh!" of disapproval, and then added, "If it had been the Lord's will, I think they might hae left out that verse."—"It hasna been his will, though," said one of the girls—"It seems sae," said John. I have entirely forgot what he was reading about, and am often vexed at having forgot the verse that John wanted expunged from the Bible. It was in some of the minor prophets.

There was another time he came to his brother-in-law's house, where I was then living, and John being the oldest man, the Bible was laid down before him to make family worship. He made no objections, but began, as was always his custom, by asking a blessing on their devotions; and when he had done, it being customary for those who make family worship to sing straight through the Psalms from beginning to end, John says, "We'll sing in your ordinary. Where is it?"—"We do not always sing in one place," said the gudeman of the house. "Na, I daresay no, or else ye'll make that place threadbare," said John, in a short crabbed style, manifestly suspecting that his friend was not regular in his family devotions. This piece of sharp wit after the worship was begun had to me an effect highly ludicrous.

When he came to give out the chapter, he remarked, that there would be no ordinary there either, he supposed. "We have been reading in Job for a long time," said the gudeman. "How long?" said John slyly, as he turned over the leaves, thinking to catch his friend at fault. "O, I dinna ken that," said the other; "but there's a mark laid in that will tell you the bit."—"If you hae read *vera* long in Job," says

John, "you will hae made him threadbare too, for the mark is only at the ninth chapter." There was no answer, so he read on. In the course of the chapter he came to these words—"Who commandeth the sun, and it riseth not."—"I never heard of Him doing that," says John. "But Job, honest man, maybe means the darkness that was in the land o' Egypt. It wad be a fearsome thing an the sun warna till rise."

A little farther on he came to these words—"Which maketh Arcturus, Orion, and Pleiades, and the chambers of the south." "I hae often wondered at that verse," says John. "Job has been a grand philosopher! The Pleiades are the se'en sterns,—I ken them; and Orion, that's the King's Ellwand; but I'm never sae sure about Arcturus. I fancy he's ane o' the plennits, or maybe him that hauds the gouden plough."

On reading the last chapter of the book of Job, when he came to the enumeration of the patriarch's live stock, he remarked, "He has had an unco sight o' creatures. Fourteen thousand sheep! How mony was that?"—"He has had seven hunder scores," said one. "Ay," said John, "it was an unco swarm o' creatures. There wad be a dreadfu' confusion at his clippings and spainings. Six thousand camels, a thousand yoke of oxen, and a thousand she-asses. What, in the wide warld, did he do wi' a' thae creatures? Wad it no hae been mair purpose-like if he had had them a' milk kie?"— "Wha wad he hae gotten to have milked them?" said one of the girls. "It's vera true," said John.

One time, during a long and severe lying storm of snow, in allusion to some chapter he had been reading, he prayed as follows: (This is from hearsay.) "Is the whiteness of desolation to lie still on the mountains of our land for ever? Is the earthly hope o' thy servants to perish frae the face of the earth? The flocks on a thousand hills are thine, and their lives or deaths wad be naething to thee—thou wad neither be the richer nor the poorer; but it is a great matter to us. Have pity, then, on the lives o' thy creatures, for beast an' body are a' thy handywark, and send us the little wee cludd out o' the sea like a man's hand, to spread and darken, and pour and plash, till the green gladsome face o' nature aince mair appear."

During the smearing season one year, it was agreed that each shepherd, young and old, should ask a blessing and return thanks at meal-time, in his turn, beginning at the eldest, and going off at the youngest; that, as there was no respect of persons with God, so there should be none shown among neighbours. John being the eldest, the graces began with him, and went decently on till they came to the youngest, who obstinately refused. Of course it devolved again on

John, who, taking off his broad bonnet, thus addressed his Maker with great fervency:—

"O our gracious Lord and Redeemer, thou hast said in thy blessed word, that those who are ashamed of thee and thy service, of them thou wilt be ashamed when thou comest into thy kingdom. Now, all that we humbly beg of thee at this time is, that Geordie may not be reckoned amang that unhappy number. Open the poor chield's heart an' his een to a sight o' his lost condition; an' though he be that prood that he'll no ask a blessing o' thee, neither for himsell nor us, do thou grant us a' thy blessing ne'ertheless, an' him amang the rest, for Christ's sake. Amen."

The young man felt the rebuke very severely, his face grew as red as flame, and it was several days before he could assume his usual hilarity. Had I lived with John a few years, I could have picked up his remarks on the greater part of the Scriptures, for to read and not make remarks was out of his power. The story of Ruth was a great favourite with him—he often read it to his family of a Sabbath evening, as "a good lesson on naturality;" but he never failed making the remark, that "it was nae mair nor decency in her to creep in beside the douss man i' the night-time when he was sleeping."

Odd Characters.

AMONG the first of these in this district was old Will o' Phaup, one of the genuine Laidlaws of Craik, where he was born in 1691. He was shepherd in Phaup for fifty-five years. For feats of frolic, strength, and agility, he had no equal in his day. In the hall of the laird, at the farmer's ingle, and in the shepherd's cot, Will was alike a welcome guest, and in whatever company he was, he kept the whole in one roar of merriment. In Will's days brandy was the common drink in this country; as for whisky, it was, like silver in the days of Solomon, nothing accounted of. Good black French brandy was the constant beverage, and a heavy neighbour Will was on it. Many a hard bouse he had about Moffat, and many a race he ran, generally for wagers of so many pints of brandy, and in all his life never was beat. He once ran at Moffat for a wager of five guineas, which one of the chiefs of the Johnstons betted on his head. His opponent was a celebrated runner from Crawford-Moor, of the name of Blaikley, on whose head, or rather on whose feet, a Captain Douglas had wagered. Will knew nothing of the match till he went to Moffat, and was very averse to it. "No that he was ony way fear'd for the chap," he said, "but he had on a' his ilkaday claes, an' as a' the leddies an' gentlemen at Moffat-wall war to be there to see the race, he didna like to appear afore them like an assie whalp."

However, he was urged, and obliged to go out and strip; and, as he told it, "a poor figure I made beside the chield wi' his grand ruffled sark. I was sae affrontit at thinking that Will o' Phaup should hae made sic a dirty shabby appearance afore sae mony grit folks an' bonny leddies, that the deil a fit I could rin mair nor I had been a diker. My sark was as din as it had been row'd amang the asse, an' my breeks a' mendit wi' clouts o' different colours. Shame fa' me gin I didna wuss mysell i' the water out-ower the lugs. The race was down on Annan-side, an' jimply a mile, out an' in; an', at the very first, the man wi' the ruffled sark flew off like a hare, an' left poor Will o' Phaup to come waughlin up ahint him like a singit cur, wi' his din sark and his cloutit breeks. I had neither heart nor power till a very queer accident befel me; for, Scots grund! disna the tying o' my cloutit breeks brek loose, and in a moment they war at my heels, and there was I standin' like a hapshekel'd staig! 'Off wi' them, Phaup! Off wi' them!' cries ane. Od, sir, I just sprang out o' them, and that instant I fand my spirits rise to the proper pitch. I kend though I had tarry breeks and a din sark, I had as bonny a skin as was on the field; an' though the leddies should turn about their backs, what could I help it. But instead o' that, the wild gillies only clappet their hands, an' shoutit out, 'Weel pro'en, Will o' Phaup! Hooray! Phaup for ever yet!' The chield was clean afore me, but I fand that if he war a eagle I wad o'ertake him, for I scarcely kend whether I was touching the grund or fleeing in the air, and as I came by Mr Welch, I heard him saying, 'By G—, Phaup has him yet!' for he saw Blaikley failing. I got by him, but I had not muckle to brag o', for he keepit the step on me till within a gun-shot o' the starting-post.

"Then there was sic a fraze about me by the winning party, and naething wad serve them but that I should dine wi' them in the public room. 'Na, fiend be there then, Mr Johnson,' says I, 'for though your leddies only leuch at my accident, if I war to dinner wi' them in this state, I kenna how they might tak it.'"

When a young lad, only sixteen years of age, and the very first year he was in Phaup, his master betted the price of his whole drove of Phaup hogs on his head, at a race with an Englishman on Stagshaw-bank. James Anderson, Esq. of Ettrickhall, was then farmer of Phaup, and he had noted at the shedding, before his young shepherd left home, that whenever a sheep got by wrong, he never did more than run straight after it, lay hold of it by sheer speed, and bring it back in his arms. So the laird having formed high ideas of Will's swiftness, without letting him know of the matter, first got an English gentleman into a heat, by bragging the English runners with Scots ones, and then proffered betting the price of his 300 wedder hogs, that he had a poor starved barefooted boy who was helping to drive them,—whom he believed to be about the worst runner in Scotland, —who would yet beat the best Englishman that could be found in Stagshawbank-fair.

The Englishman's national pride was aroused, as well it might, his countrymen being well known as the superior runners. The bet was taken, and Will won it with the greatest ease for his master, without being made aware of the stake for which he ran. This he never knew till some months afterwards, that his master presented him with a guinea, a pair of new shoes, and a load of oat-meal, for winning him the price of the Phaup hogs. Will was exceedingly proud of the feat he had performed, as well as of the present, which, he remarked, was as much to him as the price of the hogs was to his master. From that day forth he was never beat at a fair race.

He never went to Moffat, that the farmers did not get him into their company, and then never did he get home to Phaup sober. The mad feats which he then performed, were, for an age, the standing jokes of the country, and many of his sayings settled into regular proverbs or by-words. His great oath was "Scots ground!" And "Scots ground, quo' Will o' Phaup," is a standing exclamation to this day—"one plash more, quo' Will o' Phaup," is another,—and there are many similar ones. This last had its origin in one of those Moffat bouses, from which the farmer of Selcouth and Will were returning by night greatly inebriated, the former riding, and Will running by his side. Moffat water being somewhat flooded, the farmer proposed taking Laidlaw on the horse behind him. Will sprang on, but, as he averred, never got seated right, till the impatient animal plunged into the water, and the two friends came off, and floated down the river, hanging by one another. The farmer got to his feet first, but in pulling out Will, lost his equilibrium a second time, and plunging headlong into the stream, down he went. Will was then in the utmost perplexity, for, with the drink and ducking together, he was quite benumbed, and the night was as dark as pitch; he ran down the side of the stream to succour his friend, and losing all sight of him, he knew not what to do; but hearing a great plunge, he made towards the place, calling out, "One plash more, sir, and I have you—One plash more," quo' Will o' Phaup; but all was silent! "Scots ground!" quo' Will o' Phaup—"a man drown'd, an' me here!" Will ran to a stream, and took his station in the middle of the water, in hopes of feeling his drowning friend come against his legs;—but the farmer got safely out by himself.

There was another time at Moffat, that he was taken in, and had to pay a dinner and drink for a whole large party of gentlemen. I have forgot how it happened, but think it was by a wager. He had not only to part with all his money, but had to pawn his whole stock of sheep. He then came home with a heavy heart, told his wife what he had done, and that he was a ruined man. She said, that since he had saved the cow, they would do well enough.

The money was repaid afterwards, so that Will did not actually lose his stock; but after that, he went seldom to Moffat. He fell upon a much easier plan of getting fun; for, at that period, there were constantly bands of smugglers passing from the Solway, through the wild region where he lived, towards the Lothians. From these Will purchased occasionally a stock of brandy, and then the gentlemen and farmers came all and drank with him, paying him at the enormous rate of a shilling per bottle, all lesser measures being despised, and out of repute at Phaup. It became a place of constant rendezvous, but a place where they drank too deep to be a safe place for gentlemen to meet. There were two rival houses of Andersons at that time that never ceased quarrelling, and they were wont always to come to Phaup with their swords by their sides. Being all exceedingly stout men, and equally good swordsmen, it may easily be supposed they were dangerous neighbours to meet in such a wild remote place. Accordingly, there were many quarrels and bloody bouts there as long as the Andersons possessed Phaup; after which, the brandy system was laid aside. Will twice saved his master's life in these affrays;—once, when he had drawn on three of Amos's tenants of Potburn, but they had mastered his sword, broken it, and were dragging him to the river by the neckcloth. Will knocked down one, cut his master's neckcloth, and defended him stoutly till he gathered his breath, and then the two jointly did thrash the Amoses to their hearts' satisfaction. And another time, from the sword of Michael of Tushielaw; but he could not help the two fighting a duel afterwards, which was the cause of much mischief, and many heart-burnings, among these haughty relatives.

Will and his master once fought a clean battle themselves two, up in a wild glen called Phaup Coom. They differed about a young horse, which the laird had sent there to graze, and which he thought had not been well treated; and so bitter did the recriminations grow between them, that the laird threatened to send Will to hell. Will defied him, on which he attacked him furiously with his cane, while the shepherd defended himself as resolutely with his staff. The combat was exceedingly sharp and severe, but the gentleman was too scientific for the shepherd, and hit him many blows about the head and shoulders, while Will could not hit him once, "all that he could thrash on." The latter was determined, however, not to yield, and fought on, although, as he termed it, "the blood began to blind his een." He tried several times to close with his master, but found him so complete in both his defences and offences, that he never could accomplish it, but always suffered for his temerity. At length he "jouked down his head, took a lounder across the shoulders, and, in the meantime, hit his master across the shins." This ungentlemanly blow quite paralysed the laird, and the cane dropped out of his hand, on which Will closed with him, mastered him with ease, laying him down, and holding him fast;— but all that he could do, he could not pacify him,—he still swore he would have his heart's blood. Will had then no resource, but to spring up, and bound away to the hill. The laird pursued for a time, but he might as well have tried to catch a roe-buck; so he went back to Phaup, took his horse in silence, and rode away home. Will expected a summons of removal next day, or next term at the farthest, but Mr Anderson took no notice of the affair, nor ever so much as mentioned it again.

Will had many pitched battles with the bands of smugglers, in defence of his master's grass, for they never missed unloading on the lands of Phaup, and turning their horses to the best grass they could find. According to his account, these fellows were exceedingly lawless, and accounted nothing of taking from the country people whatever they needed in emergencies. The gipsies, too, were then accustomed to traverse the country in bands of from twenty to forty, and were no better than freebooters. But to record every one of Will o' Phaup's heroic feats, would require a volume. I shall, therefore, only mention one trait more of his character, which was this—

He was the last man of this wild region, who heard, saw, and conversed with the fairies, and that not once or twice, but at sundry times and seasons. The shealing at which Will lived all the better part of his life, at Old Upper Phaup, was one of the most lonely and dismal situations that ever was the dwelling of human creatures. I have often wondered how such a man could live so long, and rear so numerous and respectable a family, in such a habitation. It is on the very outskirts of Ettrick Forest, quite out of the range of social intercourse, a fit retirement for lawless banditti, and a genial one for the last retreat of the spirits of the glen—before taking their final leave of the land of their love, in which the light of the gospel then grew too bright for their tiny moonlight forms. There has Will beheld them riding in long and beautiful array, by the light of the moon, and even in the summer twilight; and there has he seen them sitting in seven circles, in the bottom of a deep ravine, drinking nectar out of cups of silver and gold, no bigger than the dew-cup flower; and there did he behold their wild unearthly eyes, all of one bright sparkling blue, turned every one upon him at the same moment, and heard their mysterious whisperings, of which he knew no word, save now and then the repetition of his own name, which was always done in a strain of pity. Will was coming from the hill in a dark misty evening in winter, and, for a good while, imagined he heard a great gabbling of children's voices, not far from him, which still grew more and more audible; it being before sunset, he had no spark of fear, but set about investigating from whence the sounds and laughter proceeded. He, at length, discovered that they issued from a deep cleugh not far distant, and thinking it was a band of gipsies, or some marauders, he laid down his bonnet and his plaid, and creeping softly over the heath, he reached the brink of the precipice, and peeping over, to his utter astonishment, beheld the fairies sitting in seven circles, on a green spot in the bottom of the dell, where no green spot ever was before. They were apparently eating and drinking; but all their motions were so quick and momentary, he could not well say what they were doing. Two or three at the queen's back appeared to be baking bread. They were all ladies, and their numbers quite countless—dressed in green pollonians, and grass-green bonnets on their heads. He perceived at once by their looks, their giggling, and their peals of laughter, that he was discovered. Still fear took no possession of his heart, for it was daylight, and the blessed sun was in heaven, although obscured by clouds; till at length he heard them pronounce his own name audibly twice; Will then began to think it might not be quite so safe to wait till they pronounced it a third time, and at that moment of hesitation it first came into his mind that it was All-hallow-eve! There was no farther occasion to warn Will to rise and run, for he well knew the fairies were privileged on that day and that night, to do what seemed good in their own eyes. "His hair," he said, "stood all up like the birses on a sow's back, an' every bit o' his body, outside and in, prinkled as it had been brunt wi' nettles." He ran home as fast as his feet could carry him, and greatly were his children astonished (for he was then a widower) to see their father come running like a madman, without either his bonnet or plaid. He assembled them to prayers, and shut the door, but did not tell them what he had seen for several years.

There was another time that he followed a whole troop of them up a wild glen called Entertrony, from one end to the other, without ever being able to come up with them, although they never appeared to be more than twenty paces in advance. Neither were they flying from him; for instead of being running at their speed, as he was doing, they seemed to be standing in a large circle. It happened to be the day after a Moffat fair, and he supposed them to be a party of his neighbours returning from it, who wished to lead him a long chase before they suffered themselves to be overtaken. He heard them speaking, singing, and laughing; and being a man so fond of sociality, he exerted himself to come up with them, but to no purpose. Several times did he hail them, and desire them to stay, and tell him the news of the fair; but he was only answered by a peal of eldrich laughter, that seemed to spread along the skies over his head. At length he began to suspect that that unearthly laugh was not altogether unknown to him. He stood still to consider, and that moment the laugh was repeated, and a voice out of the crowd called to him in a shrill laughing tone, "Ha, ha, ha! Will o' Phaup, look to your ain hearthstane the night." Will again threw off every encumbrance, and fled home to his lonely cot, the most likely spot on the estate for the fairies to congregate; but it is wonderful what safety concentres round a man's own hearth and family circle.

There was another time, when he was a right old man, that he was sitting on a little green hillock at the end of his house, in the evening, resting himself, that there came three little boys up to him, all exactly like one another, when the following short dialogue ensued between Will and them.

"Good e'en t'ye, Will Laidlaw."

"Good e'en t'ye, creatures. Where ir ye gaun this gate?"

"Can ye gie us up-putting for the night?"

"I think three sickan bits o' shreds o' hurchins winna be ill to put up.—Where came ye frae?"

"Frae a place that ye dinna ken. But we are come on a commission to you."

"Come away in then, an' tak sic cheer as we hae."

Will rose and led the way into the house, and the little boys followed; and as he went, he said carelessly, without looking back, "What's your commission to me, bairns?" He thought they were some gentleman's sons come from his master.

"We are sent to demand a silver key that you have in your possession."

Will was astounded; and standing still to consider of some old transaction, he said, without lifting his eyes from the ground,—

"A silver key? In God's name, where came ye from?"

There was no answer, on which Will wheeled round and round, and round; but the tiny beings were all gone, and Will never saw them more. At the name of God, they vanished in the twinkling of an eye. It is curious that I never should have heard the secret of the silver key, or indeed, whether there was such a thing or not.

But Will once saw a vision which was more unaccountable than this still. On his way from Moffat one time, about midnight, he perceived a light very near to the verge of a steep hill, which he knew perfectly well, but I have forgot whether it was on the lands of Bodsbeck or Selcouth, though I think it was on the latter. The light appeared exactly like one from a window, and as if a lamp moved frequently within. His path was by the bottom of the hill, and the light being almost close at the top, he had at first no thoughts of visiting it; but as it shone in sight for a full mile, his curiosity to see what it was continued still to increase as he approached nearer. At length, on coming to the bottom of the steep bank, it appeared so bright and so nigh, that he determined to climb the steep and see what it was. There was no moon, but it was a starry night and not very dark, and so Will ventured on his perilous expedition, clambering up the precipice with the greatest difficulty, as well as fatigue. He went straight to the light, which he found to be an opening into an extensive cavern, about the size and dimensions of an ordinary barn. The opening was a square one, and just big enough for a man to have crept in. Will set in his head and beheld a row of casks from one end to the other, and two men with long beards, buff belts about their waists, and torches in their hands, who seemed busy in writing something on each cask. They were not the small casks used by smugglers, but large ones, about one half bigger than common tar-barrels, and all of a size, save two very huge ones at the further end. The cavern was all neat and clean, but there was an appearance of mouldiness about the casks, as if they had stood there for ages. The men were both at the farther end when Will looked in, and busily engaged; but at length one of them came towards him, holding his torch above his head, and, as Will thought, having his eyes fixed on him. Will never got such a fright in his life;—many a fright he got with unearthly creatures, but this was the most frightful of them all. He was a man of gigantic size, with grizly features, and his beard hanging down to his belt. Will ran with all his might, but to his dying day could never recollect in what direction. It was not long, however, till he missed his feet and fell, and the hill being almost perpendicular, he hurled down with great celerity, soon reached the bottom of the steep, and pursued his way home, it may well be conceived, in the utmost terror and amazement; but the light from the cavern was extinguished on the instant—he saw it no more.

Will apprized all the people within his reach, the next morning, of the wonderful discovery he had made; but the story was so like a fantasy or a dream, that several of them were hard of belief;—some there were who never did believe it, but ascribed all to the Moffat brandy. However, they sallied out in a body, armed with cudgels and two or three rusty rapiers, to reconnoitre; but the entrance into the cave they could not find, nor has it ever been discovered again to this day. Many a place they tried to open that day, but Will was satisfied the whole time, that none of them were in the least like the entrance he discovered. He left a part of the men standing on the hill, and took others away to the spot from whence he first saw the light. He knew also within a few yards of the place, where he first left his path to climb the steep, at which time he said it was right opposite to him. But with regard to this, Will's philosophy was a little deranged, when he was told that two things were always right opposite to one another. There were, however, some strong corroborative proofs in Will's favour. It was manifest that he had been there, which was directly out of his road, for they found the sloat that he had made in hurling down the hill from the top to the bottom; and when they discovered that track, they thought they had the prize. They soon found that they were as far from it as ever, for Will, in the midst of his terror and confusion, neither knew in what direction he was running when he fell, nor how far he had run. There were, moreover, evident marks of two horses having been fastened that night in a wild cleuch-head, at a short distance from the spot they were searching.

If the whole of this was an optical delusion, it was the most singular I ever heard or read of. For my part, I do not believe it was; I believe there was such a cavern existing at that day, and that vestiges of it may still be discovered. It was an unfeasible story altogether for a man to invent; and, moreover, though Will was a man whose character had a deep tinge of the superstitions of his own country, he was besides a man of probity, truth, and honour, and never told that for the truth, which he did not believe to be so. Peace be to his ashes, and blest be his memory! I remember him very well;—he died in my father's house, old, and full of days, and was the first human being whom I saw depart from this stage of existence.

His sons inherited his agility, though not perhaps in an equal degree. One of them, however, never was beat, save by a Mr Bryden of Corsecleuch, who beat him two races out of six. This latter was a man below the common size; but, save by Robert Laidlaw, he remained unconquered in the race, and even disputed the palm very hardly with him. Will's great-grandsons are, at this time, among the swiftest runners of the Forest; but old people say they are greatly degenerated from the speed of their fathers. He was a young man, near to his prime, in the year 1715; and having fled with his ewes into Annandale from a snow storm, he saw the Galloway and Nithsdale men marching to the Border. Happening to be in Annandale again in the winter of 1745, he saw Prince Charles and his clans marching northward, towards Dumfries. One of his sons is still alive, near to a hundred years of age, with all his faculties complete; and as he well remembers all his father's legends and traditions, what a living chronicle remains there of past ages!

There was a contemporary of Laidlaw's, who died about the same period, but an older man, who was also a very remarkable man in his day, superstitious in the extreme; many of his stories and traditions were of a visionary nature. But in legendary lore he was altogether unequalled—he was master of it; a sovereign over that department of literature, making it his boast and pride that he could sing every song and ballad that ever his country produced. He had not only all the old ballads since published in the Border Minstrelsy, but as many more of a nature too romantic, trivial, or indelicate, to be admitted into that work. Andrew was a man of strong sound sense, keen feelings, and quick discernment, but, like his contemporary and acquaintance, had many encounters with beings of another and an unknown world. Nor was it any wonder these patriarchs should have been superstitious; they lived under the ministry of the far-famed and Reverend Thomas Boston, a great divine and a saintly character, but than whom a more superstitious man never existed.

Daft Jock Amos was another odd character, of whom many droll sayings are handed down. He was a lunatic; but having been a scholar in his youth, he was possessed of a sort of wicked wit, and wavering uncertain intelligence, that proved right troublesome to those who took it on them to reprove his eccentricities. As he lived close by the church, Mr Boston and he were constantly coming in contact, and many of their little dialogues are preserved.

"The mair fool are ye, quo' Jock Amos to the minister," is a constant by-word in Ettrick to this day. It had its origin, simply as follows:—Mr Boston was taking his walk one fine summer evening after sermon, and in his way came upon Jock, very busy cutting some grotesque figures in wood with his knife. Jock, looking hastily up, found he was fairly caught, and not knowing what to say, burst into a foolish laugh—"Ha! ha! ha! Mr Boston, are you there? Will you coup a good whittle wi' me?"

"Nay, nay, John, I will not exchange knives to-day."

"The mair fool are ye," quo' Jock Amos to the minister.

"But, John, can you repeat the fourth commandment?—I hope you can—Which is the fourth commandment?"

"I daresay, Mr Boston, it'll be the ane after the third."

"Can you not repeat it?"

"I'm no sure about it—I ken it has some wheeram by the rest."

Mr Boston repeated it, and tried to show him his error in working with knives on the Sabbath day. John wrought away till the divine added,

"But why won't you rather come to church, John? What is the reason you never come to church?"

"Because you never preach on the text I want you to preach on."

"What text would you have me to preach on?"

"On the nine-and-twenty knives that came back from Babylon."

"I never heard of them before."

"It is a sign you have never read your Bible. Ha, ha, ha, Mr Boston, sic fool sic minister."

Mr Boston searched long for John's text that evening, and at last finding it recorded in Ezra, i.9, he wondered greatly at the acuteness of the fool, considering the subject on which he had been reproving him.

"John, how auld will you be?" said a sage wife to him one day, when talking of their ages.

"O, I dinna ken," said John. "It wad tak a wiser head than mine to tell you that."

"It is unco queer that you dinna ken how auld you are," returned she.

"I ken weel enough how auld I am," said John; "but I dinna ken how auld I'll be."

An old man, named Adam Linton, once met him running from home in the grey of the morning. "Hey, Jock Amos," said he, "where are you bound for so briskly this morning?"

"Aha! He's wise that wats that, an' as daft wha speers," says Jock, without taking his eye from some object that it seemed to be following.

"Are you running after anybody?" said Linton.

"I am that, man," returned Jock; "I'm rinning after the deil's messenger. Did you see ought o' him gaun by?"

"What was he like?" said Linton.

"Like a great big black corbie," said Jock, "carrying a bit tow in his gab. An' what do you think?—he has tauld me a piece o' news the day! There's to be a wedding ower by here the day, man. Ay, a wedding! I maun after him, for he has gien me an invitation."

"A wedding? Dear Jock, you are raving. What wedding can there be to-day?" said Linton.

"It is Eppy Telfer's, man. Auld Eppy Telfer's to be wed the day; an' I'm to be there; an' the minister is to be there, an' a' the elders. But Tammie, the Cameronian, he darena come, for fear he should hae to dance wi' the kimmers. There will be braw wark there the day, Aedie Linton,—braw wark there the day!" And away ran Jock towards Ettrickhouse, hallooing and waving his cap for joy. Old Adam came in, and said to his wife, who was still in bed, that he supposed the moon was at the full, for Jock Amos was gane quite gyte awthegither, and was away shouting to Ettrickhouse to Eppy Telfer's wedding.

"Then," said his wife, "if he be ill, she will be waur, for they are always affected at the same time; and, though Eppy is better than Jock in her ordinary way, she is waur when the moon-madness comes ower her." This woman was likewise subject to lunatic fits of insanity, and Jock had a great ill will at her; he could not even endure the sight of her.

The above little dialogue was hardly ended before word came in that Eppy Telfer had "put down" herself over night, and was found hanging dead in her own little cottage at day-break. Mr Boston was sent for, who, with his servant man and one of his elders, attended, but in a state of such perplexity and grief, that he seemed almost as much dead as alive. The body was tied on a deal, carried to the peak of the Wedder Law, and interred there, and all the while Jock Amos attended, and never in his life met with an entertainment that appeared to please him more. While the men were making the grave, he sat on a stone near by, jabbering and speaking one while, always addressing Eppy, and laughing most heartily at another. They heard him at one time saying, "Ha, ha, ha, Eppy, lass, but ye will see finely about you here! You will see when Tam Boston's kie gang i' the corn, and Willie Blake's.—Hoo, hie-nout! Ha, ha, ha! Then you will see a' the braw fo'ks gang by to the kirk, light shod and light shankit. But they'll be a' laden when they gang back again—laden wi' Tam Boston's gospel, but it will a' gae by poor Eppy. Never you mind, Eppy, lass. You and I may laugh at them a' out here."

After this high fit John lost his spirits entirely, and never more recovered them. He became a complete nonentity, and lay mostly in his bed till the day of his death.

Another notable man of that day was William Stoddart, nicknamed Candlem, one of the feuars of Ettrickhouse. He was simple, unlettered, and rude, as all his sayings that are preserved testify. Being about to be married to one Meggie Coltard, a great penny-wedding was announced, and the numbers that came to attend it were immense. Candlem and his bride went to Ettrick church to be married, and Mr Boston perceiving such a motley crowd following them, repaired into the church; and after admitting a few respectable witnesses, he set his son John, and his servant John Currie, to keep the two doors, and restrain the crowd from entering. Young Boston let in a number at his door, but John Currie stood manfully in the breach, refusing entrance to all. When the minister came to put the question, "Are you willing to take this woman," &c.

"I wat weel I was thinking sae," says Candlem. "Haud to the door, John Currie."

When the question was put to Meggie, she bowed assent like a dumb woman, but this did not satisfy Willie Candlem.—"What for d'ye no answer, Meggie?" says he. "Dinna ye hear what the honest man's speering at ye?"

In due time Willie Candlem and Meggie had a son, and as the custom then was, it was decreed that the first Sabbath after he was born he should be baptized. It was about the Martinmas time, the day was stormy and the water flooded; however, it was agreed that the baptism could not be put off, for fear of the fairies; so the babe was well rolled up in swaddling clothes, and laid on before his father on the white mare,—the stoutest of the kimmers stemming the water on foot. Willie Candlem rode the water slowly and cautiously. "What are they squeeling at?" said he to himself, but durst not look back for fear of his charge. After he had crossed the river safely, and a sand-bed about as wide, Willie wheels his white mare's head about, and exclaims—"Why, the deil haet I hae but the slough!" Willie had dropped the child into the flooded river, without missing it out of the huge bundle of clothes; but luckily, one of the kimmers picked him up, and as he showed some signs of life, they hurried into a house at Goosegreen, and got him brought round again. In the afternoon he was so far recovered, that the kimmers thought he might be taken up to church for baptism, but Willie Candlem made this sage remark— "I doubt he's rather unfeiroch to stand it;—he has gotten enough o' the water for ae day." On going home to his poor wife in the straw, his first address to her was—"Ay, ye may take up your handywark, Meggie, in making a slough open at baith ends. What signifies a thing that's open at baith ends?"

The boy lingered on till the beginning of summer and then died; on which occasion Willie's consolatory address to his wife was delivered, and still deservedly preserved inviolate: "Ay, ye may take up your winter's wark now, Meggie;—there it's a' gane in ae kink," (a fit of coughing.)

Another time, in harvest, it came a rainy day, and the Ettrick began to look very big in the evening. Willie Candlem perceiving his crop in danger, yoked the white mare in the sledge, and was proceeding to lead his corn out of watermark; but out came Meggie, and began expostulating with him on the sinfulness of the act, which rather damped Willie's good resolves.—"Put in your beast again, like a good Christian man, Willie," said she, "and dinna be setting an ill example to a' the parish. Ye ken, that this vera day the minister bade us lippen to Providence in our straits, and we wad never rue't. He'll take it very ill off your hand, the setting of sic an example on the Lord's day; therefore, Willie, my man, take his advice an' mine, and lippen to Providence this time."

Willie Candlem was obliged to comply, for who can withstand the artillery of a woman's tongue? So he put up his white mare, and went to bed with a heavy heart; and the next morning, by break of day, when he arose and looked out, behold, the greater part of his crop was gone.—"Ye may take up your Providence now, Meggie! Where's your Providence now? A' down the water wi' my good corn! Deil that you had your Providence and your minister baith buckled on your back!"

Meggie answered him meekly, as her duty and custom was—"O Willie! dinna rail at Providence, but down to the meadow-head and claim first." Willie Candlem took the hint, galloped on his white mare down to the Ettrick meadows, over which the river spread, and they were covered with floating sheaves; so Willie began and hauled out, and carried out, till he had at least six times as much corn as he had lost. At length one man came, and another, but Willie refused all participation. "Ay, ye may take up your corn now where ye can find it, lads," said Willie; "I keppit nane but my ain. Yours is gane farther down. Had ye come when I came, ye might have keppit it a'."

So Willie drove and drove, till the stackyard was full.—"I think the crop has turn'd no that ill out after a'," said Meggie.—"I say, he's no sic an ill chap, that Providence o' yours, Meggie; he has done unco weel at this bout; but I dinna ken about trusting him as far every day."

William Bryden of Aberlosk was another very singular man, but an age later than the heroes of whom we have been treating; he was the first who introduced the draining of sheep pasture, which has proved of such benefit to this country; but in all other things he made a point of letting them remain as God made them. He castrated no males, weaned no lambs, and baptized no children.

Dreams and Apparitions. Containing

George Dobson's Expedition to Hell,

and

The Souters of Selkirk.

THERE is no phenomenon in nature less understood, and about which greater nonsense is written, than dreaming. It is a strange thing. For my part, I do not understand it, nor have I any desire to do so; and I firmly believe that no philosopher that ever wrote knows a particle more about it than I do, however elaborate and subtle the theories he may advance concerning it. He knows not even what sleep is, nor can he define its nature, so as that any common mind can comprehend him; and how can he define that ethereal part of it, wherein the soul holds intercourse with the external world?—how, in that state of abstraction, some ideas force themselves upon us, in spite of all our efforts to get rid of them; while others, which we have resolved to bear about with us by night as well as by day, refuse us their fellowship, even at periods when we most require their aid?

No, no; the philosopher knows nothing about either; and if he says he does, I entreat you not to believe him. He does not know what mind is; even his own mind, to which one would think he has the most direct access; far less can he estimate the operations and powers of that of any other intelligent being. He does not even know, with all his subtlety, whether it be a power distinct from his body, or essentially the same, and only incidentally and temporarily endowed with different qualities. He sets himself to discover at what period of his existence the union was established. He is baffled; for consciousness refuses the intelligence, declaring, that she cannot carry him far enough back to ascertain it. He tries to discover the precise moment when it is dissolved, but on this consciousness is altogether silent, and all is darkness and mystery; for the origin, the manner of continuance, and the time and mode of breaking up of the union between soul and body, are in reality undiscoverable by our natural faculties—are not patent, beyond the possibility of mistake: but whosoever can read his Bible, and solve a dream, can do either, without being subjected to any material error.

It is on this ground that I like to contemplate, not the theory of dreams, but the dreams themselves; because they prove to the unlettered and contemplative mind, in a very forcible manner, a distinct existence of the soul, and its lively and rapid intelligence with external nature, as well as with a world of spirits with which it has no acquaintance, when the body is lying dormant, and the same to it as if sleeping in death.

I account nothing of any dream that relates to the actions of the day; the person is not then sound asleep; there is no division between matter and mind, but they are mingled together in a sort of chaos—what a farmer would call compost—fermenting and disturbing one another. I find, that in all these sort of dreams, every calling and occupation of men have their own, relating in some degree to their business; and in the country, at least, their imports are generally understood. Every man's body is a barometer. A thing made up of the elements must be affected by their various changes and convulsions, and so it assuredly is. When I was a shepherd, and all the comforts of my life so much depending on good or ill weather, the first thing I did every morning was strictly to overhaul the dreams of the night, and I found that I could better calculate from them than from the appearance and changes of the sky. I know a keen sportsman, who pretends that his dreams never deceive him. If he dream of angling, or pursuing salmon in deep waters, he is sure of rain; but if fishing on dry ground, or in waters so low that the fish cannot get from him, it forebodes drought; hunting or shooting hares, is snow, and moorfowl, wind, &c. But the most extraordinary professional dream on record is, without all doubt, that well-known one of George Dobson, coach-driver in Edinburgh, which I shall here relate; for though it did not happen in the shepherd's cot, it has often been recited there.

George was part proprietor and driver of a hackney-coach in Edinburgh, when such vehicles were scarce; and one day there comes a gentleman to him whom he knew, and says:—"George, you must drive me and my son here out to a certain place," that he named, somewhere in the vicinity of Edinburgh.—"Sir," says George, "I never heard tell of such a place, and I cannot drive you to it unless you give me very particular directions."

"It is false," returned the gentleman; "there is no man in Scotland who knows the road to that place better than you do. You have never driven on any other road all your life, and I insist on your taking us."

"Very well, sir," says George, "I'll drive you to hell if you have a mind, only you are to direct me on the road."

"Mount and drive on, then," said the other, "and no fear

of the road."

George did so, and never in his life did he see his horses go at such a noble rate; they snorted, they pranced, and they flew on; and as the whole road appeared to lie down hill, he deemed that he should soon come to his journey's end. Still he drove on at the same rate, far far down hill,—and so fine an open road he never travelled,—till by degrees it grew so dark that he could not see to drive any farther. He called to the gentleman, inquiring what he should do; who answered, that this was the place they were bound to, so he might draw up, dismiss them, and return. He did so, alighted from the dickie, wondered at his foaming horses, and forthwith opened the coach-door, held the rim of his hat with the one hand, and with the other demanded his fare.

"You have driven us in fine style, George," said the elder gentleman, "and deserve to be remembered; but it is needless for us to settle just now, as you must meet us here again tomorrow precisely at twelve o'clock."

"Very well, sir," says George, "there is likewise an old account, you know, and some toll-money;" which indeed there was.

"It shall all be settled to-morrow, George, and moreover, I fear there will be some toll-money to-day."

"I perceived no tolls to-day, your honour," said George.

"But I perceived one, and not very far back neither, which I suspect you will have difficulty in repassing without a regular ticket. What a pity I have no change on me!"

"I never saw it otherwise with your honour," said George, jocularly; "what a pity it is you should always suffer yourself to run short of change!"

"I will give you that which is as good, George," said the gentleman; and he gave him a ticket written with red ink, which the honest coachman could not read. He, however, put it into his sleeve, and inquired of his employer where that same toll was which he had not observed, and how it was that they did not ask toll from him as he came through? The gentleman replied, by informing George that there was no road out of that domain, and that whoever entered it must either remain in it, or return by the same path; so they never asked any toll till the person's return, when they were at times highly capricious; but that ticket would answer his turn. And he then asked George if he did not perceive a gate, with a number of men in black standing about it.

"Oho! Is yon the spot?" says George; "Then, I assure your honour, yon is no toll-gate, but a private entrance into a great man's mansion; for do not I know two or three of yon to be gentlemen of the law, whom I have driven often and often; and as good fellows they are too, as any I know—men who never let themselves run short of change. Good day.—Twelve o'clock to-morrow?"

"Yes, twelve o'clock noon, precisely;" and with that, George's employers vanished in the gloom, and left him to wind his way out of that dreary labyrinth the best way he could. He found it no easy matter, for his lamps were not lighted, and he could not see an ell before him—he could not even perceive his horses' ears; and what was worse, there was a rushing sound, like that of a town on fire, all around him, that stunned his senses, so that he could not tell whether his horses were moving or standing still. George was in the greatest distress imaginable, and was glad when he perceived the gate before him, with his two identical friends of the law still standing. George drove boldly up, accosted them by their names, and asked what they were doing there; but they made him no answer, but pointed to the gate and the keeper. George was terrified to look at this latter personage, who now came up and seized his horses by the reins, refusing to let him pass. In order to introduce himself in some degree to this austere toll-man, George asked him, in a jocular manner, how he came to employ his two eminent friends as assistant gate-keepers?

"Because they are among the last comers," replied the ruffian, churlishly. "You will be an assistant here, to-morrow."

"The devil I will, sir?"

"Yes, the devil you will, sir."

"I'll be d— if I do then—that I will."

"Yes, you'll be d— if you do—that you will."

"Let my horses go in the meantime then, sir, that I may proceed on my journey."

"Nay."

"Nay?—Dare you say nay to me, sir? My name is George Dobson, of the Pleasance, Edinburgh, coach driver, and coach proprietor too; and I'll see the face of the man d— who will say nay to me, as long as I can pay my way. I have his Majesty's licence, and I'll go and come as I choose—and that I will. Let go my horses there, and say what is your demand."

"Well, then, I'll let your horses go," said the keeper; "but I'll keep yourself for a pledge." And with that he let go the horses, and seized honest George by the throat, who struggled in vain to disengage himself, and cursed, swore, and threatened, by his own confession, most bloodily. His horses flew off like the wind, so swift, that the coach was flying in the air, and scarcely stotting on the earth once in a quarter of a mile. George was in furious wrath, for he saw that his grand coach and harness would all be broken to pieces, and his gallant pair of horses maimed or destroyed; and how was his family's bread now to be won!—He struggled, swore, threatened, and prayed in vain;—the intolerable toll-man was deaf to all remonstrances. He once more appealed to his two genteel acquaintances of the law, reminding them how he had of late driven them to Roslin on a Sunday, along with two ladies, who, he supposed, were their sisters, from their familiarity, when not another coachman in town would engage with them. But the gentlemen, very ungenerously, only shook their heads, and pointed to the gate. George's circumstances now became desperate, and again he asked the hideous toll-man what right he had to detain him, and what were his charges.

"What right have I to detain you, sir, say you? Who are you that make such a demand here? Do you know where you are, sir?"

"No, faith, I do not," returned George; "I wish I did. But I *shall* know, and make you repent your insolence too. My name, I told you, is George Dobson, licensed coach-hirer in Edinburgh, Pleasance; and to get full redress of you for this unlawful interruption, I only desire to know where I am."

"Then, sir, if it can give you so much satisfaction to know where you are," said the keeper, with a malicious grin, "you *shall* know, and you may take instruments by the hands of your two friends there, instituting a legal prosecution . Your redress, you may be assured, will be most ample, when I inform you that you are in Hell, and out of this gate you return no more."

This was rather a damper to George, and he began to perceive that nothing would be gained in such a place by the strong hand, so he addressed the inexorable toll-man, whom he now dreaded more than ever, in the following terms. "But I must go home, at all events, you know, sir, to unyoke my two horses, and put them up, and to inform Chirsty Halliday, my wife, of my engagement. And, bless me! I never recollected till this moment, that I am engaged to be back here to-morrow at twelve o'clock, and see here is a free ticket for my passage this way."

The keeper took the ticket with one hand, but still held George with the other. "Oho! were you in with our honourable friend, Mr R** of L***?" said he. "He has been on our books for a long while,—however, this will do, only you must put your name to it likewise; and the engagement is this—You, by this instrument, en- gage your soul, that you will return here by to-morrow at noon."

"Catch me there, billy!" says George. "I'll engage no such thing, depend on it;—that will I not."

"Then remain where you are," said the keeper, "for there is no other alternative. We like best for people to come here in their own way, in the way of their business;" and with that he flung George backward, heels-over-head down hill, and closed the gate.

George, finding all remonstrance vain, and being desirous once more to see the open day, and breathe the fresh air, and likewise to see Chirsty Halliday, his wife, and set his house and stable in some order, came up again, and in utter desperation, signed the bond, and was suffered to depart. He then bounded away on the track of his horses, with more than ordinary swiftness, in hopes to overtake them; and always now and then uttered a loud wo! in hopes they might hear and obey, though he could not come in sight of them. But George's grief was but beginning, for at a well-known and dangerous spot, where there was a tan-yard on the one hand, and a quarry on the other, he came to his gallant steeds overturned, the coach smashed to pieces, Dawtie with two of her legs broken, and Duncan dead. This was more than the worthy coachman could bear, and many degrees worse than being in hell. There his pride and manly spirit bore him up against the worst of treatment; but here his heart entirely failed him, and he laid himself down, with his face on his two hands, and wept bitterly, bewailing, in the most deplorable terms, his two gallant horses, Dawtie and Duncan.

While lying in this inconsolable state, behold there was one took hold of his shoulder, and shook it; and a well-known voice said to him, "Geordie! What is the matter wi' ye, Geordie?" George was provoked beyond measure at the insolence of the question, for he knew the voice to be that of Chirsty Halliday, his wife. "I think you needna ask that, seeing what you see," said George. "O my poor Dawtie, where are a' your jinkings and prancings now, your moopings and your wincings? I'll ne'er be a proud man again—bereaved o' my bonny pair."

"Get up, George; get up, and bestir yourself," said Chirsty Halliday, his wife. "You are wanted directly, to bring in the Lord President to the Parliament House. It is a great storm, and he must be there by nine o'clock.—Get up—rouse yourself, and make ready —his servant is waiting for you."

"Woman, you are demented!" cried George. "How can I go and bring in the Lord President, when my coach is broken in pieces, my poor Dawtie lying with twa of her legs broken, and Duncan dead? And, moreover, I have a previous engagement, for I am obliged to be in hell before twelve o'clock."

Chirsty Halliday now laughed outright, and continued long in a fit of laughter, but George never moved his head from the pillow, but lay and groaned, for, in fact, he was all this while lying snug in his bed; while the tempest without was roaring with great violence, and which circumstance may perhaps account for the rushing and deafening sound which astounded him so much in hell. But so deeply was he impressed with the realities of his dream that he would do nothing but lie and moan, persisting and believing in the truth of all he had seen. His wife now went and informed her neighbours of her husband's plight, and of his singular engagement with Mr R** of L***y at twelve o'clock. She persuaded one friend to harness the horses, and go for the Lord President; but all the rest laughed immoderately at poor coachy's predicament. It was, however, no laughing to him; he never raised his head, and his wife becoming at last uneasy about the frenzied state of his mind, made him repeat every circumstance of his adventure to her, (for he would never believe or admit that it was a dream,) which he did in the terms above narrated; and she perceived, or dreaded, that he was becoming somewhat feverish. She went over and told Dr Wood of her husband's malady, and of his solemn engagement to be in hell at twelve o'clock.

"He maunna keep it, dearie. He maunna keep that engagement at no rate," said Dr Wood. "Set back the clock an hour or twa, to drive him past the time, and I'll ca' in the course of my round. Are ye sure he hasna been drinking hard?" She assured him he had not. "Weel, weel, ye maun tell him that he maunna keep that engagement at no rate. Set back the clock and I'll come and see him. It is a frenzy that maunna be trifled with. Ye maunna laugh at it, dearie,—maunna laugh at it. Maybe a nervish fever, wha kens."

The Doctor and Chirsty left the house together, and as their road lay the same way for a space, she fell a-telling him of the two young lawyers whom George saw standing at the gate of hell, and whom the porter had described as two of the last comers. When the Doctor heard this, he staid his hurried stooping pace in one moment, turned full round on the woman, and fixing his eyes on her that gleamed with a deep unstable lustre, he said, "What's that ye were saying, dearie? What's that ye were saying? Repeat it again to me every word." She did so. On which the Doctor held up his hands, as if palsied with astonishment, and uttered some fervent ejaculations. "I'll go with you straight," said he, "before I visit another patient. This is wonderfu'! It is terrible! The young gentlemen are both at rest—both lying corpses at this time!—fine young men—I attended them both—died of the same exterminating disease.—Oh this is wonderful; this is wonderful!"

The Doctor kept Chirsty half running all the way down the High Street and St Mary's Wynd, at such a pace did he walk, never lifting his eyes from the pavement, but always exclaiming now and then, "It is wonderfu'! most wonderfu'!" At length, prompted by woman's natural curiosity, she inquired at the Doctor if he knew anything of their friend Mr R** of L***y? But he shook his head, and replied, "Na, na, dearie,—ken naething about him. He and his son are baith in London,—ken naething about him; but the tither is awfu'—it is perfectly awfu'!"

When Dr Wood reached his patient, he found him very low, but only a little feverish, so he made all haste to wash his head with vinegar and cold water, and then he covered the crown with a treacle plaster, and made the same application to the soles of his feet, awaiting the issue. George revived a little, when the Doctor tried to cheer him up by joking him about his dream; but on mention of that he groaned, and shook his head. "So you are convinced, dearie, that it is nae dream?" said the Doctor.

"Dear sir, how could it be a dream?" said the patient. "I was there in person, with Mr R** and his son; and see here are the marks of the porter's fingers on my throat." Dr Wood looked, and distinctly saw two or three red spots on one side of his throat, which confounded him not a little. "I assure you, sir," continued George, "it was no dream, which I know to my sad experience. I have lost my coach and horses, and what more have I?—signed the bond with my own hand, and in person entered into the most solemn and terrible engagement."

"But ye're no to keep it, I tell ye," said Dr Wood. "Ye're to keep it at no rate. It is a sin to enter into a compact wi' the deil, but it is a far greater ane to keep it. Sae let Mr R** and his son bide where they are yonder, for ye sanna stir a foot to bring them out the day."

"Oh, oh! Doctor!" groaned the poor fellow, "this is not a thing to be made a jest o'! I feel that it is an engagement I cannot break. Go I must, and that very shortly. Yes, yes, go I must, and go I shall, though I should borrow David Barclay's pair." With that he turned his face towards the wall, groaned deeply, and fell into a lethargy, while Dr Wood caused them to let him alone, thinking if he would sleep out the appointed time, which was at hand, he would be safe; but all the time he kept feeling his pulse, and by degrees showed symptoms of uneasiness. The wife ran for a clergyman of famed abilities, to pray and converse with her husband, in hopes by that means to bring him to his senses; but after his arrival, George never spoke more, save calling to his horses, as if encouraging them to run with great speed, and thus in imagination driving at full career into hell, he went off in a paroxysm after a terrible struggle, precisely within a few minutes of twelve o'clock.

What made this singular professional dream the more remarkable and unique in all its parts, was not known at the time of George's death. It was a terrible storm on the night of the dream, as has been already mentioned, and during the time of the hurricane, a London smack went down off Wearmouth about three in the morning. Among the sufferers were the Hon. Mr R** of L***y, and his son! George could not know aught of this at break of day, for it was not known in Scotland till the day of his interment; and as little knew he of the deaths of the two young lawyers, who both died of the small-pox the evening before.

I have heard another amusing story of a man of the same name, which brings it to my remembrance at present. This last was a shoemaker, a very honest man, who lived at the foot of an old street, called the Back Row, in the town of Selkirk. He was upwards of thirty, unmarried, had an industrious old stepmother, who kept house for him, and of course George was what is called "a bein bachelor," or "a chap that was gayan weel to leeve." He was a cheerful happy fellow, and quite sober, except when on the town-council, when he sometimes took a glass with the magistrates of his native old borough, of whose loyalty, valour, and antiquity, there was no man more proud.

Well, one day, as George was sitting in his *shop*, as he called it, (for no man now-a-days would call that a shop in which there was nothing to sell,) sewing away at boots and shoes for his customers, whom he could not half hold in whole leather, so great was the demand over all the country for George Dobson's boots and shoes— he was sitting, I say, plying away, and singing with great glee,—

> "Up wi' the souters o' Selkirk,
>   An' down wi' the Earl o' Hume,
>   An' up wi' a' the brave billies
>   That sew the single-soled shoon!
> An' up wi' the yellow, the yellow,
>   The yellow and green hae doon weel;
>   Then up wi' the lads of the forest,
>   "But down wi' the Merse to the deil!"

The last words were hardly out of George's mouth, when he heard a great noise enter the Back Row, and among the voices one making loud proclamation, as follows:—

> "Ho yes!—Ho yes!
> Souters ane, souters a',
> Souters o' the Back Raw,
> There's a gentleman a-coming
> Wha will ca' ye souters a'."

"I wish he durst," says George. "That will be the Earl o' Hume wha's coming. He has had us at ill will for several generations. Bring my aik staff into the shop, callant, and set it down beside me here—and ye may bring ane to yoursell too. I say, callant, stop.—Bring my grandfather's auld sword wi'ye. I wad like to see the Earl o' Hume, or ony o' his cronies, come and cast up our honest calling and occupation till us!"

George laid his oak staff on the cutting-board before him, leaned the old two-edged sword against the shop wall, at his right hand—the noise of the proclamation went out at the head of the Back Row, and died in the distance; and then George began again, and sung the Souters of Selkirk with more obstreperous glee than ever.—The last words were not out of his mouth, when a grand gentleman stepped into the shop, clothed in light armour, with a sword by his side and pistols in his breast. He had a liveryman behind him, and both the master and man were all shining in gold.—This is the Earl o' Hume in good earnest, thought George to himself; but, nevertheless, he sanna danton me.

"Good morrow to you, Souter Dobson," says the gentleman. "What the devil of a song is that you were singing?" George would have resented the first address with a vengeance, but the latter question took him off it unawares, and he only answered, "It is a very good sang, sir, and ane of the auldest—What objections have you to it?"

"Nay, but what is it about?" returned the stranger; "I want to hear what you say it is about."

"I'll sing you it over again, sir," said George, "and then you may judge for yoursell. Our sangs up here awa dinna speak in riddles and parables; they're gayan downright;" and with that George gave it him over again full birr, keeping at the same time a sharp look out on all his guest's movements, for he had no doubt now that it was to come to an engagement between them, but he was determined not to yield an inch, for the honour of old Selkirk.

When the song was done, however, the gentleman commended it, saying, it was a spirited old thing, and, without doubt, related to some of the early border feuds. "But how think you the Earl of Hume would like to hear this?" added he. George, who had no doubt all this while that the Earl of Hume was speaking to him, said good-naturedly, "We dinna care muckle, sir, whether the Earl o' Hume take the sang ill or weel. I'se warrant he has heard it mony a time ere now, and, if he were here, he wad hear it every day when the school looses, an' Wattie Henderson wad gie him it every night."

"Well, well, Souter Dobson, that is neither here nor there. That is not what I called about. Let us to business. You must make me a pair of boots in your very best style," said the gentleman, standing up, and stretching forth his leg to be measured.

"I make you no boots, sir," says George, nettled at being again called Souter. "I have as many regular customers to supply as hold me busy from one year's end to another. I cannot make your boots—you may get them made where you please."

"You *shall* make them, Mr Dobson," says he; "I am determined to try a pair of boots of your making, cost what they will. Make your own price, but let me have the boots by all means; and, moreover, I want them before to-morrow morning."

This was so conciliatory and so friendly of the Earl, that George, being a good-natured fellow, made no farther objection, but took his measure, and promised to have them ready. "I will pay them now," said the gentleman, taking out a purse of gold; but George refused to accept of the price till the boots were produced. "Nay, but I will pay them now," said the gentleman; "for, in the first place, it will insure me of the boots, and, in the next place, I may probably leave town to-night, and make my servant wait for them. What is the cost?"

"If they are to be as good as I can make them, sir, they will be twelve shillings."

"Twelve shillings, Mr Dobson! I paid thirty-six for these I wear in London, and I expect yours will be a great deal better. There are two guineas, and be sure to make them good."

"I cannot, for my life, make them worth the half of that money," says George. "We have no materials in Selkirk that will amount to one-third of it in value." However, the gentleman flung down the gold and went away, singing the Souters of Selkirk.

"He is a most noble fellow that Earl of Hume," says George to his apprentice. "I thought he and I should have had a battle, but we have parted on the best possible terms."

"I wonder how you could bide to be *souter'd* yon gate?" said the boy.

George scratched his head with the awl, bit his lip, and looked at his grandfather's sword. He had a great desire to follow the insolent gentleman, for he found that he had inadvertently suffered a great local insult to be passed on him without offering any retaliation. He could do nothing now but keep it to himself.

After George had shaped the boots with the utmost care, and of the best and finest Kendal leather, he went up the Back Row to seek assistance, so that he might have them done at the stated time; but never a stitch of assistance could George obtain, for the gentleman had trysted a pair of boots in every shop in the Row, paid for them all, and called every one of the shoemakers souters twice over.

Never was there such a day in the Back Row of Selkirk! What could it mean? Had the gentleman a whole regiment coming up, all of the same size, and the same measure of legs? Or was he not rather an army agent, come to take specimens of the best workmen in the country? This last being the prevailing belief, every Selkirk souter threw off his coat, and fell a slashing and cutting of Kendal leather; and such a forenoon of cutting, and sewing, and puffing, and roseting, never was in Selkirk since the battle of Flodden-field.

George's shop was the nethermost of the street, so that the stranger guests came all to him first; so, scarcely had he taken a mouthful of a hurried dinner, and begun to sew again, and, of course, to sing, when in comes a fat gentleman, exceedingly well mounted, with sword and pistols; he had fair curled hair, red cheeks that hung over his stock, and a liveryman behind him. "Merry be your heart, Mr Dobson, but what a plague of a song is that you are singing?" said he. George looked very suspicious-like at him, and thought to himself, now I could bet any man two gold guineas that this is the Duke of Northumberland, another enemy to our town; but I'll not be cowed by him neither, only I could have wished I had been singing another song when his Grace came into *the shop*. These were the thoughts that run through George's mind in a moment, and at length he made answer —"We reckon it a good sang, my lord, and ane o' the auldest."

"Would it suit your convenience to sing that last verse over again?" said the fat gentleman with the fair curled hair, and the red cheeks hanging over his cravat; and at the same time he laid hold of his gold-handled pistols.

"O certainly, sir," said George; "but at the same time I must take a lesson in manners from my superiors;" and with that he seized his grandfather's cut-and-thrust sword, and cocking that up by his ear, he sang out with fearless glee—

"The English are dults, to a man, a man—
Fat puddings to fry in a pan, a pan—
    Their Percies and Howards
    We reckon but cowards—
Ay, turn the blue bonnets wha can, wha can!"

George now set his joints in that manner, that the moment the
Duke of Northumberland presented his pistol, he might be ready to
cleave him, or cut off his right hand, with his grandfather's cut-and-
thrust sword; but the fat man with the curled hair durst not venture
the issue—he took his hand from his pistol, and laughed till his big
sides shook. "You are a great original, Dobson," said he; "but you are
nevertheless a brave fellow—a noble fellow—a souter among a thousand, and I am glad I have met with you in this mood too. Well, then,
let us proceed to business. You must make me a pair of boots in your
very best style, George, and that without any loss of time."

"O Lord, sir, I would do that with the greatest pleasure, but it is a
thing entirely out of my power," said George with a serious face.

"Pooh, pooh, I know the whole story," said the fat gentleman with
the fair curled hair and the red cheeks. "You are all hoaxed and
made fools of this morning; but the thing concerns me very much,
and I'll give you five guineas, Mr Dobson, if you will make me a pair
of good boots before to-morrow at this time."

"I wad do it cheerfully for the fifth part o' the price, my lord," said
George; "but it is needless to speak about that, it being out o' my
power. But what way are we hoaxed? I dinna account ony man made
a fool of wha has the cash in his pocket as weel as the goods in his
hand."

"You are all made fools of together, and I am the most made a fool
of any," said the fat gentleman. "I betted a hundred guineas with a
young Scottish nobleman last night, that he durst not go up the Back
Row of Selkirk, calling all the way, 'Souters ane, souters a', souters o'
the Back-raw;' and yet, to my astonishment, you have let him call it,
and insult you all with impunity; and he has won."

"Deil confound the rascal!" exclaimed George. "If we had but
taken him up! But we took him for our friend, come to warn us, and
lay all in wait for the audacious fellow who was to come up behind."

"And a good amends you took of him when he came," said the fat
gentleman. "Well, after I had taken the above bet, up speaks another
of our company, and he says—'Why make such account of a few poor
cobblers, or souters, or how do you call them? I'll bet a hundred
guineas, that I'll go up the Back Row after that gentleman has set

them all agog, and I'll call every one of them souter twice over to his face.' I took the bet in a moment: 'You dare not, for your blood, sir,' says I. 'You do not know the spirit and bravery of the men of Selkirk. They will knock you down at once, if not tear you to pieces.' But I trusted too much to your spirit, and have lost my two hundred guineas, it would appear. Tell me, in truth, Mr Dobson, did you suffer him to call you souter twice to your face without resenting it?"

George bit his lip, scratched his head with the awl, and gave the lingels such a yerk, that he made them both crack in two. "D——n it! we're a' affrontit thegither!" said he in a half whisper, while the apprentice boy was like to burst with laughter at his master's mortification.

"Well, I have lost my money," continued the gentleman, "but I assure you, George, the gentleman wants no boots. He has accomplished his purpose, and has the money in his pocket; but as it will avail me I may not say how much, I entreat that you will make me a pair. Here is the money,—here are five guineas, which I leave in pledge; only let me have the boots. Or suppose you make these a little wider, and transfer them to me; that is very excellent leather, and will do exceedingly well; I think I never felt better;" and he stood leaning over George, handling the leather. "Now, do you consent to let me have them?"

"I can never do that, my lord," says George, "having the other gentleman's money in my pocket. If you would offer me ten guineas, it would be the same thing."

"Very well, I will find those who will," said he, and off he went, singing, "Turn the blue bonnets wha can, wha can."

"This is the queerest day about Selkirk that I ever saw," said George; "but really this Duke of Northumberland, to be the old hereditary enemy of our town, is a real fine frank fellow."

"Aye, but he souter'd ye, too," said the boy.

"It is a lee, ye little blackguard."

"I heard him ca' you a souter amang a thousand, master; an' that taunt will be heard tell o' yet."

"I fancy, callant, we maun let that flee stick to the wa'," says George; and sewed away, and sewed away, and got the boots finished the next day by twelve o'clock. Now, thought he to himself, I have thirty shillings by this bargain, and so I'll treat our magistrates to a hearty glass this afternoon; I hae muckle need o' a slockening, and the Selkirk bailies never fail a friend. George put his hand in his pocket to clink his two gold guineas. The devil a guinea was in George's pocket, nor plack either! His countenance changed, and fell so much, that the apprentice noticed it, and suspected the cause; but George would confess nothing, though, in his own mind, he strongly suspected the Duke of Northumberland of the theft, *alias*, the fat gentleman with the fair curled hair, and the red cheeks hanging over his stock.

George went away up among his brethren of the awl in the Back Row, and called on them every one; but he soon perceived, from their blank looks, and their disinclination to drink that night, that they were all in the same predicament with himself. The fat gentleman with the curled hair had called on them every one, and got measure of a pair of ten-guinea boots, but had not paid any of them; and somehow or other, every man had lost the price of the boots which he had received in the morning. Who to blame for this, nobody knew; for the whole day over, and a good part of the night, from the time the proclamation was made, the Back Row of Selkirk was like a cried fair; all the idle people in the town and the country about were there, wondering after the man who had raised such a demand for boots. After all, the souters of Selkirk were left neither richer nor poorer than they were at the beginning, but every one of them had been four times called a *souter* to his face,—a title of great obloquy in that town, although the one of all others that the townsmen ought to be proud of. And it is curious that they are proud of it, when used collectively; but apply it to any of them as a term of reproach, and you had better call him the worst name under heaven.

This was the truth of the story; and the feat was performed by the late Duke of Queensberry, when Earl of March, and two English noblemen, on a tour through this country. Every one of them gained his bet, through the simplicity of the honest souters; but certainly the last had a difficult part to play, having staked two hundred guineas that he would take all the money from the souters that they had received from the gentleman in the morning, and call every one of them *souter* to his face. He got the price entire from every one, save Thomas Inglis, who had drunk the half of his before he got to him; but this being proven, the English gentleman won.

George Dobson took the thing most amiss. He had been the first taken in all along, and he thought a good deal about it. He was moreover a very honest man, and in order to make up the boots to the full value of the money he had received, he had shod them with silver, which took two Spanish dollars, and he had likewise put four silver tassels to the tops, so that they were splendid boots, and likely to remain on his hand. In short, though he did not care about the loss, he took the hoax sore amiss, and thought a good deal about it.

Shortly after this, he was sitting in his shop, working away, and not singing a word, when in comes a fat gentleman, with fair curled hair, and red cheeks, but they were *not* hanging over his cravat; and he says, "Good morning, Dobson. You are very quiet and contemplative this morning."

"Ay, sir, fo'ks canna be aye alike merry."

"Have you any stomach for taking measure of a pair of boots this morning?"

"Nah! I'll take measure o' nae mae boots to strangers; I'll stick by my auld customers."—He is very like my late customer, thought George, but his tongue is not the same. If I thought it were he, I would nick him.

"I have heard the story of the boots, George," says he, "and never heard a better one. I have laughed very heartily at it; and I called principally to inform you, that if you will call at Widow Wilson's, in Hawick, you will get the price of your boots."

"Thank you, sir," says George, and the gentleman went away; and then Dobson was persuaded he was *not* the Duke of Northumberland, though astonishingly like him. George had not sewed a single yerking, ere the gentleman comes again into the shop, and says, "You had better measure me for these boots, Dobson, I intend to be your customer in future."

"Thank you, sir, but I would rather not, just now."

"Very well, call then at Widow Wilson's, in Hawick, and you shall get *double* payment for the boots you have made." George thanked him again, and away he went; but in a very short space he enters the shop again, and again requested George to measure him for a pair of boots. George became suspicious of the gentleman, and rather uneasy, as he continued to haunt him like a ghost; and so, merely to be quit of him, he took the measure of his leg and foot. "It is very near the measure of these fine silver-mounted ones, sir," says George, "you had better just take them."

"Well, so be it," said the stranger. "Call at Widow Wilson's, in Hawick, and you shall have *triple* payment for your boots. Good day."

"O this gentleman is undoubtedly wrong in his mind," says George to himself. "This beats all the customers I ever met with! Ha—ha—ha! Come to Widow Wilson's, and you shall have payment for your boots,—*double* payment for your boots,—*triple* payment for your boots! Oh! the man's as mad as a March hare! He—he—he—he!"

"Hilloa, George," cried a voice close at his ear, "what's the matter wi' ye? Are ye gaun daft? Are ye no gaun to rise to your wark the day?"

"Aich! Gudeness guide us, mother, am I no up yet?" cries George, springing out of his bed; for he had been all the while in a sound sleep, and dreaming. "What gart ye let me lie so long? I thought I had been i' the shop!"

"Shop!" exclaimed she; "I daresay then, you thought you had found a fiddle in't. What were ye gaffawing and laughing at?"

"O! I was laughing at a fat man, an' the payment of a pair o' boots at Widow Wilson's, in Hawick."

"Widow Wilson's, i' Hawick!" exclaimed the wife, holding up both her hands; "Gude forgie me for a great liar, if I hae dream'd about onybody else, frae the tae end o' the night to the tither."

"Houts, mother, haud your tongue; it is needless to heed your dreams, for ye never gie ower dreaming about somebody."

"An' what for no, lad? Hasna an auld body as good a right to dream as a young ane? Mrs Wilson's a through-gawn quean, and clears mair than a hunder a-year by the tannage. I'se warrant there sall something follow thir dreams; I get the maist o' my dreams redd."

"How can you say that, when it was but the other night you dreamed that Lord Alemoor brought you down in his wood, for a grey hen?"

"I wat that was nae lee, lad; an' tuffled my feathers weel, when he had me down. There's nae saying what may happen, Geordie; but I wish your wing as weel fledged as a Mrs Wilson aneath it."

George was greatly tickled with his dream about the fat gentleman and the boots, and so well convinced was he that there was some sort of meaning in it, that he resolved to go to Hawick the next market day, and call on Mrs Wilson, and settle with her; although it was a week or two before his usual term of payment, he thought the money would scarcely come wrong. So that day he plied and wrought as usual; but instead of his favourite ditties relating to the Forest, he chanted, the whole day over, one as old as any of them; but I am sorry I recollect only the chorus and a few odd stanzas of it.

SING ROUND ABOUT HAWICK, &c.

We'll round about Hawick, Hawick,
Round about Hawick thegither;
We'll round about Hawick, Hawick,
And in by the bride's gudemither.
Sing round about Hawick, &c.

And as we gang by we will rap,
  And drink to the luck o' the bigging;
For the bride has her tap in her lap,
  And the bridegroom his tail in his rigging.
    Sing round about Hawick, &c.

There's been little luck i' the deed,
  We're a' in the dumps thegither;
Let's gie the bridegroom a sheep's head,
  But gie the bride brose and butter.
    Sing round about Hawick, &c.

Then a' the gudewives i' the land
  Came flockin' in droves thegither,
A' bringin' their bountith in hand,
  To please the young bride's gudemither.
    Sing round about Hawick, &c.

The black gudewife o' the Braes
  Gae baby-clouts no worth a button;
But the auld gudewife o' Penchrice
  Came in wi' a shouder o' mutton.
    Sing round about Hawick, &c.

Wee Jean o' the Coate gae a pun',
  A penny, a plack, and a bodle;
But the wife at the head o' the town
  Gae nought but a lang pin-todle.*
    Sing round about Hawick, &c.

The mistress o' Bortugh cam ben,
  Aye blinkin' sae couthy an' canny:
But some said she had in her han'
  A kipple o' bottles o' branny.
    Sing round about Hawick, &c.

And some brought dumples o' woo,
  And some brought flitches o' bacon,

* A pin-cushion. *Vide* Dr Jamieson.

And kebbucks and cruppocks enow;
   But Jenny Muirhead brought a capon.
     Sing round about Hawick, &c.

Then up came the wife o' the Mill,
   Wi' the cog, an' the meal, an' the water;
For she likit the joke sae weel
   To gie the bride brose and butter.
     Sing round about Hawick, &c.

And first she pat in a bit bread,
   And then she pat in a bit butter,
And then she pat in a sheep's head,
   Horns an' a' thegither!

Sing round about Hawick, Hawick,
   Round about Hawick thegither;
Round about Hawick, Hawick,
   Round about Hawick for ever. +

On the Thursday following, George, instead of going to *the shop*, dressed himself in his best Sunday clothes, and, with rather a curious face, went ben to his step-mother, and inquired "what feck o' siller she had about her?"

"Siller! Gudeness forgie you, Geordie, for an evendown waster and a profligate! What are ye gaun to do wi' siller the day?"

"I have something ado ower at Hawick, an' I was thinking it wad be as weel to pay her account when I was there."

"Oho, lad! Are ye there wi' your dreams and your visions o' the night, Geordie? Ye're aye keen o' sangs, man; I can pit a vera gude ane i' your head. There's an unco gude auld thing they ca', '*Wap at the widow, my laddie.*' D'ye ken it, Geordie? Siller! quo he! Hae ye ony feck o' siller, mother! Whew! I hae as muckle as will pay the widow's account sax times ower! Ye may tell her that frae me; and tell her that I bade you play your part as weel as old lucky could play her's. Siller! Lack-a-day! But, Geordie, my man—Auld wives' dreams are no to be regardit, ye ken. Eh?"

"Whisht now, mother, and mind the grey hen in the Haining wood."

"Heyti-teyti, you an' your grey hen! Stand ye to your tackle, billy.

+ This very old local song, we believe, never was published.—C.N.

Dinna come ower soon hame at night; an' good luck to a' honest intentions."

After putting half a dozen pairs of trysted shoes, and the identical silver-mounted boots into the cadger's creels—then the only regular carriers—off set George Dobson to Hawick market, a distance of nearly eleven new-fashioned miles, but then accounted only eight and three quarters; and after parading the Sandbed, Slitterick Bridge and the Tower Knowe, for the space of an hour, and shaking hands with some four or five acquaintances, he ventured east the gate to pay Mrs Wilson her account. He was kindly welcomed, as every good and regular customer was, by Mrs Wilson, who made it a point always to look after the one thing needful. They settled amicably, as they always had done before; and in the course of business George ventured several sly jocular hints, to see how they would be taken, vexed that his grand and singular dream should go for nothing. No, nothing would pass there but sterling *cent per cent*. The lady was deaf and blind to every effort of gallantry, valuing her own abilities too highly ever to set a man a second time at the head of her flourishing business. Nevertheless, she could not be blind to George's qualifications—he knew that was impossible,—for in the first place he was a goodly person, with handsome limbs and broad square shoulders; of a very dark complexion, true, but with fine shrewd manly features; was a burgess and councillor of the town of Selkirk, and as independent in circumstances as she was.

Very well; Mrs Wilson knew all this—valued George Dobson accordingly, and would not have denied him any of those good points more than Gideon Scott would to a favourite Cheviot tup, in any society whatever; but she had that sharp cold business-manner, that George could discover no symptoms where the price of the boots was to come from. In order to conciliate matters as far as convenient, if not even to stretch a point, he gave her a farther order, larger than the one just settled; but all that he elicited was thanks for his custom, and one very small glass of brandy; so he drank her health, and a good husband to her. Mrs Wilson only curtsied and thanked him coldly, and away George set west the street, with a quick and stately step, saying to himself that the expedition of the silver-mounted boots was all up.

As he was posting up the street, an acquaintance of his, a flesher, likewise of the name of Wilson, eyed him, and called him aside. "Hey, George, come this way a bit. How are ye? How d'ye do, sir? What news about Selkirk? Grand demand for boots there just now, I hear? Eh? Needing any thing in my way the day?—Nae beef like that about your town. Come away in, and taste the gudewife's bottle. I want to hae a crack wi' ye, and get measure of a pair o' boots. The grandest story yon, sir, I ever heard. Eh? Needing a leg o' beef?—Better? Never mind, come away in."

George was following Mr Wilson into the house, having as yet scarcely got a word said, and he liked the man exceedingly, when one pulled his coat, and a pretty servant girl smirked in his face and said, "Maister Dabsen, thou maun cum awa yest the geate and speak till Mistress Wulsin; there's sumtheyng forgwot atween ye. Thou maun cum directly."

"Haste ye, gae away, rin!" says Wilson, pushing him out at the door, "that's a better bait than a poor flesher's dram. There's some comings an' gangings yonder. A bien birth and a thrifty dame. Grip to, grip to, lad! I'se take her at a hunder pund the quarter. Let us see you as ye come back again."

George went back, and there was Mrs Wilson standing in the door to receive him.

"I quite forgot, Mr Dobson—I beg pardon. But I hope, as usual, you will take a family dinner with me to-day?"

"Indeed, Mrs Wilson, I was just thinking to mysell that you were fey, and that we two would never bargain again, for I never paid you an account before that I did not get the offer of my dinner."

"A very stupid neglect! But, indeed, I have so many things to mind, and so hard set with the world, Mr Dobson; you cannot conceive, when there's only a woman at the head of affairs—"

"Ay, but sic a woman," said George, and shook his head.

"Well, well, come at two. I dine early. No ceremony, you know. Just a homely dinner, and no drinking." So saying, she turned and sailed into the house very gracefully; and then turning aside, she looked out at the window after him, apostrophising him thus—"Ay, ye may strut away west the street, as if I were looking after you. Shame fa' the souter-like face o' ye; I wish you had been fifty miles off the day! If it hadna been fear for affronting a good steady customer, ye shoudna hae been here. For there's my brother coming to dinner, and maybe some o' his cronies; and he'll be sae ta'en wi' this merry souter chield, that I ken weel they'll drink mair than twice the profits o' this bit order. My brother maun hae a' his ain will too! Fo'ks maun aye bow to the bush they get bield frae, else I should take a staup out o' their punch cogs the night."

George attended at ten minutes past two, to be as fashionable as the risk of losing his kale would permit—gave a sharp wooer-like rap at the door, and was shown by the dimpling border maid into the

ROOM,—which, in those days, meant the only sitting apartment of a
house. Mrs Wilson being absent about the dinner getting up, and no
one to introduce the parties to each other, think of George's utter
amazement, and astonishment, and dumfounderment,—for there is
no term half strong enough to express it by,—when he saw the
identical fat gentleman, who came to him thrice in his dream, and
ordered him to come to Widow Wilson's, and get payment of his
boots. He was the very identical gentleman in every respect, every
inch of him, and George could have known him among a thousand.
It was not the Duke of Northumberland, but he that was so very like
him, with fair curled hair, and red cheeks, which did not hang over
his cravat. George felt as if he had been dropped into another state of
existence, and knew hardly what to think or say. He had at first very
nigh run up and taken the gentleman's hand, and addressed him as
an old acquaintance, but luckily he recollected the equivocal circumstances in which they met, which was not actually in *the shop*, but in
George's little bed-closet in the night, or early in the morning.

In short, the two sat awkward enough, till, at last, in came Mrs
Wilson, in most brilliant attire, and really a handsome fine woman;
and with her a country lady, with something in her face extremely
engaging. Mrs Wilson immediately introduced the parties to each
other thus:— "Brother, this is Mr Dobson, boot and shoemaker in
Selkirk;—as honest a young man, and as good a payer as I know.—
Mr Dobson, this is Mr Turnbull, my brother, the best friend I ever
had, and this is his daughter Margaret."

The parties were acquainted in one minute, for Mr Turnbull was
a frank kind-hearted gentleman; ay, they were more than acquainted, for the very second or third look that George got of Margaret
Turnbull, he loved her. And during the whole afternoon, every word
that she spoke, every smile that she smiled, and every happy look that
she turned on another, added to his flame; so that long ere the sun
leaned his elbow on Skelfhill Pen, he was deeper in love than, perhaps, there ever was a souter in this world. It is needless to describe
Miss Turnbull—she was *exquisite*, that is enough—just what a woman
should be, and not exceeding twenty-five years of age. What a mense
she would be to the town of Selkirk, and to a boot and shoemaker's
parlour, as well as to the top of the councillors' seat every Sunday!

When the dinner was over, the brandy bottle went round, accompanied with the wee wee glass, in shape of the burr of a Scots thistle.
When it came to Mr Turnbull, he held it up between him and the
light,—"Keatie, whaten a niff-naff of a glass is that? let us see a
feasible ane."

"If it be over little, you can fill it the oftener, brother. I think a big dram is so vulgar!"

"That's no the thing, Keatie. The truth is, that ye're a perfect she Nabal, and ilka thing that takes the value of a plack out o' your pocket, is vulgar, or improper, or something that way. But I'll tell you, Keatie, my woman, what you shall do. Set down a black bottle on this hand o' me, and twa clear anes on this, and the cheeny bowl atween them, and I'll let you see what I'll do. I ken o' nane within the ports o' Hawick can afford a bowl better than you. Nane o' your half bottles and quarter bottles at a time; now Keatie, ye hae a confoundit trick o' that; but I hae some hopes that I'll learn ye good manners by and by."

"Dear brother, I'm sure you are not going to drink your bottles here. Think what the town would say, if I were to keep cabals o' drinkers in my sober house."

"Do as I bid you now, Keatie, and lippen the rest to me. Ah, she is a niggard, Mr Dobson, and has muckle need of a little schooling to open her heart."

The materials were produced, and Mr Turnbull, as had been predicted, did not spare them. There were other two Wilsons joined them immediately after dinner, the one a shoemaker, and the other our friend the flesher, and a merrier afternoon has seldom been in Hawick. Mr Turnbull was perfectly delighted with George;—he made him sing "The Souters o' Selkirk," "Turn the Blue Bonnets," and all his best things; but when he came to "Round about Hawick," he made him sing it six times over, and was never weary of laughing at it, and identifying the characters with those then living. Then the story of the boots was an inexhaustible joke, and the likeness between Mr Turnbull and the Duke of Northumberland an acceptable item. At length Mr Turnbull got so elevated, that he said, "Ay, man! and they are shod wi' silver, and silver tossels round the top? I wad gie a bottle o' wine for a sight o' them."

"It shall cost you nae mair," says George, and in three minutes he set them on the table. Mr Turnbull tried them on, and walked through and through the room with them, singing—

"With silver he was shod before—
With burning gold behind."

They fitted exactly; and before sitting down, he offered George the original price, and got them.

It became late rather too soon for our group, but the young lady grew impatient to get home, and Mr Turnbull was obliged to prepare for going; nothing, however, would please him, save that George should go with him all night; and George being, long before this time, over head and ears in love, accepted of the invitation, and the loan of the flesher's bay mare, and went with them. Miss Margaret had soon, by some kind of natural inspiration, discovered our jovial souter's partiality for her; and in order to open the way for a banter, the best mode of beginning a courtship, she fell on and rallied him most severely about the boots and the *soutering*, and particularly about letting himself be robbed of the two guineas. This gave George an opportunity of retaliating so happily, that he wondered at himself, for he acknowledged that he said things that he never believed he had the face to say to a lady before.

The year after that, the two were married in the house of Mrs Wilson, and Mr Turnbull paid down a hundred pounds to George on the day he brought her from that house a bride. Now, thought George to himself, I have been twice most liberally paid for my boots in that house. My wife, perhaps, will stand for the third payment, which I hope will be the best of all; but I still think there is to be another one beside. He was not wrong, for after the death of his worthy father-in-law, he found himself entitled to the third of his whole effects; the transfer of which, nine years after his marriage, was made over to him in the house of his friend, Mrs Wilson.

Dreams and Apparitions.—Part II.
Containing

Tibby Hyslop's Dream,
and the Sequel.

In the year 1807, when on a jaunt through the valleys of Nith and Annan, I learned the following story on the spot where the incidents occurred, and even went and visited all those connected with it, so that there is no doubt with regard to its authenticity.

In a wee cottage called Know-back, on the large farm of Drumlochie, lived Tibby Hyslop, a respectable spinster, about the age of forty I thought when I saw her, but, of course, not so old when the first incidents occurred which this singular prophetic tale relates. Tibby was represented to me as a good and sincere Christian, not in name and profession only, but in word and in deed; and I believe I may add, in heart and in soul. Nevertheless, there was something in her manner and deportment different from other people—a sort of innocent simplicity, bordering on silliness, together with an instability of thought, that, in the eyes of many, approached to abstraction.

But then Tibby could repeat the book of the Evangelist Luke by heart, and many favourite chapters both of the Old and New Testaments; while there was scarcely one in the whole country who was so thoroughly acquainted with those Books from beginning to end; for, though she had read a portion every day for forty years, she had never perused any other books but the Scriptures. They were her week-day books, and her Sunday books, her books of amusement, and books of devotion. Would to God that all our brethren and sisters of the human race—the poor and comfortless, as well as the great and wise, knew as well how to estimate these books as Tibby Hyslop did!

Tibby's history is shortly this. Her mother was married to a sergeant of a recruiting party. The year following he was obliged to go to Ireland, and from thence nobody knew where; but neither he nor his wife appeared again in Scotland. Before their departure, however, they left Tibby, then a helpless babe, with her grandmother, who lived in a hamlet somewhere about Tinwald; and with that grandmother was she brought up to read her Bible, card and spin, and work at all kinds of country labour to which women are accustomed. Jane Hervey was her grandmother's name, a woman then scarcely past her prime, certainly within forty years of age; but an elder sister, named Douglas, lived also with her, and with these two were the early years of Tibby Hyslop spent, in poverty, contentment, and devotion.

At the age of eighteen, Tibby was hired at the Candlemas fair, for a great wage, to be byre-woman to Mr Gilbert Forret, then farmer at Drumlochie. Tibby had then acquired a great deal of her mother's dangerous bloom—dangerous, when attached to poverty, and so much simplicity of heart; and when she came home and told what she had done, her mother and aunty, as she always denominated the two, marvelled much at the extravagant conditions, and began to express some fears regarding her new master's designs, till Tibby put them all to rest by the following piece of simple information.

"Dear, ye ken, ye needna be feared that Mr Forret has ony design o' courting me, for, dear, ye ken, he has a wife already, and five bonny bairns; and he'll never be sae daft as fa' on and court anither ane. I'se warrant he finds ane enow for him, honest man!"

"Oh, then, you are safe enough, since he is a married man, my bairn," said Jane.

> "Ay, but wha on Monanday's morn has seen
> The gerse and the dew-cup growing green,
> Where a married man and a maid had been?"

said old aunty Douglas; but she spoke always in riddles and mysteries, and there was no more of it. But the truth was, that Mr Forret was notorious in his neighbourhood for the debauching of young and pretty girls, and was known in Dumfries market by the name of Gibby Gledger, from the circumstance of his being always looking slyly after them; and perceiving Tibby so comely, and at the same time so simple, he judged her a fine prey, hired her at nearly double wages, and moreover gave her a crown as arle-money.

So home Tibby went to her service, and being a pliable, diligent creature, she was beloved by all about the town. Her master attended much about the byre, commended her for her neatness, and whenever a quiet opportunity offered, would pat her rosy cheek, and say kind things. Tibby took all these in good part, judging them tokens of approbation of her good services, and was proud of them; and if he once or twice whispered a place and an hour of assignation, she took it for a joke, and paid no farther attention to it. Mr Forret was much from home, kept much company, and had few opportunities of meeting with his pretty dairymaid privately;

and the fewer, that between the stable and byres there was only a half wall.

In short, a whole year passed over without the worthy farmer having accomplished his cherished purpose regarding poor Tibby; still he was quite convinced that it was a matter which might be accomplished with perfect ease, and would lead to a very pleasant diversity in a farmer's monotonous life. With this laudable prospect, when the Candlemas fair came round again, he hired Tibby to remain another year, still on the former high conditions, and moreover he said to her: "I wish your grandmother and grand-aunt would take my pleasant cottage of Know-back. They should have it for a mere trifle, a week's shearing or so, as long as you remain in my service; and as it is likely to be a long while before you and I part, if I get my will, it would be better to have them near you, that you might see them often, and attend to their wants. I could give them plenty of work through the whole year, on the best conditions. What think you of this proposal, Rosy?"—a familiar name he often called her by.

"O, I'm sure, sir, I think ye are the kindest man that ever the Almighty made. What a blessing is it when riches open up the heart to acts of charity an' benevolence! My poor auld mother an' aunty will be blithe to grip at the kind offer, for they sit under a hard master yonder, and the Almighty will bestow a blessing on you for this, sir; and they will gie you their blessing, an' I sall bestow my poor blessing on you too, sir."

"Well, I'll rather have that than all the rest. Come, bestow it, then. Nay, I see I must take it, after all."

So saying, he kissed her. Tibby neither blushed nor proffered refusal, because it was the way that the saints of old saluted one another; and away she went with the joyful news to her poor mother and aunty. Now, they had of late found themselves quite easy in their circumstances, owing to the large wages Tibby received, every farthing of which was added to the common stock; and though Tibby appeared a little brawer at the meeting-house, it was her grandmother who laid it out on her, without any consent on her part. "I am sure," said her grandmother, when Tibby told the story of her master's kindness and attention, "I am sure it was the kindest intervention o' Providence that ever happened to poor things afore, when ye fell in wi' that kind worthy man, i' the mids o' a great hiring market, where ye might just as easily hae met wi' a knave, or a niggard, or a sinner,—wha wad hae thought naething o' working your ruin,—as wi' this man o' sickan charity an' mercy."

"Ay; the wulcat maun hae his collop,
   An' the raven maun hae his part,
An' the tod will creep through the hether,
   For the bonny moorhen's heart,"

said old Douglas Hervey, poking in the fire all the while with the tongs, and speaking only as if speaking to herself—"Hech-wow, an' lack-a-day! but the times are altered sair since I first saw the sun! 'How are they altered, kerlin?' Because the gospel's turn'd like a gainder, and Sin a fine madam. How d'ye do, sweet Madam Sin? Come in by here, and be a sharer o' our bed and board. Hope ye left a' friends weel in your cozy hame? But, on the tither hand, ca' away that dirty, wearysome bird; fling stanes an' glaur at him. What is he aye harp, harp, harping there for?—Thraw his neck about. Poor, poor Religion, waes me for her! She was first driven out o' the lord's castle into the baron's ha'; out o' the baron's ha', into the farmer's bien dwelling; and at last out o' that, into the poor cauldrife shiel, where there's nae ither comfort but what she brings wi' her."

"What has set ye onna thae reflections the day, aunty?" cried Tibby aloud at her ear; for she was half deaf, and had so many flannel mutches on, besides a blue napkin, which she always wore over them all, that her deafness was nearly completed altogether.

"Oogh! what's the lassie saying?" said she, after listening a good while, till the sounds actually reached the interior of her ear, "what's the young light-head saying about the defections o' the day? what kens she about them?—oogh! Let me see your face, dame, and find your hand, for I hae neither seen the ane, nor felt the tither, this lang and mony a day." Then taking her grand-niece by the hand, and looking close into her face through the spectacles, she added—"Ay, it is a weel-faured sonsy face, very like the mother's that bore ye; and hers was as like *her* mother's; and there was never as muckle common sense amang a' the three as to keep a brock out o' the kail-yard. Ye hae an unco good master, I hear—oogh! I'm glad to hear't—hoh-oh -oh-oh!—verra glad. I hope it will lang continue, this kindness. Poor Tibby!—as lang as the heart disna gang wrang, we maun excuse the head, for it'll never aince gang right. I hope they were baith made for a better warld, for nane o' them were made for this."

When she got this length, she sat hastily down, and began her daily and hourly task of carding wool for her sister's spinning, abstracting herself from all external considerations.

"I think aunty's unco parabolical the day," said Tibby to her grandmother; "what makes her that gate?"

"O dear, hinny, she's aye that gate now. She speaks to naebody but hersell," said Jane. "But—lownly be it spoken—I think whiles there's ane speaks till her again that my een canna see."

"The angels often conversed wi' good folks langsyne," said Tibby. "I ken o' naething that can hinder them to do sae still, if they're sae disposed. But weel wad I like to hear ane o' thae preevat apologies, (perhaps meaning apologues,) for my auntie has something in her aboon other earthly creatures."

"Ye may hear enow o' them aince we war leeving near you again; there's ane every midnight, and another atween daylight and the sun. It is my wonder that she's no ta'en for a witch; for, troth, d'ye ken, hinny, I'm whiles a wee feared for her mysell. And yet, for a' that, I ken she's a good Christian."

"Ay, that she is—I wish there were mony like her," said Tibby, and so the dialogue closed for the present.

Mr Forret sent his carts at the term, and removed the old people to the cottage of Know-back, free of all charge, like a gentleman as he was, and things went on exceedingly well. Tibby had a sincere regard for her master; and as he continued to speak to her, when alone, in a kind and playful manner, she had several times ventured to broach religion to him, trying to discover the state of his soul. Then he would shake his head, and look demure in mockery, and repeat some grave, becoming words. Poor Tibby thought he *was* a blessed man. Then, when he would snatch a kiss or two, Tibby did not in the least comprehend the drift of this; but, convinced in her heart that it could only mean something holy, and good, and kind, she tried not further to reflect on it, for she could not; but she blessed him in her heart, and was content to remain in her ignorance of human life.

But in a short time his purposes were divulged in such a manner as to be no more equivocal. That morning immediately preceding the developement of this long-cherished atrocity, Jane Hervey was awaked at an early hour by the following unintelligible dialogue in her elder sister's bed.

"Have ye seen the news o' the day, kerlin?"

"Ooh?"

"Have ye seen the news o' the day?"

"Ay, that I hae, on a braid open book, without clasp or seal. Whether will you or the deil win?"

"That depends on the citadel. If it stand out, a' the powers o' hell winna shake the fortress, nor sap a stane o' its foundation."

"Ah, the fortress is a good ane, and a sound ane; but the poor head captain!—ye ken what a sweet-lipped, turnip-headit brosey he is."

"Ay; and the weapons o' sin are grown strang and powerfu' now-a-days, kerlin."

"Sae they say, sae they say. They hae gotten a new forge i' the fire o' hell, made out o' despised ordinances. O, lack-a-day, my poor Tibby Hyslop!—my innocent, kind, thowless Tibby Hyslop! Now for the tod or the moorhen!"

Jane was frightened at hearing such a colloquy, but particularly at that part of it where her darling child was mentioned in such a way. She sprung from her own bed to that of her sister, and cried in her ear with a loud voice,—"Sister, sister Douglas, what is that you are saying about our dear bairn?"

"Oogh? I was saying naething about your bairn. She is turned intil a spring-gun, is she?—or a man-trap rather is it? I trow little whilk o' them it is, poor stupit creature. She lies in great jeopardy yonder; but nane as yet. Gang awa' to your bed—wow, but I was sound asleep."

"There's naebody can make ought out o' her but nonsense," said Jane, as she went to put a few sticks and peat clods on the scarcely living embers. But, after the two had risen from their scanty but happy breakfast, which Douglas had blessed with more fervency than ordinary, she could not settle at her carding, but always stopped short, and began mumbling and speaking to herself. At length, after a long pause, she looked over her shoulder, and said,—"Jeanie, warna ye speaking o' ganging ower to see our bairn the day? Haste thee an' gang away, then; and stay nouther to put on clean bussing, kirtle, nor barrie, else ye may be an antrin meenut or twa ower lang."

Jane made no reply, but, drawing the skirt of her gown over her shoulders, she set out for Drumlochie, a distance of nearly a mile; and as she went by the corner of the byre, she weened she heard her bairn's voice, in great passion or distress, and ran straight into the byre, crying out, "What's the matter wi' you, Tibby? what ails you, my bairn?" but, receiving no answer, she thought her voice must have been somewhere outside the house, and slid quietly out, looking everywhere, and at length went down to the kitchen.

Tibby had run a hard risk that hour, not from any proffer of riches or finery—these had no temptations for her—she could not even understand the purport or drift of them. But she did escape, however; and it was, perhaps, her grandmother's voice that saved her.

Mr Forret, *alias* Gledging Gibby, had borne the brunt of incensed kirk-sessions before that time, and also the unlicensed tongues of mothers, roused into vehemence by the degradation of beloved daughters; but never in his life did he bear such a rebuke as he did that day from the tongue of one he had always viewed as a mere simpleton. It was a lesson to him—a warning of the most sublime and terrible description, couched in the pure and emphatic language of Scripture. Gibby cared not a doit for these things, but found himself foiled, and exposed to his family, and the whole world, if this fool chose to do it. He was, therefore, glad to act a part of deep hypocrisy, pretending the sincerest contrition, regretting, with tears, his momentary derangement, and want of self-control; attributing it wholly to the temptations of the wicked one, and praising poor Tibby to the skies for saving him in an hour of utter depravity. He likewise made her a present of a sum of money he had offered her before, saying, he did not give it her as a bribe, but as the reward of honesty, virtue, and truth, for all of which he had the highest regard, and that he would esteem her the more for her behaviour that day, as long as he lived.

Poor Tibby readily believed and forgave him; and thinking it hard to ruin a repentant sinner in his worldly and family concerns, she promised never to divulge what had passed; and he knowing well the value of her word, was glad at having so escaped.

Jane found her grand-daughter terribly flushed in the countenance, and flurried in her speech that day, but Jane's stupid head could draw no inferences from these, or anything else. She asked if she was well enough, and the other saying she was, Jane took it for granted that she was so, and only added, "Your crazed auntie would gar me believe ye war in some jeopardy, and hurried me away to see you, without giving me leave to change a steek." One may easily conceive Tibby's astonishment at hearing this, considering the moment at which her grandmother arrived. As soon as the latter was gone, she kneeled before her Maker, and poured out her soul in grateful thanksgiving for her deliverance; and, in particular, for such a manifest interference of some superior intelligence in her behalf.

"How did ye find our poor bairn the day, titty Jean? Was the trial ower afore ye wan? Or did ye gie a helping-hand at raising the siege?—Ooogh?"

"Whaten siege? I saw nae siege, nor heard tell of ony."

"The great siege o' the castle o' Man-soul, that Bunyan speaks about, ye ken. Was it ower? Or is it to try for again? Oh! ye dinna understand me! Did ye ever understand onything a' your days? Did our bairn no tell ye onything?"

"She tauld me naething, but said she was very weel."

"She's ae fool, and ye're another! If I had been her, I wad hae blazed it baith to kirk and council;—to his wife's ear, and his minister's teeth! I wad hae gart heaven sab, and hell girn at it! Isna the resetter waur than the thief? The cowardly butcher that conceals the lambs and kills them, waur than the open fauld-brikker and sheep-reiver? And isna the sweet-lippit kiss-my-lufe saint waur than the stouthright reprobate? Figh—fie! A dish o' sodden turnips at the best. She's very weel, is she?—Oogh! Red an' rosy like a boiled lobster? Aye. Hoh—oh—oh—oh!—silly woman—silly woman— Hoh—oh—oh!"

In a few weeks, Mr Forret's behaviour to his simple dairymaid altered very materially. He called her no more by the endearing name of Rosy; poor ideot was oftener the term; and finding he was now safe from accusation, his malevolence towards her had scarcely any bounds. She made out her term with difficulty, but he refused to pay the stipulated wage, on pretence of her incapacity; and as she had by that time profited well at his hand, she took what he offered, thanked him, and said no more about it. She was no more hired as a servant, but having at the first taken a long lease of the cottage, she continued, from year to year, working on the farm by the day, at a very scanty allowance. Old Douglas in a few years grew incapable of any work, through frailty of person, being constantly confined to bed, though in mind as energetic and mysterious as ever. Jane wrought long, till at length a severe illness in 1799 rendered her unfit to do anything further than occasionally knit a piece of a stocking; and poor Tibby's handywork had all three to maintain. They had brought her up with care and kindness amid the most pinching poverty, and now, indeed, her filial affection was hardly put to the proof; but it was genuine, and knew no bounds. Night and day did she toil for the sustenance of her aged and feeble relations, and a murmur or complaint never was heard to drop from her lips. Many a blessing was bestowed on her as they raised their palsied heads to partake of her hard-earned pittance; and many a fervent prayer was poured out, when none heard but the Father of the spirits of all flesh.

Times grew harder and harder. Thousands yet living remember what a time that was for the poor, while the meal for seasons was from four to five shillings a-stone, and even sometimes as high as seven. Tibby grew fairly incapable of supporting herself and her aged friends. She stinted herself for their sakes, and that made her still more incapable; yet often with tears in her eyes did she feed these frail beings, her heart like to melt because she had no more to give them. There are no poor-rates in that country. Know-back is quite retired —nobody went near it, and Tibby complained to none, but wrought on, and fought away, night and day, in sorrow and anxiety, but still with a humble and thankful heart.

In this great strait, Mrs Forret was the first who began, unsol-
icited, to take compassion on the destitute group. She could not
conceive how they existed on the poor creature's earnings. So she
went privately to see them, and when she saw their wretched state,
and heard their blessings on their dear child, her heart was moved to
pity, and she determined to assist them in secret, for her husband was
such a churl, that publicly she durst not venture to do it. Accordingly, whenever she had an opportunity, she made Tibby come into
the kitchen, and get a meal for herself; and often the considerate lady
slid a small loaf, or a little tea and sugar, into her lap, quietly, for the
two aged invalids;—for gentle woman is always the first to pity, and
the first to relieve.

Poor Tibby! how her heart expanded with gratitude on receiving
these little presents, for her love for the two old dependent creatures
was of so pure and sacred a sort, as scarcely to retain in its element
any of the common feelings of humanity. There was no selfish principle there—they were to her as a part of her own nature. And it was
observed, that whenever she got these little presents, enabling her to
give the aged and infirm a better meal, and one more suited to their
wasted frames, she had not patience to walk home to Know-back—
she ran all the way.

Tibby never went into the kitchen unless the mistress desired her,
or sent her word by some of the other day-labourers to come in as she
went home; and one evening having got word in this last way, she
went in, and the lady of the house, with her own hand, presented her
with a little bowl full of beat potatoes, and some sweet milk to them.
This was all, and one would have thought it was an aliment so
humble and plain, that scarcely any person would have grudged it to
a hungry dog. However, it so happened that as Tibby was sitting
behind backs enjoying her little savoury meal, Mr Forret chanced to
come into the kitchen to give orders anent something that had come
into his mind; and perceiving Tibby, his old friend, so comfortably
engaged, he, without speaking a word, seized her by the neck with
one hand, and by the shoulder with the other, and hurrying her out
at the back-door into the yard, he flung her, with all his might, on a
dunghill. "Wha the devil bade you come into my house, and eat up
the meat that was made for others?" cried he, in a demoniac voice,
choking with rage; and then he swore a terrible oath, which I do not
choose to set down, that "if he found her again at such employment,
he would cut her throat, and fling her to the dogs."

Poor Tibby was astounded beyond the power of utterance, or even

of rising from the place where he had thrown her down, until lifted by
two of the servant-maids, who tried to comfort her as they supported
her part of the way home; and bitterly did they blame their master,
saying it would have been a shame to any one who had the feelings of
a man, to do such an act; but as for their master, he scarcely had the
feelings of a beast. Tibby never opened her mouth, neither to curse,
blame, nor complain, but went on her way crying till her heart was
like to break.

She had no supper for the old famishing pair that night. They had
tasted nothing from the time that she left them in the morning; and as
she had accounted herself sure of receiving something from Mrs
Forret that night, she had not asked her day's wages from the grieve,
glad to let a day run up now and then, when able to procure a meal in
any other honest way. She had nothing to give them that night, so
what could she do? She was obliged, with a sore heart, to kiss them
and tell them so; and then, as was her custom, she said a prayer over
their couch, and laid herself down to sleep drowned in tears.

She had never so much as mentioned Mr Forret's name either to
her grandmother or grand-aunt that night, or by the least insin-
uation given them to understand that he had either used her ill or
well; but no sooner were they composed to rest, and all the cottage
quiet, than old Douglas began abusing him with great vehemence
and obstreperousness, and Tibby, to her astonishment, heard some of
his deeds spoken of with great familiarity, which she was sure never
had been whispered to the ear of flesh; and many more of the same
stamp which Tibby had never heard mentioned before, which,
nevertheless, from obvious circumstances, might have been but too
true. But what shocked her most of all, was the following terrible
prognostication, which she heard repeated three several times:—
"Na, na, I'll no see it, for I'll never see aught earthly again beyond
the wa's o' this cottage, but Tibby will live to see it;—ay, ay, she'll see
it." Then a different voice asked—"What will *she* see, kerlin?" "She'll
see the craws picking his banes at the back o' the dyke."

Tibby's heart grew cauld within her when she heard this terrible
announcement, because, for many years bygone, she had been convinced, from sensible demonstration, that old Douglas Hervey had
commerce with some superior intelligence; and after she had heard
the above sentence repeated again and again, she shut her ears, that
she might hear no more; committed herself once more to the hands of
a watchful Creator, and fell into a troubled sleep.

The elemental spirits that weave the shadowy tapestry of dreams,
were busy at their aerial looms that night in the cottage of Know-

back, bodying forth the destinies of men and women in brilliant and quick succession. One only of these delineations I shall here relate, precisely as it was related to me, by my friend the worthy clergyman of that parish, to whom Tibby related it the very next day. There is no doubt that her grand-aunt's disjointed prophecy formed the groundwork of the picture; but be that as it may, this was her dream; and it was for the sake of telling it, and tracing it to its fulfilment, that I began this story.

Tibby Hyslop dreamed, that on a certain spot which she had never seen before, between a stone-dyke and the verge of a woody precipice, a little, sequestered, inaccessible corner, of a triangular shape,—or, as she called it to the minister, "a three-neukit crook o' the linn," she saw Mr Forret lying without his hat, with his throat slightly wounded, and blood running from it; but he neither appeared to be dead, nor yet dying, but in excellent spirits. He was clothed in a fine new black suit, had full boots on, which appeared likewise to be new, and yellow spurs gilt. A great number of rooks and hooded crows were making free with his person;—some picking out his eyes, some his tongue, and some tearing out his bowels. But in place of being distressed by their voracity, he appeared much delighted, encouraging them on all that he could, and there was a perfectly good understanding between the parties. In the midst of this horrible feast, down came a majestic raven from a dark cloud close above this scene, and, driving away all the meaner birds, fell a-feasting himself; —opened the breast of his victim, who was still alive, and encouraging him on; and after preying on his vitals for some time, at last picked out his heart, and devoured it; and then the mangled wretch, after writhing for a short time in convulsive agonies, groaned his last.

This was precisely Tibby's dream as it was told to me, first by my friend Mr Cunningham of Dalswinton, and afterwards by the clergyman to whom she herself related it next day. But there was something in it not so distinctly defined, for though the birds which she saw devouring her master, were rooks, blood-crows, and a raven, still each individual of the number had a likeness by itself, distinguishing it from all the rest; a certain character, as it were, to support; and these particular likenesses were so engraven on the dreamer's mind, that she never forgot them, and she could not help looking for them both among "birds and bodies," as she expressed it, but never could distinguish any of them again; and the dream, like many other distempered visions, was forgotten, or only remembered now and then with a certain tremor of antecedent knowledge.

Days and seasons passed over, and with them the changes incident to humanity. The virtuous and indefatigable Tibby Hyslop was assisted by the benevolent, who had heard of her exertions and patient sufferings; and the venerable Douglas Hervey had gone in peace to the house appointed for all living, when one evening in June, John Jardine, the cooper, chanced to come to Know-back, in the course of his girding and hooping peregrinations. John was a living and walking chronicle of the events of the day, all the way from the head of Glen-breck to the bridge of Stoneylee. He knew every man, and every man's affairs—every woman, and every woman's failings; and his information was not like that of many others, for it was generally to be depended on. How he got his information so correctly, was a mystery to many, but whatever John the cooper told as a fact, was never disputed, and any woman, at least, might have ventured to tell it over again.

"These are hard times for poor folks, Tibby. How are you and auld granny coming on?"

"Joost fighting on as we hae done for mony a year. She is aye contentit, poor body, an' thankfu', whether I hae little to gie her, or muckle. This life's naething but a fight, Johnie, frae beginning to end."

"It's a' true ye say, Tibby," said the cooper, interrupting her, for he was afraid she was going to begin on religion, a species of conversation that did not accord with John's talents or dispositions, "It's a' true ye say, Tibby; but your master will soon be sic a rich man now, that we'll a' be made up, and you amang the lave will be made a lady."

"If he get his riches honestly, an' the blessing o' the Almighty wi' them, John, I shall rejoice in his prosperity, but neither me nor ony ither poor body will ever be muckle the better o' them. What way is he gaun to get sickan great riches? If a' be true that I hear, he is gaun to the wrang part to seek them?"

"Aha, lass, that's a' that ye ken about it. Did ye no hear that he had won the law-plea on his laird, whilk has been afore the Lords for mair than seven years? An' did ye no hear that he had won ten pleas afore the courts o' Dumfries, a' rising out o' ane anither, like ash girderings out o' ae root, and that he's to get, on the hale, about twenty thousand punds worth o' damages?"

"That's an unco sight o' siller, John. How muckle is that?"

"Aha, lass, ye hae fixed me now; but they say it will come to as muckle goud as six men can carry on their backs. And we're a' to get twenties, and thirties, and forties o' punds for bribes, to gar us gie faithfu' and true evidences at the great concluding trial afore the

Lords; and you are to be bribit amang the rest, to gar ye tell the hale truth, and nothing but the truth."

"There needs nae waste o' siller to gar me do that. But, Johnie, I wad like to ken whether that mode o' taking oaths, solemn and sacred oaths, about the miserable trash o' this warld, be according to the tenor o' gospel revelation, and the third o' the Commands?"

"Aha, lass! ye *hae* fixed me now! That's rather a kittle point, but I believe it's a' true that ye say. However, ye'll get the offer of a great bribe in a few days; an' take ye my advice, Tibby,—Get haud o' the bribe afore hand; for if ye lippen to your master's promises, you will never finger a bodle after the job's done."

"I'm but a poor simple body, Johnie, an' canna manage ony sickan things. But I shall need nae fee to gar me tell the truth, an' I winna tell an untruth for a' my master's estate, an' his sax backfu's o' goud into the bargain. If the sin o' the soul, Johnie——"

"Ay, ay, that's very true, Tibby! very true, indeed, about the sin o' the soul! But as ye were saying about being a simple body—What wad ye think if I were to cast up that day Gledging Gibby came here to gie you your lesson—I could maybe help you on a wee bit—What wad you gie me if I did?"

"Alack, I hae naething to gie you but my blessing; but I shall pray for the blessing o' God on ye."

"Ay, ay, as ye say. I daresay there might be waur things. But could you think o' naething else to gie a body wha likes as weel to be paid aff hand as to gie credit? That's the very thing I'm cautioning you against."

"I dinna expect ony siller frae that fountain-head, Johnie: It is a dry ane to the puir and the needy, and an unco sma' matter wad gar me make over my rights to a pose that I hae neither faith nor hope in. But ye're kend for an auld-farrant man; if ye can bring a little honestly this way, I shall gie you the half o't; for weel I ken it will never come this way by ony art or shift o' mine."

"Ay, ay, that's spoken like a sensible and reasonable woman, Tibby Hyslop, as ye are and hae always been. But think you that nae way could be contrived"—and here the cooper gave two winks with his left eye—"by the whilk ye could gie me it a', and yet no rob yoursel of a farthing?"

"Na, na, Johnie Jardine, that's clean aboon my comprehension: But ye're a cunning draughty man, and I leave the hale matter to your guidance."

"Very weel, Tibby, very weel. I'll try to ca' a gayan substantial gird round your success, if I can hit the width o' the chance, and the

girth o' the gear. Gude day to you the day, an' think about the plan
o' equal-aqual that I spake o'."

Old maids are in general very easily courted, and very apt to take
a hint. I have indeed known a great many instances in which they
took hints very seriously, before ever they were given. Not so with
Tibby Hyslop. There had such a heavy charge lain upon her the
greater part of her life, that she had never turned her thoughts to any
earthly thing beside, and she knew no more what the cooper was
aiming at, than if the words had not been spoken. When he went
away, her grandmother called her to the bedside, and asked if the
cooper was gone away. Tibby answered in the affirmative; on which
granny said, "What has he been havering about sae lang the day? I
thought I heard him courting ye."

"Courting me! Dear granny, he was courting nane o' me; he was
telling me how Mr Forret had won as muckle siller at the law as sax
men can carry on their backs, and how we are a' to get a part of it."

"Dinna believe him, hinny; the man that can win siller at the law,
will lose it naewhere. But, Tibby, I heard the cooper courting you,
and I thought I heard you gie him your consent to manage the
matter as he likit. Now you hae been a great blessing to me. I thought
you sent to me in wrath, as a punishment of my sins, but I have found
that you were indeed sent to me in love and in kindness. You have
been the sole support of my old age, and of hers wha is now in the
grave, and it is natural that I should like to see you put up afore I
leave you. But, Tibby Hyslop, John Jardine is not the man to lead a
Christian life with. He has nae mair religion than the beasts that
perish—he is frighted for it, and shuns it as a body would do a
loathsome or poisonous draught: And besides, it is weel kend how
sair he neglected his first wife. Hae naething to do wi' him, my dear
bairn, but rather live as you are. There is neither sin nor shame in
being unwedded, but there may be baith in joining yourself to an
unbeliever."

Tibby wondered at this information. She did not know she had
been courted, and she found that she rather thought the better of the
cooper for what it appeared he had done. Accordingly, she made no
promises to her grandmother, but only remarked, that "it was a pity
no to gie the cooper a chance o' conversion, honest man."

The cooper kept watch about Drumlochie and the hinds' houses,
and easily found out all the sly Gibby's movements, and even the
exact remuneration he could be urged to give to such as were pleased
to remember aright. Indeed it was believed that the most part of the
hinds and labouring people remembered nothing of the matter

farther than he was pleased to inform them, and that in fact they gave evidence to the best of their knowledge or remembrance, although that evidence might be decidedly wrong.

One day Gibby took his gun, and went out towards Know-back. The cooper also, guessing what was in his head, went thither by a circuitous route, so as to come in as it were by chance; but ere he arrived, Mr Forret had begun his queries and instructions to Tibby. —The two could not agree by any means; Tibby either could not recollect the yearly crops on each field on the farm of Drumlochie, or recollected wrong—But at length, in comes the cooper, when the calculations were at the keenest, and at every turn he took Mr Forret's side, with the most strenuous asseverations, abusing Tibby for her stupidity and want of recollection.

"Hear me speak, Johnie Jardine, afore ye condemn me aff-loof: Mr Forret says that the crooked holm was pease in the 96, and corn in the 97; I say it was corn baith the years. How do ye say about that?"

"Mr Forret's right—perfectly right. It grew pease in the 96, and aits, good Angus aits, in the 97. Poor gouk! dinna ye think that he has a' these things merkit down in black an' white, and what good could it do to him to mislead you? Depend on't, he is right there."

"Could ye tak your oath on that, Johnie Jardine?"

"Ay, this meenint,—sax times repeated, if it were necessary."

"Then I yield—I am but a poor silly woman, liable to mony errors and shortcomings—My recollection is playing at hide-an'-seek wi' me—I maun be wrang, and I yield that it is sae. But I am sure, John, you cannot but remember this sae short a while syne, for ye shore wi' us that har'st. Was the lang field niest Robie Johnston's farm growing corn in the dear year, or no? I say it was."

"It was the next year, Tibby, my woman," said Mr Forret; "you are confounding one year with another again; and I see what is the reason. It was oats in 99, grass in 1800, and oats again in 1801; now you never remember any of the intermediate years, but only those that you shore on these fields. I cannot be mistaken in a rule I never break."

The cooper had now got his cue. He perceived that the plea ultimately depended on proof relating to the proper cropping of the land throughout the lease; and he supported the farmer so strenuously, that Tibby, in her simplicity, fairly yielded, although hardly convinced; but the cooper assured the farmer that he would put her all to rights, provided she received a handsome acknowledgment, for there was not the least doubt that Mr Forret was right in every particular.

This speech of the cooper's gratified the farmer exceedingly, as his whole fortune now depended upon the evidence to be elicited in the court at Dumfries, on a day that was fast approaching, and he was willing to give anything to secure the evidence on his side; so he made a long set speech to Tibby, telling her how necessary it was that she should adhere strictly to the truth—that, as it would be an awful thing to make oath to that which was false, he had merely paid her that visit to instruct her remembrance a little in that which was the truth, it being impossible, on account of his jottings, that he could be mistaken; and finally it was settled, that for thus telling the truth, and nothing but the truth, Tibby Hyslop, a most deserving woman, was to receive a present of L.15, as wages for time bygone. This was all managed in a very sly way by the cooper, who assured Forret that all should go right, as far as related to Tibby Hyslop and himself, which elated the farmer exceedingly; for the spirit of litigation had of late possessed him to such a degree, and he had ventured such a stake on the issue, that if he had been master of the realm, he would have parted with the half of it to beat his opponents.

The day of the trial arrived, and counsel attended from Edinburgh for both parties, to take full evidence before the two Circuit Lords and Sheriff. The evidence was said to have been unsatisfactory to the Judges, but upon the whole in Mr Forret's favour. The cooper's was decidedly so, and the farmer's counsel were crowing and bustling immoderately, when at length Tibby Hyslop was called to the witnesses' box. At the first sight of her master's counsel, and the Dumfries writers and notaries that were hanging about him, Tibby was struck dumb with amazement, and almost bereaved of sense. She at once recognised them, all and severally, as the birds that she saw, in her dream, devouring her master, and picking the flesh from his bones; while the great lawyer from Edinburgh was, in feature, eye, and beak, the identical raven which at last devoured his vitals and heart.

This singular coincidence brought reminiscences of such a nature over her spirit, that, on the first questions being put, she could not answer a word. She knew from thenceforward that her master was a ruined man, and her heart failed, on thinking of her kind mistress and his family. The counsel then went, and whispering Mr Forret, inquired what sort of a woman she was, and if her evidence was likely to be of any avail. As the cooper had behaved so well, and had likewise answered for Tibby, the farmer was intent on not losing her evidence, and answered his counsel that she was a worthy honest woman, who would not swear to a lie for the king's dominions, and that he must not lose her evidence. This intelligence the lawyer announced to the bench with great consequence and pomposity, and the witness was allowed a little time to recover her spirits.

Isabella Hyslop, spinster, was again called, answered to her name, and took the oath distinctly, and without hesitation, until the official querist came to the usual question, "Now, has no one instructed you what to say, or what you are to answer?" When Tibby replied, with a steady countenance, "Nobody except my master!" The counsel and client stared at one another, while the Court could hardly maintain their gravity of deportment. The querist went on—

"What? Do you say your master instructed you what to say?"

"Yes."

"And did he promise or give you any reward for what you were to say?"

"Yes."

"How much did he give or promise you for answering as he directed you?"

"He gave me fifteen pound notes."

Here Mr Forret and his counsel, losing all patience, interrupted the proceedings, the latter addressing the Judges, with pompous vehemence, to the following purport:—

"My Lords, in my client's name, and in the names of justice and reason, I protest against proceeding with this woman's evidence, it being manifest that she is talking through a total derangement of intellect. At first she is dumb, she cannot answer nor speak a word, and now she is answering in total disregard of all truth and propriety. I appeal to your Lordships if such a farrago as this can be at all inferential or relevant?"

"Sir, it was but the other minute," said the junior Judge, "that you announced to us with great importance, that this woman was a person noted for honesty and worth, and one who would not tell a lie for the king's dominions. Why not then hear her evidence to the end? For my own part, I perceive no tokens of discrepancy in it, but rather a scrupulous conscientiousness. Of that, however, we will be better able to judge when we have heard her out. I conceive that, for the sake of both parties, this woman should be strictly examined."

"Proceed with the evidence, Mr Wood," said the senior Lord, bowing to his assistant.

Tibby was reminded that she was on her great oath, and examined over again; but she adhered strictly to her former answers.

"Can you repeat anything to the Court that he desired you to say?"

"Yes; he desired me over and over again to tell the whole truth, and nothing but the truth."

"And, in order that you should do this, he paid you down fifteen pounds sterling?"

"Yes."

"This is a very singular transaction: I cannot perceive the meaning of it. You certainly must be sensible that you made an advantageous bargain?"

"Yes."

"But you depone that he charged you to tell only the truth?"

"Yes, he did, and before witnesses, too."

Here Mr Forret's counsel began to crow amain, as if the victory had been his own; but the junior Judge again took him short by saying, "Have patience, sir, the woman may be right, and your client in the wrong; at least I think I can perceive as much. Now, my good woman, I esteem your principles and plain simplicity very highly. We want only to ascertain the truth, and you say your master there charged you to tell that only. Tell me this, then—did he not inform you what that truth was?"

"Yes. It was for that purpose he came over to see me, to help my memory to what was the truth, for fear I should hae sworn wrang, which wad hae been a great sin, ye ken."

"Yes, it would so. I thought that would be the way.—You may now proceed with your questions regularly, Mr Wood."

"Are you quite conscious, now, that those things he brought to your remembrance were actually the truth?"

"No."

"Are you conscious they were *not* the truth?"

"Yes; at least, some of them, I am sure, were not."

"Please to condescend on one instance."

"He says he has it markit on his buik, that the crookit houm, that lies at the back o' the wood, ye ken, grew pease in the ninety-sax, and corn in the ninety-se'en; now, it is unco queer that he should hae settin't down wrang, for the houm was really and truly aits baith the years."

"It is a long time since; perhaps your memory may be at fault?"

"If my master had not chanced to mention it, I could not have been sure, but he set me a-calculating and comparing; and my mother and me have been consulting about it, and have fairly settled it."

"And you are quite positive it was oats both years?"

"Yes."

"Can you mention any circumstance on which you rest your conclusions?"

"Yes; there came a great wind ae Sabbath day, in the ninety-sax, and that raised the shearers' wages, at Dumfries, to three shillings the day. We began to the crookit houm on a Monanday's morning, at three shillings a-day, and that very day twalmonth, we began till't again at tenpence. We had a good deal o' speaking about it, and I said to John Edie, 'What need we grumble! I made sae muckle at shearing, the last year, that it's no a' done yet.' And he said, 'Ah, Tibby, Tibby, but wha can hain like you?'"

"Were there any others that you think your master had marked down wrong?"

"There was ane at any rate—the lang field niest Robie Johnston's march: He says it was clover in the drouthy dear year, and aits the niest; but that's a year I canna forget; it was aits baith years. I lost a week's shearing on it the first year, waiting on my auntie, and the niest year she was dead; and I shore the lang field niest Robie Johnston's wi' her sickle heuk, and black ribbons on my mutch."

The whole of Tibby's evidence went against Mr Forret's interest most conclusively, and the Judges at last dismissed her, with high compliments of her truth and integrity. The cause was again remitted to the Court of Session for revisal after this evidence taken, and the word spread over all the country that Mr Forret had won. Tibby never contradicted this, nor disputed it, but she was thoroughly convinced, that in place of winning, he would be a ruined man.

About a month after the examination at Dumfries, he received a letter from his agents in Edinburgh, buoying him up with hopes of great and instant success, and urging the utility of his presence in town at the final decision of the cause on which all the minor ones rested. Accordingly he equipped himself, and rode into Dumfries in the evening, to be ready for the coach the following morning, saying to his wife, as he went away, that he would send home his mare with the carrier, and that as he could not possibly name the day on which he would be home, she was to give herself no uneasiness. The mare was returned the following night, and put up in her own stall, nobody knew by whom; but servants are such sleepy, careless fellows, that few regarded the circumstance. This was on a Tuesday night; and a whole week passed over, and still Mrs Forret had no word from her husband, which kept her very uneasy, as their whole fortune, being, and subsistence, now depended on the issue of this great law-suit, and she suspected that the case still continued dubious, or was found to be going against him.

But, behold, on the arrival of the Edinburgh papers next week, the whole case, so important to farmers, was detailed; and it was there stated, that the great farmer and improver, Mr Forret of Drumlochie, had not only forfeited his whole fortune by improper husbandry and manifest breaches of the conditions on which he held his lease, but that criminal letters had been issued against him for attempts to pervert justice, and rewards offered for his detention or seizure. This was terrible news for the family at Drumlochie, but there were still sanguine hopes entertained that the circumstances were mistated, or at all events that the husband and father would make his escape; and as there was no word from him day after day, this latter sentiment began to be cherished by the whole family as their only remaining and forlorn hope.

But one day, as poor Tibby Hyslop was going over to the Cat Linn, to gather a burden of sticks for firewood, she was surprised, on looking over the dike, to see a great body of crows collected, all of which were so intent on their prey, that they seemed scarcely to regard her presence as a sufficient cause for their desisting; she waved her burden-rope at them over the dike, but they refused to move. Her heart nearly failed her, for she remembered of having before seen something of the same scene, with some fearful concomitants. But pure and unfeigned religion, the first principle of which teaches a firm reliance on divine protection, can give courage to the weakest of human beings. Tibby climbed over the dike, drove the vermin away, and there lay the corpse of her late unfortunate master, woefully defaced by these voracious birds of prey. He had bled himself to death in the jugular vein, was lying without the hat, and clothed in a fine new black suit of clothes, top boots, which appeared likewise to be new, and gilt spurs; and the place where he lay was a little three-cornered sequestered spot, between the dike and the precipice, and inaccessible by any other way than through the field. It was a spot that Tibby had never seen before.

A city dream is nothing but the fumes of a distempered frame, and a more distempered imagination; but let no man despise the circumstantial and impressive visions of a secluded Christian; for who can set bounds to the intelligences existing between the soul and its Creator?

The only thing more I have to add is, that the Lord President, having made the remark that he paid more regard to that poor woman, Isabella Hyslop's evidence, than to all the rest elicited at Dumfries, the gainers of the great plea became sensible that it was principally owing to her candour and invincible veracity that they were successful, and sent her a present of twenty pounds. She was living comfortably at Know-back when I saw her, a contented and happy old maiden. The letter was found in Mr Forret's pocket, which had blasted all his hopes and driven him to utter distraction; he had received it at Dumfries, returned home, and put up his mare carefully in the stable, but not having courage to face his ruined family, he had hurried to that sequestered spot, and perpetrated the woeful deed of self-destuction.

Dreams and Apparitions,
containing
Smithy Cracks, &c.
Part III.

"HAVE you heard anything of the apparition which has been seen about Wineholm Place?" said the Dominie.

"Na, I never heard o' sic a thing as yet," quoth the smith; "but I wadna wonder muckle that the news should turn out to be true."

The Dominie shook his head, and uttered a long "h'm—h'm—h'm," as if he knew more than he was at liberty to tell.

"Weel, that beats the world," said the smith, as he gave over blowing the bellows, and looked over the spectacles at the Dominie's face.

The Dominie shook his head again.

The smith was now in the most ticklish quandary; eager to learn particulars, and spread the astounding news through the whole village, and the rest of the parish to boot, but yet afraid to press the inquiry, for fear the cautious Dominie should take the alarm of being reported as a tatler, and keep all to himself. So the smith, after waiting till the wind-pipe of the great bellows ceased its rushing noise, and he had covered the gloss neatly up with a mixture of small coals, culm, and cinders; and then, perceiving that nothing more was forthcoming from the Dominie, he began blowing again with more energy than before—changed his hand—put the other sooty one in his breeches-pocket—leaned to the horn—looked in a careless manner to the window, or rather gazed on vacancy, and always now and then stole a sly look at the Dominie's face. It was quite immovable. His cheek was leaned on his open hand, and his eyes fixed on the glowing fire. It was very teazing this for poor Clinkum the smith. But what could he do? He took out his glowing iron, and made a shower of fire sweep through the whole smithy, whereof a good part, as intended, sputtered upon the Dominie, but he only shielded his face with his elbow, turned his shoulder half round, and held his peace. Thump, thump! clink, clink! went the hammer for a space; and then when the iron was returned to the fire, "Weel, that beats the world!" quoth the smith.

"What is this that beats the world, Mr Clinkum?" said the

Dominie, with the most cool and provoking indifference.

"This story about the apparition," quoth the smith.

"What story?" said the Dominie.

Now really this insolence was hardly to be borne, even from a learned Dominie, who, with all his cold indifference of feeling, was sitting toasting himself at a good smithy fire. The smith felt this, for he was a man of acute feeling, and therefore he spit upon his hand and fell a clinking and pelting at the stithy with both spirit and resignation, saying within himself, "These dominie bodies just beat the world!"

"What story?" reiterated the Dominie. "For my part I related no story, nor have ever given assent to a belief in such story that any man has heard. Nevertheless, from the results of ratiocination, conclusions may be formed, though not algebraically, yet corporately, by constituting a quantity, which shall be equivalent to the difference, subtracting the less from the greater, and striking a balance in order to get rid of any ambiguity or paradox."

At the long adverb, *nevertheless*, the smith gave over blowing, and pricked up his ears, but the definition went beyond his comprehension.

"Ye ken that just beats the whole world for deepness," said the smith; and again began blowing the bellows.

"You know, Mr Clinkum," continued the Dominie, "that a proposition is an assertion of some distinct truth, which only becomes manifest by demonstration. A corollary is an obvious, or easily inferred consequence *of* a proposition; while an hypothesis is a *sup*-position, or concession made, during the process of demonstration. Now, do you take me along with you? Because if you do not, it is needless to proceed?"

"Yes, yes, I understand you middling weel; but I wad like better to hear what other fo'ks say about it than you."

"And why so? Wherefore would you rather hear another man's demonstration than mine?" said the Dominie sternly.

"Because, ye ken, ye just beat the whole world for words," quoth the smith.

"Ay, ay! that is to say, words without wisdom," said the Dominie, rising and stepping away. "Well, well, every man to his sphere, and the smith to the bellows."

"Ye're quite wrang, master," cried the smith after him. "It isna the *want* o' wisdom in you that plagues me, it is the owerplush o't."

This soothed the Dominie, who returned, and said mildly—"By the by, Clinkum, I want a leister of your making, for I see there is no other tradesman makes them so well. A five-grained one make it; at your own price."

"Very weel, sir. When will you be needing it?"

"Not till the end of close-time."

"Ay, ye may gar the three auld anes do till then."

"What do you wish to insinuate, sir? Would you infer, because I have three leisters, that therefore I am a breaker of the laws? That I, who am placed here as a pattern and monitor of the young and rising generation, should be the first to set them an example of insubordination?"

"Ye ken, that just beats a' in words! but we ken what we ken, for a' that, master."

"You had better take a little care what you say, Mr Clinkum; just a *little* care. I do not request you to take particular care, for of that your tongue is incapable, but a very little is a necessary correlative of consequences. And mark you—don't go to say that I said this or that about a ghost, or mentioned such a ridiculous story."

"The crabbitness o' that body beats the world!" said the smith to himself, as the Dominie went halting homeward.

The very next man who entered the smithy door was no other than John Broadcast, the new laird's hind, who had also been hind to the late laird for many years, and who had no sooner said his errand than the smith addressed him thus:—"Have *you* ever seen this ghost that there is such a noise about?"

"Ghost? Na, goodness be thankit, I never saw a ghost in my life, save aince a wraith. What ghost do you mean?"

"So you never saw nor heard tell of any apparition about Wineholm-place, lately?"

"No, I hae reason to be thankfu' I have not."

"Weel, that beats the world! Whow, man, but ye are sair in the dark! Do you no think there are siccan things in nature, as fo'k no coming fairly to their ends, John?"

"Goodness be wi' us! Ye gar a' the hairs o' my head creep, man. What's that you're saying?"

"Had ye never ony suspicions o' that kind, John?"

"No; I canna say that I had."

"None in the least? Weel, that beats the world!"

"O, haud your tongue, haud your tongue! We hae great reason to be thankfu' that we are as we are!"

"How as you are?"

"That we are nae stocks or stones, or brute beasts, as the Minister o' Traquair says. But I hope in God there is nae siccan a thing about my master's place as an unearthly visitor."

The smith shook his head, and uttered a long hem, hem, hem! He had felt the powerful effect of that himself, and wished to make the same appeal to the feelings and longings after immortality of John Broadcast. The bait took; for the latent spark of superstition was kindled in the heart of honest John, and there being no wit in the head to counteract it, the portentous hint had its full sway. John's eyes stelled in his head, and his visage grew long, assuming meanwhile something of the hue of dried clay in winter. "Hech, man, but that's an awsome story!" exclaimed he. "Fo'ks hae great reason to be thankfu' that they are as they are. It is truly an awsome story."

"Ye ken, it just beats the world for that," quoth the smith.

"And is it really thought that this laird made away wi' our auld master?" said John. The smith shook his head again, and gave a strait wink with his eyes.

"Weel, I hae great reason to be thankfu' that I never heard siccan a story as that!" said John. "Wha was it tauld you a' about it?"

"It was nae less a man than our mathewmatical Dominie, he that kens a' things," said the smith; "and can prove a proposition to the nineteenth part of a hair. But he is terrified the tale should spread; and therefore ye maunna say a word about it."

"Na, na; I hae great reason to be thankfu' I can keep a secret as weel as the maist part o' men, and better than the maist part o' women. What did he say? Tell us a' that he said."

"It is not so easy to repeat what he says, for he has sae mony lang-nebbit words. But he said, though it was only a supposition, yet it was easily made manifest by positive demonstration."

"Did you ever hear the like o' that! Now, have we na reason to be thankfu' that we are as we are? Did he say it was by poison that he was taken off, or that he was strangled?"

"Na; I thought he said it was by a collar, or a collary, or something to that purpose."

"Then, it wad appear, there is no doubt of the horrid transaction? I think, the Doctor has reason to be thankfu' that he's no taken up. Is not that strange?"

"O, ye ken, it just beats the world."

"He deserves to be torn at young horses' tails," said the ploughman.

"Ay, or nippit to death with red-hot pinchers," quoth the smith.

"Or harrowed to death, like the children of Ammon," said the ploughman.

"Na, I'll tell you what should be done wi' him—he should just be docked and fired like a farcied horse," quoth the smith. "Od help ye, man, I could beat the world for laying on a proper poonishment."

John Broadcast went home full of terror and dismay. He told his wife the story in a secret—she told the dairymaid with a tenfold degree of secrecy; and as Dr Davington, or the New Laird, as he was called, sometimes kissed the pretty dairymaid for amusement, it gave her a great deal of freedom with her master, so she went straight and told him the whole story to his face. He was unusually affected at hearing such a terrible accusation against himself, and changed colour again and again; and as pretty Martha, the dairymaid, supposed it was from anger, she fell to abusing the Dominie without mercy, for he was session-clerk, and had been giving her some hints about her morality, of which she did not approve; she therefore threw the whole blame upon him, assuring her master that he was the most spiteful and malicious man on the face of God's earth; "and to show you that, sir," said Martha, wiping her eyes, "he has spread it through the hale parish that I am ower sib wi' my master, and that you and I baith deserve to sit wi' the sacking-gown on us."

This enraged the Doctor still farther, and he forthwith dispatched Martha to desire the Dominie to come up to the Place and speak with her master, as he had something to say to him. Martha went, and delivered her message in so exulting a manner, that the Dominie suspected there was bad blood a-brewing against him; and as he had too much self-importance to think of succumbing to any man alive, he sent an impertinent answer to the laird's message, bearing, that if Dr Davington had any business with him, he would be so good as attend at his class-room when he dismissed his scholars. And then he added, waving his hand toward the door, "Go out. There is contamination in your presence. What hath such a vulgar fraction ado to come into the halls of uprightness and science?"

When this message was delivered, the Doctor being almost beside himself with rage, instantly dispatched two village constables with a warrant to seize the Dominie, and bring him before him, for the Doctor was a justice of the peace. Accordingly, the poor Dominie was seized at the head of his pupils, and dragged away, crutch and all, up before the new laird, to answer for such an abominable slander. The Dominie denied everything anent it, as indeed he might, save having asked the smith the simple question, *if he had heard ought of a ghost at the Place?* But he refused to tell *why* he asked that question. He had his own reasons for it, he said, and reasons that to *him* were quite sufficient, but as he was not obliged to disclose them, neither would he.

The smith was then sent for, who declared that the Dominie had told him of the ghost being seen, and a murder committed, which he called a *rash assassination*, and said it was obvious, and easily inferred that it was done by a collar.

How the Dominie did storm! He even twice threatened to knock down the smith with his crutch; not for the slander, he cared not for that nor the Doctor a pin, but for the total subversion of his grand case in geometry; and he therefore denominated the smith's head *the logarithm to number one*, a term which I do not understand, but the appropriation of it pleased the Dominie exceedingly, made him chuckle, and put him in better humour for a good while. It was in vain that he tried to prove that his words applied only to the definition of a problem in geometry, he could not make himself understood; and the smith maintaining his point firmly, and apparently with conscientious truth, appearances were greatly against the Dominie, and the Doctor pronounced him a malevolent and dangerous person.

"O, ye ken, he just beats the world for that," quoth the smith.

"I a malevolent and dangerous person, sir!" said the Dominie, fiercely, and altering his crutch from one place to another of the floor, as if he could not get a place to set it on. "Dost thou call me a malevolent and dangerous person, sir? What then art thou? If thou knowest not I will tell thee. Add a cipher to a ninth figure, and what does that make? Ninety you will say. Ay, but then put a cipher *above* a nine, and what does that make? ha—ha—ha—I have you there. Your case exactly in higher geometry! for say the chord of sixty degrees is radius, then the sine of ninety degrees is equal to the radius, so the secant of o, that is nickle-nothing, as the boys call it, is radius, and so is the co-sine of o. The versed sine of 90 degrees is radius, (that is nine with a cipher added, you know,) and the versed sine of 180 degrees is the diameter; then of course the sine increases from o (that is cipher or nothing) during the first quadrant till it becomes radius, and then it decreases till it becomes nothing. After this you note it lies on the *contrary* side of the diameter, and consequently, if positive before, is negative now, so that it must end in o, or a cipher above a nine at most."

"This unintelligible jargon is out of place here, Mr Dominie, and if you can show no better reasons for raising such an abominable falsehood, in representing me as an incendiary and murderer, I shall procure you a lodgement in the house of correction."

"Why, sir, the long and short of the matter is this—I only asked at that fellow there, that logarithm of stupidity! if he had heard ought of

a ghost having been seen about Wineholm-place. I added nothing
farther, either positive or negative. Now, do you insist on my reasons
for *asking* such a question?"

"I insist on having them."

"Then what will you say, sir, when I inform you, and depone to
the truth of it, that *I saw the ghost myself?*—yes, sir—that I saw the
ghost of your late worthy father-in-law myself, sir; and though I said
no such thing to that decimal fraction, yet it told me, sir—Yes, the
spirit of your father-in-law told me, sir, that you were a murderer."

"Lord, now what think ye o' that?" quoth the smith. "Ye had
better hae letten him alane; for od, ye ken, he's the deevil of a body
that ever was made. He just beats the world."

The Doctor grew as pale as a corpse, but whether out of fear or
rage, it was hard to say at that time. "Why, sir, you are mad! stark,
raving mad," said the Doctor; "therefore for your own credit, and for
the peace and comfort of my amiable young wife and myself, and our
credit among our retainers, you must unsay every word that you
have now said regarding that ridiculous falsehood."

"I'll just as soon say that the parabola and the ellipsis are the
same," said the Dominie; "or that the diameter is not the longest line
that can be drawn in the circle; or that I want eyes, ears, and
understanding, which that I have, could all be proven by equation.
And now, sir, since you have forced me to divulge what I was in
much doubt about, I have a great mind to have the old Laird's grave
opened to-night, and have the body inspected before witnesses."

"If you dare, for the soul of you, disturb the sanctuary of the
grave," said the Doctor vehemently; "or with your unhallowed
hands touch the remains of my venerable and revered predecessor, it
had been better for you, and all who make the attempt, that you
never had been born. If not then for my sake, for the sake of my wife,
the sole daughter of the man to whom you have all been obliged, let
this abominable and malicious calumny go no farther, but put it
down; I pray of you to put it down, as you would value your own
advantage."

"I have seen him, and spoke with him—that I aver," said the
Dominie. "And shall I tell you what he said to me?"

"No, no! I'll hear no more of such absolute and disgusting nonsense," said the Laird.

"Then, since it hath come to this, I will declare it in the face of the
whole world, and pursue it to the last," said the Dominie, "ridiculous
as it is, and I confess that it is even so. I have seen your father-in-law
within the last twenty hours; at least a being in his form and hab-

iliments, and having his aspect and voice. And he told me, that he believed you were a very great scoundrel, and that you had helped him off the stage of time in a great haste, for fear of the operation of a *will*, which he had just executed, very much to your prejudice. I was somewhat aghast, but ventured to remark, that he must surely have been sensible whether you murdered him or not, and in what way. He replied, that he was not absolutely certain, for at the time you put him down, he was much in his customary way of nights,—very drunk; but that he greatly suspected you had hanged him, for, ever since he had died, he had been troubled with a severe crick in his neck. Having seen my late worthy patron's body deposited in the coffin, and afterwards consigned to the grave, these things overcame me, and a kind of mist came ower my senses; but I heard him saying as he withdrew, what a pity it was that my nerves could not stand this disclosure. Now, for my own satisfaction, I am resolved that to-morrow, I shall raise the village, with the two ministers at the head of the multitude, and have the body, and particularly the neck of the deceased minutely inspected."

"If you do so, I shall make one of the number," said the Doctor. "In the mean time, measures must be taken to put a stop to a scene of madness and absurdity so disgraceful to a well regulated village, and a sober community."

"There is but one direct line that can be followed, and any other would either be an acute or obtuse angle," said the Dominie; "therefore I am resolved to proceed right forward, on mathematical principles, in the diagonal, and if the opposite vertices of the quadrilateral fall in with these, the case is proven;" and away he went, skipping on his crutch, to arouse the villagers to the scrutiny.

The smith remained behind, concerting with the Doctor, how to controvert the Dominie's profound scheme of unshrouding the dead; and certainly the smith's plan, viewed professionally, was not amiss. "O, ye ken, sir, we maun just gie him another heat, and try to saften him to reason, for he's just as stubborn as Muirkirk ir'n. He beats the world for that."

While the two were in confabulation, Johnston, the old house-servant, came in and said to the Doctor—"Sir, your servants are going to leave the house, every one, this night, if you cannot fall on some means to divert them from it. The old laird is, it seems, risen again, and come back among them, and they are all in the utmost consternation. Indeed, they are quite out of their reason. He appeared in the stable to Broadcast, who has been these two hours dead with terror, but is now recovered, and telling such a tale down stairs, as never was heard from the mouth of man."

"Send him up here," said the Doctor. "I shall silence him. What does the ignorant clown mean by joining in this unnatural clamour?"

John came up, with his broad bonnet in his hand, shut the door with hesitation, and then felt twice with his hand if it really was shut. "Well, John," said the Doctor, "what an absurd lie is this that you are vending among your fellow servants, of having seen a ghost?" John picked some odds and ends of threads out of his bonnet, that had nothing ado there, and said nothing. "You are an old super-stitious dreaming dotard," continued the Doctor; "but if you propose in future to manufacture such stories, you must, from this instant, do it somewhere else than in my service, and among my domestics. What have you to say for yourself?"

"Indeed, sir, I hae naething to say but this, that we hae a' muckle reason to be thankfu' that we are as we are."

"And whereon does that wise saw bear? What relation has that to the seeing of a ghost? Confess then this instant, that you have forged and vended a deliberate lie, or swear before Heaven, and d—n yourself, that you *have* seen a ghost."

"Indeed, sir, I hae muckle reason to be thankfu'—"

"For what?"

"That I never tauld a deliberate lee in my life. My late master came and spake to me in the stable; but whether it was his ghaist or himsell—a good angel or a bad ane, I hae reason to be thankfu' I never said; for I *do—not—ken.*"

"Now, pray let us hear from that sage tongue of yours, so full of sublime adages, what this doubtful being said to you?"

"I wad rather be excused, an it were your honour's will, an' wad hae reason to be thankfu'."

"And why would you decline telling this?"

"Because I ken ye wadna believe a word o't. It is siccan a strange story! O sirs, but fo'ks hae muckle reason to be thankfu' that they are as they are!"

"Well, out with this strange story of yours. I do not promise to credit it, but shall give it a patient hearing, provided you swear that there is no forgery in it."

"Weel, as I was suppering the horses the night, I was dressing my late kind master's favourite mare, and I was just thinking to mysell, an he had been leevin' I wadna hae been my lane the night, for he wad hae been standing over me cracking his jokes, and swearing at me in his ain good-natured hamely way. Ay, but he's gane to his lang account, thinks I, an' we poor frail dying cratures that are left ahind hae muckle reason to be thankfu' that we are as we are. When behold I looks up, and there's my auld master standing leaning against the trivage, as he used to do, and looking at me. I canna but say my heart was a little astoundit, and maybe lap up through my midriff into my breath-bellows; I couldna say, but in the strength o' the Lord I was enabled to retain my senses for a good while. 'John Broadcast,' says he, with a deep and angry tone.—'John Broadcast, what the d—l are you thinking about? You are not currying that mare half. What a d—d lubberly way of dressing a horse is that?'

" 'L—d make us thankfu', master!' says I, 'are you there?'

" 'Where else would you have me be at this hour of the night, old blockhead?' says he.

" 'In another hame than this, master,' says I; 'but I fear me it is nae good ane, that ye are sae soon tired o't.'

" 'A d—d bad one, I assure you,' says he.

" 'Ay, but, master,' says I, 'ye hae muckle reason to be thankfu' that ye are as ye are.'

" 'In what respects, dotard?' says he.

" 'That ye hae liberty to come out o't a start now and then to get the air,' says I; and oh, my heart was sair for him when I thought o' his state! and though I was thankfu' that I was as I was, my heart and flesh began to fail me, at thinking of my being speaking face to face wi' a being frae the unhappy place. But out he briks again wi' a grit round o' swearing about the mare being ill keepit; and he ordered me to cast my coat and curry her weel, for that he had a lang journey to take on her the morn.

" 'You take a journey on her!' says I, 'Ye forget that she's flesh and blood. I fear my new master will dispute that privilege with you, for he rides her himsell the morn.'

" 'He ride her!' cried the angry spirit. 'If he dares for the soul of him lay a leg over her, I shall give him a downcome! I shall gar him lie as low as the gravel among my feet. And soon soon shall he be levelled with it at ony rate! The dog! the parricide! first to betray my child, and then to put down myself. But he shall not escape! he shall not escape!' cried he with such a hellish growl, that I fainted and heard no more."

"Weel, that beats the world!" quoth the smith; "I wad hae thought the mare wad hae luppen ower yird and stane, or fa'en down dead wi' fright."

"Na, na," said John, "in place o' that, whenever she heard him fa' a-swearing, she was sae glad that she fell a-nickering."

"Na, but that beats the hale world a'thegither!" quoth the smith.

"Then it has been nae ghaist ava, ye may depend on that."

"I little wat what it was," said John, "but it was a being in nae good or happy state o' mind, and is a warning to us a' how muckle reason we hae to be thankfu' that we are as we are."

The Doctor pretended to laugh at the absurdity of John's narrative, but it was with a ghastly and doubtful expression of countenance, as though he thought the story far too ridiculous for any clodpole to have contrived out of his own head; and forthwith he dismissed the two dealers in the marvellous, with very little ceremony, the one protesting that the thing beat the world, and the other that they had both reason to be thankfu' that they were as they were.

The next morning the villagers, small and great, were assembled at an early hour to witness the lifting of the body of their late laird, and headed by the established and dissenting clergymen, and two surgeons, they proceeded to the tomb, and soon extracted the splendid coffin, which they opened with all due caution and ceremony. But instead of the murdered body of their late benefactor, which they expected in good earnest to find, there was nothing in the coffin but a layer of gravel, of about the weight of a corpulent man!

The clamour against the new laird then rose all at once into a tumult that it was impossible to check, every one declaring aloud that he had not only murdered their benefactor, but, for fear of the discovery, had raised the body, and given, or rather sold it, to the dissectors. The thing was not to be borne! so the mob proceeded in a body up to Wineholm-Place, to take out their poor deluded lady, and burn the Doctor and his basely acquired habitation to ashes. It was not till the multitude had surrounded the house that the ministers and two or three other gentlemen could stay them, which they only did by assuring the mob that they would bring out the Doctor before their eyes, and deliver him up to justice. This pacified the throng; but on inquiry at the hall, it was found that the Doctor had gone off early that morning, so that nothing further could be done for the present. But the coffin, filled with gravel, was laid up in the aisle and kept open for inspection.

Nothing could now exceed the consternation of the simple villagers of Wineholm at these dark and mysterious events. Business, labour, and employment of every sort, were at a stand, and the people hurried about to one another's houses, and mingled together in one heterogeneous mass of theoretical speculation. The smith put his hand to the bellows, but forgot to blow till the fire went out; the weaver leaned on his beam, and listened to the legends of the ghastly tailor. The team stood in the mid furrow, and the thresher agaping

over his flail; and even the Dominie was heard to declare that the
geometrical series of events was increasing by no *common* measure,
and therefore ought to be calculated rather arithmetically than by
logarithms; and John Broadcast saw more and more reason for being
thankful that he was as he was, and neither a stock nor a stone, nor a
brute beast.

Every thing that happened was more extraordinary than the last;
and the most puzzling of all was the circumstance of the late laird's
mare, saddle, bridle and all, being off before day the next morning; so
that Dr Davington was obliged to have recourse to his own, on which
he was seen posting away on the road towards Edinburgh. It was
thus but too obvious that the ghost of the late laird had ridden off on
his favourite mare, the Lord only knew whither! for as to that point
none of the sages of Wineholm could divine. But their souls grew chill
as an iceberg, and their very frames rigid at the thoughts of a spirit
riding away on a brute beast to the place appointed for wicked men.
And had not John Broadcast reason to be thankful that he was as he
was?

However the outcry of the community became so outrageous, of
murder, and foul play in so many ways, that the officers of justice
were compelled to take note of it; and accordingly the Sheriff-
substitute, the Sheriff-clerk, the Fiscal, and two assistants, came in
two chaises to Wineholm to take a precognition, and there a court
was held which lasted the whole day, at which, Mrs Davington, the
late laird's only daughter, all the servants, and a great number of the
villagers, were examined on oath. It appeared from the evidence that
Dr Davington had come to the village and set up as a surgeon—that
he had used every endeavour to be employed in the laird's family in
vain, as the latter detested him. That he, however, found means of
seducing his only daughter to elope with him, which put the laird
quite beside himself, and from thenceforward he became drowned in
dissipation. That such, however, was his affection for his daughter,
that he caused her to live with him, but would never suffer the Doctor
to enter his door—that it was nevertheless quite customary for the
Doctor to be sent for to his lady's chamber, particularly when her
father was in his cups; and that on a certain night, when the laird had
had company, and was so overcome that he could not rise from his
chair, he had died suddenly of apoplexy; and that no other skill was
sent for, or near him, but this his detested son-in-law, whom he had
by will disinherited, though the legal term for rendering that will
competent had not expired. The body was coffined the second day
after death, and locked up in a low room in one of the wings of the

building; and nothing farther could be elicited. The Doctor was missing, and it was whispered that he had absconded; indeed it was evident, and the Sheriff acknowledged, that from the evidence taken collectively, the matter had a very suspicious aspect, although there was no direct proof against the Doctor. It was proved that he had attempted to bleed the patient, but had not succeeded, and that at that time the laird was black in the face.

When it began to wear nigh night, and nothing farther could be learned, the Sheriff-clerk, a quiet considerate gentleman, asked why they had not examined the wright who made the coffin, and also placed the body in it? The thing had not been thought of; but he was found in court, and instantly put into the witness's box and examined on oath. His name was James Sanderson, a stout-made, little, shrewd-looking man, with a very peculiar squint. He was examined thus by the Procurator-fiscal.

"Were you long acquainted with the late laird of Wineholm, James?"

"Yes, ever since I left my apprenticeship; for I suppose about nineteen years."

"Was he very much given to drinking of late?"

"I could not say. He took his glass gayen heartily."

"Did you ever drink with him?"

"O yes, mony a time."

"You must have seen him very drunk then? Did you ever see him so drunk that he could not rise, for instance?"

"O never! for, lang afore that, I could not have kend whether he was sitting or standing."

"Were you present at the corpse-chesting?"

"Yes, I was."

"And were you certain the body was then deposited in the coffin?"

"Yes; quite certain."

"Did you screw down the coffin-lid firmly then, as you do others of the same make?"

"No, I did not."

"What were your reasons for that?"

"They were no reasons of mine—I did what I was ordered. There were private reasons, which I then wist not of. But, gentlemen, there are some things connected with this affair, which I am bound in honour not to reveal—I hope you will not compel me to divulge them at present."

"You are bound by a solemn oath, James, which is the highest of all obligations; and for the sake of justice, you must tell everything you know; and it would be better if you would just tell your tale straight forward, without the interruption of question and answer."

"Well, then, since it must be so: That day, at the chesting, the Doctor took me aside, and says to me, 'James Sanderson, it will be necessary that something be put into the coffin to prevent any unpleasant flavour before the funeral; for, owing to the corpulence, and inflamed state of the body by apoplexy, there will be great danger of this.' 'Very well, sir,' says I—'what shall I bring?'

" 'You had better only screw down the lids lightly at present, then,' said he, 'and if you could bring a bucket-full of quicklime, a little while hence, and pour it over the body, especially over the face, it is a very good thing, an excellent thing for preventing any deleterious effluvia from escaping.'

" 'Very well, sir,' says I; and so I followed his directions. I procured the lime; and as I was to come privately in the evening to deposit it in the coffin, in company with the Doctor alone, I was putting off the time in my workshop, polishing some trifle, and thinking to myself that I could not find in my heart to choke up my old friend with quicklime, even after he was dead, when, to my unspeakable horror, who should enter my workshop but the identical laird himself, dressed in his dead-clothes in the very same manner in which I had seen him laid in the coffin, but apparently all streaming in blood to the feet. I fell back over against a cart-wheel, and was going to call out, but could not; and as he stood straight in the door, there was no means of escape. At length the apparition spoke to me in a hoarse trembling voice, enough to have frightened a whole conclave of bishops out of their senses; and it says to me, 'Jamie Sanderson! O, Jamie Sanderson! I have been forced to appear to you in a d—d frightful guise.' These were the very first words it spoke; and they were far frae being a lie, but I hafflins thought to mysell, that a being in such circumstances might have spoke with a little more caution and decency. I could make no answer, for my tongue refused all attempts at articulation, and my lips would not come together; and all that I could do, was to lie back against my new cart-wheel, and hold up my hands as a kind of defence. The ghastly and blood-stained apparition, advancing a step or two, held up both its hands flying with dead ruffles, and cried to me in a still more frightful voice, 'O, my faithful old friend! I have been murdered! I am a murdered man, Jamie Sanderson! and if you do not assist me in bringing the wretch to a due retribution, you will be d—d to hell, sir.' "

"This is sheer raving, James," said the Sheriff, interrupting him. "These words can be nothing but the ravings of a disturbed and heated imagination. I entreat you to recollect, that you have appealed to the great Judge of heaven and earth for the truth of what you assert here, and to answer accordingly."

"I know what I am saying, my Lord Sheriff," said Sanderson; "and am telling naething but the plain truth, as nearly as my state of mind at the time permits me to recollect. The appalling figure approached still nearer and nearer to me, breathing threatenings if I would not rise and fly to its assistance, and swearing like a sergeant of dragoons at both the Doctor and myself. At length it came so close on me, that I had no other shift but to hold up both feet and hands to shield me, as I had seen herons do when knocked down by a goshawk, and I cried out; but even my voice failed me, so that I only cried like one through his sleep.

" 'What the devil are you lying gaping and braying at there?' said he, seizing me by the wrists, and dragging me after him. 'Do you not see the plight I am in, and why won't you fly to succour me?'

"I now felt to my great relief, that this terrific apparition was a being of flesh, bones, and blood, like myself; that, in short, it was indeed my kind old friend the laird popped out of his open coffin, and come over to pay me an evening visit, but certainly in such a guise as earthly visit was never paid. I soon gathered up my scattered senses, took my kind old friend into my room, bathed him all over, and washed him well in lukewarm water; then put him into a warm bed, gave him a glass or two of warm punch, and he came round amazingly. He caused me to survey his neck a hundred times I am sure; and I had no doubt that he had been strangled, for there was a purple ring round it, which in some places was black, and a little swollen; his voice creaked like a door-hinge, and his features were still distorted. He swore terribly at both the Doctor and myself; but nothing put him half so mad as the idea of the quicklime being poured over him, and particularly over his face. I am mistaken if that experiment does not serve him for a theme of execration as long as he lives."

"So he is then alive, you say?" asked the Fiscal.

"O yes, sir! alive and tolerably well, considering. We two have had several bottles together in my quiet room; for I have still kept him concealed, to see what the Doctor would do next. He is in terror for him somehow, until sixty days be over from some date that he talks of, and seems assured that that dog will have his life by hook or crook, unless he can bring him to the gallows betimes, and he is absent on that business to-day. One night lately, when fully half-seas over, he set off to the schoolhouse, and frightened the Dominie; and last night he went up to the stable, and gave old Broadcast a hearing for not keeping his mare well enough.

"It appeared that some shaking motion in the coffining of him had brought him to himself, after bleeding abundantly both at mouth and nose; that he was on his feet ere ever he knew how he had been disposed of, and was quite shocked at seeing the open coffin on the bed, and himself dressed in his grave-clothes, and all in one bath of blood. He flew to the door, but it was locked outside; he rapped furiously for something to drink; but the room was far removed from any inhabited part of the house, and none regarded. So he had nothing for it but to open the window, and come through the garden and the back loaning to my workshop. And as I had got orders to bring a bucket-full of quicklime, I went over in the forenight with a bucket-full of heavy gravel, as much as I could carry, and a little white lime sprinkled on the top of it; and being let in by the Doctor, I deposited that in the coffin, screwed down the lid, and left it, and the funeral followed in due course, the whole of which the laird viewed from my window, and gave the Doctor a hearty day's cursing for daring to support his head and lay it in the grave. And this, gentlemen, is the substance of what I know concerning this enormous deed, which is I think quite sufficient. The laird bound me to secrecy until such time as he could bring matters to a proper bearing for securing of the Doctor; but as you have forced it from me, you must stand my surety, and answer the charges against me."

The laird arrived that night with proper authority, and a number of officers, to have the Doctor, his son-in-law, taken into custody; but the bird had flown; and from that day forth he was never seen, so as to be recognised in Scotland. The laird lived many years after that; and though the thoughts of the quicklime made him drink a great deal, yet from that time he never suffered himself to get *quite* drunk, lest some one might have taken it into his head to hang him, and he not know anything about it. The Dominie acknowledged that it was as impracticable to calculate what might happen in human affairs as to square the circle, which could only be effected by knowing the ratio of the circumference to the radius. For shoeing horses, vending news, and awarding proper punishments, the smith to this day just beats the world. And old John Broadcast is as thankful to Heaven as ever that things are as they are.

Mount-Benger, May 15.

Dreams and Apparitions.—Part IV.

The Laird of Cassway

THERE is an old story which I have often heard related, about a great laird of Cassway, in an outer corner of Dumfries-shire, of the name of Beattie, and his two sons; but whether it is a dream or an apparition, as it partakes of the nature of both, I cannot decide. This Beattie had occasion to be almost constantly in England, because, as my informant said, he took a great hand in government affairs, from which I deem that the tradition had its rise about the time of the civil wars; for about the close of that time, the Scotts took the advantage of the times to put the Beatties down, who, for some previous ages, had maintained the superiority of that district.

Be that as it may, the laird of Cassway's second son, Francis, fell desperately in love with a remarkably beautiful girl, the eldest daughter of Henry Scott of Drumfielding, a gentleman, but still only a retainer, and far beneath Beattie of Cassway, both in wealth and influence. Francis was a scholar newly returned from the university —was tall, handsome, of a pale complexion, and gentlemanly appearance, while Thomas, the eldest son, was fair, ruddy, and stout made, a perfect picture of health and good-humour,—a sportsman, a warrior, and a jovial blade; one who would not suffer a fox to get rest in the whole moor district, nor a pretty girl to sleep quietly in her bed. He rode the best horse, kept the best hounds, played the best fiddle, danced the best country bumpkin, and took the best refreshment of mountain dew of any man between Erick brae and Teviot stone, and was altogether that sort of a young man, that whenever he cast his eyes on a pretty girl, either at chapel or weapon-shaw, she would hide her face, and giggle as if tickled by some unseen hand.

Now, though Thomas, or the Young Laird, as he was called, had only spoke once to Ellen Scott in his life, at which time he chucked her below the chin, and bid the deil take him if ever he saw as bonny a face in his whole born days; yet, for all that, Ellen loved him. It could not be said that she was *in love* with him, for a maiden's heart must be won before it is given absolutely away; but hers gave him the preference to any other young man. She loved to see him, to hear of him, and to laugh at him; and it was even observed by the domestics, that Tam Beattie o' the Cassway's name came oftener into her conversation than there was any occasion for.

Such was the state of affairs when Francis came home, and fell desperately in love with Ellen Scott; and his father being in England, and he under no restraint, he went forthwith and paid his addresses to her. She received him with a kindness and affability that pleased him to the heart; but he little wist that this was only a spontaneous and natural glow of kindness toward him because of his connexions, and rather because he was the young Laird of Cassway's only brother, than the poor but accomplished Francis Beattie, the scholar from Oxford.

He was, however, so much delighted with her, that he asked her father's permission to pay his addresses to her, and, in one word, court her for his wife. Her father, who was a prudent and sensible man, answered him in this wise—"That nothing would give him greater delight than to see his beloved Ellen joined with so accomplished and amiable a young gentleman in the bonds of holy wedlock, provided his father's assent was previously attained. But as he himself was subordinate to another house, not on the best terms with the house of Cassway, he would not take it on him to sanction any such connexion without old Squire Beattie's full consent. That, moreover, as he, Francis Beattie, was just setting out in life, as a lawyer, there was but too much reason to doubt that a matrimonial connexion with Ellen at that time, would be highly imprudent; therefore it was not to be thought further of till the old Squire was consulted. In the meantime, he should always be welcome to his house, and to his daughter's company, as he had the same dependence on his honour and integrity, as if he had been a son of his own."

The young man thanked him affectionately, and could not help acquiescing in the truth of his remarks, promised not to mention matrimony further, till he had consulted his father, and added—"But indeed you must excuse me, if I avail myself of your permission to visit here often, as I am sensible it will be impossible for me to live for any space of time out of my dear Ellen's sight." He was again made welcome, and the two parted mutually pleased with each other.

Henry Scott of Drumfielding was a widower, with six daughters, over whom presided Mrs Jane Jerdan, their maternal aunt, a right old maid, with fashions and ideas even more antiquated than herself. No sooner had the young wooer taken his leave, than in she bounces to the room, the only sitting apartment in the house, and says, in a loud important whisper, "What's that young swankey of a lawyer wanting, that he's aye hankering sae muckle about our town? I'll tell

you what, brother Harry, it strikes me that he wants to make a
wheel-wright o' your daughter Nell. Now, gin he axes your consent
to ony sickan thing, dinna ye grant it. That's a'. Take an auld fool's
advice gin ye wad prosper. Fo'ks are a' wise ahint the hand, and sae
will ye be."

"Dear, Mrs Jane, what objections can you have to Mr Francis
Beattie, the most accomplished young gentleman of the whole country?"

"'Complished gentleman! 'Complished kirn-milk, float-whey,
and jeelaberry! I'll tell you what, brother Harry, afore I were a
landless lady, I wad rather be a tailor's layboard, and hae the red-het
goose gaun bizzing up my rumple. What has he to maintain a lady
spouse with? The wind o' his lungs, forsooth!—thinks to sell that for
goud in goupings. Hech me! Crazy wad they be wha wad buy it; and
they wha trust to crazy people for their living will live but crazily.
Take an auld fool's advice gin ye wad prosper, else ye'll be wise ahint
the hand. Have nae mair to do with him—Nell's bread for his betters,
tell him that. Or, by my certy, gin I meet wi' him face to face, I'll tell
him."

"It would be unfriendly in me to keep aught a secret from you,
sister, considering the interest you have taken in my family. I *have*
given him my consent to visit my daughter, but at the same time have
restricted him from mentioning matrimony untill he have consulted
his father."

"An' what is the visiting to gang for then? Sack possets and
blawflummery? Blaw the soup, dawtie, that it dinna blister the sweet
gab o' you! O, it is sae savoury and sweet, this courting and cooing
between a pennyless maid and a briefless lawyer! Fiend hae me, gin I
wadna rather ride the stang through the great burrough of Lochmaben, afore I were set down to woo, and hadna either marriage or
some waur thing to converse about. Away wi' him! Our Nell's food
for his betters. What wad you think an she could get the young laird
his brother wi' a blink o' her ee?"

"Never speak to me of that, Mrs Jane. I wad rather see the poorest
of his shepherd lads coming about my child than he;" and with these
words Henry left the room.

Mrs Jane stood long, making faces, shaking her apron with both
hands, nodding her head, and sometimes giving a stamp with her
foot. "I have set my face against that connexion," said she; "our
Nell's no made for a lady to a London lawyer. It wad set her rather
better to be Lady of Cassway. The young laird for me! I'll hae the
branks of love thrown over the heads o' the twasome, tie the tangs

thegither, and then let them gallop like twa kippled grews. My brother Harry's a simple man; he disna ken the credit that he has by his daughters—thanks to some other body than he! Niece Nell has a shape, an ee, and a lady manner that wad kilhab the best lord o' the kingdom, were he to come under their influence and my manoovres. She's a Jerdan a' through, and that I'll let them ken! Fo'ks are a' wise ahint the hand; credit only comes by catch an' keep. Goodnight to a' younger brothers, puffings o' love vows, and sabs o' wind! Gie me the good green hills, the gruff wedders, and bob-tail'd ewes; and let the law and the gospel men sell the wind o' their lungs as dear as they can."

In a few days, Henry of Drumfielding was called out to attend his chief on some expedition; on which Mrs Jane, not caring to trust her message to any other person, went over to Cassway, and invited the young laird to see her niece, quite convinced that her charms and endowments would at once enslave the elder brother as they had done the younger. Tam Beattie was delighted at finding such a good back friend as Mrs Jane, for he had for a twelvemonth had designs upon Ellen Scott; he had scarcely considered of what nature, but was quite convinced of the necessity of some love affair between the beauty and himself, and it was only sheer want of leisure that had prevented him from putting it in execution. In the height of his romance, however, he, either through chance or design, asked Mrs Jane if the young lady was privy to this invitation.

"*She* privy to it!" exclaimed Mrs Jane, shaking her apron. "Ha, weel I wat, no! She wad soon hae flown in my face wi' her gibery and her jaukery, had I tauld her my errand; but the gowk kens what the tittling wants, although it is not aye crying, *Give, give,* like the horse loch-leech."

"Does the horse-leech really cry that, Mrs Jane? I should think, from a view of its mouth, that it could scarcely cry anything," said Tom.

"Are ye sic a reprobate as to deny the words o' the Scripture, sir? Hech, wae's me! what some folks hae to answer for! We're a' wise ahint the hand. But hark ye,—come ye ower in time, else I am feared she may be settled for ever out o' your reach. Now, I canna bide to think on that, for I have always thought you twa made for ane anither. Let me take a look o' you frae tap to tae—O yes—made for ane anither, as leel as ever the hart was made for the hind, or the sheath for the sword. Come ower in time, before billy Harry come hame again; and let your visit be in timeous hours, else I'll gie you the back of the door to keep. Wild reprobate, to deny that the horse loch-leech can speak! Ha—he—he is the man for me. Down wi' a' courting, and kissing, and sighing, and sabbing, without a motive! for they wha gang to seek an errand generally find one."

Thomas Beattie was true to his appointment, as may be supposed, and Mrs Jane having her niece rigged out in eminent style, he was perfectly charmed with her; and really it cannot be denied that Ellen was as much delighted with him. She was young, gay, and frolicsome, and Tom had no sooner met with her, even in her aunt's presence, than he began a-flattering her, and from that to toying and romping with her; so that Ellen never spent a more joyous and happy after-noon, or knew before what it was to be in a presence that delighted her. True, he never mentioned the word *marriage*, though Mrs Jane gave him plenty of opportunities, but Ellen liked his company a great deal the better. It had always proved a chilling, damping sort of term, that, to her; and in the buoyancy of youthful spirits, innocence, and gaiety, she liked better that it should be set aside for the present; and never two lovers came better on than Tom Beattie of Cassway and the beautiful Ellen of Drumfielding.

There were two beds in the room with running doors, all of which stood delightfully open, in order to show the beautiful coverlets within; and as Ellen had become very teasing, Mrs Jane ventured to remind the laird of the above circumstances, adding, that she deemed the wild gilly well deserved to feel the metal of a gentleman's beard, as none of her former lovers had been blessed with such a privilege. The laird took the hint, and tried, at a gentle wrestle, to place Ellen on the stock of one of the beds, but he could not, without being more rude, than, even in that rude age, good manners allowed; and in this gentle exercise were the two engaged, altogether by themselves, when the room-door opened, and in popped Francis Beattie! Ellen's face was flushed with laughter and animated exer-tion, and when she saw her devoted lover at her side, she blushed still deeper, and her glee was damped in a moment. She looked rather like a condemned criminal, or at least a guilty creature, than what she really was,—a being over whose mind the cloud of guilt had never cast its shadow.

Francis loved her above all things on earth or in heaven, and the moment he saw her standing abashed, and extricating herself gently from the hands of his brother, his spirit was moved to jealousy—to maddening and uncontrollable jealousy. His ears rang, his hair stood on end, and the contour of his face became like a bent bow. He walked up to his brother with his hand on his hilt, and almost inarticulately addressed him thus, while his teeth ground together like a horse-rattle:

"Pray, sir, may I ask you of your intentions, and of what you are seeking here?"

"I know not, Frank, what right you have to ask any such questions; but you will allow that I have a right to ask at you what the devil you are seeking here at present, seeing you come so very inopportunely."

"Do you know what you are doing, sir, what you have done, or what you have attempted? That maiden, sir, is my maiden—my beloved and betrothed maiden—dearer to me than life and all its enjoyments; and ere you touch that dear maiden with a foul finger, sir, you shall sooner touch my heart's blood! Dare you put it to the issue of the sword this moment?"

"Come now, dear Francis, don't fall on to act the fool and the madman both at a time, for this maiden is *not* your maiden, nor ever will be either your maiden or your wife; and rather than bring such a dispute to the issue of the sword between two brothers who never had a quarrel in their lives, I propose that we bring it to a much more temperate and decisive issue here where we stand, by giving the maiden her choice. Stand you there at that corner of the room, I at this, and Ellen Scott in the middle; let us both ask her, and to whomsoever she comes, the prize be his. Why should we try to decide, by the loss of one of our lives, what we cannot decide, and what may be decided in a friendly and rational way in one minute?"

"It is easy for you, sir, to talk temperately and with indifference on such a trial, but not so with me. This young lady is dear to my heart."

"Well, but so is she to mine."

"I have asked her of her father as my wife, and have his consent. I have asked herself, and have not been denied; and here again if I do ask her, I ask her only as my wife."

"Well, Frank, then you have the advantage of me, and it is but justice you should avail yourself of it. For I have *not* asked her father, nor do I intend it; and when I ask her here from you, I ask her only as my mistress."

"And have you the arrogance to suppose that this peerless young maiden, this flower of the Border, would listen to a suit so degrading and ruinous?"

"No man can tell, Frank, to what a woman will listen, or to what she will not listen; all that I say is, that I am willing to take my chance and abide by the consequences. I was not aware of any engagement between you and her when I made the proposal; and though I find I am now placed at a manifest disadvantage, I am willing to abide by

her fiat; for what do a man's pretensions signify, without the countenance and assent of the object of his affection? Let us, therefore,
appeal to the lady at once, whose claim is the best, and as your
pretensions are the highest, do you ask her first."

"My dearest Ellen," said Francis, humbly and affectionately,
"you know that my whole soul is devoted to your love, and that I
aspire to it only in the most honourable way; confirm then my appeal
by coming to my arms, and suffering me to embrace you as my own
loved and betrothed dame, in the presence of this unlicensed and
presumptuous libertine."

Ellen stood dumb and motionless, looking stedfastly down at the
hem of her green jerkin, which she was nibbling with both her hands.
She dared not lift an eye to either of the brothers, though apparently
conscious that she ought to have flown into the arms of Francis.

"Ellen, I need not tell you that I love you, for a woman knows that
by instinct," said Thomas. "Nor need I attempt to tell how dearly
and how long I will love you, for in faith I cannot. My pretensions, it
is true, are not of the most honourable description, as some men
count honour; but in truth, I love you so well, that I doubt very much
if I can live without you in one way or other. I know you love me
better than perhaps you ought to do. Put reason to her cradle then,
and suffer nature to have her own way, and I am sure of my Ellen for
them all."

Ellen looked up. There was a smile on her lovely face; an arch,
mischievous, and happy smile, but it turned not on Thomas. Her face
turned to the contrary side, but yet the beam of that smile fell not on
Francis, who stood in a state of as terrible suspense between hope and
fear, as a sinner at the gate of heaven, who has implored of St Peter to
open the gate, and awaits a final answer. The die of his fate was soon
cast, for Ellen Scott looking one way, yet moving another, straight-
way threw herself into Thomas Beattie's arms, exclaiming, "Ah,
Tom! Tom! I fear I am doing that which I shall rue, but I must trust
to your generosity, for bad as you are, I like you the best."

Thomas was deeply affected by this appeal of the young and
splendid beauty to his generosity. He took her in his arms, and
embraced and kissed her; but before he could say a word in return,
the despair and rage of his brother breaking forth over every barrier
of reason, interrupted him. "This is the trick of a coward, to screen
himself from the chastisement he deserves," cried Francis, shaking his
sword at his brother. "A mean and infamous appeal to the agitated
passions of an inexperienced and infatuated girl. But you escape me
not thus! Follow me if you dare!" And he rushed from the house,

shaking his naked sword at his brother.

Ellen trembled with agitation at the young man's rage; and while Thomas still pressed her to his bosom, and assured her of his unalterable affection, in came Mrs Jane Jerdan, shaking her apron, and tucking it so as to make it twang like a bowstring.

"What's a' this, Squire Tummas? Are we to be habbled out o' house an' hadding by this rapacious young lawyer o' yours? By the souls o' the Jerdans, I'll kick up sic a stoure about his lugs as shall blind the juridical een o' him! It's queer that men should study the law only to learn to break it. Sure am I nae gentleman that hasna been bred a lawyer wad come into a neighbour's house bullyragging that gate wi' sword in hand, malice prepense in his eye, and venom on his tongue. Just as a lassie hadna her ain freedom o' choice, because a fool has been pleased to ask her! Haud the grip ye hae, Niece Nell, ye hae made a wise choice for aince. Tam's the man for my money! Fo'ks are a' wise ahint the hand, but real wisdom lies in taking time by the forelock. But, Squire Tam, the thing that I want to ken is this—Are you going to put up wi' a' that bullying and threatening? Or do ye propose to chastise the fool according to his folly?"

"In truth, Mrs Jane, I am very sorry for my brother's behaviour, and could not with honour yield any more than I did to pacify him. But he must be humbled. It will not do to suffer him to carry matters with so high a hand."

"Now, wad ye be but advised and leave him to me, I would play him sic a plisky as he shouldna forget till his dying day. By the souls o' the Jerdans, I would! Now promise to me that ye winna fight him."

"O promise, promise!" cried Ellen vehemently, "for the sake of heaven's love, promise my aunt that."

Thomas smiled and shook his head as much as if he had said, "you do not know what you are asking." Mrs Jane went on.

"Do it then—do it with a vengeance, and remember this, that wherever ye set the place o' combat, be it in hill or dale, deep linn or moss hagg, I shall have a thirdsman there to encourage thee on. I shall give you a meeting you little wot of."

Thomas Beattie took all this for words of course, as Mrs Jane was well known for a raving, ranting old maid, whose vehemence few regarded, but a great many respected her for the care she had taken of her sister's family, and a greater number still regarded her with terror, as a being possessed of superhuman powers; so after many expressions of the fondest love for Ellen, he took his leave, his mind being made up how it behoved him to deal with his brother.

I forgot to mention before, that old Beattie lived at Nether Cassway with his family; and his eldest son Thomas at Over Cassway, who, on his father entering into a second marriage, was put in possession of that castle, and these lands. Francis, of course, lived in his father's house when in Scotland, and it was thus that his brother knew nothing of his frequent visits to Ellen Scott.

Well, that night, as soon as Thomas went home, he dispatched a note to his brother to the following purport: That he was sorry for the rudeness and unreasonableness of his behaviour. But if, on coming to himself, he was willing to make an apology before his mistress, then he (Thomas) would gladly extend to him the right hand of love and brotherhood; but if he refused this, he would please to meet him on the crook of Glen-dearg next morning by the sun-rising. Francis returned for answer that he would meet him at the time and place appointed, and make his asseverations good to his heart. There was then no farther door of reconciliation left open, but Thomas still had hopes of managing him even on the combat field.

Francis slept little that night, being wholly set on revenge for the disgraceful way in which he had lost his beloved mistress; and a little after daybreak he arose, and putting himself in light armour, proceeded to the place of rendezvous. He had farther to go than his elder brother, and on coming in sight of the crook of Glen-dearg, he perceived the latter there before him. He was wrapt in his cavalier cloak, and walking up and down the crook with impassioned strides, on which Francis soliloquised as follows, as he hasted on:—"Ah ha! so Tom is here before me! This is what I did not expect, for I did not think the flagitious dog had so much spirit or courage in him as to meet me. I am glad he has! for how I long to chastise him, and draw some of the pampered blood from that vain and insolent heart, which has bereaved me of all I held dear on earth!"

In this way did he cherish his wrath till close at his brother's side, and then addressing him in the same insolent terms, he desired him to cease his cowardly cogitations and draw. His opponent instantly wheeled about, threw off his horseman's cloak, and presented his sword; and behold the young man's father stood before him armed and ready for action! The sword fell from Francis's hand, and he stood appalled as if he had been a statue, unable either to utter a word or move a muscle.

"Take up thy sword, caitiff, and let it work thy ruthless work of vengeance here. Is it not better that thou shouldst pierce this old heart, worn out with care and sorrow, and chilled by the ingratitude of my race, than that of thy gallant and generous brother, the representative of our house, and the chief of our name? Take up thy sword, I say, and if I do not chastise thee as thou deservest, may Heaven reft the sword of justice from the hand of the avenger!"

"The God of Heaven forbid that I should ever lift my sword against my honoured father!" said Francis.

"Thou darest not, thou traitor and coward!" returned the father. —"I throw back the disgraceful terms in thy teeth which thou used'st to thy brother. Thou camest here boiling with rancour, to shed his blood, and when I appear in person for him, thou darest not accept the challenge."

"You never did me wrong, my dear father; but my brother has wronged me in the tenderest part."

"Thy brother never wronged thee intentionally, thou deceitful and sanguinary fratricide; and where no previous intention exists, there is no offence committed. It was thou alone who forced this quarrel upon him, and I have great reason to suspect that thou designed'st to cut him off, that the inheritance and the maid might both be thine own. But here I swear by the arm that made me, and the Redeemer that saved me, if thou wilt not go straight and kneel to thy brother for forgiveness, confessing thy injurious treatment, and swearing submission to thy natural chief, I will banish thee from my house and presence for ever, and load thee with a parent's curse, which shall never be removed from thy soul till thou art crushed to the lowest hell."

The young scholar, being utterly astounded at his father's words, and at the awful and stern manner in which he addressed him, whom he had never before reprimanded, was wholly overcome. He kneeled to his parent, and implored his forgiveness, promising, with tears, to fulfil every injunction which it would please him to enjoin; and on this understanding, the two parted on amicable and gracious terms.

Francis went straight to the tower of Over Cassway, and inquired for his brother, resolved to fulfil his father's stern injunctions to the very letter. He was informed his brother was in his chamber in bed, and indisposed. He asked the porter farther, if he had not been forth that day, and was answered, that he had gone forth early in the morning in armour, but had quickly returned, apparently in great agitation, and betaken himself to his bed. He then requested to be taken to his brother, to which the servant instantly assented, and led him up to the chamber, never suspecting that there could be any animosity between the two only brothers; but on John Burgess opening the door, and announcing THE TUTOR, Thomas, being in a nervish state, was a little alarmed. "Remain in the room there,

Burgess," said he. "What, brother Frank, are you seeking here at this hour, armed capapee? I hope you are not come to assassinate me in my bed?"

"God forbid, brother," said the other; "here, John, take my sword down with you, I want some private conversation with Thomas." John did so, and the following conversation ensued; for as soon as the door closed, Francis dropt on his knees, and said, "O, my dear brother, I have erred grievously, and am come to confess my crime, and implore your pardon."

"We have both erred, Francis, in suffering any earthly concern to incite us against each other's lives. We have both erred, but you have my forgiveness cheerfully; here is my hand on it, and grant me thine in return. Oh, Francis, I have got an admonition that never will be erased from my memory, this morning, and which has caused me to see my life in a new light. What or whom think you I met an hour ago on my way to the crook of Glen-dearg to encounter you?"

"Our father, perhaps."

"You have seen him then?"

"Indeed I have, and he has given me such a reprimand for severity, as son never received from a parent."

"Brother Frank, I must tell you, and when I do, you will not believe me—It *was not* our father whom we both saw this morning."

"It was no other whom I saw. What do you mean? Do you suppose that I do not know my own father?"

"I tell you it was not, and could not be. I had an express from him yesterday. He is two hundred miles from this, and cannot be in Scotland sooner than three weeks hence."

"You astonish me, Thomas. This is beyond human comprehension."

"It is true—that I avouch, and the certainty of it has sickened me at heart. You must be aware that he came not home last night, and that his horse and retinue have not arrived."

"He was not at home, it is true, nor have his horse and retinue arrived in Scotland. Still there is no denying that our father is here, and that, at least, it was he who spoke to and admonished me."

"I tell you it is impossible. A spirit hath spoke to us in our father's likeness, for he is not, and cannot be in Scotland at this time. My faculties are altogether confounded by the event, not being able to calculate on the qualities or condition of our monitor. An evil spirit it certainly could not be, for all its admonitions pointed to good. I sorely dread, Francis, that our father is no more—that there hath been another engagement, that he hath lost his life, and that his soul hath been lingering around his family before taking its final leave of this sphere. I believe that our father is dead; and for my part, I am so sick at heart, that my nerves are all in a flame. Pray, do you take horse and post off for Salop, from whence his commission to me yesterday was dated, and see what hath happened to our reverend father."

"I cannot, for my life, give credit to this, brother, or that it was any other being who rebuked me, but my father himself. Pray allow me to tarry another day at least, before I set out on such a wild-goose chase. Perhaps our father may appear in the neighbourhood, and may be concealing himself for some secret purpose. Did you tell him of our quarrel?"

"No. He never asked me concerning it, but charged me sharply with my intent on the first word, and adjured me by my regard for his blessing, and my hope in heaven, to desist from my purpose."

"Then he knew it all intuitively; for when I first went in view of the spot appointed for our meeting, I perceived him walking sharply to and fro, wrapped in his military cloak. He never so much as deigned to look at me, till I came close to his side, and thinking it was yourself, I fell to upbraiding him, and desired him to draw. He then threw off his cloak, drew his sword, and telling me he came in your place, dared me to the encounter. But he knew all the grounds of our quarrel minutely, and laid the blame on me. I own I am a little puzzled to reconcile circumstances, but am convinced my father is near at hand. I heard his words, saw his eyes flashing anger and indignation. Unfortunately I did not touch him, which would have put an end to all doubts; for he did not present the hand of recon-ciliation to me, as I expected he would have done, on my yielding implicitly to all his injunctions."

The two brothers then parted, with protestations of mutual for-bearance in all time coming, and with an understanding, as that was the morning of Saturday, that if their father, or some word of him, did not reach home before the next evening, the Tutor of Cassway, as Francis was denominated, I know not why, was to take horse for the county of Salop, early on Monday's morning.

Thomas, being thus once more left to himself, could do nothing but toss and tumble in his bed, and reflect on the extraordinary occurrence of that morning; and, after many troubled cogitations, it at length occurred to his recollection what Mrs Jane Jerdan had said to him:—"Do it then. Do it with a vengeance!—But remember this, that wherever ye set the place of combat, be it in hill or dale, deep linn, or moss hagg, I shall have a thirdsman there to encourage you on. I shall give you a meeting you little wot of."

If he was confounded before, he was ten times more so at the remembrance of these words, of most ominous import.

At the time he totally disregarded them, taking them for mere rhodomontade; but now the idea to him was terrible, that his father's spirit, like the prophet's of old, should have been conjured up by witchcraft; and then again he bethought himself that no witch would have employed her power to prevent evil. In short, he knew not what to think, and so, taking the hammer from its rest, he gave three raps on the pipe drum, for there were no bells in the towers of those days, and up came old John Burgess, Thomas Beattie's henchman, huntsman, and groom of the chambers, one who had been attached to the family for fifty years, and he says, in his slow West Border tongue, "How's tou now, callan'?—Is tou ony betterlins? There has been tway stags seen in the Bloodhope-Linns tis mworning already."

"Ay, and there has been something else seen, John, that lies nearer to my heart, to-day." John looked at his master with an inquisitive eye and quivering lip, but said nothing. The latter went on, "I am very unwell to-day, John, and cannot tell what is the matter with me. I think I am bewitched."

"It's very likely thou is, callan'. I pits nae doubt on't at a'."

"Is there anybody in this moor district whom you ever heard blamed for the horrible crime of witchcraft?"

"Ay, that there is; mair than ane or tway. There's our neighbour, Lucky Jerdan, for instance, and her niece, Nell, the warst o' the pair, I doubt." John said this with a sly stupid leer, for he had admitted the old hen to an audience with his master the day before, and had eyed him afterwards bending his course towards Drumfielding.

"John, I am not disposed to jest at this time; for I am disturbed in mind, and very ill. Tell me, in reality, did you ever hear Mrs Jane Jerdan accused of being a witch?"

"Why, look thee, master, I dares nae say she's a wotch, for Lucky has mony good points in her character. But it is weel kenned she has mair power nor her ain, for she can stwop a' the plews in Eskdale wi' a wave o' her hand, and can raise the dead out o' their graves, just as a matter o' course."

"That, John, is an extraordinary power, indeed. But did you never hear of her sending any living men *to* their graves? For as that is rather the danger that hangs over me, I wish you would take a ride over and desire Mrs Jane to come and see me. Tell her I am ill, and request of her to come and see me."

"I shall do that, callan'. But are tou sure it is the auld wotch I'm to bring? For it strikes me the young ane maybe has done the deed; an' if sae, she is the fittest to effect the cure. But I sall bring the auld ane. Dinna flee intil a rage, for I sall bring the auld ane—though, gude forgi'e me, it is unco like bringing the houdy."

Away went John Burgess to Drumfielding, but Mrs Jane would not move at his entreaties. She sent word back to his master to "rise out o' his bed, for he wad be waur if onything ailed him; an' if he had ought to say to auld Jane Jerdan, she would be ready to hear it at hame, though he behoved to remember that it wasna ilka subject under the sun that she could thole to be questioned anent."

With this answer John was forced to return, and there being no accounts of old Beattie having been seen in Scotland, the young men remained over the Sabbath-day in the utmost consternation at the apparition of their father which they had seen, and the appalling rebuke they had received from it. The most incredulous mind could scarce doubt that they had had communion with a supernatural being; and not being able to draw any other conclusion themselves, they became persuaded that their father was dead; and accordingly both prepared for setting out early on Monday morning towards the county of Salop, from whence they had last heard of him.

But just as they were ready to set out, when their spurs were buckled on and their horses bridled, Andrew Johnston, their father's confidential servant, arrived from the place to which they were bound. He had rode night and day, never once stinting the light gallop, as he said, and had changed his horse seven times. He appeared as if his ideas were in a state of derangement and confusion; and when he saw his young masters standing together, and ready-mounted for a journey, he stared at them as if he scarcely believed his own senses. They of course asked immediately for the cause of his express, but his answers were equivocal, and he appeared not to be able to assign any motive. They asked him anent their father, and if anything extraordinary had happened to him. He would not say either that there had, or that there had not, but he inquired in his turn if nothing extraordinary had happened with them at home. They looked to one another, and returned him no answer; but at length the youngest said, "Why, Andrew, you profess to have ridden express for the distance of two hundred miles; now, you surely must have some guess for what purpose you have done this? Say, then, at once, what is the purport of your message? Is our father alive?"

"Ye—es, I think he is."

"You *think* he is. Are you uncertain, then?"

"I am certain he is not *dead*,—at least was not when I left him.

But—hum—certainly there has a change taken place. Hark ye, masters—can a man be said to be in life when he is out of himself?"

"Why, thou provoking and ambiguous rascal, say at once the purport of thy message, and keep us not in this thrilling suspense. Is our father well?"

"No—not *quite* well. I am sorry to say, honest gentleman, that he is not. But the truth is, my masters, now that I see you well and hearty, and about to take a journey in company, I begin to suspect that I have been posted all this way on a fool's errand; and the devil another syllable will I speak on the subject, till I have had some refreshment, and if you still insist on hearing a ridiculous story, you shall hear it then."

"You shall as soon have my right hand!" exclaimed the passionate Francis, "as you shall either taste meat or drink in my father's hall, till you have said every word of his message to us."

"Why, hark you, Mr Tutor," said the important Andrew, "I think I can command as much as I please to eat and to drink in the Castle of Cassway, without your interference, or with it; and by the spirits of all the Johnstons of Annandale, I'll keep my word. I am neither my master's serf nor his hound, to cour beneath the menace of a boy; and if my message imports aught, which I aver not that it does, it bears nothing favourable to you in its substance, Mr Tutor; and, therefore, in one word, I begin no long stories, pining with fatigue, with hunger, and thirst." But Thomas, who knew his man better, had him instantly conveyed to a private apartment; and, after he had been amply supplied with the best that the larder and cellar could produce, Andrew Johnston began as follows:—

"Why, faith, you see, my masters, it is not easy to say my errand to you, for in fact I have none. Therefore, all that I can do is to tell you a story,—a most ridiculous one it is, as ever sent a poor fellow out on the gallop for the matter of two hundred miles or so. On the morning before last, right early, little Isaac, the page, comes to me, and he says,—'Johnston, thou must go and visit measter. He's bad.'

"'Bad!' says I. 'Whaten way is he bad?'

"'Why, by not being good,' says he. 'He's so far ill as he's not well, and desires to see you without one moment's delay. He's in fine taking, and that you'll find; but whatfor do I stand here? Lword, I never got such a fright. Why, Johnston, does thou know that measter hath lwost himself?'

"'How lost himself? Rabbit,' says I, 'speak plain out, else I'll have thee lug-hauled, thou dwarf! thou merlin! thou bratchet of an elfin;' for my blood rose at the crimp, for fooling at any mishap of my master's. But my choler only made him worse, for there is not a greater deil's-buck in all the five dales.

"'Why, man, it is true that I said,' quoth he, laughing; 'the old gurly squoir hath lwost himself; and it will be grand sport to see thee going calling him at all the stane-crosses in the kingdom, in this here way—Ho yes! and a two times ho yes! and a *three* times ho yes! Did onybody no see the better half of my measter, laird of the twa Cassways, Bloodhope, and Pantland, which was amissing overnight, and is supposed to have gone a-woolgathering? If anybody hath seen that better part of my measter, whilk contains as mooch wit as a man could drive on a hurlbarrow, let them restore it to me, Andrew Johnston, piper, trumpeter, whacker, and wheedler, to the same great noble squoir, and high shall be his reward. Ho yes!'

"'The devil restore thee to thy rights!' said I, knocking him down, and leaving him sprawling in the kennel, and then hasted to my master, whom I found, indeed, on the very north-west turret of derangement; feverish, restless, and raving, and yet with a fervency of demeanour that stunned and terrified me. He seized my hand in both his, which were burning like fire, and gave me such a look of despair as I shall never forget. 'Johnston, I am ill,' said he, 'grievously ill, and know not what is to become of me. Every nerve in my body is in a burning flame, and my soul is as it were torn to fritters with amazement. Johnston, as sure as you are in the body, something most deplorable hath happened to me.'

"'Yes, as sure as I am in the body there has, master,' says I. 'But I'll have you bled and doctored in style; and you shall soon be as sound as a roach,' says I, 'for a gentleman must not lose heart altogether for a little fire-raising in his outworks, if it does not reach the citadel,' says I to him. But he cut me short by shaking his head and flinging my hand from him.

"'A truce with your talking,' says he. 'That which hath befallen me is as much above your comprehension as the sun is above the earth, and never will be comprehended by mortal man. But I must inform you of it, as I have no other means of gaining the intelligence that I yearn for, and which I am incapable of gaining personally. Johnston, there never was a mortal man suffered what I have suffered since midnight. I believe I have had doings with hell; for I have been disembodied and embodied again, and the intensity of my tortures has been as far above a parallel as my own comprehension. I was at home this morning at day-break.'

"'At home at Cassway?' says I. 'I am sorry to hear you say so, master, because you know, or should know, that the thing is impossible, you being in the ancient town of Shrewsbury on the King's business.'

"'I was at home in very deed, Andrew,' returned he; 'but whether in the body, or out of the body, I cannot tell—the Lord only knoweth. But there I was in this guise, and with this heart and all its feelings within me, where I saw scenes, heard words, and spoke others, which I will here relate to you. I had finished my dispatches last night by midnight, and was sitting musing on the hard fate and improvidence of my sovereign master, when, ere ever I was aware, a neighbour of ours, Mrs Jane Jerdan of Drumfielding, a mysterious character, with whom I have had some strange doings in my time, came suddenly into the chamber and stood before me. I accosted her with doubt and terror, asking what had brought her so far from home.'

"'You are not so far from home as you imagine,' said she; 'and it is fortunate for some that it is so, for your two sons have quarrelled about the possession of my niece Ellen, and though the eldest is blameless of the quarrel, yet has he been forced into it, and they are engaged to fight at day-break at the crook of Glen-dearg. There they will assuredly fall by each other's hands, if you interpose not; for there is no other authority now on earth that can prevent this woful calamity.'

"'Alas! how can I interfere,' said I, 'at this distance? It is already within a few hours of the meeting, and before I get from among the windings of the Severn, their swords will be bathed in each other's blood. I must trust to the interference of Heaven.'

"'Is your name and influence, then, to perish for ever?' said she. 'Is it so soon to follow your master's, the great Maxwell of the Dales, into utter oblivion? Why not rather rouse into requisition the energies of the spirits that watch over human destinies? At least step aside with me, that I may disclose the scene to your eyes. You know I can do it; and you may then act according to your natural impulse.'

"'Such were the import of the words she spoke to me, if not the very words themselves. I understood them not at the time, nor do I yet. But when she had done speaking, she took me by the hand, and hurried me towards the door of the apartment, which she opened, and the first step we took over the threshold, we stepped into a void space, where I knew of none, and fell downward. I was going to call out, but felt my descent so rapid, that my voice was stifled, and I could not so much as draw my breath. I expected every moment to fall against something, and be dashed to pieces; and I shut my eyes, clenched my teeth, and held by the dame's hand with a frenzied grasp, in expectation of the catastrophe. But down we went—down and down, with a celerity which tongue cannot describe, without light, breath, or intervention of any sort. I now felt assured that we had both at once stepped from off the earth, and were hurled into the immeasurable void; and now that I really felt it had taken place, I wondered how it had not happened to many others beside ourselves. The airs of darkness sung in my ears with a booming din as I rolled down the steeps of everlasting night, an outcast from nature and all its harmonies, and a journeyer into the depths of hell.

"'I still held my companion's hand, and felt the pressure of hers; and so long did this our alarming descent continue, that I at length caught myself breathing once more, but as quick as if I had been in the height of a fever. I then tried every effort to speak, but they were all unavailing; for I could not emit one sound, although my lips and tongue fathomed the words. Think, then, of my astonishment, when my companion sung out the following stanza with great glee:—

> 'Here we roll,
> Body and soul,
> Down to the deeps of the paynim's goal—
> With speed and with spell,
> With yo and with yell,
> This is the way to the palace of hell—
> Sing Yo! Ho!
> Level and low,
> Down to the Valley of Vision we go!'

"'Ha, ha, ha! Tam Beattie,' added she, 'where is a' your courage now? Cannot ye lift up your voice and sing a stave wi' your auld crony? And cannot ye lift up your een, and see what region you are in now?'

"'I did force open my eyelids, and beheld light, and apparently worlds, or huge lurid substances gliding by me with speed, beyond that of the lightning of heaven. I certainly perceived light, though of a dim, uncertain nature; but so precipitate was my descent, I could not distinguish from whence it proceeded, or of what it consisted, whether of the vapours of elemental wastes, or the streamers of hell. So I again shut my eyes closer than ever, and waited the event in terror unutterable.

"'We at length came upon something which interrupted our further progress. I had no feeling as we fell against it, but merely as if we came in contact with some soft substance that impeded our descent; and immediately afterwards I perceived that our motion had ceased.

"'What a terrible tumble we hae gotten, laird!' said my companion. 'But ye are now in the place where you should be, an' deil speed the coward!'

"'So saying, she quitted my hand, and I felt as if she were wrested from me by a third object; but still I durst not open my eyes, being convinced that I was lying in the depths of hell, or some hideous place not to be dreamed of; so I lay still in despair, not even daring to address a prayer to my Maker. At length I lifted my eyes slowly and fearfully, but they had no power of distinguishing objects in the place where I now sojourned. All that I perceived was a vision of something in nature, with which I had in life been too well acquainted. It was a glimpse of green glens, long withdrawing ridges, and one high hill, with a cairn on its summit. I rubbed my eyes to divest them of the enchantment, but when I opened them again, the illusion was still brighter and more magnificent. Then springing to my feet, I perceived that I was lying in a little fairy ring, not one hundred yards from the door of my own hall!

"'I was, as you may well conceive, dazzled with admiration; still I felt that something was not right with me, and that I was struggling with an enchantment; but recollecting the hideous story told me by the beldame, of the deadly discord between my two sons, I hasted to watch their motions, for the morning was yet but dawning. In a few seconds after recovering my senses, I perceived my eldest son Thomas leave his tower armed, and pass on towards the place of appointment. I waylaid him, and remarked to him that he was very early astir, and I feared on no good intent. He made me no answer, but stood like one in a stupor, and gazed at me. 'I know your purpose, son Thomas,' said I; 'so it is vain for you to equivocate. You have challenged your brother, and are going to meet him in deadly combat; but as you value your father's blessing, and would deprecate his curse—as you value your hope in heaven, and would escape the punishment of hell—abandon the hideous and cursed intent, and be friends with your only brother.'

"'On this, my dutiful son Thomas kneeled to me, and presented his sword, disclaiming, at the same time, all intentions of taking away his brother's life, and all animosity for the vengeance sought against himself, and thanked me in a flood of tears for my interference. I then ordered him back to his couch, and taking his cloak and sword, hasted away to the crook of Glen-dearg, to wait the arrival of his brother.'"

Here Andrew Johnston's narrative detailed the self-same

circumstances recorded in a former part of this tale, as having passed between the father and his younger son, so that it is needless to recapitulate them; but beginning where that broke off, he added, in the words of the old laird, "'As soon as my son Francis had left me, in order to be reconciled to his brother, I returned to the fairy knowe and ring where I first found myself seated at daybreak. I know not why I went there, for though I considered with myself, I could discover no motive that I had for doing so, but was led thither by a sort of impulse which I could not resist, and from the same feeling spread my son's mantle on the spot, laid his sword down beside it, and laid me down to sleep. I remember nothing farther with any degree of accuracy, for I instantly fell into a chaos of suffering, confusion, and racking dismay, from which I was only of late released by awaking from a trance, on the very seat and in the same guise in which I was the evening before. I am certain I was at home in body or in spirit—saw my sons—spake these words to them, and heard theirs in return. How I returned I know even less than how I went, for in that instance it seemed to me as if the mysterious force that presses us to this sphere, and supports us on it, was in my case withdrawn or subverted, and that I merely fell from one part of the earth's surface and alighted on another. Now I am so ill that I cannot move from this couch; therefore, Andrew, do you mount and ride straight for home. Spare no horse flesh, by night or by day, to bring me word of my family, for I dread that some evil hath befallen them. If you find them in life, give them many charges from me of brotherly love and affection; if not—what can I say, but in the words of the patriarch, If I am bereaved of my children, I am bereaved.'"

The two brothers, in utter amazement, went together to the green ring on the top of the knoll above the castle of Cassway, and there found the mantle lying spread, and the sword beside it. They then, without letting Johnston into the awful secret, mounted straight, and rode off with him to their father. They found him still in bed, and very ill; and though rejoiced at seeing them, they soon lost hope of his recovery, his spirits being broken and deranged in a wonderful manner. Their conversations together were of the most solemn nature, the visitation deigned to them having been above their capacity. On the third or fourth day, their father was removed by death from this terrestrial scene, and the minds of the young men were so much impressed by the whole of the circumstances, that it made a great alteration in their after life. Thomas, as solemnly charged by his father, married Ellen Scott, and Francis was well known afterward as the celebrated Dr Beattie of Amherst. Ellen was mother to twelve sons, and on the night that her seventh son was born, her aunt Jerdan was lost, and never more heard of, either living or dead.

This will be viewed as a most romantic and unnatural story, as without doubt it is; but I have the strongest reasons for believing that it is founded on a literal fact, of which all the three were sensibly and positively convinced. It was published in England in Dr Beattie's lifetime and by his acquiescence, and owing to the respectable source from whence it came, was never disputed in that day as having had its origin in truth. It was again republished, with some miserable alterations, in a London collection of 1770, by J. Smith, at No. 15, Paternoster-row; and though I have seen none of those, but relate the story wholly from tradition, yet the assurance attained from a friend of the existence of these, is a curious and corroborative circumstance, and proves that, if the story was not true, the parties believed it to have been so. It is certainly little accordant with any principle of nature or reason, but so also are many other well authenticated traditionary stories; therefore, the best way is to admit their veracity without saying why or wherefore.

Mount Benger, July 7, 1827.

Class IX.
Fairies, Brownies, and Witches.

Mary Burnet

IN this class of my pastoral legends, I must take a date, in some instances, a century earlier than the generality of those of the other classes, and describe a state of manners more primitive and visionary than any I have witnessed, simple and romantic as these have been; and I must likewise relate scenes so far out of the way of usual events, that the sophisticated gloss and polish thrown over the modern philosophic mind, may feel tainted by such antiquated breathings of superstition. Nevertheless, be it mine to cherish the visions that have been, as well as the hope of visions yet in reserve, far in the ocean of eternity, beyond the stars and the sun. For, after all, what is the soul of man without these? What but a cold phlegmatic influence, so inclosed within the walls of modern scepticism, as scarcely to be envied by the spirits of the beasts that perish?

However, as all my legends hitherto have been founded on facts, or are of themselves traditionary tales that seem originally to have been founded on facts, I should never have thought of putting the antiquated and visionary tales of my friends, the Fairies and Brownies, among them, had it not been for the late advice of a highly valued friend, who held it as indispensable, that these most popular of all traditions by the shepherd's ingle-side, should have a place in his Calendar. At all events, I pledge myself to relate nothing that has not been handed down to me by tradition. How these traditions have originated, I leave to the professors of moral philosophy, in their definitions of pneumatology, to determine.

The following incidents are related as having occurred at a shepherd's house, not a hundred miles from St Mary's Loch; but, as the descendants of one of the families still reside in the vicinity, I deem it requisite to use names which cannot be recognised, save by those who have heard the story.

John Allanson, the farmer's son of Inverlawn, was a handsome, roving, and incautious young man, enthusiastic, amorous, and fond of adventure, and one who could hardly be said to fear the face of either man, woman, or spirit. Among other love adventures, he fell a-courting Mary Burnet, of Kirkstyle, a most lovely and innocent maiden, and one who had been bred up in rural simplicity. She loved him, but yet she was afraid of him; and though she had no objection to meeting with him among others as oft as convenient, yet she carefully avoided meeting him alone, though often and earnestly urged to it. One day, the sinful young man, finding an opportunity, at Our Lady's Chapel, after mass, urged his suit for a private meeting so ardently, and with so many vows of love and sacred esteem, that poor Mary was won; at least so far won, as to promise, that *perhaps* she would come and meet him.

The trysting place was a little green sequestered spot, on the very verge of the lake, well known to many an angler, and to none better than the writer of this old tale; and the set time when the King's Elwand (now foolishly termed the Belt of Orion) set his first golden knob above the hill. Allanson came too early; for his heart yearned to clasp his beloved Mary all alone; and he watched the evening autumnal sky with such eagerness and devotion, that he thought every little star that arose in the south-east the top knob of the King's Elwand; but no second one following in the regular time, he began to think the Gowden Elwand was lost for that night, or withheld by some spiteful angel, out of envy at the abundance of his promised enjoyment. The Elwand did at last arise in good earnest, and then the youth, with a heart palpitating with agitation, had nothing for it but to watch the heathery brow by which bonny Mary Burnet was to descend. No Mary Burnet made her appearance, even although the King's Elwand had now measured its own equivocal length five or six times up the lift.

Young Allanson now felt all the most poignant miseries of disappointment; and, as the story goes, uttered in his heart some unhallowed wish, and even repeated it so often, as to give the vagrant spirits of the wild a malicious interest in the event. He wished that some witch or fairy would influence his Mary to come to him in spite of her maidenly scruples and overstrained delicacy. In short, it is deemed that he wished to have her there, by whatever means or agency.

This wish was thrice repeated with all the energy of disappointed love. It was thrice repeated, and no more, when, behold, Mary appeared on the brae, with wild and eccentric motions, speeding to the appointed place. Allanson's enthusiasm, or rather excitement, seems to have been more than he was able to bear, as he instantly became delirious with joy, and always professed that he could remember nothing of their first meeting, save that Mary remained silent, and spoke not a word, neither good nor bad. He had no doubt, he said, that his words and actions both were extravagant; but he had no conception that they could be anything but respectful; yet, for all that, Mary, who had never uttered a word, fell a-sobbing and weeping, refusing to be comforted. This melting tenderness the youth had not construed aright; for, on offering some further blandishments, the maid uttered a piercing shriek, sprung up, and ran from him with amazing speed.

At this part of the loch, which, as I said, is well known to many, the shore is overhung by a precipitous cliff, of no great height, but still inaccessible, either from above or below. Save in a great drought, the water comes to within a yard of the bottom of this cliff, and the intermediate space is filled with rough unshapely pieces of rock fallen from above. Along this narrow and rude space, hardly passable by the angler at noon, did Mary bound with the swiftness of a kid, although surrounded with darkness. Her lover, pursuing with all his energy, called out, "Mary! Mary! my dear Mary, stop and speak with me. I'll conduct you home, or anywhere you please, but do not run from me. Stop, my dearest Mary—stop!"

Mary would not stop; but ran on, till, coming to a little cliff that jutted into the lake, round which there was no passage, and, perceiving that her lover would there overtake her, she uttered another shriek, and plunged into the lake. The loud sound of her fall into the still lake rung in the young man's ears like the knell of death; and if before he was crazed with love, he was now as much so with despair. He saw her floating lightly away from the shore towards the deepest part of the loch; but, in a short time, she began to sink, and gradually disappeared, without uttering a throb or a cry. A good while previous to this, Allanson had flung off his bonnet, shoes, and coat, and plunged in after the treasure of his soul. He swam to the place where she disappeared; but there was neither boil nor gurgle on the water, nor even a bell of departing breath, to mark the place where his beloved had sunk. Being strangely impressed, at that trying moment, either to live or die with her, he tried to dive, in hopes either to bring her up or to die in her arms; and he thought of their being so found on the shore of the lake with a melancholy satisfaction; but by no effort of his could he reach the bottom, nor knew he what distance he was still from it. With an exhausted frame, and a despairing heart, he was obliged again to seek the shore, and, dripping wet as he was, and half naked, he ran to her father's house with the woful tidings. Everything there was quiet. The old shepherd's family, of whom Mary was the youngest, and sole daughter, were all sunk in quiet repose; and oh how the distracted lover wept at the thoughts of wakening them to hear the doleful tidings! But waken them he must; so, going to the little window close by the goodman's bed, he called, in a melancholy tone, "Andrew! Andrew Burnet, are you waking?"

"Troth, man, I think I be: or, at least, I'm half-an'-half. What hast thou to say to auld Andrew Burnet at this time o' night?"

"Are you waking, I say?"

"Gudewife, am I waking? Because if I be, tell that stravaiger sae. He'll maybe tak' your word for it, for mine he winna tak'."

"O Andrew, none of your humour to-night;—I bring you tidings the most woful, the most dismal, the most heart-rending, that ever were brought to an honest man's door."

"To his window, you mean," cried Andrew, bolting out of bed, and proceeding to the door. "Gude sauff us, man, come in, whaever you be, an' tell us your tidings face to face; an' then we'll can better judge of the truth of them. If they be in concord wi' your voice, they are melancholy indeed. Have the reavers come, and are our kye driven?"

"Oh, alas! waur than that—a thousand times waur than that! Your daughter—your dear beloved and only daughter, Mary—"

"What of Mary?" cried the gudeman. "What of Mary?" cried her mother, shuddering and groaning with terror; and at the same time she kindled a light.

The sight of their neighbour, half-naked, and dripping with wet, and madness and despair in his looks, sent a chillness to their hearts, that held them in silence, and they were unable to utter a word, till he went on thus—"Mary is gone; your darling and mine is lost, and sleeps this night in a watery grave,—and I have been her destroyer."

"Thou art mad, John Allanson," said the old man, vehemently, "raving mad; at least I hope so. Wicked as thou art, thou hadst not a heart to kill my dear child. O yes, you are mad—God be thanked, you are mad. I see it in your looks and whole demeanour. Heaven be praised, you are mad! You *are* mad, but you'll get better again. But what do I say?" continued he, as recollecting himself,—"We can soon convince our own senses. Wife, lead the way to our daughter's bed."

With a heart throbbing with terror and dismay, old Jean Linton led the way to Mary's chamber, followed by the two men, who were eagerly gazing, one over each of her shoulders. Mary's little apartment was in the farther end of the long narrow cottage; and as soon as they entered it, they perceived a form lying on the bed, with the bed-clothes drawn over its head; and on the lid of Mary's little chest, that stood at the bed-side, her clothes were lying neatly folded, as they wont to be. Hope seemed to dawn on the faces of the two old people when they beheld this, but the lover's heart sunk still deeper in despair. The father called her name, but the form on the bed returned no answer; however, they all heard distinctly the sobs, as of one weeping. The old man then ventured to pull down the clothes from her face; and, strange to say, there indeed lay Mary Burnet, drowned in tears, yet apparently nowise surprised at the ghastly appearance of the three naked figures. Allanson gasped for breath, for he remained still incredulous. He touched her clothes—he lifted her robes one by one,—and all of them were dry, neat, and clean, and had no appearance of having sunk in the lake.

There can be no doubt that Allanson was confounded by the strange event that had befallen him, and felt like one struggling with a frightful vision, or some energy beyond the power of man to comprehend. Nevertheless, the assurance that Mary was there in life, weeping although she was, put him once more beside himself with joy; and he kneeled at her bedside, beseeching but to kiss her hand. She, however, repulsed him with disdain, uttering these words with great emphasis—"You are a bad man, John Allanson, and I entreat you to go out of my sight. The sufferings that I have undergone this night, have been beyond the power of flesh and blood to endure; and by some cursed agency of yours have these sufferings been brought about. I therefore pray you, in His name, whose law you have transgressed, to depart out of my sight."

Wholly overcome by conflicting passions, by circumstances so contrary to one another, and so discordant with everything either in the works of Nature or Providence, the young man could do nothing but stand like a rigid statue, with his hands lifted up, and his visage like that of a corpse, until led away by the two old people from their daughter's apartment. They then lighted up a fire to dry him, and began to question him with the most intense curiosity; but they could elicit nothing from him, but the most disjointed exclamations—such as, "Lord in Heaven, what can be the meaning of this!" And at other times—"It is all the enchantment of the devil; the evil spirits have got dominion over me!"

Finding they could make nothing of him, they began to form conjectures of their own. Jean affirmed that it had been the Mermaid of the loch that had come to him in Mary's shape, to allure him to his destruction; "and he had muckle reason to be thankful that he had keepit in some bounds o' decency wi' her, else he wad hae been miserable through life, an' a thousand times waur through eternity."

But Andrew Burnet, setting his bonnet to one side, and raising his left hand to a level with that, so that he might have full scope to

motion and flourish with it, suiting his action to his words, thus
began, with a face of sapience never to be excelled:—

"Gudewife, it doth strike me that thou art very wide of the mark.
It must have been a spirit of a great deal higher quality than a
meer-maiden, who played this ex-tra-ōrdinary prank. The meer-
maiden is not a spirit, but a beastly sensitive creature, with a
malicious spirit within it. Now, what influence could a cauld clatch of
a creature like that, wi' a tail like a great saumont-fish, hae ower our
bairn, either to make her happy or unhappy? Or where could it
borrow her claes, Jean? Tell me that. Na, na, Jean Linton, depend on
it, the spirit that courtit wi' poor sinfu' Jock there, has been a fairy;
but whether a good ane or an ill ane, it is hard to determine."

How long Andrew's disquisition might have lasted, will never be
known, for it was interrupted by the young man falling into a fit of
trembling that was fearful to look at, and threatened soon to terminate his existence. Jean ran for the family cordial, observing, by
the way, that "though he was a wicked person, he was still a fellow-
creature, and might live to repent;" and influenced by this spark of
genuine humanity, she made him swallow two horn-spoonfuls of
strong aquavitæ, while Andrew brought out his best Sunday shirt,
and put it on him in place of his wet one. Then putting a piece of
scarlet thread round each wrist, and taking a strong rowan-tree staff
in his hand, he conveyed his trembling and astonished guest home,
giving him at parting this sage advice:—

"I'll tell you what it is, Jock Allanson,—ye hae run a near risk o'
perdition, an' escaping that for the present, o' losing your right
reason. But tak' an auld man's advice—never gang again out by
night to beguile ony honest man's daughter, lest a worse thing befall
thee."

Next morning Mary dressed herself more neatly than usual, but
there was manifestly a deep melancholy settled on her lovely face,
and at times the unbidden tear would start into her eye. She spoke no
word, either good or bad, that ever her mother could recollect, that
whole morning; but she once or twice observed her daughter gazing
at her, as with an intense and melancholy interest. About nine
o'clock in the morning, she took a hay-raik over her shoulder, and
went down to a meadow at the east end of the loch, to coil a part of
her father's hay, her father and brother engaging to join her about
noon, when they came from the sheep-fold. As soon as old Andrew
came home, his wife and he, as was natural, instantly began to
converse on the events of the preceding night; and in the course of
their conversation, Andrew said, "Gudeness be about us, Jean, was

not yon an awfu' speech o' our bairn's to young Jock Allanson last night?"

"Ay, it was a downsetter, gudeman, and spoken like a good Christian lass."

"I'm no sae sure o' that, Jean Linton. My good woman, Jean Linton, I'm no sae sure o' that. Yon speech has gi'en me a great deal o' trouble o' heart, for d'ye ken, an take my life,—ay, an take your life, Jean,—nane o' us can tell whether it was in the Almighty's name, or the devil's, that she discharged her lover."

"O fy, Andrew, how can ye say sae? How can ye doubt that it was in the Almighty's name?"

"Couldna she have said sae then, and that wad hae put it beyond a' doubt? An' that wad hae been the natural way too; but instead of that, she says, 'I pray you, in the name of him whose law you have transgressed, to depart out o' my sight.' I confess I'm terrified when I think about yon speech, Jean Linton. Didna she say, too, that 'her sufferings had been beyond what flesh an' blood could have endured?' What was she but flesh and blood? Didna that remark infer that she was something mair than a mortal creature? Jean Linton, Jean Linton! what will you say, if it should turn out that our daughter *is* drowned, and that yon was the fairy we had in the house a' the night and this morning?"

"O haud your tongue, Andrew Burnet, an' dinna make my heart cauld within me. We hae aye trusted in the Lord yet, an' he has never forsaken us, nor will he yet giè the wicked power ower us or ours."

"Ye say very weel, Jean, an' we maun e'en hope for the best," quoth old Andrew; and away he went, accompanied by his son Alexander, to assist their beloved Mary on the meadow.

No sooner had Andrew set his head over the bents, and come in view of the meadow, than he said to his son, "I wish Jock Allanson maunna hae been east the loch fishing for geds the day; for I think my Mary has made very little progress in the meadow."

"She's ower muckle ta'en up about other things this while, to mind her wark," said Alexander: "I wadna wonder, father, if that lassie gangs a black gate yet."

Andrew uttered a long and a deep sigh, that seemed to ruffle the very fountains of life, and, without speaking another word, walked on to the hay field. It was three hours since Mary had left home, and she ought at least to have put up a dozen coils of hay each hour. But, in place of that, she had put up only seven altogether, and the last was unfinished. Her own hay-raik, that had an M and a B neatly cut on the head of it, was leaning on the unfinished coil, and Mary was wanting. Her brother, thinking she had hid herself from them in sport, ran from one coil to another, calling her many bad names, playfully; but, after he had turned them all up, and several deep swathes besides, she was not to be found. Now, it must be remarked, that this young man, who slept in the byre, knew nothing of the events of the foregoing night, the old people and Allanson having mutually engaged to keep them a profound secret. So that, when old Andrew said, "What in the world can hae come o' the lassie?" his son replied, with a lightsome air, "Off wi' some o' the lads, to be sure, on some daft errand. Od ye ken little about her; she wad rin through fire an' water to be wi' a handsome young lad. I believe, if the deil himsell war to come to her in the form of a braw, bonny lad, he might persuade her to do ought ever he likit."

"Whisht, callant, how can ye speak that gate about your only sister? I'm sure, poor lassie, she has never gi'en ane o' us a sair heart in a' her life—till now," added Andrew, after a long pause; and the young man, perceiving his father looking so serious and thoughtful, dropped his raillery, and they began to work at the hay. Andrew could work none; he looked this way and that way, but in no way could he see Mary approaching: so he put on his coat, and went away home, to pour his sorrows into the bosom of his old wife; and in the meantime, he desired his son to run to all the neighbouring farm-houses and cots, every one, and make inquiries if anybody had seen Mary.

When Andrew went home and informed his wife that their darling was missing, the grief and astonishment of the aged couple knew no bounds. They sat down, and wept together, and declared, over and over, that this act of Providence was too strange for them, and too high to be understood. Jean besought her husband to kneel instantly, and pray urgently to God to restore their child to them; but he declined it, on account of the wrong frame of his mind, for he declared, that his rage against John Allanson was so extreme, as to unfit him for approaching the throne of his Maker. "But if the profligate refuses to listen to the entreaties of an injured parent," added he, "he shall feel the weight of an injured father's arm."

Andrew went straight away to Inverlawn, though without the least hope of finding young Allanson at home, for he had no doubt that he had seduced his daughter from her duty; but, on reaching the place, to his still farther amazement, he found the young man lying ill of a burning fever, raving incessantly of witches, spirits, and Mary Burnet. To such a height had his frenzy arrived, that when Andrew went there, it required three men to hold him in the bed. Both his parents testified their opinions openly, that their son was bewitched, or possessed of a demon, and the whole family was thrown into the greatest consternation. The good old shepherd, finding enough of grief there already, was obliged to confine his to his own bosom, and return disconsolate to his little family circle, in which there was a woful blank that night.

His son returned also from a fruitless search. No one had seen any traces of his sister, but an old crazy woman, at a place called Oxcleuch, said that she had seen her go by in a grand chariot with young Jock Allanson, toward the Birkhill Path, and by that time they were at the Cross of Dumgree. The young man said he asked her what sort of a chariot it was, as there was never such a thing in that country as a chariot, nor yet a road for one. But she replied, that he was widely mistaken, for that a great number of chariots sometimes passed that way, though never any of them returned. These words appearing to be merely the ravings of superannuation, they were not regarded; but when no other traces of Mary could be found, old Andrew went up to consult this crazy dame once more, but he was not able to bring any such thing to her recollection. She spoke only in parables, which to him were incomprehensible.

Bonny Mary Burnet was lost. She left her father's house at nine o'clock on a Wednesday morning, the 17th of September, neatly dressed in a white jerkin and green bonnet, with her hay-raik over her shoulder; and that was the last sight she was doomed ever to see of her native cottage. She seemed to have had some presentiment of this, as appeared from her demeanour that morning before she left it. Mary Burnet of Kirkstyle was lost, and great was the sensation produced over the whole country by the mysterious event. There was a long ballad extant at one period on the melancholy catastrophe, which was supposed to have been composed by the chaplain of St Mary's, but I have only heard tell of it, without ever hearing it sung or recited. Many of the verses concluded thus:—

> "But bonny Mary Burnet
> We will never see again."

The story soon got abroad, with all its horrid circumstances, and there is little doubt that it was grievously exaggerated. The gossips told of a love-tryst by night, at the side of the loch—of the young profligate's rudeness, which was carried to that degree, that she was obliged to throw herself into the lake, and perish, rather than submit to infamy and sin. In short, there was no obloquy that was not thrown on the survivor, who certainly in some degree deserved it, for, instead of growing better, he grew ten times more wicked than he was before.

In one thing the whole country agreed, that it had been the real Mary Burnet who was drowned in the loch, and that the being which was found in her bed, lying weeping and complaining of suffering, and which vanished the next day, had been a fairy, an evil spirit, or a changeling of some sort, for that it never spoke save once, and that in a mysterious manner; nor did it partake of any food with the rest of the family. Her father and mother knew not what to say or what to think, but they wandered through this weary world like people wandering in a dream.

Everything that belonged to Mary Burnet was kept by her parents as the most sacred relics, and many a tear did her aged mother shed over them. Every article of her dress brought the once comely wearer to mind. The handsome shoes that her feet had shaped, and even the very head of her hay-raik, with an M and B cut upon it, were laid carefully by in the little chest that had once been hers, and served as dear memorials of one that was now no more. Andrew often said, "That to have lost the darling child of their old age in any way would have been a great trial, but to lose her in the way that they had done, was really mair than human frailty could endure."

Many a weary day did he walk by the shores of the loch, looking eagerly for some vestige of her garments, and though he trembled at every appearance, yet did he continue to search on. He had a number of small bones collected, that had belonged to lambs and other minor animals, and, haply, some of them to fishes, from a fond supposition that they might once have formed joints of her toes or fingers. These he kept concealed in a little bag, in order, as he said, "to let the doctors see them." But no relic, besides these, could he ever discover of his Mary's body.

Young Allanson recovered from his raging fever scarcely in the manner of other men, for he recovered all at once, after a few days' raving and madness. Mary Burnet, it appeared, was by him no more remembered. He grew ten times more wicked than before, and hesitated at no means of accomplishing his unhallowed purposes. His passion for women grew into a mania, that blinded the eyes of his understanding, and hindered him from perceiving the path of moral propriety, or even that of common decency. This total depravity the devout shepherds and cottagers around him regarded as an earthly and eternal curse fixed on him; a mark like that which God put upon Cain, that whosoever knew him might shun him. They detested him, and, both in their families and in the wild, when there was no ear to hear but that of Heaven, they prayed protection from his devices, as if he had been the wicked one; and they all prophesied that he would make a bad end.

One fine day, about the middle of October, when the days begin to get very short, and the nights long and dark, on a Friday morning, the next year but one after Mary Burnet was lost, a memorable day in the fairy annals, John Allanson, younger of Inverlawn, went to a great hiring fair at a village called Moffat in Annandale, in order to hire a housemaid. His character was so notorious, that not one pretty maiden in the district would serve in his father's house; so away he went to the fair at Moffat, to hire the prettiest and loveliest girl he could there find, with the generous intention of seducing her as soon as she came home. This was no supposititious accusation, for he acknowledged his plan to Mr David Welch of Cariferan, who rode down to the market with him, and seemed to boast of it, and dwell on it, with delight. But the maidens of Annandale had a guardian angel in the fair that day, of which neither he nor they were aware.

Allanson looked through the hiring market, and through the hiring market, and at length fixed on one, which indeed was not difficult to do, for there was no such form there for elegance and beauty. She had all the appearance of a lady, but she had the badge of servitude in her bosom, a little rose of Paradise, without the leaves, so that Allanson knew she was to hire. He urged her for some time, with emotions of the wildest delight, and at length meeting with his young companion, Mr David Welch, he pointed her out to him, and asked how she would suit.

Mr Welch answered, that he was in great luck indeed, if he acquired such a mistress as that. "*If* ?" said he,—"I think you need hardly have put an *if* to it. Stop there for a small space, and I will let you see me engage her in five minutes." Mr Welch stood still and eyed him. He took the beauty aside. She was clothed in green, and as lovely as a new blown rose.

"Are you to hire, pretty maiden?"

"Yes, sir."

"Will you hire with me?"

"I care not though I do. But if I hire with you, it must be for the long term."

"Certainly. The longer the better. What are your wages to be?"

"You know, if I hire, I must be paid in kind. I must have the first living creature that I see about Inverlawn to myself."

"I wish it may be me, then. But what the devil do you know about Inverlawn?"

"I think I *should* know about it."

"Bless me! I know the face as well as I know my own, and better. But the name has somehow escaped me. Pray, may I ask your name?"

"Hush! hush!" said she solemnly, and holding up her hand at the same time; "Hush, hush, you had better say nothing about that here."

"I am in utter amazement!" exclaimed he. "What is the meaning of this? I conjure you to tell me your name?"

"It is Mary Burnet," said she, in a soft whisper; and at the same time she let down a green veil over her face.

If Allanson's death-warrant had been announced to him at that moment, it could not have deprived him so completely of sense and motion. His visage changed into that of a corpse, his jaws fell down, and his eyes became glazed, so as apparently to throw no reflection inwardly. Mr Welch, who had kept his eye steadily on them all the while, perceived his comrade's dilemma, and went up to him. "Allanson?—Mr Allanson? What the deuce is the matter with you, man?" said he. "Why, the girl has bewitched you, and turned you into a statue!"

Allanson made some sound with his voice, as if attempting to speak, but his tongue refused its office, and he only jabbered. Mr Welch, conceiving that he was seized with some fit, or about to faint, supported him into the Johnston Arms, and got him something to drink; but he either could not, or would not, grant him any explanation. Welch being, however, resolved to see the maiden in green once more, persuaded Allanson, after causing him to drink a good deal, to go out into the hiring-market again, in search of her. They ranged the market through and through, but the maiden in green was gone, and not to be found. She had vanished in the crowd the moment she divulged her name, and even though Welch had his eye fixed on her, he could not discover which way she went. Allanson appeared to be in a kind of stupor as well as terror, but when he found that she had left the market, he screwed his courage to the sticking place once more, and resolving to have a winsome housemaid from Annandale, he began again to look out for the top of the market.

He soon found one more beautiful than the last. She was like a sylph, clothed in robes of pure snowy white, with green ribbons. Again he pointed this new flower out to Mr David Welch, who declared that such a perfect model of beauty he had never in his life seen. Allanson, being resolved to have this one at any wages, took her aside, and put the usual question.

"Do you wish to hire, pretty maiden?"

"Yes, sir."

"Will you hire with me?"

"I care not though I do."

"What, then, are your wages to be? Come—say? And be reasonable; I am determined not to part with you for a trifle."

"My wages must be in kind; I work on no other conditions. Pray, how are all the good people about Inverlawn?"

Allanson's breath began to cut, and a chillness to creep through his whole frame, and he answered, with a faltering tongue,—

"I thank you,—much in their ordinary way."

"And your aged neighbours," rejoined she, "are they still alive and well?"

"I—I—I think they are," said he, panting for breath. "But curse me, if I know who I am indebted to for these kind recollections."

"What," said she, "have you so soon forgot Mary Burnet of Kirkstyle?"

Allanson started as if a bullet had gone through his heart. The lovely sylph-like form glided into the crowd, and left the astounded libertine once more standing like a rigid statue, until aroused by his friend, Mr Welch. He tried a third fair one, and got the same answers, and the same name given. Indeed, the first time ever I heard the tale, it bore that he tried *seven*, who all turned out to be Mary Burnets of Kirkstyle; but I think it unlikely that he would try so many, as he must long ere that time have been sensible that he laboured under some power of enchantment. However, when nothing else would do, he helped himself to a good proportion of strong drink. While he was thus engaged, a phenomenon of beauty and grandeur came into the fair, that caught the sole attention of all present. This was a lovely dame, riding in a gilded chariot, with two liverymen before, and two behind, clothed in green and gold; and never sure was there so splendid a meteor seen in a Moffat fair. The word instantly circulated in the market, that this was the Lady Elizabeth Douglas, eldest daughter to the Earl of Morton, who then sojourned at Auchincastle, in the vicinity of Moffat, and which lady at that time was celebrated as a great beauty all over Scotland. She was afterwards Lady Keith; and the mention of this name in the tale, as it were by mere accident, fixes the era of it in the reign of James the Fourth, at the very time that fairies, brownies, and witches, were at the rifest in Scotland.

Every one in the market believed the lady to be the daughter of the Earl of Morton, and when she came to the Johnston Arms, a gentleman in green came out bareheaded, and received her out of the carriage. All the crowd gazed at such unparalleled beauty and grandeur, but none was half so much overcome as Allanson. His heart, being a mere general slave to female charms, was smitten in proportion as this fair dame excelled all others he had ever seen. He had never conceived aught half so lovely either in earth, or heaven, or fairyland, and his heart, at first sight, burned with an inextinguishable flame of love towards her. But alas, there is reason to fear there was no spark of that refined and virtuous love in him, which is the delight of earth and heaven. It might be more fervent and insufferable, but it wanted the sweet serenity and placid delights of the former. His was not a ray from the paradise above, but a burning spark from the regions below. From thence it arose, and in all its wanderings, thitherward it pointed again.

While he stood in this burning fever of love and admiration, his bosom panting, and his eyes suffused with tears, think of his astonishment, and the astonishment of the countless crowd that looked on, when this brilliant and matchless beauty beckoned him towards her! He could not believe his senses, but looked hither and thither to see how others regarded the affair; but she beckoned him a second time, with such a winning courtesy and smile, that immediately he pulled off his beaver cap and hasted up to her; and without more ado she gave him her arm, and the two walked into the hostel.

Allanson conceived that he was thus distinguished by Lady Elizabeth Douglas, the flower of the land, and so did all the people of the market; and greatly they wondered who the young farmer could be that was thus particularly favoured; for it ought to have been mentioned that he had not one personal acquaintance in the fair save Mr David Welch of Cariferan. But no sooner had she got him into a private room, than she began to inquire kindly of his health and recovery from the severe malady by which he was visited. Allanson thanked her ladyship with all the courtesy he was master of; and being by this time persuaded that she was in love with him, he became as light as if treading on the air. She next inquired after his father and mother. "Oho!" thinks he to himself, "poor creature, she is terribly in for it! but her love *shall not* be thrown away upon a backward or ungrateful object."

He answered her with great politeness, and at length began to talk of her noble father and young Lord William, but she cut him short by asking if he did not recognise her.

"Oh, yes! He knew who her ladyship was, and remembered that he had seen her comely face often before, although he could not recall to his memory the precise time or places of their meeting."

She asked him for his old neighbours of Kirkstyle, and if they were still in life and health!!

Allanson felt as if his heart were a piece of ice. A chillness spread over his whole frame; he sank back on a seat, and remained motionless; but the beautiful and adorable creature soothed him with kind words, and even with blandishments, till he again gathered courage to speak.

"What!" said he; "and has it been your own lovely self who has been playing tricks on me this whole day? "

"A first love is not easily extinguished, Mr Allanson," said she. "You may guess, from my appearance, that I have been fortunate in life; but, for all that, my first love for you has continued the same, unaltered and unchanged, and you must forgive the little freedoms I used to-day to try your affections, and the effects my appearance would have on you."

"It argues something for my good taste, however, that I never pitched on any face for beauty to-day but your own," said he. "But now that we have met once more, we shall not so easily part again. I will devote the rest of my life to you, only let me know the place of your abode."

"It is hard by," said she, "only a very little space from this; and happy, happy, would I be to see you there to-night, were it proper or convenient. But my lord is at present from home, and in a distant country."

"I should not conceive that any particular hinderance to my visit," said he; "for, in truth, I account it one of the most fortunate events that has happened to me; and visit you I will, and visit you I shall, this night,—that you may depend upon."

"But I hope, Mr Allanson, you are not of the same rakish disposition that you were on our first acquaintance? for, if you are, I could not see your face under my roof on any account."

"Why, the truth is, madam, that the country people reckon me a hundred degrees worse; but I know myself to be, in fact, many thousand degrees better. However, let it suffice, that I have no scruples in visiting my old sweetheart in the absence of her lord, nor are they increased by his great distance from home."

With great apparent reluctance she at length consented to admit of his visit, and offered to leave one of her gentlemen, whom she could trust, to be his conductor; but this he positively refused. It was his desire, he said, that no eye of man should see him enter or leave her happy dwelling. She said he was a self-willed man, but should have his own way; and after giving him such directions as would infallibly lead him to her mansion, she mounted her chariot and was driven away.

Allanson was uplifted above every sublunary concern. Sinful as the adventure was, he gloried in it, for such adventures were his supreme delight. Seeking out his friend, David Welch, he imparted to him his extraordinary good fortune, but he did not tell him that she was not the Lady Elizabeth Douglas. Welch insisted on accompanying him, but this he would in nowise admit; the other, however, set him on the way, and refused to turn back till he came to the very point of the road next to the lady's splendid mansion; and in spite of all that Allanson could say, Welch remained there till he saw his comrade enter the court-gate, which glowed with lights as innumerable as the stars of the firmament.

"Ah, what a bad girl that Lady Elizabeth Douglas must be for all her beauty," said Mr Welch to himself. "But, oh! that I had had that wild fellow's fortune to-night!" David Welch did not think so before that day eight days. Let no man run on in evil, and expect that good will spring out of it.

Allanson had promised to his father and mother to be home on the morning after the fair to breakfast. He came not either that day or the next; and the third day the old man mounted his white pony, and rode away towards Moffat in search of his son. He called at Cariferan on his way, and made inquiries at Mr Welch. The latter manifested some astonishment that the young man had not returned; nevertheless he assured his father of his safety, and desired him to return home; and then with reluctance confessed that the young man was engaged in an amour with the Earl of Morton's beautiful daughter; that he had gone to the castle by appointment, and that he, David Welch, had accompanied him to the gate, and seen him enter, and it was apparent that his reception had been a kind one, since he had tarried so long.

The old man lifted off his bonnet with the one hand, and with the other wiped a tear from his eye, saying, at the same time, "Then I'll never see him alive again! For several years I have foreseen that women would infallibly be the end of him; and now that he is gone upon his wild adventures in the family of the proud Earl Douglas of Morton, how is it likely that he shall ever escape the fate that in reality he deserves? How inscrutable are the divine decrees! My son was born to the doom that has overtaken him. On the night that he was born, there was a weeping and wailing of women all around our house, and even in the bed where his mother was confined; and as it was a brownie that brought the midwife, no one ever knew who she was, or whence she came. His life has been one of mystery, and his end will be the same."

Mr Welch, seeing the old man's distress, was persuaded to accompany him on his journey, as the last who had seen his son and seen him enter the castle. On reaching Moffat they found his steed standing at the hostel, whither it had returned in the night of the fair before the company broke up; but the owner had not been heard of since seen in company with Lady Elizabeth Douglas. The old man set out for Auchincastle, taking Mr David Welch along with him; but long ere they reached the place, Mr Welch assured him he would not find his son there, as it was nearly in a different direction that they rode, by appointment, on the evening of the fair. However, to the castle they went, and were admitted to the Earl, who laughed heartily at the old man's tale, and seemed to consider him in a state of derangement. He sent for his daughter Elizabeth, and questioned her concerning her meeting with the son of the old respectable country-man—of her appointment with him on the night of the preceding Friday, and concluded by saying he hoped she had him still in some safe concealment about the castle.

The lady, hearing her father talk thus flippantly, and seeing the serious and dejected looks of the old man towards her, knew not what to say, and asked an explanation. But Mr Welch put a stop to it by declaring to old Allanson that the Lady Elizabeth was not the lady with whom his son made the appointment, for he had seen her, had considered her lineaments very minutely, and would engage to know her again among ten thousand; nor was that the castle to which he had conducted his son, nor anything like it. "But go with me," continued he, "and though I am a stranger in this district, I think I can take you to the very place."

Away they went again; and Mr Welch traced the road from Moffat, by which young Allanson and he had gone to the appointed place, until, after travelling several miles, they came to a place where a road struck off to the right at an angle. "Now I know we are right," said Welch; "for here we stopped, and your son intreated me to return, which I refused, and accompanied him to yon large tree, and a little way beyond it, from whence I saw him received in at the splendid gate. We shall now be in sight of the mansion in three minutes."

They passed on to the tree, and a space beyond it; but then Mr Welch lost the use of his speech, as he perceived that there was neither palace nor gate there, but a tremendous gulf, fifty fathoms deep, and a dark stream foaming and boiling below.

"How is this?" said old Allanson. "There is neither mansion nor habitation of man here!"

Welch's tongue for a long space refused its office, and there he stood like a statue, gazing on the altered and awful scene. "He only who made the spirits of men," said he, at last, "and all the spirits that sojourn in the earth and air, can tell how this is. We are wandering in a world of enchantment, and have been influenced by some agencies above human nature, or without its pale; for here of a certainty did I take leave of your son—and there, in that direction, and apparently either on the verge of that gulf, or the space above it, did I see him received in at the court-gate of a mansion, splendid beyond all conception. How can human comprehension make anything of this?"

They went forward to the verge, Mr Welch leading the way to the very spot on which he saw the gate opened, and there they found marks where a horse had been plunging. Its feet had been over the brink, but it seemed to have recovered itself, and deep, deep down, and far within, lay the mangled corpse of John Allanson; and in this manner, mysterious beyond all example, terminated the career of that wicked and flagitious young man. What a beautiful moral may be extracted from this fairy tale!

But among all these turnings and windings, there is no account given, you will say, of the fate of Mary Burnet; for this last appearance of hers at Moffat seems to have been altogether a phantom or illusion. Gentle and kind reader, I can give you no account of the fate of that maiden; for though the ancient fairy tale proceeds, it seems to me to involve her fate in ten times more mystery than what is previously related, for, if she was not a changeling, or the Queen of the Fairies herself, I can make nothing of her.

The yearly return of the day on which Mary was lost, was observed as a day of mourning by her aged and disconsolate parents, —a day of sorrow, of fasting, and humiliation. Seven years came and passed away, and the seventh returning day of fasting and prayer was at hand. On the evening previous to it, old Andrew was moving along the sands of the loch, still looking for some relic of his beloved Mary, when he was aware of a little shrivelled old man, who came posting towards him. The creature was not above five spans in height, and had a face scarcely like that of a human creature; but he was, nevertheless, civil in his deportment, and sensible in speech. He bade Andrew a good evening, and asked him what he was looking for. Andrew answered, that he was looking for that which he would never find.

"Pray, what is your name, ancient shepherd?" said the stranger; "for methinks I should know something of you, and perhaps have a commission to you."

"Alas! why should you ask after my name?" said Andrew. "My name is now nothing to any one."

"Had not you once a beautiful daughter, named Mary?" said the stranger.

"It is a heart-rending question, man," said Andrew; "but certes, I had once a beloved daughter named Mary."

"What became of her?" said the stranger.

Andrew shook his head, turned round, and began to move away; it was a theme that his heart could not brook. He sauntered along the loch sands, his dim eye scanning every white pebble as he passed along. There was a hopelessness apparent in his stooping form, his gait, his eye, his features,—in every step that he took there was a hopeless apathy. The dwarf followed him along, and began to expostulate with him. "Old man, I see you are pining under some real or fancied affliction," said he. "But in continuing to do so, you are neither acting according to the dictates of reason nor true religion. What is man that he should fret, or the son of man that he should repine, under the chastening hand of his Maker?"

"I am far frae justifying mysell," returned Andrew, surveying his shrivelled monitor with some degree of astonishment. "But there are some feelings that neither reason nor religion can o'ermaster; and there are some that a parent may cherish without sin."

"I deny the position," said the stranger, "taken either absolutely or in relative degree. All repining under the Supreme decree is leavened with unrighteousness. But, subtleties aside, I ask you, as I did before, What became of your daughter?"

"Ask the Father of her spirit, and the framer of her body," said Andrew, solemnly; "ask Him into whose hands I committed her from childhood. He alone knows what became of her, but *I do not.*"

"How long is it since you lost her?"

"It is seven years to-morrow."

"Ay! you remember the time well. And are you mourning for her all this while?"

"Yes; and I will go down to the grave mourning for my only daughter, the child of my age, and of all my affection. O, thou unearthly-looking monitor, knowest thou aught of my darling child? for if thou dost, thou wilt know, that she was not like other women. There was a simplicity, a purity, and a sublimity about my lovely Mary, that was hardly consistent with our frail nature."

"Wouldst thou like to see her again?" said the dwarf, snappishly.

Andrew turned round his whole frame, shaking as with a palsy, and gazed on the audacious shrimp. "See her again, creature!" cried he vehemently—"Would I like to see her again, say'st thou?"

"I said so," said the dwarf, "and I say farther, Dost thou know this token? Look and see if thou dost."

Andrew took the token, and looked at it, then at the shrivelled stranger, and then at the token again; and at length he burst into tears, and wept aloud; but they were tears of joy, and his weeping seemed to have some breathings of laughter intermingled in it. And still as he kissed and kissed the token, he brayed out in broken and convulsive sentences,—"Yes, auld body, I *do* know it!—I *do* know it!—I *do* know it! It is indeed the same golden Edward, with three holes in it, with which I presented my Mary on her birth day, in her eighteenth year, to buy her a new suit for the holidays. But when she took it, she said—ay, I mind weel what my bonny woman said,—'It is sae bonny and sae kenspeckle,' said she, 'that I think I'll keep it for the sake of the giver.' O, dear, dear! and blessed little creature, tell me how she is, and where she is? Is she living, or is she dead? Is she in earth or in heaven? for I ken weel she is in ane of them."

"She is living, and in good health," said the dwarf; "and better, and brawer, and happier, and lovelier than ever; and if you make haste, you will see her and her family at Moffat to-morrow afternoon. They are to pass there on a journey, but it is an express one, and I am sent to you with that token, to inform you of the circumstance, that you may have it in your power to see and embrace your beloved daughter once before you die."

"And am I to meet my Mary at Moffat? Come away, little, dear, welcome body, thou blessed of heaven, come away, and taste of an auld shepherd's best cheer, and I'll gang foot for foot with you to Moffat, and my auld wife shall gang foot for foot with us too. I tell you, little, blessed, and welcome crile, come along with me."

"I may not tarry to enter your house, or taste of your cheer, good shepherd," said the being. "May plenty still be within your walls, and a thankful heart to enjoy it. But my directions are neither to taste meat nor drink in this country, but to haste back to her that sent me. Go—haste, and make ready, for you have no time to lose."

"At what time will she be there?" cried Andrew, flinging the plaid from him, to run home with the tidings.

"Precisely when the shadow of the Holy Cross falls due east," cried the dwarf; and turning round, he hasted on his way.

When old Jean Linton saw her husband coming hobbling and

running home without his plaid, and having his doublet flying wide open, she had no doubt that he had lost his wits; and, full of anxiety, she met him at the side of the kail-yard. "Gudeness preserve us a' in our right senses, Andrew Burnet, what's the matter wi' you?"

"Stand out o' my gate, wife, for, d'ye see, I'm rather in a haste."

"I see that, indeed, gudeman; but stand still, an' tell me what has putten you *in* sic a haste. Ir ye drunken or ir ye dementit?"

"Na, na; but I'm gaun awa till Moffat."

"O, gudeness pity the poor auld body! How can ye gang to Moffat, man? Or what have ye to do at Moffat? Dinna ye mind that the morn is the day o' our solemnity?"

"Haud out o' my gate, auld wife, an' dinna speak o' solemnities to me. I'll keep it at Moffat the morn.—Ay, gudewife, an' ye shall keep it at Moffat, too. What d'ye think o' that, woman? Too-whoo, ye dinna ken the mettle that's in an auld body till it be tried."

"Andrew—Andrew Burnet!"

"Get away wi' your frightened looks, woman; an' haste ye, gang an' fling me out my Sabbath-day claes. An', Jean Linton, my woman, d'ye hear, gang an' pit on your bridal gown, and your silk hood, for ye maun be at Moffat the morn too; an' it is mair nor time we were away. Dinna look sae bumbazed, woman, till I tell ye, that our ain Mary is to meet us at Moffat the morn."

"O, Andrew! dinna sport wi' the last feelings of an auld forsaken heart."

"Gude forbid, my auld wife, that I ever sported wi' feeling o' yours," cried Andrew, clasping her in his arms, and bursting into tears; "they are a' as sacred to me as breathings frae the Throne o' Grace. But it is true that I tell ye; our dear bairn is to meet us at Moffat the morn, wi' a son in every hand; an' we maun e'en gang an' see her aince again, an' kiss her an' bless her afore we dee."

The tears now rushed from the old woman's eyes like fountains, and dropped from her sorrow-worn cheeks to the earth, and then, as with a spontaneous movement, she threw her skirt over her head, kneeled down at her husband's feet, and poured out her soul in thanksgiving to her Maker. She then rose up quite deprived of her senses through joy, and ran crouching away on the road towards Moffat, as if hasting beyond her power to be at it. But Andrew brought her back; and they prepared themselves for their journey.

Kirkstyle being twenty miles from Moffat, they set out on the afternoon of Tuesday, the 16th of September; slept that night at a place called Turnberry Sheil, and were in Moffat next day by noon. Wearisome was the remainder of the day to that aged couple; they wandered about conjecturing by what road their daughter would come, and how she would come attended. "I have made up my mind on baith these matters," said Andrew; "at first I thought it was likely that she would come out o' the east, because a' our blessings come frae that airt; but finding now that that would be o'er near to the very road we hae come oursells, I now take it for granted she'll come frae the south; an' I just think I see her leading a bonny boy in every hand, an' a servant lass carrying a bit bundle ahint her."

The two now walked out on all the southern roads, in hopes to meet their Mary, but always returned to watch the shadow of the Holy Cross; and, by the time it fell due east, they could do nothing but stand in the middle of the street, and look round them in all directions. At length, about half a mile out on the Dumfries road, they perceived a poor beggar woman approaching with two children following close to her, and another beggar a good way behind. Their eyes were instantly riveted on these objects; for Andrew thought he perceived his friend the dwarf in the one that was behind; and now all other earthly objects were to them nothing, save these approaching beggars. At that moment a gilded chariot entered the village from the south, and drove by them at full speed, having two livery men before, and two behind, clothed in green and gold. "Ach-wow! the vanity of worldly grandeur!" said Andrew, as the splendid vehicle went thundering by; but neither he nor his wife deigned to look at it farther, their whole attention being fixed on the group of beggars. "Ay, it is just my woman," said Andrew, "it is just herself; I ken her gang yet, sair pressed down wi' poortith although she be. But I dinna care how poor she be, for baith her an' hers sall be welcome to my fireside as lang as I hae ane."

While their eyes were thus strained, and their hearts melting with tenderness and pity, Andrew felt something embracing his knees, and, on looking down, there was his Mary, blooming in splendour and beauty, kneeling at his feet. Andrew uttered a loud hysterical scream of joy, and clasped her to his bosom; and old Jean Linton stood trembling, with her arms spread, but durst not close them on so splendid a creature, till her daughter first enfolded her in a fond embrace, and then she hung upon her and wept. It was a wonderful event—a restoration without a parallel. They indeed beheld their Mary, their long-lost darling; they held her in their embraces, believed in her identity, and were satisfied. Satisfied, did I say? They were happy beyond the lot of mortals. She had just alighted from her chariot; and, perceiving her aged parents standing together, she ran and kneeled at their feet. They now retired into the hostel, where

Mary presented her two sons to her father and mother. They spent the evening in every social endearment; and Mary loaded the good old couple with rich presents, watched over them till midnight, when they both fell into a deep and happy sleep, and then she remounted her chariot, and was driven away. If she was any more seen in Scotland, I never heard of it; but her parents rejoiced in the thoughts of her happiness till the day of their death.

Mount Benger, Jan 10, 1828.

The Witches of Traquair

THERE was once a young man, a native of Traquair, in the county of Peebles, whose name was Colin Hyslop, and who suffered more by witchcraft, and the intervention of supernatural beings, than any man I ever heard of. But the tale is a very old one, and sorry am I to say that I cannot vouch for the truth of it, which I have hitherto, for the most part, been accustomed to do, and which I feel greatly disposed to do at all times, provided the tale bears the marks. of authenticity impressed on the leading events, whether I know of a verity that every individual incident related *did* happen or not.

Traquair was a terrible place then! There was a witch almost in every hamlet, and a warlock here and there besides. There were no fewer than twelve witches in one straggling hamlet, called Taniel-Burn, and five in Kirk-Row. What a desperate place Traquair had been in those days! But there is no person who is so apt to overshoot his mark as the Devil. He must be a great fool in the main; for, with all his high-flying and democratic principles, he often runs himself into the most confounded blunders that ever the leader of an opposition got into the midst of. Throughout all the annals of the human race, it is manifest, that whenever he was aiming to do the most evil, he was uniformly bringing about the most good; and it seems to have been so in the age to which my tale refers.

The truth is, that Popery was then on its last legs, and the Devil, finding it (as then exercised) a very convenient and profitable sort of religion, exerted himself beyond measure to give its motley hues a little more variety; and the plan of making witches and warlocks, and of holding nocturnal revels with them, where every sort of devilry was exercised, was at that time with him a favourite measure. It was also favourably received by the meaner sort of the populace. Witches gloried in their power, and warlocks in their foreknowledge of events, and the energies of their master. Women, beyond a certain age, when the pleasures and hopes of youth delighted no more, flew to it as an excitement of a higher and more terrible nature; and men, whose tempers had been soured by disappointment and ill usage, betook themselves to the Prince of the Power of the Air, enlisting under his banner, in hopes of obtaining revenge on their oppressors. However extravagant this may appear, there is no doubt of the fact, that, in those days, the hopes of attaining some energies beyond the reach of mere human capability, inflamed the ignorant and wicked to attempts and acts of the most diabolical nature; for hundreds acknowledged their principles, and gloried in them, before the tribunals that adjudged them to the stake.

"I am now fairly under the power of witchcraft," said Colin Hyslop, as he sat on the side of the Feathen Hill, with his plaid drawn over his head, the tears running down his brown manly cheek, and a paper marked with uncouth lines and figures in his hand,—"I am now fairly under the power of witchcraft, and must submit to my fate; I am entangled, enchained, enslaved; and the fault is all my own, for I have committed that degree of sin which my sainted and dying father assured me would subject me to the snares of my hellish neighbours and sworn adversaries. My pickle sheep have a' been bewitched, and a great part o' them have died dancing hornpipes an' French curtillions. I have been changed, and ower again changed, into shapes and forms that I darena think of, far less name; and a' through account of my ain sin. Hech! but it is a queer thing that sin! It has sae mony inroads to the heart, and outlets by the senses, that we seem to live and breathe in it. And I canna trow that the Deil is the wyte of a' our sins neither. Na, na; black as he is, he canna be the cause and the mover of a' our transgressions, for I find them often engendering and breeding in my heart as fast as maggots on tainted carrion, and then it is out o' the power of man to keep them down. My father tauld me, that if I aince let the Deil get his little finger into *ane* o' my transactions, he wad soon hae his haill hand into them a'. Now, I hae found it in effect, but not in belief; for, from a' that I can borrow frae Rob Kirkwood, the warlock, and my aunty Nans, the wickedest witch in Christendye, the Deil appears to me to be a gayan obliging chap. That he is wayward and fond o' sin, I hae nae doubt; but in that he has mony neighbours. And then his great power over the senses and conditions of men, over the winds, the waters, and the element of flame, is to me incomprehensible, and shows him to be rather a sort of vicegerent over the outskirts and unruly parts of nature, than an opponent to its lawful lord.—What then shall I do with this?" looking at the scroll; "shall I subscribe to the conditions, and enlist under his banner, or shall I not? O love, love! were it not for thee, all the torments that old Mahoun and his followers could inflict should not induce me to quit the plain path of Christianity. But that disdainful, cruel, and lovely Barbara! I must and will have her, though my repentance should be without measure and without end. So then it is settled! Here I will draw blood from my arm—blot out the sign of the cross with it, and form that of the crescent, and these other things, the meaning of which I do not know.—Hilloa! What's that? Two beautiful deers, as I am a sinner, and one of them lame. What a prey for poor ruined Colin! and fairly off the royal bounds, too. Now for it, Bawty, my fine dog! now for a clean chase! A' the links o' the Feathen-wood winna hide them from your infallible nose, billy Bawty. Halloo! off you go, sir! and now for the bow and the broad arrow at the head slap!—What! ye winna hunt a foot-length after them, will ye no? Then, Bawty, there's some mair mischief in the wind for me! I see what your frighted looks tell me. That they dinna leave the scent of other deers on their track, but ane that terrifies you, and makes your blood creep. It is hardly possible, ane wad think, that witches could assume the shapes of these bonny harmless creatures; but their power has come to sic a height hereabouts, that nae man alive can tell what they can do. There's my aunty Nans has already turned me into a goat, then to a gander, and last of a' into a three-legged stool.

"I am a ruined man, Bawty! your master is a ruined man, and a lost man, that's far waur. He has sold himself for love to one beautiful creature, the comeliest of all the human race. And yet that beautiful creature must be a witch, else how could a' the witches o' Traquair gie me possession o' her?

"Let me consider and calculate. Now, suppose they are deceiving me—for that's their character; and suppose they can never put me in possession of her, then I hae brought myself into a fine habble. How terrible a thought this is! Let me see; is all over? Is this scroll signed and sealed; and am I wholly given up to this unknown and untried destiny?" (Opens his scroll with trembling agitation, and looks over it.) "No, thanks to the Lord of the universe, I am yet a Christian. The cross stands uncancelled, and there is neither sign nor superscription in my blood. How did this happen? I had the blood drawn—the pen filled—and the scroll laid out. Let me consider what it was that prevented me? The deers? It was, indeed, the two comely deers. What a strange intervention this is! Ah! these were no witches! but some good angels, or happy fays, or guardian spirits of the wild, sent to snatch an abused youth from destruction. Now, thanks be to Heaven, though poor and reduced to the last extremity, I am yet a free man, and in my Maker's hand. My resolution is changed—my promise is broken, and here I give this mystic scroll to the winds of the glen.

"Alas, alas! to what a state sin has reduced me! Now shall I be tortured by night, and persecuted by day; changed into monstrous shapes, torn by cats, pricked by invisible bodkins, my heart racked by insufferable pangs of love, until I either lose my reason, and yield to the dreadful conditions held out to me, or lose all hope of earthly happiness, and yield up my life. Oh, that I were as free of sin as that day my father gave me his last blessing! then might I withstand all their charms and enchantments. But that I will never be. So as I have brewed so must I drink. These were his last words to me, which I may weel remember:—'You will have many enemies of your soul to contend with, my son; for your nearest relations are in compact with the devil; and as they have hated and persecuted me, so will they hate and persecute you; and it will only be by repeating your prayers evening and morning, and keeping a conscience void of all offence towards God and towards man, that you can hope to escape the snares that will be laid for you. But the good angels from the presence of the Almighty will, perhaps, guard my poor orphan boy, and protect him from the counsels of the wicked.'

"Now, in the first place, I have never prayed at all; and, in the second place, I have sinned so much, that I have long ago subjected myself to their snares, and given myself up for lost. What will become of me? flight is in vain, for they can fly through the air, and follow me to Flanders. And then, Barbara,—O that lovely and bewitching creature! in leaving her I would leave life and saul behind!"

After this long and troubled soliloquy, poor Colin burst into tears, and wished himself a dove, or a sparrow-hawk, or an eagle, to fly away and be seen no more; but, in either case, to have bonny Barbara for his mate. At this instant Bawtie began to cock up his ears, and turn his head first to the one side and then to the other; and, on Colin looking up, he beheld two hares cowering away from a bush behind him. There was nothing that Colin was so fond of as a hunt. He sprung up, pursued the hares, and shouted, Halloo, halloo! to Bawty. No, Bawty would not pursue them a foot, but whenever he came to the place where he had seen them, and put his nose to the ground, ran back, hanging his tail, and uttering short barks, as he was wont to do when attacked by witches in the night. Colin's hair rose up on his head, for he instantly suspected that the two hares were Robin Kirkwood and his aunt Nans, watching his motions, and the fulfilment of his promise to them. Colin was horrified, and knew not what to do. He did not try to pray, for he could not; but he wished, in his heart, that his father's dying-prayer for him had been heard.

He rose, and hastened away in the direction contrary to that the hares had taken, as may well be supposed; and as he jogged along, in melancholy mood, he was aware of two damsels, who approached him slowly and respectfully. They were clothed in white, with garlands on their heads; and, on their near approach, Colin perceived that the one of them was lame, and the other supported her by the hand. The two comely hinds that had come upon him so suddenly and unexpectedly, and had prevented him, at the very decisive moment, from selling his salvation for sensual enjoyment, instantly came over Colin's awakened recollection, and he was struck with indescribable awe. Bawty was affected somewhat in the same manner with his master. He did not manifest the same sort of dismay as when attacked by witches and warlocks, but crept close to the ground, and turning his face half away from the radiant objects, uttered a sort of stifled murmur, as if moved both by respect and fear. Colin perceived, from these infallible symptoms, that the beings with whom he was now coming in contact were not the subjects of the Power of Darkness.

Colin, throwing his plaid over his shoulder in the true shepherd-style, took his staff below his left arm, so that his right hand might be at liberty to lift his bonnet when the fair damsels accosted him, and, not choosing to run straight on them, face to face, he paused at a respectful distance, straight in their path. When they came within a few paces of him, they turned gently from the path, as if to pass him on the left side, but all the while kept their bright eyes fixed on him, and whispered to each other. Colin was grieved that so much comeliness should pass by without saluting him, and kept his regretful eyes steadily on them. At length they paused, and one of them called, in a sweet but solemn voice, "Ah, Colin Hyslop, Colin Hyslop! you are on the braid way for destruction."

"How do ye ken that, madam?" returned Colin. "Do you ca' the road up the Kirk-rigg the braid way to destruction?"

"Ay, up the rigg or down the rigg, cross the rigg or round the rigg, all is the same for you, Colin. You are a lost man; and it is a great pity. One single step farther on the path you are now treading, and all is over."

"What wad ye hae me to do, sweet madam? Wad ye hae me to stand still an' starve here on the crown o' the Kirk-rigg?"

"Better starve in a dungeon than take the steps you are about to take. You were at a witch and warlock meeting yestreen."

"It looks like as gin you had been there too, madam, that you ken sae weel."

"Yes, I *was* there, but under concealment, and not for the purpose

of making any such vows and promises as you made. O wretched
Colin Hyslop, what is to become of you!"

"I did naething, madam, but what I couldna help; and my heart is
sair for it the day."

"Can you lay your hand on that heart and say so?"

"Yes, I can, dear madam, and swear to it too."

"Then follow us down to this little green knowe, and recount to us
the circumstances of your life, and I will inform you of a secret I
heard yestreen."

"Aha, madam, but yon is a fairy ring, and I hae gotten sae mony
cheats wi' changelings, that I hae muckle need to be on my guard.
However, things can hardly be waur wi' me. Lead on, and I shall
e'en follow."

The two female figures walked before him to a fairy knowe, on the
top of the Feathen-hill, and sat down, with their faces towards him,
till he recounted the incidents of his life, which were of a horrible
kind, and not to be set down. The outline was thus:—His father was a
sincere adherent of the Reformers, and a good Christian; but poor
Colin was born at Taniel-Burn, in the midst of Papists and witches;
and the nearest relation he had, a maternal aunt, was the leading
witch of the whole neighbourhood. Consequently, Colin was nur-
tured in sin, and inured to iniquity, until all the kindly and humane
principles of his nature were erased, or so much distorted, as to
appear like their very opposites; and when this was accomplished, his
wicked aunt and her associate hags, judging him fairly gained, without the pale of redemption, began to exercise cantrips, the most
comical, and, at the same time, the most refined in cruelty, at his
expense; and at length, on being assured of every earthly enjoyment,
he engaged to join their hellish community, only craving three days
to study their mysteries, bleed himself, and, with the blood extracted
from his veins, extinguish the sign of the cross, thereby renouncing his
hope in mercy, and likewise make some hieroglyphics of strange
shapes and mysterious efficacy, and finally subscribe his name to the
whole.

When the relation was finished, one of the lovely auditors said,—
"You are a wicked and abandoned person, Colin Hyslop. But you
were reared up in iniquity, and know no better; and the mercy of
Heaven is most readily extended to such. You have, besides, some
good points in your character still; for you have told us the truth,
however much to your own disadvantage."

"Aha, madam! How do you ken sae weel that I hae been telling
you a' the truth?"

"I know all concerning you better than you do yourself. There is little, very little, of a redeeming nature in your own history; but you had an upright and devout father, and the seed of the just may not perish for ever. I have been young, and now am old, yet have I never seen the good man forsaken, nor his children cast out as vagabonds in the land of their fathers."

"Ah, na, na, madam! ye canna be auld. It is impossible! But goodness kens! there are sad changelings now-a-days. I hae seen an auld wrinkled wife blooming o'er night like a cherub."

"Colin, you are a fool! And folly in youth leads to misery in old age. But I am your friend, and you have not another on earth this night but myself and sister here, and one more. Pray, will you keep this little vial, and drink it for my sake?"

"Will it no change me, madam?"

"Yes, it will."

"Then I thank you; but keep it. I have had enow of these kind o' drinks in my life."

"But suppose it change you for the better? Suppose it change you to a new creature?"

"Weel, suppose it should, what will that creature be? Tell me that first. Will it no be a fox, nor a gainder, nor a bearded gait, nor a three-fitted stool?"

"Ah, Colin, Colin!" exclaimed she, smiling through tears, "your own wickedness and unbelief gave the agents of perdition power over you. It is that power which I wish to counteract. But I will tell you nothing more. If you will not take this little vial, and drink it, for my sake; why, then, leave it, and follow on your course."

"O, dear madam! ye ken little thing about me. I was only joking wi' you for the sake o' hearing your sweet answers. For were that bit glass fu' o' rank poison, and were it to turn me intil a taed or a worm, I wad drink it aff at your behest. I hae been sae little accustomed to hear aught serious or friendly, that my very heart clings to you as it wad do to an angel coming down frae heaven to save me. Ay, and ye said something kind and respecfu' about my auld father too. That's what I hae been as little used to. Ah, but he was a douce man! Wasna he, mem? Drink that bit bottle o' liquor for your sake! Od, I wish it were fu' to the brim, and that's no what it is by twa thirds."

"Ay, but it has this property, Colin, that drinking will never exhaust it; and the langer you drink it, the sweeter it will become."

"Say you sae? Then here's till ye. We'll see whether drinking winna exhaust it or no."

Colin set the vial to his lips, with intent of draining it; but the first portion that he swallowed made him change his countenance, and shudder from head to heel.

"Ah! sweeter did you say, madam? by the faith of my heart, it has muckle need; for sickan a potion for bitterness never entered the mouth of mortal man. Oh, I am ruined, poisoned, and undone!"

With that poor Colin drew his plaid over his head, fell flat on his face, and wept bitterly, while his two comely visitants withdrew, smiling at the success of their mission. As they went down by the side of the Feathen-wood, the one said to the other, "Did you not perceive two of that infatuated community haunting this poor hapless youth to destruction? Let us go and hear their schemes, that we may the better counteract them."

They skimmed over the lea fields, and, in a thicket of brambles, briers, and nettles, they found—not two hares, but the identical Rob Kirkwood, the warlock, and auntie Nans, in close and unholy consultation. This bush has often been pointed out to me as the scene of that memorable meeting. It perhaps still remains at the side of a little hollow, nigh to the east corner of the Feathen arable fields, and the spots occupied by the witch and warlock, without a green shrub on them, are still as visible as on the day they left them. The two sisters, having chosen a disguise that completely concealed them, heard the following dialogue, from beginning to end.

"Kimmer, I trow the prize is won. I saw his arm bared; the red blood streaming; the scroll in the one hand, and the pen in the other."

"He's ours! he's ours!"

"He's nae mair yours."

"We'll ower the kirkstyle an' away wi' him."

"I liked not the appearance of yon two pale hinds at such a moment. I wish the fruit of all our pains be not stolen from us when ready for our lord and master's board. How he will storm and misuse us if this has befallen!"

"What of the two hinds? What of them, I say? I like to see blood. It is a beautiful thing blood."

"Thou art as gross as flesh and blood itself, and hast nothing in thee of the true sublimity of a supernatural being. I love to scale the thunder-cloud; to ride on the topmost billow of the storm; to roost by the cataract, or croon the anthem of hell at the gate of heaven. But *thou* delightest to see blood,—rank, reeking, and baleful Christian blood. What is in that, dotard?"

"Humph! I like to see Christian blood, howsomever. It bodes luck, kimmer—it bodes luck."

"It bodes that thou art a mere block, Rob Kirkwood; but it is needless to upbraid thee, senseless as thou art. Listen then to me:—It has been our master's charge to us these seven years to gain that goodly stripling, my nephew; and you know that you and I engaged to accomplish it; if we break that engagement, woe unto us. Our master bore a grudge at his father; but he particularly desires the son, because he knows that, could we gain him, all the pretty girls of the parish would flock to our standard.—But, Robin Kirkwood, I say, Robin Kirkwood, what two white birds are these always hopping around us? I dinna like their looks unco weel. See, the one of them is lame too; and they seem to have a language of their own to one another. Let us leave this place, Robin; my heart is quaking like an aspin."

"Let them hap on. What can wee bits o' birdies do till us? Come, let us try some o' yon cantrips the deil learned us. Grand sport yon, Nans."

"Robin, did not you see that the birds hopped three times round us? I am afraid we are charmed to the spot."

"Never mind, auld fool! It's a very good spot.—Some of our cantrips! some of our cantrips!"

What cantrips they performed is not known; but, on that day fortnight, the two were found still sitting in the middle of the bush, the two most miserable and disgusting figures that ever shocked humanity. Their cronies came with a hurdle to take them home; but Nans expired by the way, uttering wild gibberish and blasphemy, and Rob Kirkwood died soon after he got home. The last words he uttered were, "Plenty o' Christian blood soon! It will be running in streams!—in streams!—in streams!"

We now return to Colin, who, freed of his two greatest adversaries, now spent his time in a state bordering on happiness, compared with the life he had formerly led. He wept much, staid on the hill by himself, and pondered deeply on something nobody knew what, and it was believed he did not know well himself. He was in love—over head and ears in love; which may account for anything in man, however ridiculous. He was in love with Barbara Stewart, an angel in loveliness as well as virtue; but she had hitherto shunned a young man so dissolute and unfortunate in connexions. To this was attributed Colin's melancholy and retirement from society; and it might be partly the case, but there were other matters that troubled his inmost soul.

Ever since he had been visited by the two mysterious dames, he had kept the vial close in his bosom, and had drunk of the bitter potion again and again. He felt a change within him, a certain renovation of his nature, and a new train of thoughts, to which he was an utter stranger; yet he cherished them, tasting oftener and oftener his vial of bitterness, and always, as he drank, the liquor increased in quantity.

While in this half-resigned, half-desponding state, he ventured once more to visit Barbara. He thought to himself that he would go and see her, if but to take farewell of her; for he resolved not to harass so dear a creature with a suit which was displeasing to her. But, to his utter surprise, Barbara received him kindly. His humbled look made a deep impression on her; and, on taking leave, he found that she had treated him with as much respect as any virtuous maiden could treat a favourite lover.

He therefore went home rather too much uplifted in spirit, which his old adversaries, the witches, perceived, and having laid all their snares open to intrap him, they in part prevailed, and he returned, in the moment of temptation, to his old courses. The day after, as he went out to the hill, he whistled and sung,—for he durst not think,— till, behold, at a distance, he saw his two lovely monitors approaching. He was confounded and afraid, for he found his heart was not right for the encounter; so he ran away with all his might, and hid himself in the Feathen-wood.

As soon as he was alone, he took the vial from his bosom, and, wondering, beheld that the bitter liquid was dried up all to a few drops, although the glass was nearly full when he last deposited it in his bosom. He set it eagerly to his lips, lest the last remnant should have escaped him; but never was it so bitter as now; his very heart and spirit failed him, and, trembling, he lay down and wept. He tried again to drain out the dregs of his cup of bitterness; but still, as he drank, it increased in quantity, and became more and more palatable; and he now continued the task so eagerly, that in a few days it was nearly full.

The two lovely strangers coming now often in his mind, he regretted running from them, and wearied once more to see them. So, going out, he sat down within the fairy ring, on the top of the Feathen Hill, with a sort of presentiment that they would appear to him. Accordingly, it was not long till they made their appearance, but still at a distance, as if travelling along the kirk-road. Colin, perceiving that they were going to pass, without looking his way, thought it his duty now to wait on them. He hasted across the moor, and met them; nor did they now shun him. The one that halted now addressed him, while she who had formerly accosted him, and presented him with the vial, looked shy, and kept a marked distance, which Colin was exceedingly sorry for, as he loved her best. The other examined him sharply concerning all his transactions since they last met. He acknowledged everything candidly—the great folly of which he had been guilty, and likewise the great terror he was in of being changed into some horrible bestial creature, by the bitter drug they had given him. "For d'ye ken, madam," said he, "I fand the change beginning within, at the very core o' the heart, and spreading aye outward and outward, and I lookit aye every minute when my hands and my feet wad change into clutes; for I expeckit nae less than to have another turn o' the gait, or some waur thing, kenning how weel I deserved it. And when I saw that I keepit my right proportions, I grat for my ain wickedness, that had before subjected me to such unhallowed influence."

The two sisters now looked to each other, and a heavenly benevolence shone through the smiles with which that look was accompanied. The lame one said, "Did I not say, sister, that there was some hope?" She then asked a sight of his vial, which he took from his bosom, and put into her hands; and when she had viewed it carefully, she returned it, without any injunction; but taking from her own bosom a medal of pure gold, which seemed to have been dipped in blood, she fastened it round his neck with a chain of steel. "As long as you keep that vial and use it," said she, "the other will never be taken from you, and with these two you may defy all the Powers of Darkness."

As soon as Colin was alone, he surveyed his purple medal with great earnestness, but could make nothing of it; there was a mystery in the character and figures of which he had no comprehension; yet he kept all in close concealment, and walked softly.

The witches now found that he was lost to their community, and, enraged beyond measure at the loss of such a prize, which they had judged fairly their own, and of which their master was so desirous, they now laid a plan to destroy him.

He went down to the castle one night to see Barbara Stewart, who talked to him much of religion and of the Bible; but of these things Colin knew very little. He engaged, however, to go with her to the house of prayer—not to the Popish chapel, where he had once been a most irreverent auditor, but to the Reformed church, which then began to divide the parish, and the pastor of which was a devout man.

On taking leave of Barbara, and promising to attend her on the following Sabbath, a burst of eldrich laughter arose close by, and a voice, with a hoarse and giggling sound, exclaimed, "No sae fast, canny lad—no sae fast. There will maybe be a whipping o' cripples afore that play be played."

Barbara consigned them both to the care of the Almighty with great fervency, wondering how they could have been watched and overheard in such a place. Colin trembled from head to foot, for he knew the laugh too well to be that of Maude Stott, the leading witch of the Traquair gang, now that his aunt was removed. He had no sooner crossed the Quair, than, at the junction of a little streamlet, called to this day *the Satyr Sike*, he was set upon by a countless number of cats, which surrounded him, making the most infernal noises, and putting themselves into the most threatening attitudes. For a good while they did not touch him, but leaped around him, often as high as his throat, screaming most furiously; but at length his faith failed him, and he cried out in utter despair. At that moment, they all closed upon him, some round his neck, some round his legs, and some endeavouring to tear out his heart and bowels. At length one or two that came in contact with the medal in his bosom fled away, howling most fearfully, and did not return. Still he was in great jeopardy of being instantly torn to pieces; on which he flung himself flat on his face in the midst of his devouring enemies, and invoked a sacred name. That moment he felt partial relief, as if some one were driving them off one by one, and on raising his head, he beheld his lovely lame visitant of the mountains, driving these infernals off with a white wand, and mocking their threatening looks and vain attempts to return. "Off with you, poor infatuated wretches!" cried she: "Minions of perdition, off to your abodes of misery and despair! Where now is your boasted whipping of cripples? See if one poor cripple cannot whip you all."

By this time the monsters had all taken their flight, save one, that had fastened its talons in Colin's left side, and was making a last and desperate effort to reach his vitals; but he, being now freed from the rest, lent it a blow with such good-will, as made it speedily desist, and fly tumbling and mewing down the brae. He shrewdly guessed who this inveterate assailant was. Nor was he mistaken; for next day Maude Stott was lying powerless on account of a broken back, and several of her cronies were in great torment, having been struck by the white rod of the Lady of the Moor.

But the great Master Fiend, seeing now that his emissaries were all baffled and outdone, was enraged beyond bounds, and set himself, with all his wit, and with all his power, to be revenged on poor Colin. As to his power, no one disputed it; but his wit and ingenuity appear always to me to be very equivocal. He tried to assault Colin's humble dwelling that same night, in sundry terrific shapes; but many of the villagers perceived a slender form, clothed in white, that kept watch at his door until the morning twilight. The next day, he haunted him on the hill in the form of a great shaggy bloodhound, infected with madness; but finding his utter inability to touch him, he uttered a howl that made all the hills quake, and, like a flash of lightning, darted into Glendean's Banks.

He now set himself, with his noted sapience, to procure Colin's punishment by other means, namely, by the hands of Christian men, the only way now left for him. He accordingly engaged his emissaries to inform against him to holy Mother Church, as a warlock and necromancer. The crown and the church had at that time joined in appointing judges of these difficult and interesting questions. The quorum consisted of seven, including the King's Advocate, being an equal number of priests and laymen, all of them in opposition to the principles of the Reformation, it being at that time obnoxious at court. Colin was seized, arraigned, and lodged in prison at Peebles; and never was there such a stir of clamour and discontent in Strathquair. The young women wept, and tore their hair, for the goodliest lad in the valley; their mothers scolded; and the old men scratched their grey polls, bit the lip, and remained quiescent, but were at length compelled to join the combination.

Colin's trial came on, and his accusers being summoned as witnesses against him, it may well be supposed how little chance he had of escaping, especially as the noted David Beaton sat that day as judge, a severe and bigoted Papist. There were many things proven against poor Colin,—as much as would have brought all the youth of Traquair to the stake; but the stories of the deponents were so monstrous, and so far out of the course of nature, that the judges were like to fall from their seats with laughing.

For instance, three sportsmen swore, that they had started a large he-fox in the Feathen-wood, and, after pursuing him all the way to Glenrath-hope, with horses and hounds, on coming up they found Colin Hyslop lying panting in the midst of the hounds, and caressing and endeavouring to pacify them. It was deponed, that he had been discovered in the shape of a huge gander sitting on eggs; in the shape of a three-legged stool, which had groaned, and given other symptoms of animation, by which its identity with Colin Hyslop was discovered, on being tossed about and overturned, as three-legged stools are apt to be.

But when they came to the story of a he-goat, which had

proceeded to attend the service in the chapel of St John the Evangelist, and which said he-goat proved to be the unhappy delinquent, Beaton growled with rage and indignation, and said, that such a dog deserved to suffer death by a thousand tortures, and to be excluded from the power of repentance by the instant infliction of them. The most of the judges were not, however, satisfied of the authenticity of this monstrous story, and insisted on examining a great number of witnesses, both young and old, many of whom happened to be quite unconnected with the horrid community of the Traquair witches. Among the rest, a girl named Tibby Frater was examined about that, as well as the three-legged stool, and her examination may here be copied verbatim. The querist, who was a cunning man, began as follows:—

"Were you in St John's Chapel, Isabel, on the Sunday after Easter?"

"Yes."

"And did you there see a man metamorphosed into a he-goat?"

"I saw a gait in the chapel that day."

"And did he, as has been declared, seem intent on disturbing divine worship?"

"He was playing some pranks. But what else could you expect of a gait?"

"Please to describe what you saw."

"Oo, he was just rampauging about, an' dinging folk ower. The clerk and the sacristan baith ran to attack him, but he soon laid them baith prostrate. Mess John prayed against him, in Latin, they said, and tried to lay him, as if he had been a deil; but he never heedit that, and just rampit on."

"Did he ever come near or molest you in the chapel?"

"Ay, he did that."

"What did he do to you?—describe it all."

"Oo, he didna do that muckle ill, after a'; but if it was the poor young man that was changed, I'll warrant he had nae hand in it, for dearly he paid the kane. Ere long there were fifty staves raised against him, and he was beaten till there was hardly life left in him."

"And what were the people's reasons for believing that this he-goat and the prisoner were the same?"

"He was found a' wounded and bruised the next day. But, in truth, I believe he never denied these changes wrought on him to his intimate friends; but we a' ken weel wha it was that effected them. Od help you! ye little ken how we are plaguit and harassed down yonder-abouts, and what loss the country suffers by the emissaries o'

Satan! If there be any amang you that ken the true marks o' the beast, you will discern plenty o' them here, about some that hae been witnessing against this poor abused and unfortunate young man."

The members of the community of Satan were now greatly astounded. Their eyes gleamed with vengeance, and they gnashed their teeth on the maiden. But the buzz ran through the assembly against them, and execrations were poured from every corner of the crowded court. Cries of—"Plenty o' proof o' what Tibby has said." —"Let the saddle be laid on the right horse."—"Down wi' the plagues o' the land," and many such exclamations were sent forth from the mouths of the good people of Traquair. They durst not meddle with the witches at home, because, when anything was done to disoblige them, the sheep and cattle were seized with new and frightful distempers, the corn and barley were shaken, and the honest people themselves quaked under agues, sweatings, and great horrors of mind. But now that they had them all collected in a court of justice, and were all assembled themselves, and holy men present, they hoped to bring the aggressors to due punishment at last. Beaton, however, seemed absolutely bent on the destruction of Colin, alleging, that the depravity of his heart was manifest in every one of his actions during the times of his metamorphoses, even although he had no share himself in effecting these metamorphoses; he therefore sought a verdict against the prisoner, as did also the King's Advocate. Sir James Stuart of Traquair, however, rose up, and spoke with great eloquence and energy in favour of his vassal, and insisted on having his accusers tried face to face with him, when, he had no doubt, it would be seen on which side the sorcery had been exercised. "For I appeal to your honourable judgments," continued he, "if any man would transform himself into a fox, for the sake of being hunted to death, and torn into pieces by hounds? Neither, I think, would any person choose to translate himself into a gander, for the purpose of bringing out a few worthless goslings. But, above all, I am morally certain, that no living woman or man would turn himself into a three-legged stool, for no other purpose but to be kicked into the mire, as the evidence shows this stool to have been. And as for a very handsome youth turning himself into a he-goat, in order to exhibit his prowess in outbraving and beating the men of the whole congregation, that would be a supposition equally absurd. But as we have a thousand instances of honest men being affected and injured by spells and enchantments, I give it as my firm opinion, that this young man has been abused grievously in this manner, and that these his accusers, afraid of exposure through his agency, are trying in this way to put him down."

Sir James's speech was received with murmurs of applause through the whole crowded court: but the principal judge continued obstinate, and made a speech in reply. Being a man of a most austere temperament, and as bloody-minded as obstinate, he made no objections to the seizing of the youth's accusers, and called to the officers to guard the door; on which the old sacristan of Traquair remarked aloud, "By my faith in the holy Apostle John, my lord governor, you must be quick in your seizures; for an ye gie but the witches o' Traquair ten minutes, ye will hae naething o' them but moorfowls an' patricks blattering about the rigging o' the kirk; and a' the offishers ye hae will neither catch nor keep them."

They were, however, seized and incarcerated. The trials lasted for three days, at which the most amazing crowds attended; for the evidence was of the most extraordinary nature ever elicited, displaying such a system of diablerie, malevolence, and unheard-of wickedness, as never came to light in a Christian land. Seven women and two men were found guilty, and condemned to be burnt at the stake; and several more would have shared the same fate, had the private marks, which were then thoroughly and perfectly known, coincided with the evidence produced. This not having been the case, they were banished out of the Scottish dominions, any man being at liberty to shoot them, if found there under any shape whatever, after sixty-one hours from that date.

There being wise men who attended the courts in those days, called Searchers or Triers, they were ordered to take Colin into the vestry, (the trials having taken place in a church,) and examine him strictly for the diabolical marks. They could find none; but in the course of their investigation they found the vial in his bosom, as well as the medal that wore the hue of blood, and which was locked to his neck, so that the hands of man could not remove it. They returned to the judge, bearing the vial in triumph, and saying they had found no private mark, as proof of the master he served, but that here was an unguent, which they had no doubt was proof sufficient, and would, if they judged aright, when accompanied by proper incantations, transform a human being into any beast or monster intended. It was handed to the judge, who shook his head, and acquiesced with the searchers. It was then handed around, and Mr Wiseheart, or Wishart, a learned man, deciphered these words on it, in a sacred language,—"The Vial of Repentance."

The judges looked at one another when they heard these ominous words so unlooked for; and Wiseheart remarked, with a solemn

assurance, that neither the term nor the cup of bitterness were calculated for the slaves of Satan, nor the bounden drudges of the land
of perdition.

The searchers now begged the Court to suspend their judgment
for a space, as the prisoner wore a charm of a bloody hue, which was
locked to his body with steel, so that no hands could loose it, and
which they judged of far more ominous import than all the proofs of
these whole trials put together. Colin was then brought into the
Court once more, and the medal examined carefully; and lo! on the
one side were engraved, in the same character, two words, the sig-
nification of which was decided to be, "Forgiveness" above, and
"Acceptance" below. On the other side was a representation of the
Crucifixion, and these words in another language, *Cruci, dum spiro,
fido*; which words I do not understand, but they struck the judges
with great amazement. They forthwith ordered the bonds to be taken
off the prisoner, and commanded him to speak for himself, and tell,
without fear and dread, how he came by these precious and holy
bequests.

Colin, who was noted for sincerity and simplicity, began and
related the circumstances of his life, his temptations, his follies, and
his disregard of all the duties of religion, which had subjected him in
no common degree to the charms and enchantments of his hellish
neighbours, whose principal efforts and energies seemed to be aimed
at his destruction. But when he came to the vision of the fair virgins
on the hill, and of their gracious bequests, that had preserved him
thenceforward, both from the devil in person, and from the vengeance of all his emissaries combined, so well did this suit the strenuous efforts then making to obtain popularity for a falling system of
faith, that the judges instantly claimed the miracle to their own side,
and were clamorous with approbation of his modesty, and cravings
of forgiveness for the insults and contumely which they had heaped
upon this favourite of Heaven. Barbara Stewart was at this time
sitting on the bench close behind Colin, weeping for joy at this
favourable turn of affairs, having, for several days previous to that,
given up all hopes of his life, when Mr David Beaton, pointing to the
image of the Holy Virgin, asked if the fair dame who bestowed these
invaluable and heavenly relics bore any resemblance to that divine
figure. Colin, with his accustomed blunt honesty, was just about to
answer in the negative, when Barbara exclaimed in a whisper behind
him, "Ah! how like!"

"How do you ken, dearest Barbara?" said he, softly, over his
shoulder.

"Because I saw her watching your door once when surrounded by fiends—Ah! how like!"

"Ah, how like!" exclaimed Colin, by way of response to one whose opinion was to him as a thing sacred, and not to be disputed. How much hung on that moment! A denial would still have subjected him to obloquy, bonds, and death, but an anxious maiden's ready expedient saved him; and now it was with difficulty that Mr Wiseheart could prevent the Catholic part of the throng from falling down and worshipping him, whom they had so lately reviled and accused of the blackest crimes.

Times were now altered with Colin Hyslop. David Beaton, the governor of the land, appointed by the court of France, took him to Edinburgh in his chariot, and presented him to the Queen Regent, who put a ring on his right hand, a chain of gold about his neck, and loaded him with her bounty. All the Catholic nobles of the court presented him with valuable gifts, and then he was caused to make the tour of all the rich abbeys of Fife and the Border; so that, without ever having one more question asked him about his tenets, he returned home the richest man of all Traquair, even richer, as men supposed, than Sir James Stuart himself. He married Barbara Stewart, and purchased the Plora from the female heirs of Alexander Murray, where he built a mansion, planted a vineyard, and lived in retirement and happiness till the day of his death.

I have thus recorded the leading events of this tale, although many of the incidents, as handed down by tradition, are of so heinous a nature as not to bear recital. It has always appeared to me to have been moulded on the bones of some ancient religious allegory, and by being thus transformed into a nursery tale, rendered unintelligible. It would be in vain now to endeavour to restore its original structure, in the same way as Mr Blore can delineate an ancient abbey from the smallest remnant, but I should like exceedingly to understand properly what was represented by the two lovely and mysterious sisters, one of whom was lame. It is most probable that they were supposed apparitions of renowned female saints; or perhaps Faith and Charity. This, however, is manifest, that it is a Reformer's tale, founded on a Catholic allegory. Of the witches of Traquair there are many traditions extant, as well as many authentic records, and so far the tale accords with the history of the times. That they were tried and suffered there is no doubt; and the Devil lost all his popularity in that district ever after, being despised by his friends for his shallow and rash politics, and hooted and held up to ridicule by his enemies. I still maintain, that there has been no great personage since the world was framed, so apt to commit a manifest blunder, and to overshoot his mark, as he is.

Mount Benger, March 10, 1828.

The Brownie of the Black Haggs

WHEN the Sprots were lairds of Wheelhope, which is now a long time ago, there was one of the ladies who was very badly spoken of in the country. People did not just openly assert that Lady Wheelhope was a witch, but every one had an aversion even at hearing her named; and when by chance she happened to be mentioned, old men would shake their heads and say, "Ah! let us alane o' her! The less ye meddle wi' her the better." Auld wives would give over spinning, and, as a pretence for hearing what might be said about her, poke in the fire with the tongs, cocking up their ears all the while; and then, after some meaning coughs, hems, and haws, would haply say, "Hech-wow, sirs! An a' be true that's said!" or something equally wise and decisive as that.

In short, Lady Wheelhope was accounted a very bad woman. She was an inexorable tyrant in her family, quarrelled with her servants, often cursing them, striking them, and turning them away; especially if they were religious, for these she could not endure, but suspected them of every thing bad. Whenever she found out any of the servant men of the laird's establishment for religious characters, she soon gave them up to the military, and got them shot; and several girls that were regular in their devotions, she was supposed to have popped off with poison. She was certainly a wicked woman, else many good people were mistaken in her character, and the poor persecuted Covenanters were obliged to unite in their prayers against her.

As for the laird, he was a stump. A big, dun-faced, pluffy body, that cared neither for good nor evil, and did not well know the one from the other. He laughed at his lady's tantrums and barley-hoods; and the greater the rage that she got into, the laird thought it the better sport. One day, when two servant maids came running to him, in great agitation, and told him that his lady had felled one of their companions, the laird laughed heartily at them, and said he did not doubt it.

"Why, sir, how can you laugh?" said they. "The poor girl is killed."

"Very likely, very likely," said the laird. "Well, it will teach her to take care who she angers again."

"And, sir, your lady will be hanged."

"Very likely; well, it will learn her how to strike so rashly again—Ha, ha, ha! Will it not, Jessy?"

But when this same Jessy died suddenly one morning, the laird was greatly confounded, and seemed dimly to comprehend that there had been unfair play going. There was little doubt that she was taken off by poison; but whether the lady did it through jealousy or not, was never divulged; but it greatly bamboozled and astonished the poor laird, for his nerves failed him, and his whole frame became paralytic. He seems to have been exactly in the same state of mind with a colley that I once had. He was extremely fond of the gun as long as I did not kill any thing with her, (there being no game laws in Ettrick Forest in those days,) and he got a grand chase after the hares when I missed them. But there was one day that I chanced for a marvel to shoot one dead, a few paces before his nose. I'll never forget the astonishment that the poor beast manifested. He stared one while at the gun, and another while at the dead hare, and seemed to be drawing the conclusion, that if the case stood thus, there was no creature sure of its life. Finally, he took his tail between his legs, and ran away home, and never would face a gun all his life again.

So was it precisely with Laird Sprot of Wheelhope. As long as his lady's wrath produced only noise and splutter among the servants, he thought it fine sport; but when he saw what he believed the dreadful effects of it, he became like a barrel organ out of tune, and could only discourse one note, which he did to every one he met. "I wish she maunna hae gotten something she has been the waur of." This note he repeated early and late, night and day, sleeping and waking, alone and in company, from the moment that Jessy died till she was buried; and on going to the churchyard as chief mourner, he whispered it to her relations by the way. When they came to the grave, he took his stand at the head, nor would he give place to the girl's father; but there he stood, like a huge post, as though he neither saw nor heard; and when he had lowered her late comely head into the grave, and dropped the cord, he slowly lifted his hat with one hand, wiped his dim eyes with the back of the other, and said, in a deep tremulous tone, "Poor lassie! I wish she didna get something she had been the waur of."

This death made a great noise among the common people; but there was no protection for the life of the subject in those days; and provided a man or woman was a true loyal subject, and a real Anti-Covenanter, any of them might kill as many as they liked. So there was no one to take cognizance of the circumstances relating to the death of poor Jessy.

After this, the lady walked softly for the space of two or three years. She saw that she had rendered herself odious, and had entirely lost her husband's countenance, which she liked worst of all. But the evil propensity could not be overcome; and a poor boy, whom the laird, out of sheer compassion, had taken into his service, being found dead one morning, the country people could no longer be restrained; so they went in a body to the Sheriff, and insisted on an investigation. It was proved that she detested the boy, had often threatened him, and had given him brose and butter the afternoon before he died; but the cause was ultimately dismissed, and the pursuers fined.

No one can tell to what height of wickedness she might now have proceeded, had not a check of a very singular kind been laid upon her. Among the servants that came home at the next term, was one who called himself Merodach; and a strange person he was. He had the form of a boy, but the features of one a hundred years old, save that his eyes had a brilliancy and restlessness, which was very extra-ordinary, bearing a strong resemblance to the eyes of a well-known species of monkey. He was froward and perverse in all his actions, and disregarded the pleasure or displeasure of any person; but he performed his work well, and with apparent ease. From the moment that he entered the house, the lady conceived a mortal antipathy against him, and besought the laird to turn him away. But the laird, of himself, never turned away any body, and moreover he had hired him for a trivial wage, and the fellow neither wanted activity nor perseverance. The natural consequence of this arrangement was, that the lady instantly set herself to make Merodach's life as bitter as it was possible, in order to get early quit of a domestic every way so disgusting. Her hatred of him was not like a common antipathy entertained by one human being against another,—she hated him as one might hate a toad or an adder; and his occupation of jotteryman (as the laird termed his servant of all work) keeping him always about her hand, it must have proved highly disagreeable.

She scolded him, she raged at him, but he only mocked her wrath, and giggled and laughed at her, with the most provoking derision. She tried to fell him again and again, but never, with all her address, could she hit him; and never did she make a blow at him, that she did not repent it. She was heavy and unwieldy, and he as quick in his motions as a monkey; besides, he generally had her in such an ungovernable rage, that when she flew at him, she hardly knew what she was doing. At one time she guided her blow towards him, and he at the same instant avoided it with such dexterity, that she knocked down the chief hind, or foresman; and then Merodach giggled so heartily, that, lifting the kitchen poker, she threw it at him with a full design of knocking out his brains; but the missile only broke every plate and ashet on the kitchen dresser.

She then hasted to the laird, crying bitterly, and telling him she would not suffer that wretch Merodach, as she called him, to stay another night in the family. "Why, then, put him away, and trouble me no more about him," said the laird.

"Put him away!" exclaimed she; "I have already ordered him away a hundred times, and charged him never to let me see his horrible face again; but he only flouts me, and tells me he'll see me at the devil first."

The pertinacity of the fellow amused the laird exceedingly; his dim eyes turned upwards into his head with delight; he then looked two ways at once, turned round his back, and laughed till the tears ran down his dun cheeks, but he could only articulate "You're fitted now."

The lady's agony of rage still increasing from this derision, she flew on the laird, and said he was not worthy the name of a man, if he did not turn away that pestilence, after the way he had abused her.

"Why, Shusy, my dear, what has he done to you?"

"What done to me! has he not caused me to knock down John Thomson, and I do not know if ever he will come to life again?"

"Have you felled your favourite John Thomson?" said the laird, laughing more heartily than before; "you might have done a worse deed than that. But what evil has John done?"

"And has he not broke every plate and dish on the whole dresser?" continued the lady, disregarding the laird's question; "and for all this devastation, he only mocks at my displeasure,—absolutely mocks me,—and if you do not have him turned away, and hanged or shot for his deeds, you are not worthy the name of man."

"O alack! What a devastation among the china metal!" said the laird; and calling on Merodach, he said, "Tell me, thou evil Merodach of Babylon, how thou dared'st knock down thy lady's favourite servant, John Thomson?"

"Not I, your honour. It was my lady herself, who got into such a furious rage at me, that she mistook her man, and felled Mr Thomson; and the good man's skull is fractured."

"That was very odd," said the laird, chuckling; "I do not comprehend it. But then, what the devil set you on smashing all my lady's delft and china ware?—That was a most infamous and provoking action."

"It was she herself, your honour. Sorry would I have been to have broken one dish belonging to the house. I take all the house-servants to witness, that my lady smashed all the dishes with a poker, and now lays the blame on me."

The laird turned his dim and delighted eyes on his lady, who was crying with vexation and rage, and seemed meditating another personal attack on the culprit, which he did not at all appear to shun, but rather encourage. She, however, vented her wrath in threatenings of the most deep and desperate revenge, the creature all the while assuring her that she would be foiled, and that in all her encounters and contests with him, she would uniformly come to the worst. He was resolved to do his duty, and there before his master he defied her.

The laird thought more than he considered it prudent to reveal; but he had little doubt that his wife would wreak that vengeance on his jotteryman which she avowed, and as little of her capability. He almost shuddered when he recollected one who had taken *something that she had been the waur of.*

In a word, the Lady of Wheelhope's inveterate malignity against this one object, was like the rod of Moses, that swallowed up the rest of the serpents. All her wicked and evil propensities seemed to be superseded by it, if not utterly absorbed in its virtues. The rest of the family now lived in comparative peace and quietness; for early and late her malevolence was venting itself against the jotteryman, and him alone. It was a delirium of hatred and vengeance, on which the whole bent and bias of her inclination was set. She could not stay from the creature's presence, for in the intervals when absent from him, she spent her breath in curses and execrations, and then not able to rest, she ran again to seek him, her eyes gleaming with the anticipated delights of vengeance, while, ever and anon, all the scaith, the ridicule, and the harm, redounded on herself.

Was it not strange that she could not get quit of this sole annoyance of her life? One would have thought she easily might. But by this time there was nothing farther from her intention; she wanted vengeance, full, adequate, and delicious vengeance, on her audacious opponent. But he was a strange and terrible creature, and the means of retaliation came always, as it were, to his hand.

Bread and sweet milk was the only fare that Merodach cared for, and he having bargained for that, would not want it, though he often got it with a curse and with ill will. The lady having intentionally kept back his wonted allowance for some days, on the Sabbath morning following, she set him down a bowl of rich sweet milk, well drugged with a deadly poison, and then she lingered in a little anteroom to watch the success of her grand plot, and prevent any other creature from tasting of the potion. Merodach came in, and the house-maid says to him, "There is your breakfast, creature."

"Oho! my lady has been liberal this morning," said he; "but I am beforehand with her.—Here, little Missie, you seem very hungry to-day—take you my breakfast." And with that he set the beverage down to the lady's little favourite spaniel. It so happened that the lady's only son came at that instant into the anteroom, seeking her, and teazing his mamma about something which took her attention from the hall-table for a space. When she looked again, and saw Missie lapping up the sweet milk, she burst from her lobby like a dragon, screaming as if her head had been on fire, kicked the bowl and the remainder of its contents against the wall, and lifting Missie in her bosom, she retreated hastily, crying all the way.

"Ha, ha, ha—I have you now!" cried Merodach, as she vanished from the hall.

Poor Missie died immediately, and very privately; indeed, she would have died and been buried, and never one have seen her, save her mistress, had not Merodach, by a luck that never failed him, popped his nose over the flower garden wall, just as his lady was laying her favourite in a grave of her own digging. She, not perceiving her tormentor, plied on at her task, apostrophizing the insensate little carcass,—"Ah! poor dear little creature, thou hast had a hard fortune, and hast drank of the bitter potion that was not intended for thee; but he shall drink it three times double, for thy sake!"

"Is that little Missie?" said the eldrich voice of the jotteryman, close at the lady's ear. She uttered a loud scream, and sunk down on the bank. "Alack for poor little Missie!" continued the creature in a tone of mockery, "My heart is sorry for Missie. What has befallen her—whose breakfast cup did she drink?"

"Hence with thee, thou fiend!" cried the lady; "what right hast thou to intrude on thy mistress's privacy? Thy turn is coming yet, or may the nature of woman change within me."

"It is changed already," said the creature, grinning with delight; "I have thee now, I have thee now! And were it not to shew my superiority over thee, which I do every hour, I should soon see thee strapped like a mad cat, or a worrying bratch. What wilt thou try next?"

"I will cut thy throat, and if I die for it, will rejoice in the deed; a deed of charity to all that dwell on the face of the earth. Go about thy business."

"I have warned thee before, dame, and I now warn thee again, that all thy mischief meditated against me will fall double on thine own head."

"I want none of your warning, and none of your instructions, fiendish cur. Hence with your elvish face, and take care of yourself."

It would be too disgusting and horrible to relate or read all the incidents that fell out between this unaccountable couple. Their enmity against each other had no end, and no mitigation; and scarcely a single day passed over on which her acts of malevolent ingenuity did not terminate fatally for some favourite thing of the lady's, while all these doings never failed to appear as her own act. Scarcely was there a thing, animate or inanimate, on which she set a value, left to her, that was not destroyed; and yet scarcely one hour or minute could she remain absent from her tormentor, and all the while, it seems, solely for the purpose of tormenting him.

But while all the rest of the establishment enjoyed peace and quietness from the fury of their termagant dame, matters still grew worse and worse between the fascinated pair. The lady haunted the menial, in the same manner as the raven haunts the eagle, for a perpetual quarrel, though the former knows that in every encounter she is to come off the loser. But now noises were heard on the stairs by night, and it was whispered among the menials, that the lady had been seeking Merodach's bed by night, on some horrible intent. Several of them would have sworn that they had seen her passing and repassing on the stair after midnight, when all was quiet; but then it was likewise well known, that Merodach slept with well fastened doors, and a companion in another bed in the same room, whose bed, too, was nearest the door. Nobody cared much what became of the jotteryman, for he was an unsocial and disagreeable person; but some one told him what they had seen, and hinted a suspicion of the lady's intent. But the creature only bit his upper lip, winked with his eyes, and said, "She had better let alone; she will be the first to rue that."

Not long after this, to the horror of the family and the whole country side, the laird's only son was found murdered in his bed one morning, under circumstances that manifested the most fiendish cruelty and inveteracy on the part of his destroyer. As soon as the atrocious act was divulged, the lady fell into convulsions, and lost her reason; and happy had it been for her had she never recovered either the use of reason, or her corporeal functions any more, for there was blood upon her hand, which she took no care to conceal, and there was too little doubt that it was the blood of her own innocent and beloved boy, the sole heir and hope of the family.

This blow deprived the laird of all power of action; but the lady had a brother, a man of the law, who came and instantly proceeded to an investigation of this unaccountable murder; but before the Sheriff arrived, the housekeeper took the lady's brother aside, and told him he had better not go on with the scrutiny, for she was sure the crime would be brought home to her unfortunate mistress; and after examining into several corroborative circumstances, and viewing the state of the raving maniac, with the blood on her hand and arm, he made the investigation a very short one, declaring the domestics all exculpated.

The laird attended his boy's funeral, and laid his head in the grave, but appeared exactly like a man walking in a trance, an automaton, without feelings or sensations, oftentimes gazing at the funeral procession, as on something he could not comprehend. And when the death-bell of the parish church fell a-tolling, as the corpse approached the kirk-stile, he cast a dim eye up towards the belfry, and said hastily, "What, what's that? Och ay, we're just in time, just in time." And often was he hammering over the name of "Evil Merodach, King of Babylon," to himself. He seemed to have some far-fetched conception that his unaccountable jotteryman had a hand in the death of his only son, and other lesser calamities, although the evidence in favour of Merodach's innocence was as usual quite decisive.

This grievous mistake of Lady Wheelhope (for every landward laird's wife was then styled Lady) can only be accounted for, by supposing her in a state of derangement, or rather under some evil influence, over which she had no control; and to a person in such a state, the mistake was not so very unnatural. The mansion-house of Wheelhope was old and irregular. The stair had four acute turns, all the same, and four landing-places, all the same. In the uppermost chamber slept the two domestics,—Merodach in the bed farthest in, and in the chamber immediately below that, which was exactly similar, slept the young laird and his tutor, the former in the bed farthest in; and thus, in the turmoil of raging passions, her own hand made herself childless.

Merodach was expelled the family forthwith, but refused to accept of his wages, which the man of law pressed upon him, for fear of farther mischief; but he went away in apparent sullenness and dis-content, no one knowing whither.

When his dismissal was announced to the lady, who was watched day and night in her chamber, the news had such an effect on her, that her whole frame seemed electrified; the horrors of remorse vanished, and another passion, which I neither can comprehend nor define, took the sole possession of her distempered spirit. "He *must* not go!—He *shall* not go!" she exclaimed. "No, no, no—he shall not—he shall not—he shall not!" and then she instantly set herself about making ready to follow him, uttering all the while the most diabolical expressions, indicative of anticipated vengeance.—"Oh, could I but snap his nerves one by one, and birl among his vitals! Could I but slice his heart off piecemeal in small messes, and see his blood lopper and bubble, and spin away in purple slays; and then to see him grin, and grin, and grin, and grin! Oh—oh—oh—How beautiful and grand a sight it would be to see him grin, and grin, and grin!" And in such a style would she run on for hours together.

She thought of nothing, she spake of nothing, but the discarded jotteryman, whom most people now began to regard as a creature that was not canny. They had seen him eat, and drink, and work like other people; still he had that about him that was not like other men. He was a boy in form, and an antediluvian in feature. Some thought he was a mule, between a Jew and an ape; some a wizard, some a kelpie, or a fairy, but most of all, that he was really and truly a Brownie. What he was I do not know, and therefore will not pretend to say; but be that as it may, in spite of locks and keys, watching and waking, the Lady of Wheelhope soon made her escape and eloped after him. The attendants, indeed, would have made oath that she was carried away by some invisible hand, for that it was impossible she could have escaped on foot like other people; and this edition of the story took in the country; but sensible people viewed the matter in another light.

As for instance, when Wattie Blythe, the laird's old shepherd, came in from the hill one morning, his wife Bessie thus accosted him.—"His presence be about us, Wattie Blythe! have ye heard what has happened at the ha'? Things are aye turning waur and waur there, and it looks like as if Providence had gi'en up our laird's house to destruction. This grand estate maun now gang frae the Sprots, for it has finished them."

"Na, na, Bessie, it isna the estate that has finished the Sprots, but the Sprots that hae finished it, an' themsells into the boot. They hae been a wicked and degenerate race, an' aye the langer the waur, till they hae reached the utmost bounds o' earthly wickedness; an' it's time the deil were looking after his ain."

"Ah, Wattie Blythe, ye never said a truer say. An' that's just the very point where your story ends, and mine commences; for hasna the deil, or the fairies, or the brownies, ta'en away our lady bodily, an' the haill country is running and riding in search o' her; and there is twenty hunder merks offered to the first that can find her, an' bring her safe back. They hae ta'en her away, skin an' bane, body an' soul, an' a', Wattie!"

"Hech-wow! but that is awsome! And where is it thought they have ta'en her to, Bessie?"

"O, they hae some guess at that frae her ain hints afore. It is thought they hae carried her after that Satan of a creature, wha wrought sae muckle wae about the house. It is for him they are a' looking, for they ken weel, that where they get the tane they will get the tither."

"Whew! Is that the gate o't, Bessie? Why, then, the awfu' story is nouther mair nor less than this, that the leddy has made a lopment, as they ca't, and run away after a blackgaird jotteryman. Hech-wow! wac's me for human frailty! But that's just the gate! When aince the deil gets in the point o' his finger, he will soon have in his haill hand. Ay, he wants but a hair to make a tether of, ony day. I hae seen her a braw sonsy lass, but even then I feared she was devoted to destruction, for she aye mockit at religion, Bessie, an' that's no a good mark of a young body. An' she made a' its servants her enemies; an' think you these good men's prayers were a' to blaw away i' the wind, and be nae mair regarded? Na, na, Bessie, my woman, take ye this mark baith o' our ain bairns and ither folk's—If ever ye see a young body that disregards the Sabbath, and makes a mock at the ordinances o' religion, ye will never see that body come to muckle good. A braw hand she has made o' her gibes an' jeers at religion, an' her mockeries o' the poor persecuted hill-folk!—sunk down by degrees into the very dregs o' sin and misery! run away after a scullion!"

"Fy, fy, Wattie, how can ye say sae? It was weel kenn'd that she hatit him wi' a perfect an' mortal hatred, an' tried to make away wi' him mae ways nor ane."

"Aha, Bessie; but nipping an' scarting are Scots folk's wooing; an' though it is but right that we suspend our judgments, there will naebody persuade me, if she be found alang wi' the creature, but that she has run away after him in the natural way, on her twa shanks, without help either frae fairy or brownie."

"I'll never believe sic a thing of any woman born, let be a lady weel up in years."

"Od help ye, Bessie! ye dinna ken the stretch o' corrupt nature. The best o' us, when left to oursells, are nae better than strayed sheep, that will never find the way back to their ain pastures; an' of a' things made o' mortal flesh, a wicked woman is the warst."

"Alack-a-day! we get the blame o' muckle that we little deserve. But, Wattie, keep ye a gayan sharp look-out about the cleuchs and the caves o' our glen, or hope, as ye ca't; for the lady kens them a' gayan weel; and gin the twenty hunder merks wad come our way, it might gang a waur gate. It wad tocher a' our bonny lasses."

"Ay, weel I wat, Bessie, that's nae lee. And now, when ye bring me amind o't, the L——— forgie me gin I didna hear a creature up in the Brock-holes this morning, skirling as if something war cutting its throat. It gars a' the hairs stand on my head when I think it may hae been our leddy, an' the droich of a creature murdering her. I took it for a battle of wulcats, and wished they might pu' out ane anither's thrapples; but when I think on it again, they war unco like some o' our leddy's unearthly screams."

"His presence be about us, Wattie! Haste ye. Pit on your bonnet —take your staff in your hand, and gang an' see what it is."

"Shame fa' me, if I daur gang, Bessie."

"Hout, Wattie, trust in the Lord."

"Aweel, sae I do. But ane's no to throw himsell ower a linn, an' trust that the Lord's to kep him in a blanket; nor hing himsell up in a raip, an' expect the Lord to come and cut him down. An' it's nae muckle safer for an auld stiff man to gang away out to a wild remote place, where there is ae body murdering another.—What is that I hear, Bessie? Haud the lang tongue o' you, and rin to the door, an' see what noise that is."

Bessie ran to the door, but soon returned an altered creature, with her mouth wide open, and her eyes set in her head.

"It is them, Wattie! it is them! His presence be about us! What will we do?"

"Them? whaten them?"

"Why, that blackguard creature, coming here, leading our leddy be the hair o' the head, an' yerking her wi' a stick. I am terrified out o' my wits. What will we do?"

"We'll *see* what they *say*," said Wattie, manifestly in as great terror as his wife; and by a natural impulse, or as a last resource, he opened the Bible, not knowing what he did, and then hurried on his spectacles; but before he got two leaves turned over, the two entered, a frightful-looking couple indeed. Merodach, with his old withered face, and ferret eyes, leading the Lady of Wheelhope by the long hair, which was mixed with grey, and whose face was all bloated with wounds and bruises, and having stripes of blood on her garments.

"How's this!—How's this, sirs?" said Wattie Blythe.

"Close that book, and I will tell you, goodman," said Merodach.

"I can hear what you hae to say wi' the beuk open, sir," said Wattie, turning over the leaves, as if looking for some particular passage, but apparently not knowing what he was doing. "It is a shamefu' business this, but some will hae to answer for't. My leddy, I am unco grieved to see you in sic a plight. Ye hae surely been dooms sair left to yourself."

The lady shook her head, uttered a feeble hollow laugh, and fixed her eyes on Merodach. But such a look! It almost frightened the simple aged couple out of their senses. It was not a look of love nor of hatred exclusively; neither was it of desire or disgust, but it was a combination of them all. It was such a look as one fiend would cast on another, in whose everlasting destruction he rejoiced. Wattie was glad to take his eyes from such countenances, and look into the Bible, that firm foundation of all his hopes and all his joy.

"I request that you will shut that book, sir," said the horrible creature; "or if you do not, I will shut it for you with a vengeance;" and with that he seized it, and flung it against the wall. Bessie uttered a scream, and Wattie was quite paralysed; and although he seemed disposed to run after his best friend, as he called it, the hellish looks of the Brownie interposed, and glued him to his seat.

"Hear what I have to say first," said the creature, "and then pore your fill on that precious book of yours. One concern at a time is enough. I came to do you a service. Here, take this cursed, wretched woman, whom you style your lady, and deliver her up to the lawful authorities, to be restored to her husband and her place in society. She is come upon one that hates her, and never said one kind word to her in his life, and though I have beat her like a dog, still she clings to me, and will not depart, so enchanted is she with the laudable purpose of cutting my throat. Tell your master and her brother, that I am not to be burdened with their maniac. I have scourged, I have spurned and kicked her, afflicting her night and day, and yet from my side she will not depart. Take her. Claim the reward in full, and your fortune is made, and so farewell."

The creature bowed and went away, but the moment his back was turned the lady fell a-screaming and struggling like one in an agony, and, in spite of all the old couple's exertions, she forced herself out of their hands, and ran after the retreating Merodach. When he saw better would not be, he turned upon her, and, by one blow with his stick, struck her down; and, not content with that, he continued to kick and baste her in such a manner as to all appearance would have killed twenty ordinary persons. The poor devoted dame could do nothing, but now and then utter a squeak like a half-worried cat, and writhe and grovel on the sward, till Wattie and his wife came up and withheld her tormentor from further violence. He then bound her hands behind her back with a strong cord, and delivered her once more to the charge of the old couple, who contrived to hold her by that means and take her home.

Wattie had not the face to take her into the hall, but into one of the outhouses, where he brought her brother to receive her. The man of the law was manifestly vexed at her reappearance, and scrupled not to testify his dissatisfaction; for when Wattie told him how the wretch had abused his sister, and that, had it not been for Bessie's interference and his own, the lady would have been killed outright,

"Why, Walter, it is a great pity that he did not kill her outright," said he. "What good can her life now do to her, or of what value is her life to any creature living? After one has lived to disgrace all connected with them, the sooner they are taken off the better."

The man, however, paid old Walter down his two thousand merks, a great fortune for one like him in those days; and not to dwell longer on this unnatural story, I shall only add, very shortly, that the Lady of Wheelhope soon made her escape once more, and flew, as by an irresistible charm, to her tormentor. Her friends looked no more after her; and the last time she was seen alive, it was following the uncouth creature up the water of Daur, weary, wounded, and lame, while he was all the way beating her, as a piece of excellent amusement. A few days after that, her body was found among some wild haggs, in a place called Crook-burn, by a party of the persecuted Covenanters that were in hiding there, some of the very men whom she had exerted herself to destroy, and who had been driven, like David of old, to pray for a curse and earthly punishment upon her. They buried her like a dog at the Yetts of Keppel, and rolled three huge stones upon her grave, which are lying there to this day. When they found her corpse, it was mangled and wounded in a most shocking manner, the fiendish creature having manifestly tormented her to death. He was never more seen or heard of in this kingdom, though all that country-side was kept in terror for him many years afterwards; and to this day, they will tell you of THE BROWNIE OF THE BLACK HAGGS, which title he seems to have acquired after his disappearance.

This story was told to me by an old man, named Adam Halliday, whose great grandfather, Thomas Halliday, was one of those that found the body and buried it. It is many years since I heard it; but, however ridiculous it may appear, I remember it made a dreadful impression on my young mind. I never heard any story like it, save one of an old fox-hound that pursued a fox through the Grampians for a fortnight, and when at last discovered by the Duke of Athole's people, neither of them could run, but the hound was still continuing to walk after the fox, and when the latter lay down the other lay down beside him, and looked at him steadily all the while, though unable to do him the least harm. The passion of inveterate malice seems to have influenced these two exactly alike. But, upon the whole, I scarcely believe the tale can be true.

MOUNT BENGER,
   Sept. 10, 1828.

NOTES

In the Notes which follow, page references include a letter enclosed in brackets: (a) indicates that the passage concerned is to be found in the first quarter of the page, while (b) refers to the second quarter, (c) to the third quarter, and (d) to the final quarter. Where it seems useful to discuss the meaning of particular phrases, this is done in the Notes; single words are dealt with in the Glossary. Quotations from the Bible in the Notes are from the Authorised King James Version, the translation familiar to Hogg and his contemporaries. For references in the Notes to plays by Shakespeare, the edition used has been *The Complete Works: Compact Edition*, ed. by Stanley Wells and Gary Taylor (Oxford: Clarendon Press, 1988).

The present edition consists of the pieces written by Hogg for publication in his 'Shepherd's Calendar' series of articles in *Blackwood's Edinburgh Magazine*. Other pieces by Hogg published under the 'Shepherd's Calendar' title are discussed at the end of the Notes.

Storms

Hogg's 'Shepherd's Calendar' series was launched in 1819 when 'The Shepherd's Calendar. Storms' appeared in the April number of *Blackwood's*. The piece proved to be a popular one, and it was reprinted three times during Hogg's lifetime. These reprintings are discussed below, in the Textual Notes on 'Storms'. The Textual Notes also record the survival of Hogg's manuscript, which is used as copy-text in the present edition. Like Scott and many other writers of his generation, Hogg has some eccentricities in spelling; and the spellings of the manuscript of 'Storms' have not been altered.

1(a) **the tablets of memory** *tablets* are a pair or set of stiff sheets of cardboard, ivory, etc., fastened together and used as a notebook for memoranda, jottings, legal documents, records, etc.

1(b) **"Mar's year"** 1715, when there was a Jacobite rising under the Earl of Mar.

1(b) **"that year the heelanders raide"** the Jacobite rising of 1745.

1(b) **the year Nine and the year Forty** in a valuable discussion of 'Storms', John MacQueen demonstrates that 1709 and 1740 were indeed years of abnormally severe cold. See MacQueen, *The Rise of the Historical Novel* (Edinburgh: Scottish Academic Press, 1989), p.204.

2(a–b) **Eskdalemoor [...] Phaup [...] Tweedsmuir [...] Thirlestane** places either in Hogg's native Ettrick Valley, or within easy reach of it. Most of the places Hogg mentions in 'Storms' can be traced in modern maps of Ettrick and the south of Scotland.

2(c) **There's walth o' kye** the 'auld sang' has not been identified.

4(c) **Thomas Beattie, lost 72 scores** Hogg's account 'is confirmed by Beattie's own journal record of the events, which gives a long description of the storm. This emphasises the significance of the storm in the country at large and supports Hogg's testimony about the date of the storm and the fairness of the winter until the storm broke' (Elaine E. Petrie, 'James Hogg: A Study in the Transition from Folk Tradition to Literature' (unpublished doctoral thesis, University of Stirling, 1980), p.178). Beattie's journal is in private ownership.

6(d) **The Black Douglasses** a family famous for their exploits in the old days of

Border warfare with England: fortified tower-houses were typical buildings of that period. The Black Douglases were based in the Borders, while the Red Douglases were the Angus line.

10(b) Douglas Burn Blackhouse farmhouse and tower are situated beside the Douglas Burn, a tributary of Yarrow.

11(a) Charles' Street the location of Hogg's Edinburgh base at this period.

11(b) "That night [...] on his hand" from Burns's 'Tam o' Shanter' (l.77).

11(b) women fo'k Hogg's well-known song 'The Women Fo'k' was first published in his *Border Garland*, [1819]. This booklet of songs is listed among the month's new Edinburgh publications, on p.243 of the May 1819 number of *Blackwood's*, the number in which the second instalment of 'Storms' appeared.

16(a) the late worthy and judicious Mr. Bryden of Crosslee Walter Bryden of Crosslee, who had been a benefactor of Hogg's parents, was killed by the fall of a tree in 1799. Further details are to be found in Hogg, *Scottish Pastorals*, ed. by Elaine Petrie (Stirling: Stirling University Press, 1988), pp.49–50.

17(a) the Chaldee Manuscript a notorious article (by various hands, including Hogg's) which created an uproar when published in the October 1817 number of *Blackwood's*. Written in biblical style, and presenting itself as a recently-discovered oriental manuscript, this article satirises the literati and booksellers of the Edinburgh of the time. Such was the outrage of some of the victims that 'legal proceedings' were indeed 'meditated, and attempted'.

17(d) Mary Beattie later married Hogg's elder brother William.

19(d) a poet for whose works I always feel disposed to have a great partiality the poet is James Hogg: and the lines quoted are from 'Glen-Avin', which forms part of *The Queen's Wake* (1813).

21(b) Altrive Hogg's farm in the Yarrow valley.

Textual Notes on 'Storms'

The first publication of 'Storms' was in *Blackwood's Edinburgh Magazine*, 5 (April and May 1819), 75–81 and 210–16). It was reprinted in Hogg's *Winter Evening Tales*, 2 vols (Edinburgh: Oliver & Boyd, 1820), II, 152–80; and again in the second edition, (Edinburgh: Oliver & Boyd, 1821), II, 152–80. It was once more reprinted in Hogg, *The Shepherd's Calendar*, 2 vols (Edinburgh: William Blackwood, 1829), II, 254–92. The *Winter Evening Tales* texts follow *Blackwood's*, with a few small variants that can safely be attributed to the printer; while the 1829 printing, in line with the pattern discussed in the Introduction of the present volume, shows clear traces of the revising hand of Robert Hogg. Hogg's manuscript of 'Storms' survives in the Blackwood Papers at the National Library of Scotland (hereafter NLS), as part of MS 4808. The manuscript is in two sections, corresponding to the two sections in which 'Storms' was published in *Blackwood's*; and each section of the manuscript has its own sequence of pagination in Hogg's hand. Both sections consist of sheets measuring 38cm x 31.5 cm; these have been folded once, giving pages measuring 31.5cm x 19cm. Both sections are watermarked with a crown and shield device, and (in the countermark) with the date 1818. A detailed discussion of the manuscript and the early printings is to be found in Douglas S. Mack, 'Notes on Editing James Hogg's "Storms"', *The Bibliotheck*, 12 (1985), 140–49. Significantly, it appears that the first printing of 'Storms' does not seriously distort the substance of Hogg's text. In accordance with the usual practice of the period, the transfer to print involves a wholesale re-casting of the author's punctuation, and a regularisation of his spelling; but the printers have reproduced the words of Hogg's text with reasonable care and accuracy.

The present edition of 'Storms' uses Hogg's manuscript as copy-text. Hogg's free and fluid punctuation in the manuscript is not always fully worked out: for example, some sentences end without a full stop, even although the next sentence begins with a capital letter. In such cases a full stop has been added silently in the present edition. In addition, the following emendations have been made, either to provide extra punctuation where it is required by the sense, or to correct what appear to be authorial blunders and slips of the pen.

1(a) traditionally]   tradionally (manuscript)
1(b) *year Forty* —these]   *year Forty* these (manuscript)
1(c) an old shepherd in]   an old sheperd in (manuscript)
1(c) once abated—the ground]   once abated the ground (manuscript)
3(b) their heads? and]   their heads?" and (manuscript)
5(a) 3 horses, 2 men, 1 woman,]   3 hores, 2 men, 1 women, (manuscript)
5(a) shepherds, (of whom]   MS: shepherds (, of whom (manuscript)
6(b) top of a height]   top of height (manuscript)
6(c) had done—he had]   had done he had (manuscript)
10(a) hours before—there were]   hours before there were (manuscript)
10(b) impassible—at length]   impassible at length (manuscript)
10(d) trance—at length]   trance at length (manuscript)
10(d) river—I had]   river I had (manuscript)
10(d) and trees]   and trees and trees (manuscript)
14(d) prodigious;]   prdigious; (manuscript)
15(d) of the storm;]   of of the storm; (manuscript)
16(d) law's]   law's law's (manuscript)

As compared with the manuscript, the *Blackwood's* printing contains additional material. Some of this new material is clearly authorial, and these additions presumably reflect changes made by Hogg while reading the proofs for *Blackwood's*. Hogg's letters suggest that he tended to read proofs of his publications if he happened to be in Edinburgh while they were being printed; and his letters also suggest that in many cases proofs were not sent to him if he happened to be away from the city. It appears from a letter to John M'Diarmid of Dumfries that Hogg was in Edinburgh in the spring of 1819, when 'Storms' was being printed. In this letter, dated 8 March 1819, he writes from his Edinburgh base at 6 Charles' Street: 'I think it is likely I will be here till nearly midsummer' (Hornel Library, Broughton House, Kirkcudbright, manuscript S20).

The following emendations have been made to the copy-text in order to incorporate from *Blackwood's* what appear to be alterations made by Hogg at the proof stage. This matter is discussed more fully in Douglas S. Mack, 'Notes on Editing James Hogg's "Storms"', *The Bibliotheck*, 12 (1985), 140–49.

4(b) the bonds with which true Christianity connects us with Heaven and with
      each other.
      MS: the bonds which true Christianity inculcates!
12(d) horns of stragglers appearing,
      MS: horns of one appearing,
17(a) for in that case as well as the latter one, legal proceedings, it is said, were
      meditated, and attempted; but lucky it was for the shepherds that they agreed
      to no reference, for such
      MS: and in that case as well as the latter one, legal proceedings were
      meditated, and attempted; but lucky it was for the shepherds that they signed
      no reference, for such
17(b) was held, that it is likely it would have fared very ill with them; at all events, it
      would
      MS: was held that it would

19(a) nights wark! What thought ye it was that cried?"

    "I didna ken what it was, it cried just like a plover."

    "Did the callans look as they war fear'd when they heard it?"

    "They lookit gay an' queer."

    "What did they say?"

    "Ane cried, 'What is that?' an' another said, 'What can it mean.' 'Hout,' · quo Jamie Fletcher, 'it's just some bit stray bird that has lost itsel.' 'I dinna ken,' quo your Will, 'I dinna like it unco weel.'"

    "'Think ye did

MS: nights wark! Think ye did

Rob Dodds

This story was first published in the number of *Blackwood's* for March 1823, under a title typical of the magazine's practice for the series: 'The Shepherd's Calendar. Class Second. Deaths, Judgments, and Providences'. It next appeared in print (with revisions by Robert Hogg) in *The Shepherd's Calendar* of 1829, (1, 1–32), under the title 'Rob Dodds'. These were the only printings in Hogg's lifetime.

Some of the *Blackwood's* titles would have lacked precision and clarity if retained when the series was reprinted in book form. Hogg addresses this problem in a letter of 12 February 1828, in which he asks Blackwood to 'leave out the classes and give every tale a kind of appropriate name for every tale must be distinct either as a chapter or *Tale* with a beginning and an end' (NLS, MS 4021, fol. 275). In the 1829 volumes an 'appropriate name' is indeed supplied for every tale. In some cases the 1829 titles offer a useful means of providing particular stories with a distinct and appropriate name. In such cases, the present edition includes the original *Blackwood's* titles, but also uses the 1829 titles.

After its promising opening with 'Storms' in 1819, Hogg's 'Shepherd's Calendar' series in *Blackwood's* did not resume until the publication of 'Rob Dodds' in 1823. Hogg had quarrelled with Blackwood in 1820; and during 1821 and 1822 a number of his articles appeared in *The Edinburgh Magazine* (formerly *The Scots Magazine*), a periodical published by William Blackwood's rival Archibald Constable. By the spring of 1823, however, Hogg had returned to the *Blackwood's* fold. 'Rob Dodds' therefore marks something of a new beginning for the 'Shepherd's Calendar' series.

22(a) on the 13 of February 1823 as this story was first published in the March 1823 number of *Blackwood's*, these words indicate clearly that we are here dealing with the present. In 'Storms', Hogg's reminiscences conveyed something of the nature of Ettrick life and society. The opening of 'Rob Dodds', the second narrative in the series, moves on from this to provide a modern context for traditional Ettrick storytelling.

22(a) the outer limits of the county of Peebles 'Rob Dodds' is set in the wild and mountainous country around Loch Skeen and the Grey Mare's Tail waterfall, near the boundary between the county of Peebles and the county of Dumfries. This area forms part of the route from St Mary's Loch and Yarrow, to Moffat and Annandale. Most of the places mentioned in 'Rob Dodds' can be readily identified in modern maps of the area.

22(a) one of his led farms a led farm is a smaller or outlying farm managed through an employee

23(c) the gait cleugh the ravine or crag where the goats are kept.

23(c) has a craw to pook has a fault to find.

23(c) thrawing your mou' twisting your mouth as a sign of displeasure.

23(d) in the saxteen and seventeen that is, in 1816 and 1817. Rural change in this period in Scotland is discussed in Laurence J. Saunders, *Scottish Democracy 1815–*

1840: The Social and Intellectual Background (Edinburgh: Oliver & Boyd, 1950).

24(a) the days o' Abel Abel 'was a keeper of sheep, but Cain was a tiller of the ground. [...] And the Lord had respect unto Abel and to his offering: But unto Cain and to his offering he had not respect' (Genesis 4.1–5).

24(a) seem no to care a bodle seem not to care in the least.

24(c) to coup the creels to die.

24(d)–25(a) the heart is hardened like Pharaoh's, and you will not let [...] go 'And the Lord said unto Moses, Pharaoh's heart is hardened, he refuseth to let the people go' (Exodus 7.14).

25(a) just at ane mae wi't at breaking point, at the point of death.

26(a) prosperity for twenty years British agriculture prospered during the Napoleonic Wars; but found conditions more difficult in the peace which followed the battle of Waterloo (1815).

26(a) laying by a little for a sair leg saving money for a time of emergency.

26(a) ye plantit vineyards after the Flood, 'Noah began to be an husbandman, and he planted a vineyard: And he drank of the wine, and was drunken; and he was uncovered within his tent' (Genesis 9.20–21).

26(a) play paw make the slightest movement.

26(b) keep the crown o' the causey keep a creditable or dominant position.

26(c) beet a mister fulfil a need, make good a deficiency.

26(d) little mair than 140 years the conversation between the shepherd and the farmer provides an opportunity for a sketch of the history of the Ettrick Forest. Hogg's interest in the history of his district is reflected in his 'Statistics of Selkirkshire', in *Prize Essays and Transactions of the Highland Society of Scotland*, 9 (1832), 281–306. Much background information on the district is also to be found in T. Craig-Brown, *The History of Selkirkshire; or, The Chronicles of Ettrick Forrest*, 2 vols (Edinburgh: David Douglas, 1886).

27(d) afore the Revolution a reference to the events of 1689–90, during which William of Orange accepted the English crown (as William III), and later the Scottish crown (as William II).

27(d) when the great Mr Boston came to Etterick Thomas Boston (1677–1732), a theologian of substantial and enduring reputation, was minister of Ettrick from 1707 till 1732.

28(a) that laid house to house, an' field to field echoes the curse in Isaiah 5.8 on those who increase their land by taking advantage of their economic strength, through exploiting the distress of neighbouring small farmers: 'Woe unto them that join house to house, that lay field to field, till there be no place, that they may be placed alone in the midst of the earth!'. Those who 'join house to house' weaken, and eventually destroy, the community.

28(a) Mr Boston wrote an epitaph St Mary's churchyard, above St Mary's Loch in the Yarrow valley, still contains the gravestone of 'Thomas Linton late tenant in Chappelhop who died July 14 1718 in the 64th year of his age'. The farm of Chapelhope lies at the head of the loch, within sight of the churchyard. The gravestone carries the following epitaph:

> All lost for Christ an hundred fold
>> Produced and he became
> A father eyes and feet unto
>> The poor the blind the lam

This is followed on the stone by references to Matthew 19.29 and to Job 29.15–16; and the epitaph is based upon these biblical passages. I am grateful to Birgit Schwiete and Lara-May Honrado, students at the University of Stirling, for help in deciphering the inscription. Further information is to be found in 'St

Mary's Kirkyard, Yarrow', *Transactions of the Hawick Archaeological Society*, (1964), 49–52 (p.51, stone 31).

29(c) a drop in the bucket before God, 'the nations are as a drop of a bucket, and are counted as the small dust of the balance' (Isaiah 40.5).

29(c) lay the axe to the root of the tree 'And now also the axe is laid unto the root of the trees; every tree therefore which bringeth not forth good fruit is hewn down, and cast into the fire' (Luke 3.9).

31(b)the band o' the hill the ridge of the hill.

31(b) a backfu' o' peats peat, the main fuel of the district, was cut on the hills and moors, and had to be carried to the houses for use.

31(c) fiend ae inch not a scrap.

34(d) a callybit spring a chalybeate spring is one impregnated with iron salts.

Textual Notes on 'Rob Dodds'
The only printings of this story during Hogg's lifetime were in *Blackwood's*, 13 (March 1823), 311–20; and in *The Shepherd's Calendar* of 1829 (1, 1–32). As the manuscript does not survive the story is here reprinted from *Blackwood's*, with the following emendations which seek to correct what appear to be errors by the printer.

24(c)   popped off before]   popped of before (*Blackwood's*)
24(c)   kail-yard."]   kail-yard. (*Blackwood's*)
24(c)   what's that you're saying to]   what's that your saying to (*Blackwood's*)
25(c)   I ken you're telling me]   I ken your telling me (*Blackwood's*)
28(a)   on a wee, wee farm]   on' a wee, wee farm (*Blackwood's*)
37(a)   impossible] impassable (*Blackwood's*)

Mr Adamson of Laverhope
Following quickly on the heels of 'Rob Dodds', the next story in Hogg's series appeared in the number of *Blackwood's* for June 1823, again under the title 'The Shepherd's Calendar. Class Second. Deaths, Judgments, and Providences'. This story next appeared in print (with revisions, as usual, by Robert Hogg) in *The Shepherd's Calendar* of 1829, under the title 'Mr Adamson of Laverhope'. The various places of the story appear to be fictional: indeed, some of the names have a biblical resonance which is in keeping with the country people's supernatural interpretation of the events. Thus 'Laverhope' suggests the Hope or Valley of Laver, a laver being a large brazen vessel for Old Testament priests' ablutions at the sacrifical altar; while 'Widehope' suggests the 'wide gate' that 'leadeth to destruction' (Matthew 7.13).

40(a) forgive you your debts as you forgive your debtors echoes the version of the Lord's Prayer traditionally used in the worship of the Church of Scotland (Matthew 6.12).

44(a) we a' ken what wad be the quotient if a dozen is divided by four, the quotient is three: a group like Jock, May Henderson, and the good lamb would appear to be envisaged.

44(b) persecutions, forays, and fairy raids this sums up three of the favourite themes of Ettrick oral tradition: the persecution of the covenanters in the religious conflicts of the late seventeenth century; the forays of the old Border reivers; and the supernatural.

45(a) the unnatural rebellion in 1745–46, Prince Charles Edward led a Jacobite rising which sought to restore the Catholic Stuarts to the throne. Maxwells were prominent among the Jacobite families of the south of Scotland.

49(b) a cataract front more than twenty feet deep a flash flood very similar to the one described in the story was reported on the front page of *The Scotsman* newspaper for 27 July 1983, under the headline 'Borders valley devastated by freak storm'. The report describes 'a wall of water twenty ft high and 200 yds wide in places' which earlier in the week had surged across a four-mile area in the valley of the Hermitage Water, killing about a hundred sheep. 'At the home of Mr and Mrs Brian Moffat, who run a wood-carving workshop near Hermitage Castle, it was not raining, but they had seen the storm about two miles away. Within minutes the flood-water was racing across the fields crashing through drystane dykes, towards them.'

51(d) to tak the gait to set off.

52(b) needless to expect [...] siccan branches an echo of Christ's words in John 15.5: 'I am the vine, ye are the branches: He that abideth in me, and I in him, the same bringeth forth much fruit: for without me ye can do nothing'.

52(b) ae wee bit text Matthew 7.1.

53(d) his bowels had gushed out after betraying Jesus for thirty pieces of silver, Judas 'purchased a field with the reward of iniquity; and falling headlong, he burst asunder in the midst, and all his bowels gushed out' (Acts 1.18).

Textual Notes on 'Mr Adamson of Laverhope'
The only printings during Hogg's lifetime were in *Blackwood's*, 13 (June 1823), 629–40; and in *The Shepherd's Calendar* of 1829 (1, 33–68). As the manuscript for 'Mr Adamson of Laverhope' does not survive, the present edition reprints the *Blackwood's* text with the following emendations which seek to correct what appear to be errors by the printer:

39(d) his sackless family]   his rackless family (*Blackwood's*)
43(a) the abusing of his ward,]   the abusing of his word, (*Blackwood's*)
46(d) had just taken place,]   had just taken place (*Blackwood's*) [There is a gap in *Blackwood's* after 'place', as if a comma has fallen out of the type.]
48(a) grim an' gurly!]   grim an' early! (*Blackwood's*)
52(c) "an' it's this,   ]   an' it's this,   (*Blackwood's*)
55(a) 18th of July, 1804.]   18th of July, 1804, (*Blackwood's*)

Dogs
First published in the number of *Blackwood's* for February 1824 as 'The Shepherd's Calendar. Class IV. Dogs', this is indeed the fourth of Hogg's 'Shepherd's Calendar' articles in *Blackwood's*. The previous two articles, however, had both been described as 'Class Second'.

Hogg had previously contributed 'Further Anecdotes of the Shepherd's Dog' to *Blackwood's*, 2 (March 1818), 621–26. This article was a response to 'Sagacity of a Shepherd's Dog' (signed 'M.'), which had appeared in *Blackwood's*, 2 (January 1818), 417–20. In the *Shepherd's Calendar* of 1829, Robert Hogg combines Hogg's 1818 and 1824 articles into a single chapter entitled 'The Shepherd's Dog'. In this compound chapter, Robert Hogg provides a brief introductory summary of the anecdote contained in 'Sagacity of a Shepherd's Dog'.

57(b–c) North [...] Sir Christy the reference is to 'Christopher North', the central figure in the 'Noctes Ambrosianae' of *Blackwood's Edinburgh Magazine*.

57(b) the Shepherd [...] the married state Hogg's long bachelorhood ended with his marriage in 1820, when he was forty-nine. 'Dogs' was first published in 1824.

58(a) Ambrose's is the Edinburgh tavern in which the *Blackwood's* writers meet, in the magazine's 'Noctes Ambrosianae'.

58(b) I once sent you an account in 'Further Anecdotes of the Shepherd's Dog', published in *Blackwood's* in 1818, and discussed above.

58(b) my own renowned Hector Hogg's poem, 'The Author's Address to his Auld Dog Hector', was included in his book *The Mountain Bard* (Edinburgh:

Constable, 1807). 'Further Anecdotes of the Shepherd's Dog' concludes with a promise by Hogg to provide a future article about Hector.

60(d) his dad's unfortunate ear for music another reference to 'Further Anecdotes of the Shepherd's Dog', in which it is recorded that Sirrah 'never heard music, but he drew towards it; and he never drew towards it, but he joined in it with all his vigour' ('Further Anecdotes', p.625).

60(d) the precenting in church in the Scottish church of Hogg's day, instrumental music was regarded as inappropriate for worship; and a precentor led the singing, by singing the line for the congregation to repeat.

61(b) "with might and majesty," this quotation has not been identified.

62(b) Alexander Laidlaw was one of Hogg's oldest and closest friends. Laidlaw (quoted by Hogg's daughter M. G. Garden) writes that 'Mr Hogg and I were in our youthful days almost inseparable companions'. In this passage, Laidlaw also writes of Hogg's death on 21 November 1835: 'I visited him on the 22nd October, and almost daily till the 19th November. After this I was in the room in which he died, never took off my clothes, but rested occasionally on a sofa — never got home till the Saturday after the funeral' (M. G. Garden, *Memorials of James Hogg* (Paisley: Alexander Gardner, [1884]), pp.326–28). Laidlaw's farm of Bowerhope is on the southern shore of St Mary's Loch.

62(d) Mr William Nicholson a portrait-painter, Nicholson (1781–1844) established himself at Edinburgh in 1814; and his portrait of Hogg was painted there in 1815. Hogg wrote to his friend William Laidlaw on 14 February 1815, asking for Lion to be sent to Edinburgh to join in sitting for this portrait (M. G. Garden, *Memorials of James Hogg*, p.83).

66(c) cost him his life at the period in question, the death sentence could be inflicted in Scotland for theft, if the theft was of a particularly serious character; and thefts of horses, cattle, or sheep were felt to be especially heinous.

Textual Notes on 'Dogs'

The manuscript does not survive; and in the present edition this part of 'The Shepherd's Calendar' is reprinted from *Blackwood's*, 15 (February 1824), 177–83. The following emendations have been made, to correct what appear to be errors by the printer.

57(a) a *knag*,]   a *snag*, (*Blackwood's*) [Although an unusual word, *knag* fits the context perfectly, while *snag* does not. In Hogg's hand *s* has a long looped shape, and might well be confused with *k*.]

61(a) minister giving]   minister, giving (*Blackwood's*)

61(a) thrice in the course]   twice in the course (*Blackwood's*)

61(c) among sheep that his father]   amomg sheep hat his father (*Blackwood's*)

62(c) "If that should really]   "If that that should really (*Blackwood's*)

The Lasses

'Dogs' had appeared in the number of *Blackwood's* for February 1824. The next number, for March 1824, contained the first instalment of 'The Shepherd's Calendar. Class V. The Lasses'; but the concluding portion was not published until the number for February 1825. Hogg wrote to Blackwood on this subject on 29 January 1825. 'I send you a Shepherd's Callander the *lasses* concluded having written it over and shortened it still it is not good   I wish North would confess having mislaid it for it is so long after the other I am ashamed of it look that I have put the proper *Class* at the beginning for I have forgot what class *the Lasses* was' (NLS, MS 4014, fol. 287).

68(c) "farmers' bonny daughters" this quotation has not been identified.

69(b) ODoherty or yourself the person addressed is 'Christopher North', a central figure in the 'Noctes Ambrosianae', and a representation of John Wilson. 'ODoherty' (William Maginn) is likewise one of the regular cast of the 'Noctes'. The Introduction of the present volume discusses the importance of the 'Noctes' in *Blackwood's Edinburgh Magazine*.

69(d) take good tent take alert notice.

70(a) to win aff to escape.

70(d) the morn tomorrow.

70(d) as the commandment requires while suicide is not explicitly forbidden in the Bible, it was felt to be wrong because of God's command to Noah about shedding human blood (Genesis 9.5–6); and also because of the sixth commandment, 'Thou shalt not kill' (Exodus 20.13).

72(a) your lane without a companion.

72(c) ance errand for the one purpose mentioned, for the single errand.

72(c) consummation devoutly to be wussed from the famous 'To be, or not to be' soliloquy in *Hamlet*, III. 1. 58–92 (at lines 65–66).

72(d)–73(a) the bonny Snaw-fleck the Snaw-fleck (snow-flake) is the snow-bunting.

74(a) cracks as crouse talks as cheerfully.

74(b) but an' ben everywhere, throughout the house.

74(c) feint a haed devil a bit, not a whit.

74(c) gang in wi' agree with.

75(c) wha the widdy who the devil.

75(c) in by indoors.

75(c) beet the mister supply the need.

75(c) out by out of doors.

76(a) the wind will blaw nae mair out o' the west the prevailing wind in Scotland is from the west.

76(b) as the auld ballant says this quotation has not been identified.

77(a) the law of Padanaram a reference to Genesis chapters 28 and 29, in which Jacob goes to Padanaram to seek a wife, and is told by Laban 'It must not be so done in our country, to give the younger [daughter] before the firstborn' (Genesis 29.26).

77(a) Bamph Banff, the town in the North-East; THE PHRASE *go to Banff* means 'go to blazes'.

77(a) ower weel giftit o' gab too glibly eloquent.

77(b) the Grand Turk whose harem would need eunuchs.

77(d) took the book that is the Bible, for family worship.

78(a) The feint a ane never a one.

78(a) Be my certy assuredly.

78(c) ashamed to praise thy Maker an echo of Matthew 10.32–33.

81(a) Vulcan the Roman god of fire and smiths.

81(b) I wat weel I must say.

81(b) Hervey's Meditations James Hervey (1714–58) was prominent in the early Methodist movement. His works, including *Meditations among the Tombs* (1746), were extremely popular.

83(a) The saxteenth o' the Romans [...] the holy kiss 'Salute one another with an holy kiss' (Romans 16.16).

84(b) auld Laban's rules discussed in a note on the law of Padanaram, 77(a) above.

84(c) brought up in the fear, nurture, and admonition o' their Maker echoes Ephesians 6.4.

84(d) he plowed with his own heifers echoes Judges 14.18.

85(c) the Golden Harrow, in the Candlemaker-Row 'David Watson's Harrow Inn, in the the Candlemaker Row' was a favourite haunt of Hogg: see M.G. Garden, *Memorials of James Hogg*, p.305.

86(d) the whip of a Leith carter whose loaded carts would have to struggle uphill to Edinburgh from Leith, the city's port.

87(b) Middleton Middleton Inn, on the road from Galashiels (one of the main Border towns) to Edinburgh, was an important coach stage in Hogg's day: see the entry for 'Middleton House' in Francis H. Groome, *Ordnance Gazetteer of Scotland*, 6 vols (Edinburgh: Thomas C. Jack, 1882–85).

88(c) Thirlstane's motto the Scotts of Thirlestane were one of the long-established families of landed proprietors in Ettrick; this family forms the subject of Hogg's poem 'Thirlestane', in *The Mountain Bard* (1807).

91(a) a flower [...] desert air from Thomas Gray's 'Elegy, Written in a Country Church-Yard' (l.55).

91(b) a grey mare proverbially, 'the grey mare is the better horse': which means that the wife rules the husband.

91(c) W.S., writer to the signet W.S. is a much-used contraction for Writer to the Signet, a member of a society of lawyers in Edinburgh.

93(a) so long with this story the first part of the story was published in *Blackwood's* for March 1824, but the second part did not appear until the number for February 1825.

Textual Notes on 'The Lasses'
This piece was first published in *Blackwood's* 15 (March 1824), 296–304; and 17 (February 1825), 180–86). It next appeared in *The Shepherd's Calendar* of 1829 (II, 1–48), where it is given the title 'Window Wat's Courtship'. These were the only printings in Hogg's lifetime. As Hogg's manuscript does not survive, 'The Lasses' is here reprinted from *Blackwood's*, with the following emendations which seek to correct what appear to be errors by the printer:
76(c)   preparing]   preparing' (*Blackwood's*)
76(c)   'The Snaw-fleck's a braw]   The Snaw-fleck's a braw (*Blackwood's*)
78(b)   eiry.']   eiry." (*Blackwood's*)
80(b)   "'Not a word]   "Not a word (*Blackwood's*)
80(b)   least not to-night.'"]   least not to-night.' (*Blackwood's*)
86(b)   [*Blackwood's* has a new paragraph at: "Gin the gouk]

General Anecdotes
After the concluding portion of 'The Lasses' appeared in the number for February 1825, there was a long gap until the next 'Shepherd's Calendar' article, 'General Anecdotes', appeared in the April 1827 *Blackwood's*. However, 1827 proved to be a vintage year, with contributions to Hogg's series appearing in the April, May, June, July and August numbers.

In the mid 1820s a good deal of Hogg's energy was directed towards farming. At a time when economic conditions were unfavourable, he had an expensive lease from the Duke of Buccleuch of the large farm of Mount Benger. Hogg discusses these matters in a letter to Scott of 28 January 1827, a year after Scott's own financial ruin: 'I have recieved word from his Grace's curators either to pay up my arrears at Whitsunday or give up my farm' (NLS, MS 3904, p.31). In the event Hogg was able to struggle on at Mount Benger until 1830, but his financial difficulties form the background to his letter to Blackwood of 24 February 1827: 'By the hand of Mr Marshall a young enthusiast in literature I send you a No of the Shepherds Callander for Maga and am determined to produce at least as much for every month

[...] I have another No ready on *dreams and apparitions* and if I knew how much would make up £100 how I would ply' (NLS, MS 4019, fol. 185). The article sent with Mr Marshall would appear to be the one published in the April 1827 number of *Blackwood's* as 'The Shepherd's Calendar. General Anecdotes'.

Hogg had borrowed from Blackwood; and on 23 March 1827 Blackwood writes: 'I recd your letter by Mr Marshall with your capital portion of the Shepherd's Calendar. It is most interesting and will be liked by every one. To show you how I value it, I have credited your acct with ten pounds for it, of which I enclose you a five pound note, and hope in this way you will soon extinguish the bill. I am very anxious to receive your next No on Dreams and Apparitions which I am sure will be excellent' (NLS, MS 30310, p.88). Blackwood's payment for 'General Anecdotes' was welcome, as can be seen from Hogg's letter of 5 April 1827: 'I got the post letter and the note safe and I think so welcome a sum hardly ever came to my hand Margaret [Hogg's wife] was just saying she had forgot the time she had money in her pocket and I replied that I had just one shilling in my possession which I had kept alone since the Border games and it had remained so long a solitary residenter that I thought it would be a lucky one While the word was in my mouth a servant opened the door and handed in your letter' (NLS, MS 4019, fol. 187).

94(b–c) Glen-Lyon [...] Tweeddale [...] Stirling [...] St Ninian's the ewe's journey would cover approximately 100 miles, from Glen-Lyon in the Grampian Mountains of the Highlands, south to Tweeddale in the Borders. Crieff lies about 30 miles from Glen-Lyon; Stirling is about twenty miles further on; and St Ninians is now a southern suburb of Stirling.

95(b) Blackhouse like most of the other places mentioned in 'General Anecdotes', Blackhouse is in Hogg's home territory of Ettrick Forest and the surrounding districts.

95(d) short sheep the firmly established breeds of sheep in the Borders in Hogg's day were the Blackface (known as *short sheep*) and the Cheviot (known as *long sheep*): see Michael J.H. Robson, *Sheep of the Borders* (Newcastleton: Michael J.H. Robson, 1988).

96(a) Willenslee Hogg was a shepherd at Willenslee while in his late teens, leaving it for Blackhouse in Yarrow in 1790: see Hogg, *Memoir of the Author's Life* and *Familiar Anecdotes of Sir Walter Scott*, ed. by Douglas S. Mack (Edinburgh: Scottish Academic Press, 1972), pp.8–9.

98(d) put thy hook in his nose [...] come back to thee 'Because thy rage against me, and thy tumult, is come up into mine ears, therefore will I put my hook in thy nose, and my bridle in thy lips, and I will turn thee back by the way by which thou camest' (Isaiah 37.29).

99(b) slogie riddles wide-meshed riddles for separating vegetables.

99(b) the year this year.

100(b–c) fling off the airmer and hairnishin' o' the law, whilk we haena proved, an' whup up the simple sling o' the gospel before fighting and defeating Goliath of Gath, David discards armour given to him by Saul: 'And David said unto Saul, I cannot go with these; for I have not proved them. And David put them off him' (1 Samuel 17.39). The idea being expressed is that the new testament, God's new covenant of the Gospel, is to be preferred in its simplicity to the much more complex old testament, the old covenant of the Law.

101(a) the great and noble Asnapper 'And the rest of the nations whom the great and noble Asnappar brought over' (Ezra 4.10).

101(b) the feats of one Sanballat in Nehemiah, Sanballat opposes the rebuilding of Jerusalem.

102(a) "Who commandeth the sun, and it riseth not." from Job 9.7.

102(a) **"Which maketh Arcturus, Orion, and Pleiades, and the chambers of the south."** Job 9.9.

102(b) **Fourteen thousand sheep!** 'So the Lord blessed the latter end of Job more than his beginning: for he had fourteen thousand sheep, and six thousand camels, and a thousand yoke of oxen, and a thousand she asses' (Job 42.12).

102(c) **The flocks on a thousand hills are thine** echoes Psalm 50.10.

102(d) **the little wee cludd out o' the sea** 'Behold, there ariseth a little cloud out of the sea, like a man's hand' (1 Kings 18.44). This cloud is the forerunner of 'a great rain' which brings a long and damaging drought to an end.

102(d) **the smearing season** the season when sheep are treated with a tar-and-grease compound, to protect the fleeces from damp and parasites.

103(a) **thou hast said in thy blessed word** the reference is to Mark 8.38.

103(b) **creep in beside the douss man** this incident is described in Ruth chapter 3.

103(c) **Will o' Phaup** Phaup (Phawhope) is at the head of the Ettrick valley. Will Laidlaw of Phaup was Hogg's grandfather; and his grave and Hogg's lie side by side in Ettrick churchyard. Will's gravestone gives the information that he was born at Craik in 1691 and died in 'the 84th year of his age'.

103(c) **like silver in the days of Solomon** 'And all king Solomon's drinking vessels were of gold, and all the vessels of the house of the forest of Lebanon were of pure gold; none were of silver: it was nothing accounted of in the days of Solomon' (1 Kings 10.21).

104(a) **deil a fit** never a foot.

104(d) **Stagshawbank** the site of an important cattle market, in the Tyne valley in the north of England.

106(b) **bands of smugglers passing from the Solway [...] towards the Lothians** readers of Scott's *Redgauntlet* (1824) will remember that the Solway coast, in the extreme south of Scotland, was a centre of smuggling in the eighteenth century. Edinburgh is in the Lothians.

111(d) **old, and full of days** 'And Isaac gave up the ghost, and died, and was gathered unto his people, being old and full of days' (Genesis 35.29).

112(a) **1715 [...] 1745** years which saw major Jacobite risings in Scotland.

112(a–b) **One of his sons is still alive [...] Border Minstrelsy** according to his gravestone in Ettrick churchyard, Hogg's uncle Will Laidlaw died on 25 March 1829. This Will Laidlaw was an important tradition-bearer, and a source from whom Hogg obtained material for Scott for use in *Minstrelsy of the Scottish Border* (1802–03). Hogg's uncle is discussed in Elaine Petrie, 'Odd Characters: Traditional Informants in James Hogg's Family', *Scottish Literary Journal*, 10 (1983), 30–41.

112(c) **Andrew** the reference is to Andrew Moore, who is discussed in 'Appendix IV: Additional Sources and Collectors' in Elaine E. Petrie, 'James Hogg: a Study in the Transition from Folk Tradition to Literature' (unpublished doctoral thesis, University of Stirling, 1980), pp.310–16.

112(c) **the far-famed and Reverend Thomas Boston** discussed in a note on 27(d), above.

113(a) **the fourth commandment** 'Remember the sabbath day, to keep it holy' (Exodus 20.8).

113(c) **Ezra, i.9** the book of Ezra tells of the return of some of the Jewish exiles to Jerusalem from Babylon; and Ezra 1.9 is part of a list of the things they bring with them: 'And this is the number of them: thirty chargers of gold, a thousand chargers of silver, nine and twenty knives'.

114(a) **Ettrickhouse** Hogg's birthplace, near Ettrick Church.

115(c) for fear of the fairies it was believed that, until it was baptised, a child was in danger of being captured by the fairies, with a changeling being left in its place.
115(c) deil haet not a particle.

Textual Notes on 'General Anecdotes'
The only printings during Hogg's lifetime were in *Blackwood's*, 21 (April 1827), 434–48; and in *The Shepherd's Calendar* of 1829 (II, 185–229). As the manuscript for 'General Anecdotes' does not survive, the present edition reprints the *Blackwood's* text with the following emendations which seek to correct what appear to be errors by the printer:
95(d)   stupid and fushionless]   stupid and actionless (*Blackwood's*)
105(c)   one of those Moffat bouses,]   one of those Moffat houses, (*Blackwood's*) [Cf. 103(d), 'Many a hard bouse he had about Moffat'.]
105(d)   —One plash more," quo' Will o' Phaup; but all]   —One plash more, quo' Will o' Phaup;" but all (*Blackwood's*)
105(d)   "Scots ground!" quo' Will o' Phaup—"a man]   "Scots ground! quo' Will o' Phaup—a man (*Blackwood's*)
113(a)   "The mair fool are ye," quo' Jock Amos to the minister.]   "The mair fool are ye, quo' Jock Amos to the minister." (*Blackwood's*)
113(d)   like?" said Linton.]   like?" said Liston. (*Blackwood's*)

George Dobson's Expedition to Hell, and The Souters of Selkirk
In his letter to Blackwood of 24 February 1827 quoted above in the Notes on 'General Anecdotes', Hogg writes that 'I have another No ready on *dreams and apparitions*' (NLS, MS 4019, fol. 185). Having started on this subject, Hogg seems to have warmed to the theme: 'Shepherd's Calendar' stories on 'Dreams and Apparitions' appeared in the May, June, July, and August numbers of *Blackwood's* in 1827. This series within a series opened in May with 'The Shepherd's Calendar. Dreams and Apparitions. Containing George Dobson's Expedition to Hell, and the Souters of Selkirk.'.
120(a) so fine an open road he never travelled 'for wide is the gate, and broad is the way, that leadeth to destruction' (Matthew 7.13).
120(c) a ticket written with red ink like Gil-Martin's book 'all intersected with red lines' in Hogg's *Confessions of a Justified Sinner* (1824), this suggests the influence of the devil.
121(c) the Pleasance a street in the Old Town of Edinburgh.
122(a) Roslin a village six miles to the south of Edinburgh.
123(d) the Lord President to the Parliament House the Lord President presided over the First Division of the Inner House of the Court of Session, the supreme civil court of Scotland. The Court of Session met in the Parliament House in Edinburgh.
124(b) Dr Wood MacQueen identifies the Dr Wood of Hogg's story as 'Alexander Wood, an Edinburgh surgeon of some distinction who lived from 1725 to 1807', and who was acquainted with Boswell (see *The Rise of the Historical Novel*, p.210).
126(b) Selkirk a town situated near the confluence of Ettrick and Yarrow, in Ettrick Forest.
126(b) weel to leeve well-off, in comfortable circumstances.
126(d) "Up wi' the souters o' Selkirk, / An' down wi' the Earl o' Hume this traditional song, a version of which appears in Scott's *Minstrelsy of the Scottish Border*, is said to refer to the battle of Flodden (1513), a disastrous defeat, by the English, of a large Scottish army commanded by James IV. According to Selkirk tradition, the Selkirk men, as royal tenants, fought bravely around their king,

and were almost all killed. Meanwhile 'the men of the Merse' (Berwickshire), under the command of the Earl of Hume, having won their immediate part of the battle, proceeded to loot the fallen English and then left the field with the spoils. This departure from the heat of the battle was perceived by Selkirk people as an act of treachery, and was the source of a long-held grudge.

126(d) the single-soled shoon it appears that the shoes made by the old souters of Selkirk were somewhat primitive, with a single thin sole: this matter is discussed in Scott's notes on the traditional song 'The Souters of Selkirk' in *Minstrelsy of the Scottish Border*.

127(a) Souters ane, souters a' Robert Chambers writes as follows in his *Popular Rhymes of Scotland* (London and Edinburgh: W. & R. Chambers, 1870), p.286.

> 'Soutors ane, soutors twa,
> Soutors in the Back Raw!

The trade of the shoemaker formerly abounded so much in Selkirk, that the burgesses in general pass to this day amongst their neighbours by the appellation of the *Soutors of Selkirk*. [...] For some inexplicable reason, the above couplet is opprobrious to the people of Selkirk; and if any of my readers will parade the main street of the old burgh, crying it at a moderate pitch of voice, he may depend upon receiving as comfortable a lapidation as his heart could desire.'

128(a) I'se warrant I'll bet, I'll be bound.

129(b) Flodden-field discussed in a note on 126(d), above.

129(c) the Duke of Northumberland, another enemy to our town as Northumberland is an English county just to the south of the border, Dukes of Northumberland were natural enemies to the Scots during the centuries of border warfare. Sir Hugh Percy (1715–86) was the first Duke of Northumberland of the third creation; he was succeeded by his son, also Sir Hugh Percy (1742–1817).

130(a) Fat puddings *pock puddin*, which means 'a dumpling' or 'steamed pudding', is a traditional Scottish nickname for an Englishman.

130(a) Percies and Howards these aristocratic English families were renowned military opponents of the Scots: thus Sir Henry Percy, called Hotspur, the son of the Earl of Northumberland, was defeated and captured by the Scots at Otterburn in 1388; while Thomas Howard, Earl of Surrey, was created Duke of Norfolk after leading the English army to victory at Flodden in 1513.

130(a) blue bonnets men's flat-topped caps, of a style much worn in Scotland. Thus the phrase is often used to mean 'Scotsmen'.

131(d) let that flee stick to the wa' say no more about a topic, drop an embarrassing subject.

132(b) like a cried fair in a state of bustle.

132(c) the late Duke of Queensberry, when Earl of March William Douglas (1724–1810), third Earl of March and fourth Duke of Queensberry, was notorious for his escapades and dissolute life. He succeeded his cousin Charles in the dukedom of Queensberry in 1778. Hogg farmed land near Queensberry's home, Drumlanrig Castle, during the Duke's final years.

134(a) had found a fiddle had got a pleasant surprise.

134(b) I get the maist o' my dreams redd most of my dreams come true.

134(c) a grey hen a female black grouse.

134(d) SING ROUND ABOUT HAWICK the town of Hawick lies to the south of its local rival Selkirk, at the junction of Slitrig Water and the River Teviot. There are several local Hawick references in the song, and in the part of the story which follows.

135(a) a sheep's head as used in the preparation of Scotch broth, a thick soup made from mutton, barley, and vegetables.

135(b) the Braes probably Branxholme Braes farm, three miles south-west of Hawick.

135(c) Penchrice is Penchrise farm, five miles south of Hawick.

135(c) the Coate Eastcote and Westcote farms both lie within two miles of Hawick, to the north-east.

135(d)Bortugh Bortaugh farm lies two miles south-west of Hawick.

135(d) Dr Jamieson a reference to John Jamieson, *An Etymological Dictionary of the Scottish Language*, 2 vols (Edinburgh: at the University Press, 1808).

136(d) 'Wap at the widow, my laddie.' this traditional song, celebrating the attractions of a rich young widow, is included in James Johnson's *The Scots Musical Museum*, 6 vols (Edinburgh: James Johnson, 1787–1803).

136(d) C.N. 'Christopher North' was the supposed editor of *Blackwood's*.

137(a) new-fashioned miles of 1,760 yards: the old Scots mile was about 1,980 yards.

137(a) the Sandbed a street in Hawick which gets its name from the sand deposit where the rivers Teviot and Slitrig are believed to have met before the Teviot altered its course.

137(a) Slitterick Bridge and the Tower Knowe Slitrig Bridge (built 1776) links the Sandbed with the Tower Knowe, the open area at the west end of Hawick High Street where Drumlanrig's Tower stands.

137(a) east the gate in an easterly direction.

137(b) the one thing needful echoes Luke 10.42.

137(c) Gideon Scott may be a reference to Gideon Scott (1765–1833), a well-known local figure whose inventions included a reaping machine.

137(c) Cheviot tup a ram of the Cheviot breed, one of the well-established breeds of Border sheep. See Michael J.H. Robson, *Sheep of the Borders*.

139(d) Skelfhill Pen a hill eight miles south of Hawick.

140(a) a perfect she Nabal Nabal, a rich man who was 'churlish and evil in his doings', meanly refuses hospitality to David in 1 Samuel chapter 25.

140(d) "With silver he was shod before the quotation has not been identified.

Textual Notes on 'George Dobson's Expedition to Hell, and the Souters of Selkirk'
The only printings during Hogg's lifetime were in *Blackwood's*, 21 (May 1827), 549–62; and in *The Shepherd's Calendar* of 1829 (1, 131–47 and 148–75), with the usual revisions by Robert Hogg. As the manuscript does not survive, the present edition reprints the *Blackwood's* text. The following emendations seek to correct what appear to be errors by the printer:

126(b) is called "a bein bachelor," or "a chap that was gayan weel to leeve."]   is called "a bien bachelor, or a chap that was gayan weel to leeve." (*Blackwood's*)

128(d) money," says George. "We]   money," says George. We (*Blackwood's*)

134(c) settle with her;]   settle with her, (*Blackwood's*)

139(d) councillors' seat]   councillor's seat (*Blackwood's*)

Tibby Hyslop's Dream, and the Sequel
The series within a series which had started in the May number continued in the June 1827 *Blackwood's* with 'The Shepherd's Calendar. Dreams and Apparitions. Part II. Containing Tibby Hyslop's Dream, and the Sequel'. Hogg wrote to Blackwood on 28 May 1827 'I hope Tibby Hyslop will be accounted a good tale? I have another Callander ready but nothing more. I am afraid my writing season is over till Winter again' (NLS, MS 4019, fol. 191).

142(a) In the year 1807, when on a jaunt through the valleys of Nith and Annan armed with the profits from his books *The Mountain Bard* and *The Shepherd's Guide*, both published in 1807, Hogg set himself up as a farmer in Nithsdale in south-west Scotland. He left the district after a couple of years because of financial difficulties, setting out to establish himself as a professional writer in Edinburgh.

142(b) Know-back [...] Drumlochie these places appear to be fictional.

142(d) Tinwald a parish near Dumfries, on the mutual border of Nithsdale and Annandale.

147(d) borne the brunt of incensed kirk-sessions the kirk session is the ruling body of each parish church of the Church of Scotland; and in the eighteenth century kirk sessions were much concerned with dealing with sexual misconduct among parishioners.

148(d) "The great siege o' the castle o' Man-soul, that Bunyan speaks about John Bunyan's *The Holy War* (1682) tells of Diabolus's assault on the town of Mansoul.

152(c) Mr Cunningham of Dalswinton James Cunningham, stonemason at Dalswinton and elder brother of Hogg's close friend, the poet Allan Cunningham. Dalswinton is a village of Nithsdale, about five miles north of Dumfries.

153(a) from the head of Glen-breck to the bridge of Stoneylee Glenbreck is a farm on the road from Moffat to Edinburgh; while Stoneylee is about thirty miles to the south, near Annan. The two places can be taken as marking the northern and southern extremities of Annandale.

153(d) afore the Lords before the judges of the Court of Session, the supreme civil court of Scotland.

153(d) afore the courts o' Dumfries the chief town of the Nithsdale and Annandale area is Dumfries; and Dumfries was one of the towns at which the High Court of Justiciary sat regularly on circuit. In Hogg's day the judges of the High Court of Justiciary were the Lord Justice-Clerk and five Lords of Session.

154(a) the third o' the Commands the third of the ten commandments is 'Thou shalt not take the name of the Lord thy God in vain; for the Lord will not hold him guiltless that taketh his name in vain' (Exodus 20.7).

155(c) the beasts that perish echoes Psalm 49.12, 20.

156(b) corn in the 97 in Scotland, *corn* normally means 'oats'.

156(d) proof relating to the proper cropping of the land 'Apart from any conditions or stipulations in his lease, the tenant of a farm in Scotland must conform to the rules of good husbandry, *i.e.* he may not scourge or deteriorate the land by undue cropping': (*Green's Encyclopædia of the Law of Scotland*, ed. by John Chisholm, 14 vols (Edinburgh: William Green, 1896–1904), IV, 2).

157(b) the two Circuit Lords and Sheriff it was the practice to appoint two judges to go to each circuit of the High Court of Justiciary; and the sheriff (the chief local judge) attended meetings of the circuit court.

Textual Notes on 'Tibby Hyslop's Dream'
The only printings during Hogg's lifetime were in *Blackwood's*, 21 (June 1827), 664–76; and in *The Shepherd's Calendar* of 1829 (I, 212–46). As the manuscript for 'Tibby Hyslop's Dream' does not survive, the present edition reprints the *Blackwood's* text with the following emendation which seeks to correct what appears to be an error by the printer:
159(a) bargain?"] bargain?' (*Blackwood's*)

Smithy Cracks
Hogg's sequence on 'Dreams and Apparitions' was continued with 'Smithy Cracks' in the number of *Blackwood's* for July 1827. This story had been written some months earlier: Hogg told Blackwood in a letter of 5 April 1827 'I have another No of the

Callender finished of the same class called "Smithy Cracks"' (NLS, MS 4019, fol. 187).

166(d) harrowed to death, like the children of Ammon a reference to 2 Samuel 12.31.

167(b) for he was session-clerk as secretary to the kirk session (the local church court of a parish), the session clerk would be much concerned with dealing with sexual misdemeanours.

168(a) *the logarithm to number one* there is no such thing as 'the logarithm to number one': so in effect the Dominie is saying that the smith is brainless.

168(c–d) put a cipher *above* **a nine [...] a cipher above a nine at most** just as a one above a two can represent a half, so a cipher (that is, zero) above a nine can be regarded as a fraction. If the value of this fraction is calculated, however, the result is zero. Thus, having asked the Doctor 'What art thou?', the Dominie provides an answer to his own question: 'Thou art nothing'. In this passage the pompous Dominie tries to bamboozle and impress his simple hearers; but in the end he appears rather foolish himself. Of course, lurking somewhere behind 'Smithy Cracks' is the figure of the Ettrick Shepherd, who (as a simple Child of Nature) cannot possibly know enough about mathematics to poke fun at a Dominie in this way. Or can he? Hogg is playing games with his readers, just as he does when he quotes Latin.

170(c) diagonal [...] vertices [...] quadrilateral the opposite vertices of a quadrilateral are connected by a diagonal.

170(d) stubborn as Muirkirk ir'n Muirkirk in Ayrshire was a centre of the iron industry.

171(d) the night tonight.

171(d) my lane on my own, by myself.

173(c) sold it, to the dissectors a topical reference in 1827. Dr Robert Knox, the Edinburgh anatomist, was an enthusiast for practical dissection. For this he needed a supply of bodies; and he was not excessively scrupulous about where the bodies came from. William Burke and his accomplice William Hare murdered various people, in order to obtain bodies for sale to Knox. Burke was hanged in 1829.

177(d) until sixty days be over before 1871, Scots law provided that someone who was technically 'on deathbed' was not considered to be competent to make a disposition of heritable property to the injury of the heir-at-law. By an Act of 1696, a sufficient defence against the objection of deathbed was provided, if the granter lived sixty days after executing the deed.

178(d) to square the circle to construct a square equal in area to a given circle is a problem incapable of a purely geometrical solution.

178(d) *Mount-Benger* Hogg's farm in Yarrow.

Textual Notes on 'Smithy Cracks'
The only printings during Hogg's lifetime were in *Blackwood's* (22 (July 1827), 64–73; and (as 'The Laird of Wineholm') in *The Shepherd's Calendar* of 1829 (I, 311–41). The 1829 printing has the usual revisions by Robert Hogg. As the manuscript for 'Smithy Cracks' does not survive, the present edition reprints the *Blackwood's* text with the following emendations which seek to correct what appear to be errors by the printer:

163(a)   seen about Wineholm Place?"]   seen about Wineholm place?" (*Blackwood's*)

170(d)   laird is, it seems, risen]   laird is, it seem, risen (*Blackwood's*)

171(c)   sage tongue]   saget ongue (*Blackwood's*)

174(a) Every thing that happened was]   Everything that happened was (*Black-wood's*) [Hogg's manuscripts usually have 'every thing', not 'everything'; and Hogg's usual form fits the context here.]

176(d) hell, sir.'"]   hell, sir.' (*Blackwood's*)

The Laird of Cassway

This story, which concludes Hogg's sequence on 'Dreams and Apparitions', was published in the August 1827 number of *Blackwood's* as 'The Shepherd's Calendar. By the Ettrick Shepherd. Dreams and Apparitions.— Part IV'. It was given the title 'The Laird of Cassway' in *The Shepherd's Calendar* of 1829. This story, and a ballad, would appear to have been enclosed with a letter to Blackwood dated 5 July 1827 in which Hogg writes 'I [...] have stretched a point for all my throng to write you rather a good ballad off hand [...] . I hope you will like the Callander but I fear it will be the last for a while' (NLS, MS 4019, fol. 193). Blackwood replied on 14 July 1827: 'I recd your's of the 5th. only on Wednesday. It was most welcome for this No of the Calendar is very good indeed, and the Ballad is capital. Both will appear in this No–' (NLS, MS 30310, p.182). The August 1827 number contained both 'The Laird of Cassway' and Hogg's ballad 'The Perilis of Wemyng', later given the title 'May of the Moril Glen'.

179(a–b) Cassway [...] Drumfielding probably based on Cassock and Dumfedling, both of which are on the White Esk in Eskdalemuir, in the hill country at the northern extremity of the former county of Dumfriesshire. Eskdalemuir lies just to the south of Ettrick, and it provides a route from there to the lower-lying and more populated districts around Dumfries.

179(c) between Erick brae and Teviot stone Erickstanebrae lies about five miles to the north of Moffat, and the rivers Annan, Tweed and Clyde rise near it. It is about a dozen miles to the west of Eskdalemuir, while the river Teviot rises about five miles to the east of Eskdalemuir.

181(a) make a wheel-wright o' to use another person for one's own ends or advancement.

181(a) ahint the hand late, after the event.

181(b) goud in goupings untold wealth.

181(b) by my certy assuredly.

181(c) ride the stang offenders against laws or local conventions were mounted astride a rough pole or tree-trunk (a stang), and carried about in public as a punishment.

181(c) Lochmaben lies ten miles north-east of Dumfries.

182(c) the gowk kens what the tittling wants proverbially, the gowk (cuckoo) and the tittling (meadow pipit) are inseparable and incongruous companions.

182(d) the words o' the Scripture 'The horseleach hath two daughters, crying, Give, give' (Proverbs 30.15).

186(a) house an' hadding house and home.

186(b) the fool according to his folly echoes Proverbs 26.4.

187(a) Nether Cassway [...] Over Cassway Over Cassock lies about three-quarters of a mile up-stream from Nether Cassock.

187(b) Glen-dearg lies about three-quarters of a mile upstream from Over Cassock.

189(a) armed capapee like the ghost of Hamlet's father, as described by Horatio: *Hamlet*, i. 2. 200.

191(a) his father's spirit, like the prophet's of old in 1 Samuel chapter 28, the spirit of the prophet Samuel is summoned up for King Saul by the witch of Endor.

191(b) Bloodhope-Linns Bloodhope lies about a mile to the north of Glendearg.

193(b) the Johnstons of Annandale the Johnstones of Annandale were a powerful family, especially in the fourteenth and fifteenth centuries. A Johnstone who is Lord of Annandale plays a central part in Hogg' poem 'Jock Johnstone the Tinkler', included in *A Queer Book* (1832).

194(a) the five dales Eskdalemuir opens out into Eskdale. To the east lie Teviotdale and Liddesdale, and to the west lie Annandale and Nithsdale.

194(a) Pantland Pentland Hill overlooks the Bloodhope Burn.

194(b) north-west turret of derangement echoes *Hamlet*, II. 2. 380–81: 'I am but mad north-north-west; when the wind is southerly, I know a hawk from a handsaw'.

195(c) Maxwell of the Dales the Maxwells were a powerful Annandale family, for long at feud with the Johnstones, and also at feud with the Douglases, earls of Morton. The misfortunes of John Maxwell, eighth or ninth Baron Maxwell (1586?–1612), are recorded in the ballad 'Lord Maxwell's Lament'.

198(c) in the words of the patriarch spoken by the patriarch Jacob in Genesis 43.14.

199(a–b) J. Smith, at No. 15, Paternoster-row an anonymous edition of Daniel Defoe's *The Secrets of the Invisible World Laid Open* was published in London in 1770. The imprint reads 'Printed for the Author, and sold by *D. Steel*, [...] and *J. Smith*, at Number 15. in Paternoster-row'. 'The Laird of Cassway' has strong similarities to (but is not identical with) the story of 'T—— H——, a gentleman of fortune', which concludes this volume's Chapter XI, 'Of Apparitions and Dreams' (see pp.133–50).

Textual Notes on 'The Laird of Cassway'
The only printings during Hogg's lifetime were in *Blackwood's*, 22 (August 1827), 173–85; and (with the usual revisions by Robert Hogg) in *The Shepherd's Calendar* of 1829 (I, 176–211). As the manuscript for 'The Laird of Cassway' does not survive, the present edition reprints the *Blackwood's* text with the following emendation, which seeks to correct what appears to be an error by the printer:
181(a) "'Complished gentleman!]   ''Complished gentleman! (*Blackwood's*)

Mary Burnet
This story was published in the February 1828 number of *Blackwood's* as 'The Shepherd's Calendar. Class IX. Fairies, Brownies, and Witches. By the Ettrick Shepherd'; and it was given the title 'Mary Burnet' in *The Shepherd's Calendar* of 1829. A new Class is introduced here, but it is not entirely clear why this Class should be Class IX. Class numbers had not been used for any 'Shepherd's Calendar' story since the conclusion of 'The Lasses' in 1825; and it may simply be that by 1828 no one could remember what the Class number ought to be.

200(b) the sophisticated gloss and polish thrown over the modern philosophic mind in an important discussion of 'Mary Burnet', John MacQueen writes 'Nowadays the word "sophisticated" has in general usage lost the pejorative overtones it formerly possessed; "sophisticated" once implied "corrupt", a sense which in Hogg's usage it certainly retains' (*The Rise of the Historical Novel*, pp.205–06).

200(d) St Mary's Loch Yarrow Water flows from this loch, which is at the heart of Ettrick Forest.

200(d) Kirkstyle the modern Kirkstead, like the Kirkstyle of the story, is near the eastern end of the loch.

201(a) Our Lady's Chapel stood on the hillside, near the eastern end of St Mary's Loch. The church has long gone, but the churchyard remains.

205(c) scarlet thread [...] rowan-tree staff traditional protections against malign supernatural influences.

206(d) three hours [...] only seven in traditional lore, the numbers seven and three have a mystical resonance.

208(a) Oxcleuch at the western end of St Mary's Loch.

208(a) the Birkhill Path a pass through steep hills leads from the western end of St Mary's Loch, past Birkhill, and on to the market town of Moffat in Annandale.

208(a) the Cross of Dumgree Dumgree, in the upper part of Annandale, was an ancient pre-Reformation parish with a church associated with the Abbey at Kelso.

208(c) a white jerkin and green bonnet colours associated with the fairies.

209(d) a mark like that which God put upon Cain the reference is to Genesis 4.15.

210(b) Cariferan Carrifran is on the route from St Mary's Loch to Moffat, via Birkhill.

212(d) Lady Elizabeth Douglas the daughter of John, second Earl of Morton: she married Robert, Lord Keith, who was killed with James IV at the battle of Flodden in 1513.

212(d) the reign of James the Fourth was from 1488 till 1513.

217(d) not above five spans in height as a span is nine inches, the creature is not more than three feet nine inches tall.

220(a) the morn is the day tomorrow is the day

220(d) Turnberry Sheil the modern Upper Tarnberry, near Birkhill, is about half-way to Moffat from St Mary's Loch.

Textual Notes on 'Mary Burnet'

The only printings during Hogg's lifetime were in *Blackwood's*, 23 (February 1828), 214–27; and (with the usual revisions by Robert Hogg) in *The Shepherd's Calendar* of 1829 (I, 247–84). As the manuscript for 'Mary Burnet' does not survive, the present edition reprints the *Blackwood's* text with the following emendations which seek to correct what appear to be errors by the printer:

204(d) Jean affirmed]   Jane affirmed (*Blackwood's*)

218(c) subtleties aside,] subtleties aside (*Blackwood's*) [In *Blackwood's*, the spacing suggests that a comma has dropped out of the type at the end of a line, after 'aside'.]

The Witches of Traquair

This story was published in the April 1828 number of *Blackwood's* as 'The Shepherd's Calendar. Class IX. Fairies, Deils, and Witches. By the Ettrick Shepherd'; and it was given the title 'The Witches of Traquair' in *The Shepherd's Calendar* of 1829. Letters exchanged by Hogg and Blackwood suggest that Hogg was working on both 'Mary Burnet' and 'The Witches of Traquair' during December 1827; and that both stories were in Blackwood's hands before the end of January 1828 (NLS, MS 4007, fols 48–49; NLS, MS 30310, pp.398–400; NLS, MS 2245, fols 110–11).

223(a) Traquair a village in the Tweed valley, about five miles from Hogg's Yarrow home of Mount Benger. Traquair House, for centuries the home of a prominent Jacobite and Catholic family, is one of the finest old mansion-houses in the south of Scotland.

223(c) Popery was then on its last legs the Scottish Reformation dates from 1560, when the Scottish Parliament passed a series of measures that ended all links with Rome.

224(a) Feathen Hill Fethan Hill lies about two miles north-west of Traquair.

225(a) the royal bounds Ettrick Forest was a royal hunting ground.

227(c) on the braid way for destruction 'for wide is the gate, and broad is the way, that leadeth to destruction' (Matthew 7.13).

229(a) I have been young [...] land of their fathers echoes Psalm 37.25.

234(a) the Quair the Quair Water flows north-eastwards past Fethan Hill, goes on through Traquair, and then joins the Tweed.

235(c) David Beaton Archbishop of St Andrews and one of the major figures of the Scottish church in the years leading up to the Reformation, Cardinal David Beaton (1494–1546) was particularly detested by the reformers.

235(d) Glenrath-hope lies about five miles west of Fethan Hill.

236(c) Mess John name for a clergyman.

236(d) paid the kane paid the penalty.

237(a) the true marks o' the beast it was believed that witches, as followers of Satan, would have the 'mark of the beast' described in Revelation chapters 13–20.

237(a) gnashed their teeth on the maiden echoes a Biblical phrase: for example, Psalm 35.16 and Acts 7.54.

238(d) Mr Wiseheart, or Wishart George Wishart (1513?–1546), a scholar and a leading Reformer in religious matters.

239(b) *Cruci, dum spiro, fido* 'while I breathe, I have faith in the Cross' (Latin).

240(b) the Queen Regent Mary of Guise, widow of James V and mother of the child who was to become Mary Queen of Scots, became Queen Regent in 1554. The Queen Regent championed the Catholic cause.

240(b) the Plora another local reference: Plora Rig and Plora Craig lie about a mile to the east of Traquair.

240(b) planted a vineyard echoes a frequent Biblical phrase.

240(c) Mr Blore Edward Blore (1787–1879), antiquarian, artist, and architect; he advised Sir Walter Scott about the planning of Abbotsford.

Textual Notes on 'The Witches of Traquair'

The only printings during Hogg's lifetime were in *Blackwood's*, 23 (April 1828), 509–19; and in *The Shepherd's Calendar* of 1829 (II, 150–84). As the manuscript for 'The Witches of Traquair' does not survive, the present edition reprints the *Blackwood's* text with the following emendation which seeks to correct what appears to be an error by the printer:

237(a)   here, about some that]   hereabout, some that (*Blackwood's*)

The Brownie of the Black Haggs

The last contribution by Hogg to appear in *Blackwood's* under the 'Shepherd's Calendar' series title was 'The Witches of Traquair', published in the number for April 1828. However, two letters from Hogg to Blackwood provide evidence that this was not the last article written for the series. The letters are simply dated 'August 1st' and 'August 6th', but mentions of events and literary works make it clear that the month in question must be August 1828, four months on from the publication of 'The Witches of Traquair'. In the first of the letters Hogg writes 'I have a series of M,Corkindale letters a grand Coronach and a calander all ready for you' (NLS, MS 4719, fol. 163); and in the second he says 'The Calender I have not got read over yet and it being a fearful and unnatural story I want to read it to Laidlaw before I send it away' (NLS, MS 4719, fol. 167). In a letter to Hogg of 27 September 1828, Blackwood mentions what is presumably Hogg's 'fearful and unnatural' story for 'The Shepherd's Calendar': 'Your Brownie I like still better since it was in types, though it is a strange wild savage affair' (NLS, MS 30969, fol. 66). This is doubtless a reference to 'The Brownie of the Black Haggs. By the Ettrick

Shepherd', which appeared soon afterwards in the October 1828 number of *Black-wood's*. A few months later the story made its second appearance, this time in *The Shepherd's Calendar* of 1829. Although 'The Brownie of the Black Haggs' was not published in *Blackwood's* under a 'Shepherd's Calendar' title, the letters quoted above suggest strongly that Hogg wrote this particular story as a continuation of the series. Perhaps Blackwood decided to drop the series title in the magazine to avoid confusion, publication of *The Shepherd's Calendar* in book form being now imminent. Be that as it may, 'The Brownie of the Black Haggs' fits very neatly into 1828's sequence of 'Class IX' Calendars on 'Fairies, Brownies, and Witches'.

242(c) religious characters [...] the poor persecuted Covenanters these references place this story in the 'Killing Time' of the 1680s. During this period the Covenanters (presbyterians who took up arms against the governments of Charles II and James VII) were liable to summary military execution.

244(b) Merodach the name of the god of Babylon, the great enemy of Israel (Jeremiah 50.2).

245(d) thou evil Merodach of Babylon Evil-merodach (mentioned in II Kings 25.27) was the son of Nebuchadnezzar, whom he succeeded on the throne of Babylon.

246(b) the rod of Moses, that swallowed up the rest of the serpents in Exodus 7.10–13.

246(d) Bread and sweet milk traditionally, the food of a brownie.

247(d) may the nature of woman change within me echoes Lady Macbeth in *Macbeth*, I. 5. 40–53.

251(b) a hair to make a tether of a trifle used as an excuse.

251(d) nipping an' scarting are Scots folk's wooing the phrase is proverbial: to scart is to scratch.

253(a) left to yoursell misguided, astray in your judgment.

254(c) like David of old in Psalm 109.

Textual Notes on 'The Brownie of the Black Haggs'
The only printings during Hogg's lifetime were in *Blackwood's*, 24 (October 1828), 489–96; and in *The Shepherd's Calendar* of 1829 (I, 285–310). As the manuscript for 'The Brownie of the Black Haggs' does not survive, the present edition reprints the *Blackwood's* text, with the following emendation.

251(d)   The best o' us, when]   The best o 'us, when (*Blackwood's*)

Other *Shepherd's Calendar* stories

The Introduction of the present volume gives an account of the way in which William Blackwood and Robert Hogg prepared *The Shepherd's Calendar* for publication in two volumes in 1829. In addition to reprinting all the stories discussed above, the 1829 volumes contain one previously unpublished story; two stories which had previously appeared in Constable's *Edinburgh Magazine* (a new series of *The Scots Magazine*); and two pieces that had previously appeared in *Blackwood's*, but not as part of the 'Shepherd's Calendar' series. These additional items may be listed as follows.

1. 'Nancy Chisholm', in *The Shepherd's Calendar* (1829), I, 230–53: previously unpublished.
2. 'The Prodigal Son', in *The Shepherd's Calendar* (1829), I, 69–111. Previously published as 'Pictures of Country Life. No.I. Old Isaac' and 'Pictures of Country Life. No. II. Continued from p.219', *Edinburgh Magazine*, 9 (1821), 219–25, 443–52.

3. 'The School of Misfortune', in *The Shepherd's Calendar* (1829), I, 112–30. Previously published as 'Pictures of Country Life. No. III. Continued from p.452. The School of Misfortune', *Edinburgh Magazine*, 9 (1821), 583–89.

4. 'The Marvellous Doctor', in *The Shepherd's Calendar* (1829), II, 108–49. Previously published as 'The Marvellous Doctor', *Blackwood's*, 22 (1827), 349–61.

5. 'A Strange Secret', in *The Shepherd's Calendar* (1829), II, 49–107. This is a completed version of 'A Strange Secret. Related in a Letter from the Ettrick Shepherd', *Blackwood's*, 23 (1828), 822–26. This piece ends with a promise that it will be continued, but no continuation appeared in *Blackwood's*.

The question remains: why were the above stories added to the *Blackwood's* 'Shepherd's Calendar' series when that series was republished in book form in 1829? The 'Advertisement' which follows the titlepage of the first volume of the 1829 edition states:

> The greater number of the Tales contained in these volumes appeared originally in Blackwood's Edinburgh Magazine. They have been revised with care; and to complete the Collection, several Tales hitherto unpublished have been added.

The attractiveness of the 1829 volumes to potential purchasers would of course be increased by the inclusion of the previously unpublished 'Nancy Chisholm'. Furthermore, 'The Prodigal Son' and 'The School of Misfortune', being little-known old tales from *The Edinburgh Magazine*, might also have been expected to pass as new. It was probably also calculated that these two rural tales would improve the respectability of the collection, as they show Hogg in a somewhat pious, moralising mood. No doubt it was also convenient to bulk out the collection with a couple of recent stories from *Blackwood's*, even although these had not been intended to form part of the magazine's 'Shepherd's Calendar' series.

The roots of the 'Shepherd's Calendar' series in *Blackwood's* can be traced back to a fairly early stage of Hogg's career. On 20 May 1813 he wrote to the Edinburgh publisher Archibald Constable: 'I have for many years been collecting the rural and traditionary tales of Scotland and I have of late been writing them over again and new-modelling them, and have the vanity to suppose they will form a most interesting work' (NLS, MS 7200, fol. 203). This project eventually bore fruit in various publications: most notably in *The Brownie of Bodsbeck; and Other Tales*, 2 vols (Edinburgh: Blackwood, 1818); in *Winter Evening Tales*, 2 vols (Edinburgh: Oliver & Boyd, 1820); and in 'The Shepherd's Calendar' itself.

The second volume of *Winter Evening Tales* contains five chapters entitled 'The Shepherd's Calendar'. The first two of these chapters reprint 'Storms', which had launched the 'Shepherd's Calendar' series in *Blackwood's* in 1819. The remaining three chapters reprint 'Tales and Anecdotes of the Pastoral Life', which first appeared in *Blackwood's*, 1 (1817), 22–25, 143–47, and 247–50. These 'Tales and Anecdotes' can be regarded as the precursors of the magazine's 'Shepherd's Calendar' series.

The present volume brings together the pieces Hogg wrote for publication in the 'Shepherd's Calendar' series in *Blackwood's*. The remaining pieces which appeared, in other contexts, under the 'Shepherd's Calendar' label will be included in due course in future volumes of the Stirling/South Carolina Edition of James Hogg.

Hyphenation List

Various words are hyphenated at the ends of lines in this edition of *The Shepherd's Calendar*. The list below indicates those cases in which such hyphens should be retained in quotation. The page number is given for each item in the list, with the line number following. In calculating line numbers, titles and running headlines have been ignored.

23, l.19	knowe-head	130, l. 8	cut-and-thrust
34, l. 4	Merkside-edge	149, l. 3	sheep-reiver
35, l.13	peat-stack	151, l.42	Know-back
38, l. 3	twenty-seven	170, l.15	to-morrow
47, l. 4	war-horse	170, l.35	house-servant
73, l.11	a-courting	174, l.21	Sheriff-substitute
85, l.13	Padan-aram	192, l.27	ready-mounted
89, l. 3	well-powdered	205, l. 5	meer-maiden
90, l. 9	Harrow-inn	205, l.17	fellow-creature
115, l. 3	penny-wedding	207, l.22	farm-houses
126, l.13	small-pox	223, l.12	Taniel-Burn
126, l.22	town-council	227, l.18	shepherd-style
128, l. 3	good-naturedly	235, l.19	Strath-quair

Glossary

THIS Glossary sets out to provide a convenient guide to the Scots of *The Shepherd's Calendar*. Those wishing to make a serious study of Hogg's Scots should consult *The Concise Scots Dictionary*, ed. by Mairi Robinson (Aberdeen: Aberdeen University Press, 1985); and *The Scottish National Dictionary*, ed. by William Grant and David Murison, 10 vols (Edinburgh: Scottish National Dictionary Association, 1931–76). In using the Glossary, it should be remembered that, in Scots, *–it* is the equivalent of the English *–ed*. The Glossary deals with single words; but where it seems useful to discuss the meaning of a phrase, this is done in the Notes. For example, 'Rob Dodds' contains the phrase *to coup the creels*. The Glossary indicates that *coup* means 'to overturn', and that a *creel* is a deep basket for carrying such things as peat and fish. In the Notes it is recorded that *to coup the creels* means 'to die'.

aboon: above
ae: one
aff-loof: without delay
aglee: awry
anent: about, concerning
antrim: single, occasional
arle-money: money paid as a token of engagement of services
ashet: a large, oval, flat plate
asse: ash, ashes
assie: ash-covered
asteer: up and about, stirring
auld-farrant: sagacious, cunning
ava: at all
awmos: alms, food or money given in charity
awmrie: a cupboard, a pantry
axe: to ask

baby-clouts: baby-clothes
baiver: hat made of heavy woollen cloth like beaver fur
band: a ridge
bannet: a bonnet, a soft flat cap worn by men and boys
barley-hood: a fit of violent ill-temper or obstinacy
barrie: a woman's undergarment
bauchle: a useless, clumsy person
baugh: sheepish, ineffective
bawbee: a halfpenny
beet: to supply something missing
beik: to warm oneself
bein: well-to-do

belyve: soon, quickly
ben: inside; in towards the inner part of a house; the inner room
bicker: a drinking vessel, especially one made of wood
bide: to remain; to endure
bield: shelter
bien: cosy, comfortable
big: to build
biggin, bigging: a building
billie, billy: a fellow, a comrade; a brother
bilsh: a contemptuous term for a person, especially a child
birkie: an active, lively fellow
birl: to whirl round, dance
birr: force, energy
birses: bristles, hairs
birth: a berth
bit: (with omission of 'of') indicates smallness, endearment, or contempt
blad: a lump, a portion
blate: bashful
blatter: to beat with violence
bleeze: a blaze
blink: a pleasant glance; to look fondly at
blowster: to brag, to boast
bodle: a copper coin, worth a sixth of an English penny
body: a person, a human being
boonmost: highest, uppermost
bore: a chink, an opening in the clouds
bouk: a carcass; the body of a person

bounds: a district
bountith: a bounty, a gift
bouster: to bolster
braid: broad, plain
branks: a kind of bridle
bratch: a female hound
bratchet: a little brat
brigg: a bridge
broo: liquid in which something has been boiled
brose: a dish of oatmeal mixed with boiling water or milk
brosey: clumsy, inactive; a stupid person
brow: (in negative) an unfavourable opinion
brownie: a benevolent household sprite; a goblin or evil spirit
brunt: burnt
buckie: a perverse person
buckle: to partner (e.g. at a dance)
buister: one who puts tar marks of ownership on sheep
buisting-iron: an instrument used in marking sheep
bumbaze: to stupefy, perplex
bussing: a linen cap worn by old women
but: the outer room of a house
by: beyond, more than
bygane: ago

ca': to drive
cadger: an itinerant dealer, a hawker
callan, callant: a young man, a boy
callybit: chalybeate, impregnated with iron
cannie, canny: lucky, of good omen; '*no cannie*', supernatural, unnatural
cantrip: a spell; a trick
carle: a man, a fellow
cat's-witted: hare-brained
cauldrife: cold, cheerless, lacking in cheerfulness or zeal
causey: a roadway, a street
certy: certes, assuredly
champ: to crush, to mash
chiel, chield: a young man, a fellow
chop: a shop
chucks: a game with marbles
claes: clothes
clash: to strike or throw forcefully (especially of anything wet or liquid)
clatch: a fat, clumsy woman

claught: to sieze forcibly
cleuch, cleugh: a narrow gorge with high sides
clippie: a shorn sheep
clocker: a broody hen
cloot: one of the divisions in the hoof of cloven-footed animals
close-time: the close season, when killing of game is forbidden
clout: to patch, to mend; a patch
cludd: a cloud
cog: a pail or bowl
come-o'-will: an illegitimate child
compluther: to mix, to fit together
conquess: to conquer, acquire
corbie: a raven
coup: to overturn; to buy, to barter, to exchange
cout: a colt
couthy: sociable, friendly
crabbit: in a bad temper, cross
crack: to gossip, to have a talk; a gossip
craig: a rock, a cliff
creel: a deep basket for carrying peats, fish, etc.
crile: a dwarf
croppen: past participle of 'to creep'
crouse: spirited, cheerful
cruppock: [not identified]

dad: to strike
daunton: to intimidate
daw: a lazy person
dawtie: darling
depone: to testify
dew-cup: lady's mantle, *Alchemilla pratensis*
dight: to wipe
diker: a builder of stone walls
ding: to strike with heavy blows
dink: neat, trim
dirle: to tingle with emotion
ditt: to shut up, to close
doit: a very small amount; to amble, to walk with a blundering step
doited: crazed, confused
dominie: a schoolmaster
dooms: extremely, very
dorts: the sulks
douce, douse, douss: sedate, respectable; pleasant, kindly
dow: a dove; dear one, a darling

dow: (chiefly in negative) to be unwilling, to lack the strength of mind (to do something)

downsetter: a crushing rebuke

drap: a drop of

draughty: inventive in plans and plots

drift: falling snow driven by the wind

droich: a dwarf

drookit: soaked, drenched

duds: clothes

dult: a dolt

dumple: a bundle

dung: struck

ee, een: eye, eyes

eldrich: belonging to or resembling the elves; weird, unearthly

ellwand, elwand: a measuring rod one ell long; the group of stars known as the Belt of Orion

elsin: a shoemaker's awl

ely: to disappear

enow: enough

erne: an eagle

fa': to fall; to befall

faggald: a faggot

fash: to trouble, inconvenience

feasible: satisfactory, respectable

feck: quantity

feint: the devil; a fiend

fey: fated to die, doomed; behaving in an odd manner as if bewitched

five-grained: with five prongs

fizzenless: without strength or efficacy

flaip: a dull, heavy, unbroken fall

flake: a hurdle or framework of crossed slats, used as a fence or gate

flesher: a butcher

forefoughten: exhausted

foregather: to assemble

forenight: the evening; the early part of the night

forret: forward

foumart: the polecat

fraze: gushing and effusive talk

funk: to kick, throw out the legs (especially of a restive horse)

furr: the strip of earth turned over by a plough

fushionless: dull, without energy, lacking vigour

gab: the mouth

gaberlunzie: a beggar

gaff: to laugh loudly, to guffaw

gair: a patch of green grass on a hillside

gait: a way, a road; a goat

gar: to cause (something to be done)

gart: caused

gash: to talk volubly

gate: way, manner

gaun: going; active, busy

gay: very; great

gayan, gay an', gayen: very

gear: possessions, movable property, wealth

gerse: grass

gi'en: giving

gillie, gilly: a wild girl

gimmer: a ewe between its first and second shearing

gin: if

girdering: one of the suckers that grow from the root of the ash, used for hoops

girn: to show the teeth in rage, to snarl

glaur: soft, sticky mud

gledge: to give a sidelong glance, to leer

gleg: quick, alert

glowr: to stare

gommeril: a fool

goodman: the head of a household

goodwife: the mistress of a house

gouff: to cackle, to talk foolishly

gouk: the cuckoo; a fool, a simpleton

goupings: the fill of the two hands held together as a bowl

gowk: the cuckoo

grat: wept

grew: a greyhound

grieve: the overseer on a farm; a farm-bailiff

grue: to shudder with fear

gudeman: the head of a household

gudemither: mother-in-law

gudewife: the mistress of a house

guide: to treat

gurly: stormy; surly

gutter: (chiefly in plural) muddy puddles, mires

gyte: mad, insane

habble: to quarrel; to babble; a predicament

hadding: a property, a holding

haed, haet: have it

hafflins: half, partly

hag, hagg: a marshy hollow piece of ground in a moor

hain: to protect, hoard, economise

hallan: an inner wall, erected between the door and the fireplace

hallanshaker: a beggar

hallikit: crazy, hare-brained

hamp: a stutter

hand-fasting: a betrothal

hanker: to loiter, to linger expectantly

hap: to hop

hapshekel: to hobble or tie up an animal to prevent it from straying

har'st-shearer: harvest reaper

haver: to talk nonsense, to gossip

hawhed: (of animals) white-faced

hech-wow: an expression of distress or regret

hempie: a mischievous girl

herd: a shepherd; a herd

heuk: a hook, a sickle

hidling: stealthily, in secret

hind: a farm servant

hinny: honey; a term of endearment

hirsel: a flock of sheep of such a size that it can be looked after by one shepherd

hirsel: to slide along a surface without getting up, to slither

hog, hogg: a young sheep from the time it is weaned till it is first shorn

hope: a small enclosed upland valley or hollow

houdy: a midwife

hough: the hollow behind the knee-joint; the thigh

houm: low-lying level ground, on the banks of a river or stream

howe: a hollow

howk: to dig, to extricate

hund: to drive

hurchin: an unkempt person

hurlbarrow: a barrow

ilk, ilka: every, each

ilkaday: everyday

illfa'red, ill-faur'd: ugly; ill-mannered

ill-scrapit: slanderous, bitter

ingle: a fire on a hearth

ingle-side: the fireside, chimney-corner

I'se: I shall

izle: a burnt-out cinder, a hot cinder

jaukery: trickery

jeelaberry: [not identified]

jimply: scarcely, barely

jink: to frolic; to move nimbly

joe: a sweetheart

jotteryman: an odd-job-man

jouk: to duck, to dodge a blow

kail-yard: a cabbage-garden, a kitchen-garden

kane: payment in kind

kebbed: used of a ewe whose lamb has died

kebbuck: cheese

keek: to peep

kelty: a double dose

kenspeckle: easily recognised

kent: a long iron-shod pole used to help a walker in rough country, a staff

kep: to catch; to keep

kerlin: an old woman

kie: cattle

kilhab: to lure, to seduce

kimmer: a female intimate or friend; a witch

kink: a fit of coughing

kinnen: a rabbit

kipple: to couple

kirk-style, kirkstyle: a narrow entrance into a churchyard, where the bier was received at funerals

kirn-milk: buttermilk

kiss-my-lufe: literally 'kiss-my-hand', a fawner, a person given to excessive compliment

kittle: difficult to solve, tricky

kittle: to tickle

knag: a peg for hanging things on

knoll: a lump, a large piece

know, knowe: a knoll, a mound

kye: cattle

laigh: low

laith: loath

lampereel: a lamprey

landward: rustic

lang-nebbit: (of words) pedantic, polysyllabic

langsyne: long ago
lave: the rest
law: a rounded, conical hill
lee: a lie
leel: loyal, faithful
lift: the sky
lin: a waterfall, a pool in a river; a
    ravine
lingel: the waxed thread used by
    shoemakers
links: land enclosed by the windings of
    a stream or river
linn: a waterfall, a pool in a river; a
    ravine
lippen: to trust, to depend on
loaning: a grassy track
loun: a rogue, a rascal
lounder: a wallop, a whack
loup: to jump
lowe: a flame
lownly: softly, quietly
Lowrie: a name for the fox, 'Reynard'
lucky: an elderly woman
lug: the ear
lum: a chimney
luppen: leapt

mae: a greater number of things; more
Mahoun: a name for the Devil
main: very
march: a boundary, a natural frontier
mattle: to nibble
maun: must
maunna: must not
mawkin: the hare
mense: honour, credit; common sense
merk: a sum of money equal to two thirds
    of a pound Scots
mim: prim
mind: to remember
mirk: darkness
misca': to abuse verbally; to disparage
mister: a want, a lack
moldwarp: the mole
mools: the earth
moop: to twitch the lips
moorburn: the controlled burning of
    moorland to encourage new growth
moor-cock: the male red grouse
morn: tomorrow, the following morning
    or day
moudie: the mole

moup: to twitch the lips
muckle: great, big; much
mudge: to laugh in a suppressed manner
murgeon: a grimace
mutch: a close-fitting cap

neal: to nail, to strike down
neist: next
nervish: nervous, easily agitated
neuk: a corner
nieve: a fist
niffer: to exchange
niff-naff: a small or trifling thing
norlan': northern
nout: cattle

ochon: alas
od, ods: a mild oath, 'God'
or: before
out-ower: over
out-wale: an outcast, an unworthy
    person
owerplush: an excess

parishen: the inhabitants of a parish
park: an enclosed piece of land, a field
patrick: a partridge
paulie: (of young animals, especially
    lambs) undersized, not thriving
paw: a slight movement
peenge: to droop, to mope, to look cold
    and miserable
pellet: a sheepskin
pendit: arched, vaulted
penny-wedding: a wedding at which a
    guest contributed towards the cost of
    the entertainment, any surplus going
    to the couple
pickle: an indefinite number of persons
    or animals
pikit, piked: pointed, spiked
plack: a small Scottish coin, valued at
    one-third of an English penny
plew: a plough
plisky: a practical joke, a trick
pluffy: plump, fleshy
poind: to seize and sell the goods of a
    debtor
pook: to pluck
poortith: poverty
port: a gateway to a walled town
pose: a collection of money hidden away

potatoe-broo: liquid in which potatoes have been boiled
pree: to try by tasting
preses: chairman
prinkle: to tingle
pro'en: proven, tried, put to the test
pross: to put on airs, to show off
pun': a pound

quean: a young woman

rabbit: an imprecation, 'drat'
ramp: to romp boisterously
reave: to rob
redd: to interpret, to explain
rede: to advise
reek: smoke
reeky: smoky
reive: to rob
resetter: a receiver of stolen goods
rhame: a rigmarole
rigg: a strip of land
rigging: a roof
rime: a frosty haze or mist
roup: an auction, to auction
roup-roll: a record of the goods put up for sale at an auction
row: to roll, to twist, to wrap
rumple: the buttocks

sacking-gown: a penitential garment
sackless: innocent, inoffensive; lacking drive or energy
sair: sorely, severely; very much; sore, severe
sand: to vanish
sark: a shirt
saumont-fish: a salmon
scaith: damage, injury
scart: to scratch
scaur: a sheer rock, a precipice
score: a crevice, a cleft in a cliff face
shambling: twisted, out of alignment
shankit: with legs covered with stockings
shear: reap crops with a sickle
shedding: the act of sorting out sheep
sheiling: a hut for shepherds on high ground
shiel: a roughly-made hut, a hovel
shirling: a bright one (?)
sib: allied with, bound by ties of affection

sic: such
siccan, sickan: such, of such a kind
sicker: securely, firmly; secure, firm
siller: money
sindry: apart
sin' syne, sinsyne: since then
sirs: short for 'God preserve us', from 'ser', to preserve
skaith, skaithe: damage, injury
skeel: (medical) skill
skelloch: a scream
skirl: to scream, to cry out
sklate-stane: a piece of slate or slate-like stone
skreigh: to shriek, screech
slack: a hollow between hills
slae-black: sloe-black
sloat: a slit, a hole in the ground
slockening: to quench
slogie-riddle: a wide-meshed sieve for separating vegetables
smeddum: spirit, energy, vigorous resourcefulness
smudge: to laugh in a suppressed manner, to smirk
snaw-fleck: the snow bunting
soncy, sonsie, sonsy: comely, plump, buxom; friendly, hearty
sore: sorely, severely
souter: a shoemaker
spain, spean: to wean an infant or suckling animal
speat: a torrent of water
speel: to climb
speer: to ask
spense: a small inner apartment
spier: to ask
spink: an attractive young person
spraughle: to struggle to extricate oneself from a restrained position
spring: a quick, lively dance tune
sprithy: abounding in rushes
spunk: to leak out, to become known
staig: a young horse, not as yet broken to work
stang: a sting; a rough pole or tree-trunk
start: a short time
staup: a stave of a wooden cask
steek: to close, to shut up; the least article of clothing, a stitch
steer: to stir, to move
steeve: substantial, thick

stell : (of the eyes) to become fixed in a stare of astonishment

stern : a star

store-farmer : a farmer of a farm (usually in the hills) on which sheep are reared and grazed

stot : to bounce

stound : a stunning blow

stoure : a conflict; flying, swirling dust

stouthright : perhaps a variant of 'stouthreif', robbery with violence

strae : a straw

stramash : an uproar, a squabble

stravaig : to roam, to wander idly

streek : to stretch

stump : a stupid fellow

swankey : a smart, strapping young man

swee : to sway

syne : ago

tack : a tenancy, especially the leasehold tenure of a farm

tane : the one (of two)

tangs : tongs

tap : top; tip; the head

tatted : shaggy, unkempt

tent : attention; to observe, take notice of

tersyversy : topsy turvey

theek : to protect with a thick covering

thir : these

thole : to endure

thowless : ineffectual, lacking energy

thrang : busy

thrapple : the windpipe

thraw : to twist

threw : twisted

tike : a dog, a mischievous child

till : to

tine : to lose

tint : lost

tip : a tap

tither : the other (of two)

tittling : the meadow pipit

titty : a sister

tocher : a bride's dowry; to provide a bride with a dowry

tod : a fox

toop : a male sheep, a ram

torfel : to come to grief, to perish

tot : the sum total

tout : to toot, to trumpet

tove : to emit smoke or flames (of a fire)

town : a farm, a farm-steading

townhead : the upper end of a farm

towsy : dishevelled, tangled

trams : the legs

trivage : a partition between two stalls in a stable

tryst : to order something in advance

tuffle : to ruffle, to rumple

tup : a ram

tyke : a dog, a cur

unco : very; extraordinary; uncanny

unfeiroch : weak, infirm

unwordy : unworthy

upsetting : arrogance

wale : to choose

wallietragle : a good-for-nothing; an undersized person

walth : abundance

wan : arrived

wap : to thrust, to fling

war : to overcome, to get the better of

wark : a fuss

wat : to know

water : a large stream, a river

waughle : to move in a clumsy way, to stumble with fatigue

waukit-woo'd : with matted, rough wool

waur : worse

wawkit : matted, shrunk and thickened in washing (of cloth)

weapon-shaw : a muster of the men under arms in a district

wear : to guard; (of a sheepdog) to stand in front of a group of sheep to prevent them from breaking loose; to drive (animals or persons) gradually in a desired direction

weather-gaw : an atmospheric appearance (e.g. a fragment of a rainbow or a mock sun) regarded as a portent of bad weather

weazel-blawn : unpleasant-looking; ill-natured

weazon : the air passage in the throat

wedder : a wether, a male sheep, especially a castrated ram

weel-faured : good-looking

wha : who

whatten : what

whaup : the curlew

wheen: a quantity, an indefinite number
wheeram: a trifle, something insignificant
whig: a Presbyterian
whiles: sometimes
whin: furze, gorse
whisht, whist: be quiet!
whittle: a knife
wick: the corner of the eye
widdy: the gallows rope
win: to make or find one's way
wince: to kick, to prance
window-sole: a window-sill
won: to make one's way
worn: past participle of 'weir', to drive
    persons or animals, to shepherd
wough: to bark in a suppressed manner

wreath, wreathe: a bank or drift of snow
writer: a lawyer
wyte: the person to blame

yammer: to raise a clamour
yerk: to thump, to strike; to tie firmly
    together (e.g. leather, in
    shoemaking); a blow
yerker: a blow
yermit: 'arnit', an edible plant root
yestreen: yesterday evening
yetlin: an article made of cast-iron
yett: a gate
yird: the earth
younker: a youngster
yowe: a ewe